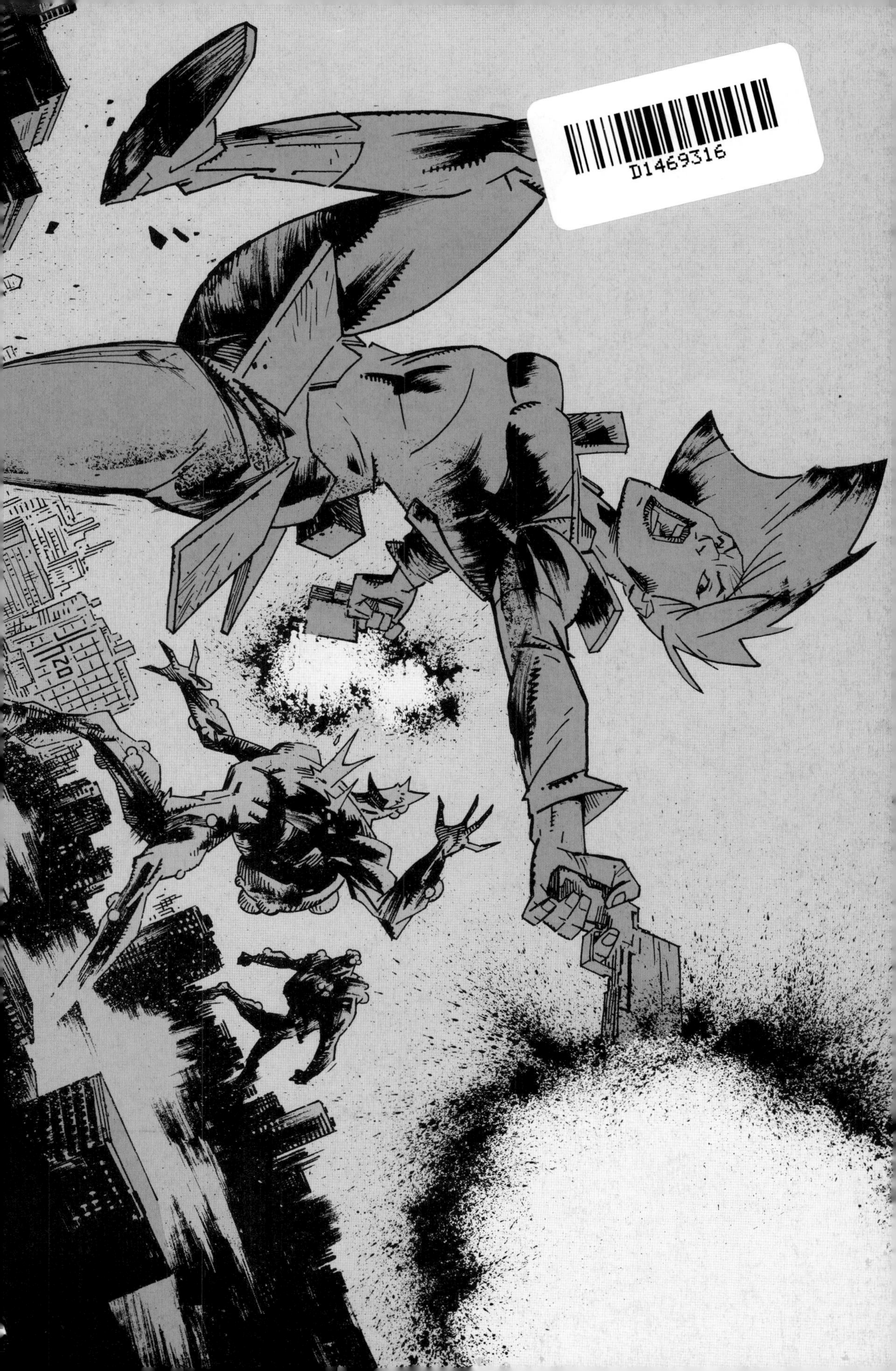

BIG GIRLS™

STORY & ART
JASON HOWARD

LETTERING
FONOGRAFIKS

IMAGE COMICS, INC. | **TODD McFARLANE** President | **JIM VALENTINO** Vice President | **MARC SILVESTRI** Chief Executive Officer **ERIK LARSEN** Chief Financial Officer | **ROBERT KIRKMAN** Chief Operating Officer | **ERIC STEPHENSON** Publisher/Chief Creative Officer **NICOLE LAPALME** Controller | **LEANNA CAUNTER** Accounting Analyst | **SUE KORPELA** Accounting & HR Manager | **MARLA EIZIK** Talent Liaison **JEFF BOISON** Director of Sales & Publishing Planning | **DIRK WOOD** Director of International Sales & Licensing | **ALEX COX** Director of Direct Market Sales | **CHLOE RAMOS** Book Market & Library Sales Manager | **EMILIO BAUTISTA** Digital Sales Coordinator | **JON SCHLAFFMAN** Specialty Sales Coordinator | **KAT SALAZAR** Director of PR & Marketing | **DREW FITZGERALD** Marketing Content Associate | **HEATHER DOORNINK** Production Director | **DREW GILL** Art Director | **HILARY DILORETO** Print Manager | **MELISSA GIFFORD** Content Manager | **TRICIA RAMOS** Traffic Manager **ERIKA SCHNATZ** Senior Production Artist | **RYAN BREWER** Production Artist | **DEANNA PHELPS** Production Artist | **IMAGECOMICS.COM**

GIRLS, VOLUME 1. First printing. March 2021. Published by Image Comics, Inc. Office of publication: PO BOX 14457, Portland, OR 97293.

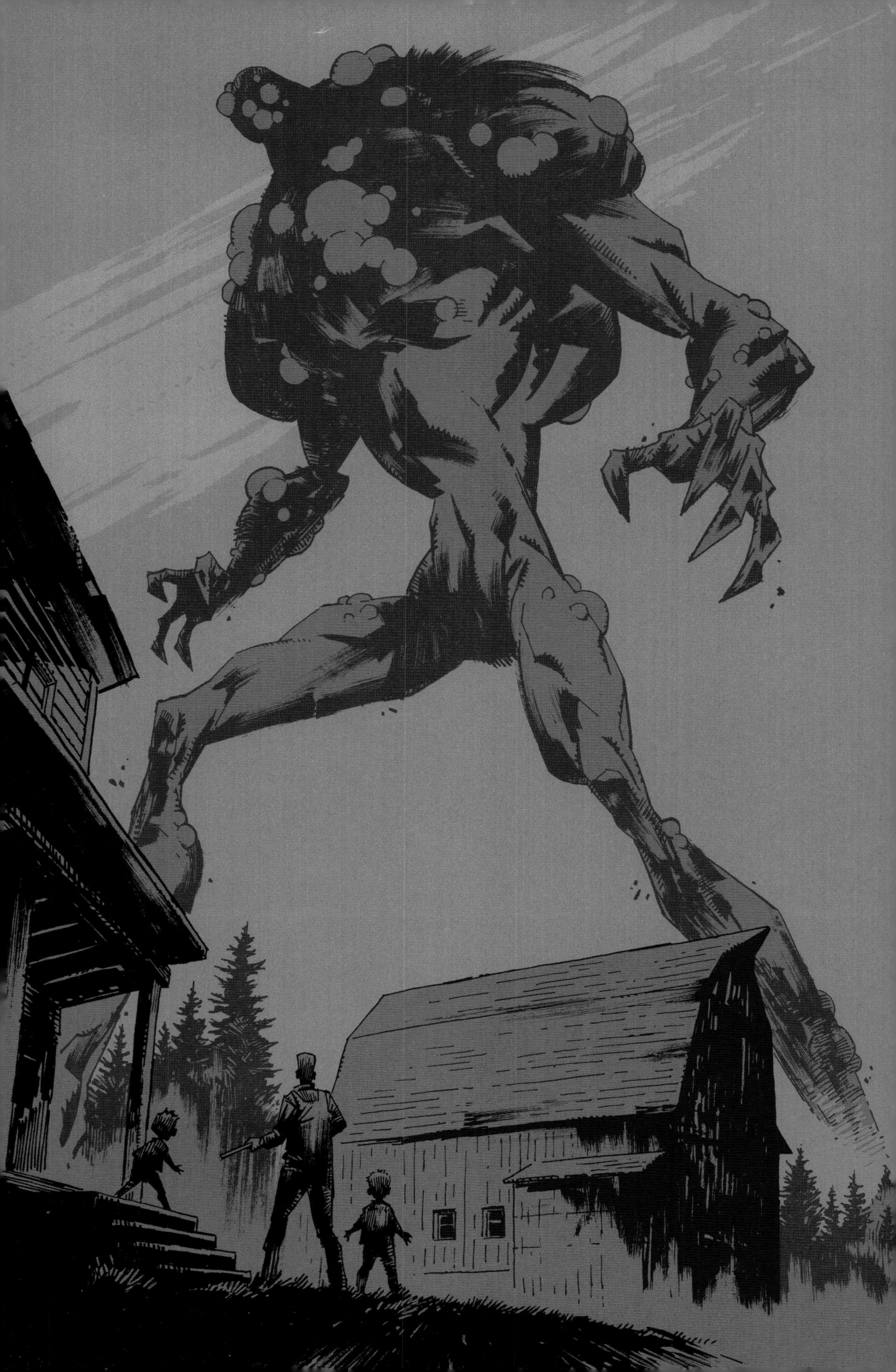

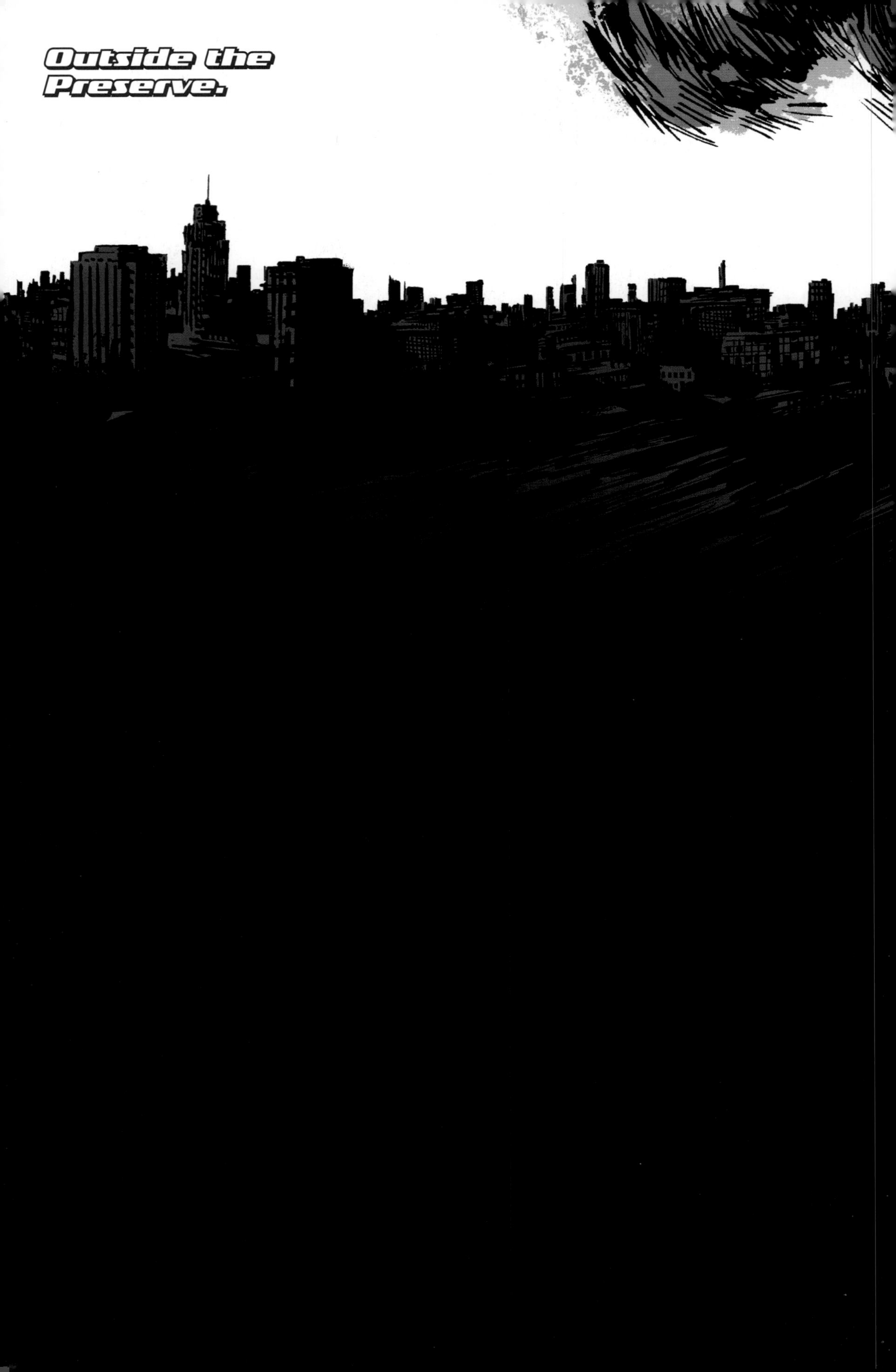
Outside the Preserve.

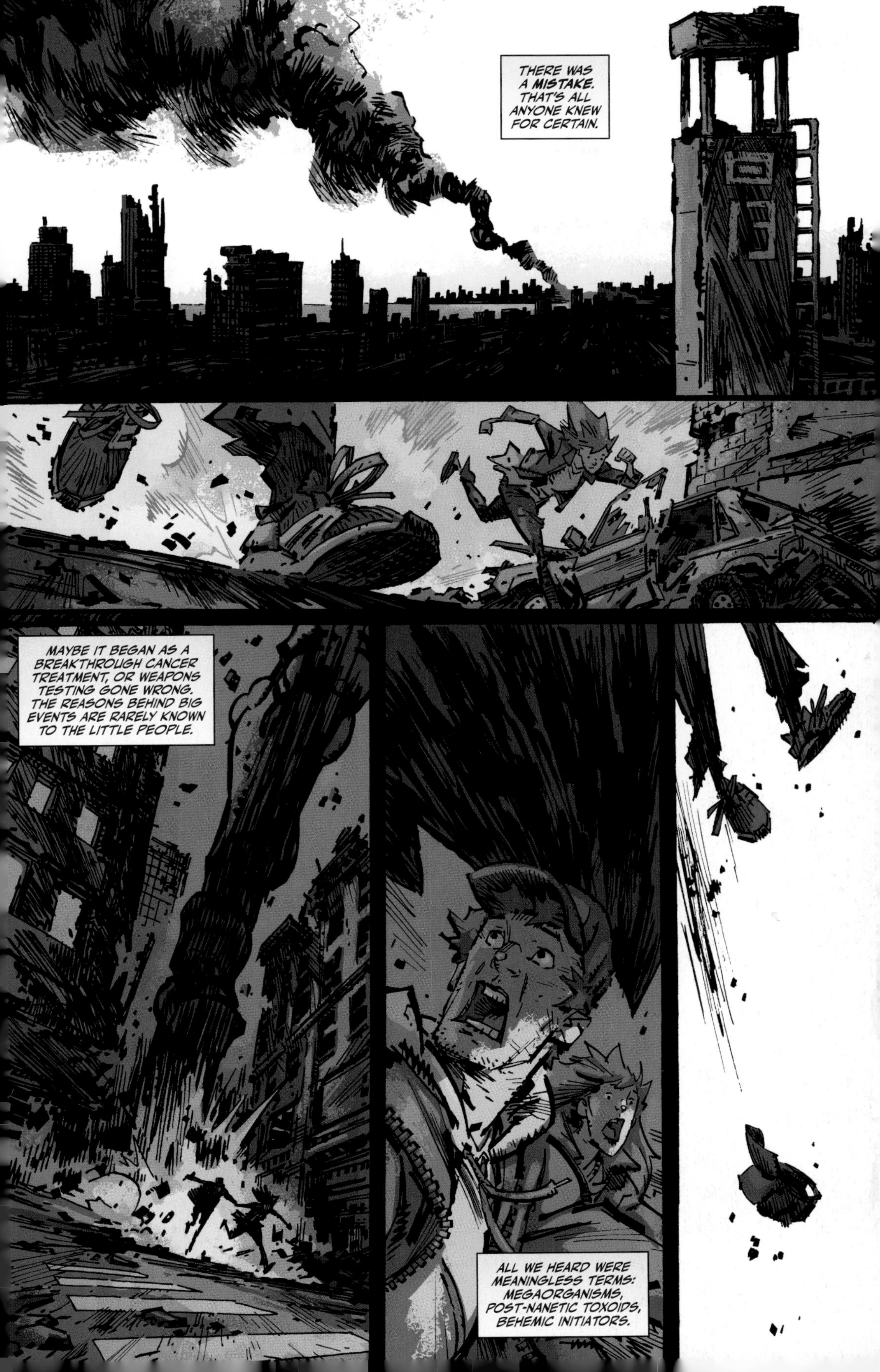
THERE WAS A MISTAKE. THAT'S ALL ANYONE KNEW FOR CERTAIN.
MAYBE IT BEGAN AS A BREAKTHROUGH CANCER TREATMENT, OR WEAPONS TESTING GONE WRONG. THE REASONS BEHIND BIG EVENTS ARE RARELY KNOWN TO THE LITTLE PEOPLE.
ALL WE HEARD WERE MEANINGLESS TERMS: MEGAORGANISMS, POST-NANETIC TOXOIDS, BEHEMIC INITIATORS.

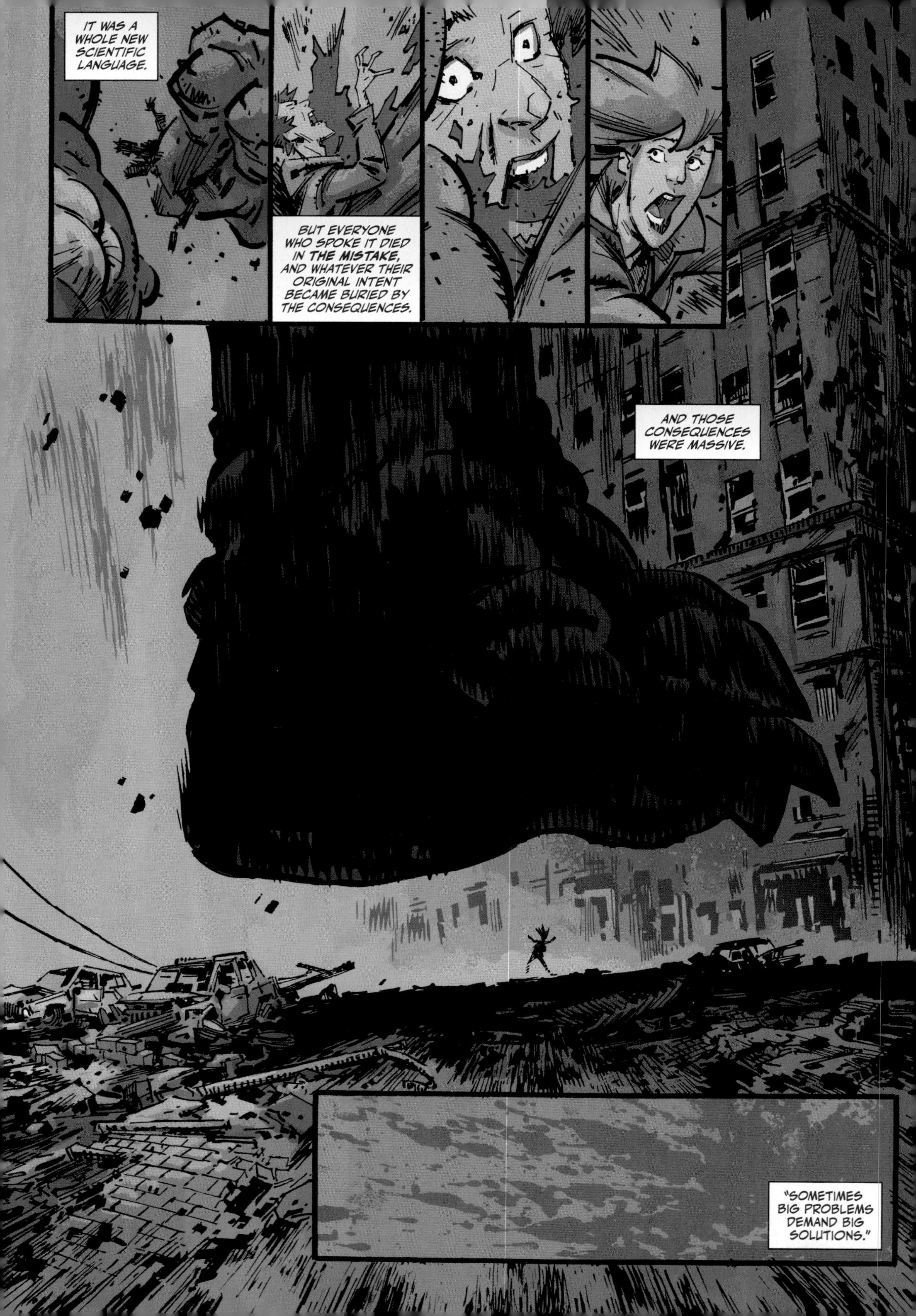
IT WAS A WHOLE NEW SCIENTIFIC LANGUAGE.
BUT EVERYONE WHO SPOKE IT DIED IN THE MISTAKE, AND WHATEVER THEIR ORIGINAL INTENT BECAME BURIED BY THE CONSEQUENCES.
AND THOSE CONSEQUENCES WERE MASSIVE.
"SOMETIMES BIG PROBLEMS DEMAND BIG SOLUTIONS."

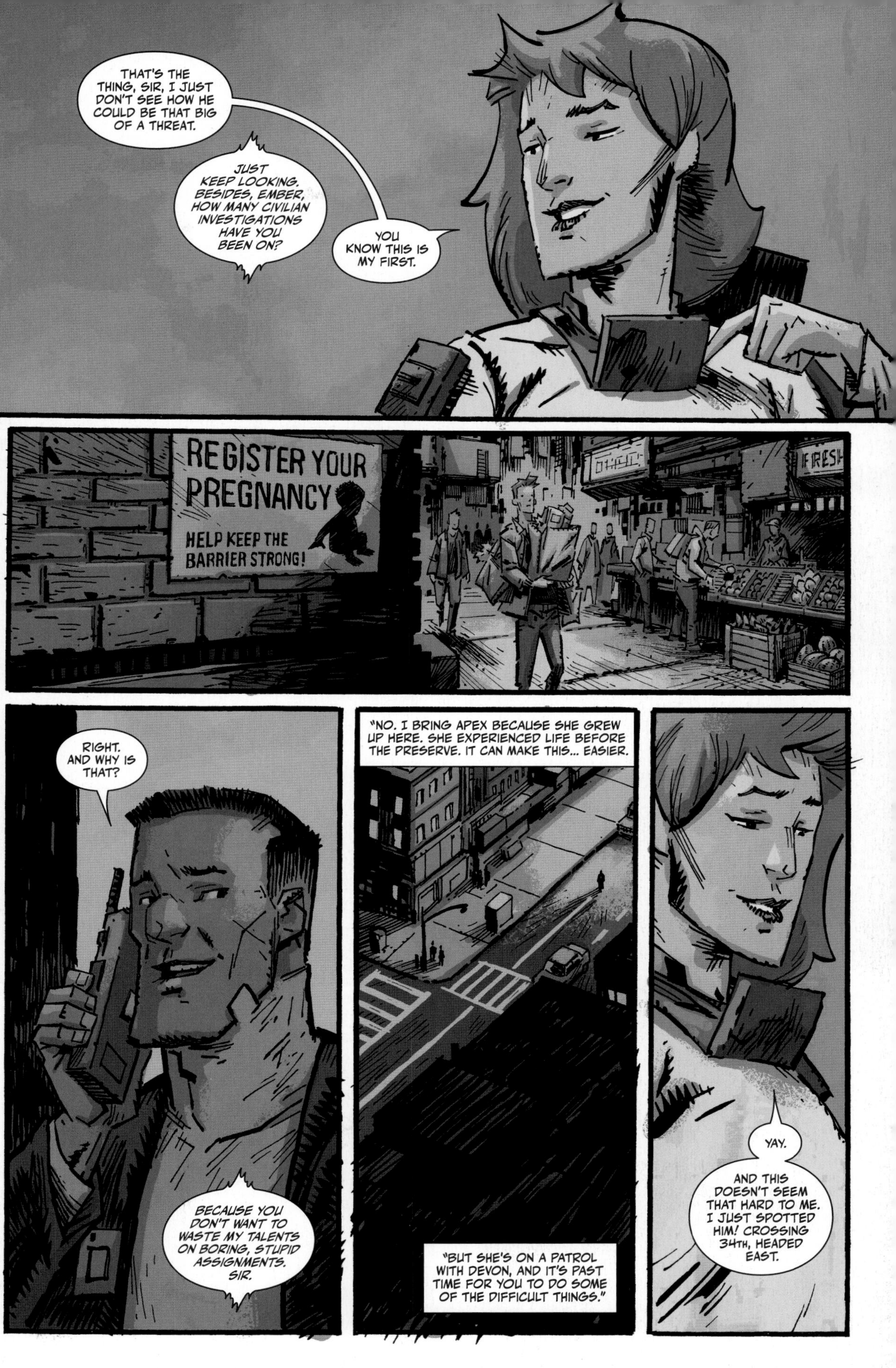
THAT'S THE THING, SIR, I JUST DON'T SEE HOW HE COULD BE THAT BIG OF A THREAT.
JUST KEEP LOOKING. BESIDES, EMBER, HOW MANY CIVILIAN INVESTIGATIONS HAVE YOU BEEN ON?
YOU KNOW THIS IS MY FIRST.
REGISTER YOUR PREGNANCY
HELP KEEP THE BARRIER STRONG!
FRESH
RIGHT. AND WHY IS THAT?
BECAUSE YOU DON'T WANT TO WASTE MY TALENTS ON BORING, STUPID ASSIGNMENTS. SIR.
"NO. I BRING APEX BECAUSE SHE GREW UP HERE. SHE EXPERIENCED LIFE BEFORE THE PRESERVE. IT CAN MAKE THIS... EASIER.
"BUT SHE'S ON A PATROL WITH DEVON, AND IT'S PAST TIME FOR YOU TO DO SOME OF THE DIFFICULT THINGS."
YAY.
AND THIS DOESN'T SEEM THAT HARD TO ME. I JUST SPOTTED HIM! CROSSING 34TH, HEADED EAST.

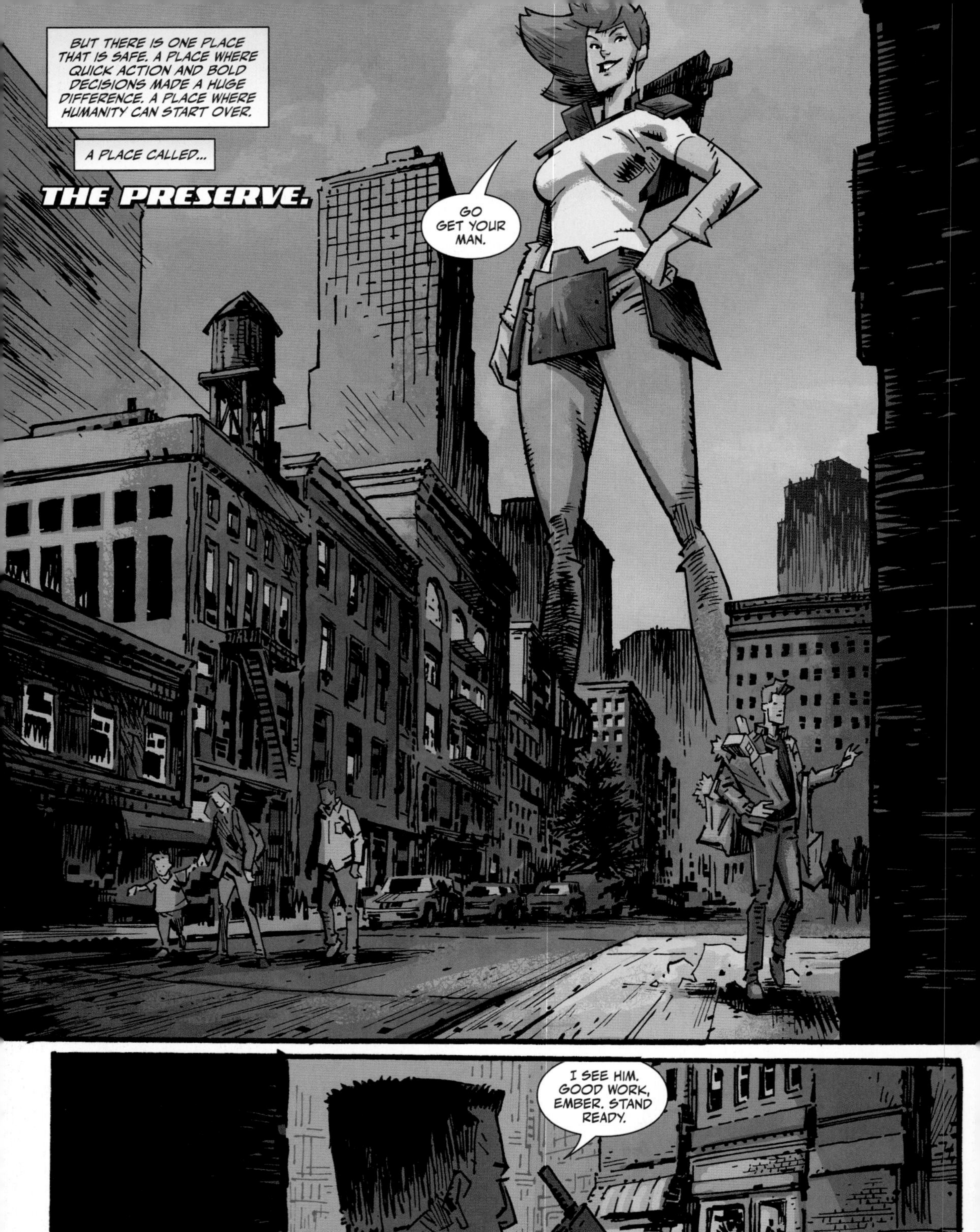
BUT THERE IS ONE PLACE THAT IS SAFE. A PLACE WHERE QUICK ACTION AND BOLD DECISIONS MADE A HUGE DIFFERENCE. A PLACE WHERE HUMANITY CAN START OVER.
A PLACE CALLED...
THE PRESERVE.
GO GET YOUR MAN.

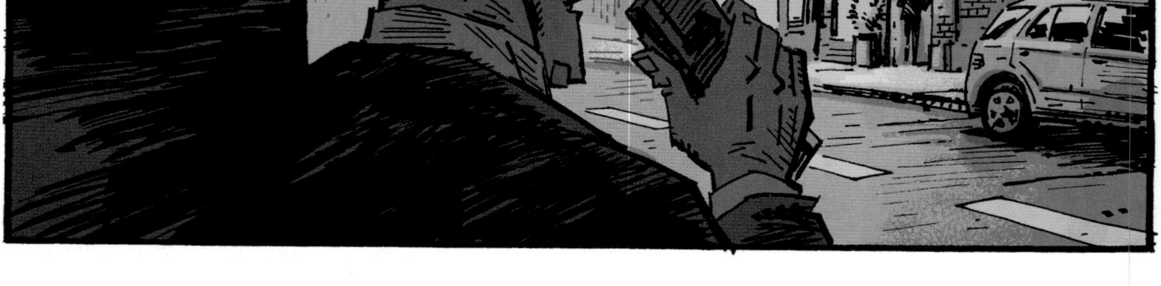
I SEE HIM. GOOD WORK, EMBER. STAND READY.

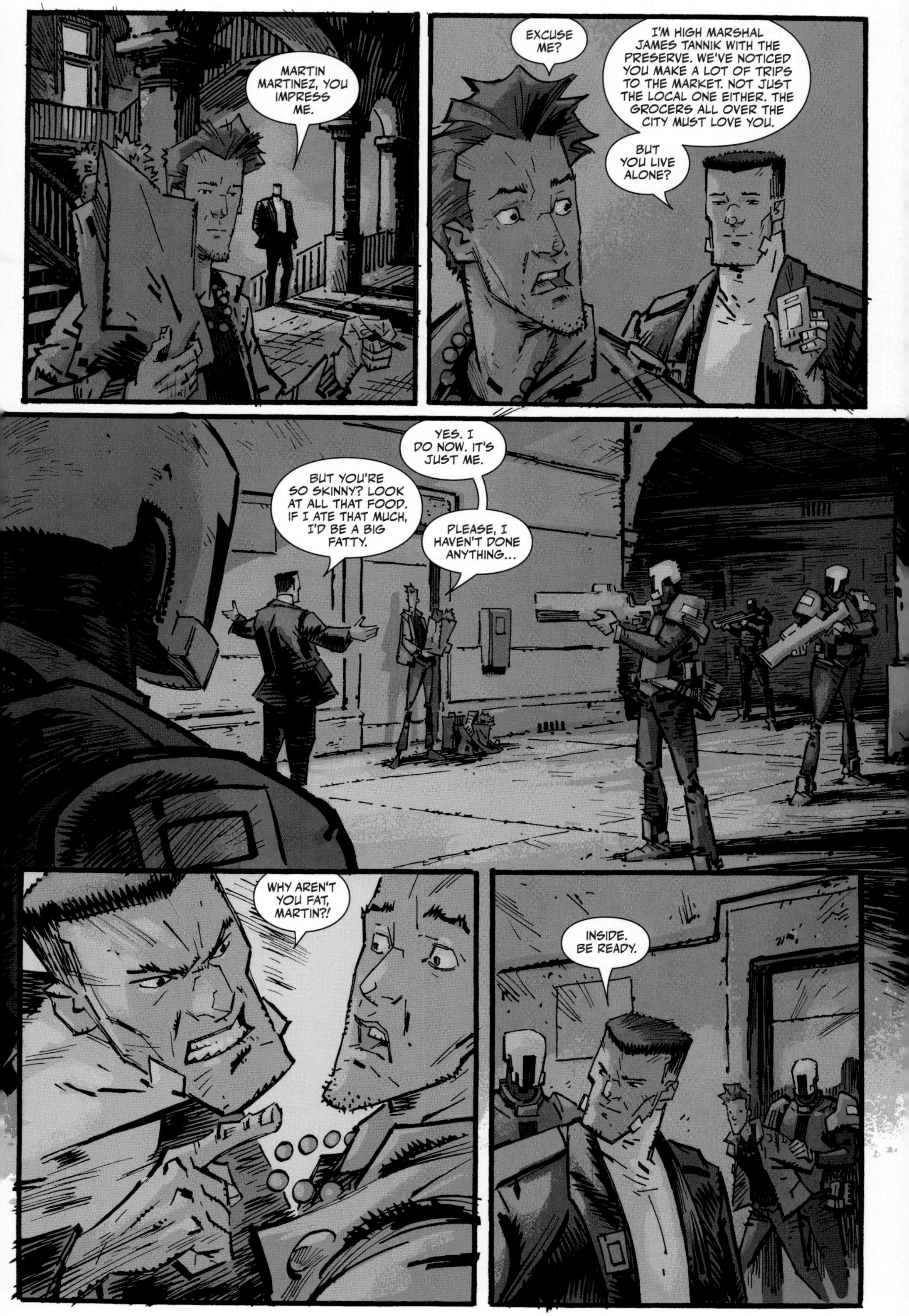
MARTIN MARTINEZ, YOU IMPRESS ME.
EXCUSE ME?
I'M HIGH MARSHAL JAMES TANNIK WITH THE PRESERVE. WE'VE NOTICED YOU MAKE A LOT OF TRIPS TO THE MARKET. NOT JUST THE LOCAL ONE EITHER. THE GROCERS ALL OVER THE CITY MUST LOVE YOU.
BUT YOU LIVE ALONE?
YES. I DO NOW. IT'S JUST ME.
BUT YOU'RE SO SKINNY? LOOK AT ALL THAT FOOD. IF I ATE THAT MUCH, I'D BE A BIG FATTY.
PLEASE, I HAVEN'T DONE ANYTHING...
WHY AREN'T YOU FAT, MARTIN?!
INSIDE. BE READY.

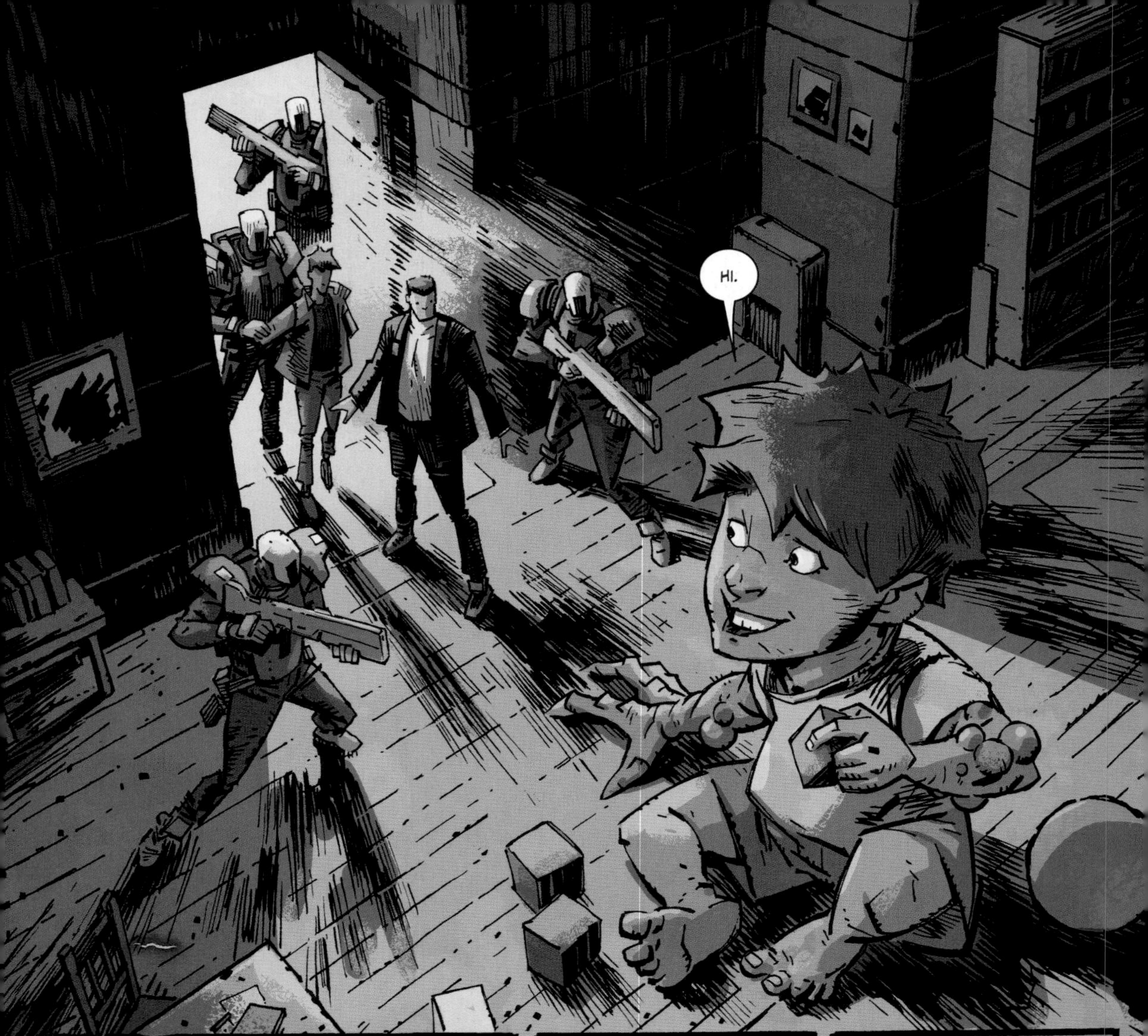
HI.

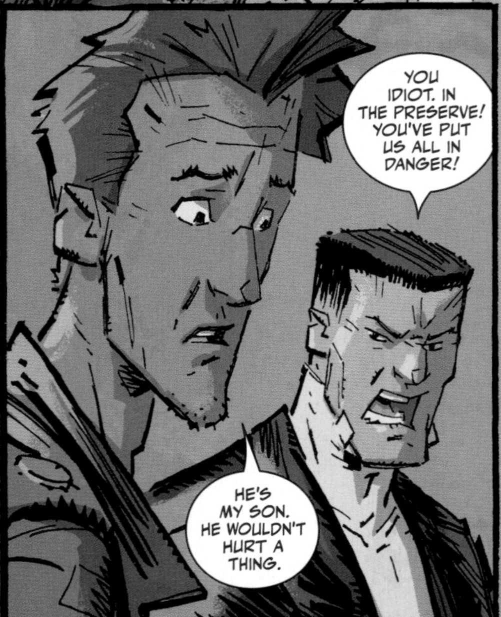
YOU IDIOT. IN THE PRESERVE! YOU'VE PUT US ALL IN DANGER!
HE'S MY SON. HE WOULDN'T HURT A THING.

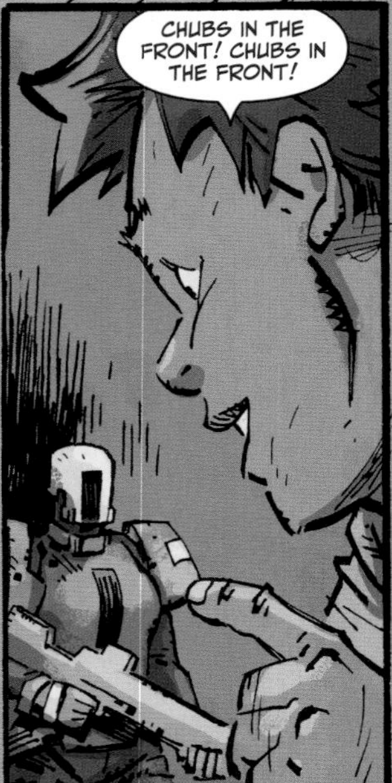
CHUBS IN THE FRONT! CHUBS IN THE FRONT!

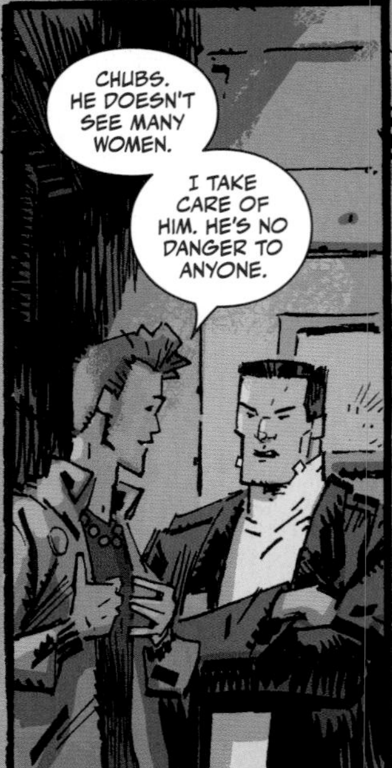
CHUBS. HE DOESN'T SEE MANY WOMEN.
I TAKE CARE OF HIM. HE'S NO DANGER TO ANYONE.

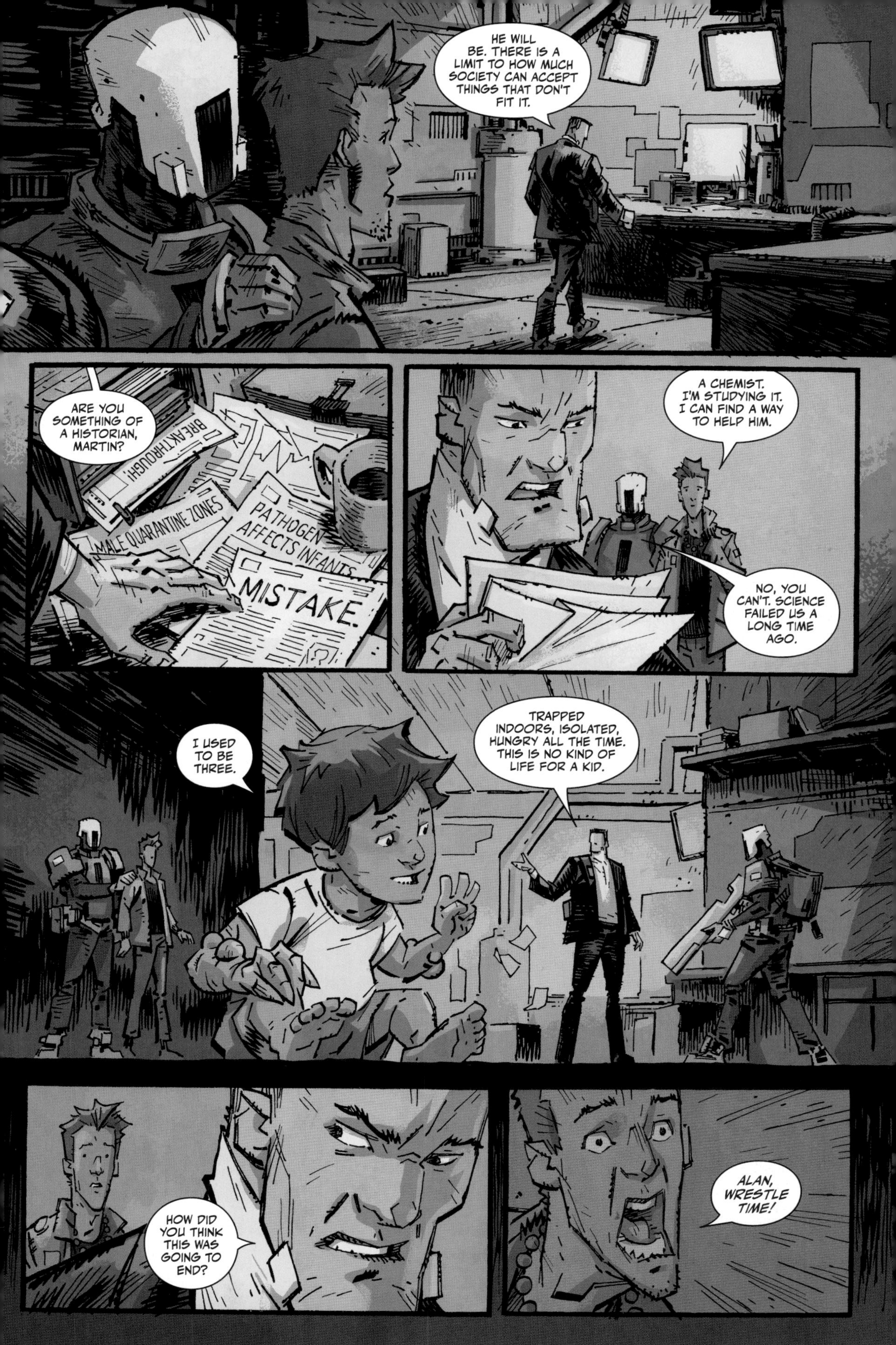
HE WILL BE. THERE IS A LIMIT TO HOW MUCH SOCIETY CAN ACCEPT THINGS THAT DON'T FIT IT.
ARE YOU SOMETHING OF A HISTORIAN, MARTIN?
BREAKTHROUGH
MALE QUARANTINE ZONES
PATHOGEN AFFECTS INFANTS
MISTAKE.
A CHEMIST. I'M STUDYING IT. I CAN FIND A WAY TO HELP HIM.
NO, YOU CAN'T. SCIENCE FAILED US A LONG TIME AGO.
I USED TO BE THREE.
TRAPPED INDOORS, ISOLATED, HUNGRY ALL THE TIME. THIS IS NO KIND OF LIFE FOR A KID.
HOW DID YOU THINK THIS WAS GOING TO END?
ALAN, WRESTLE TIME!

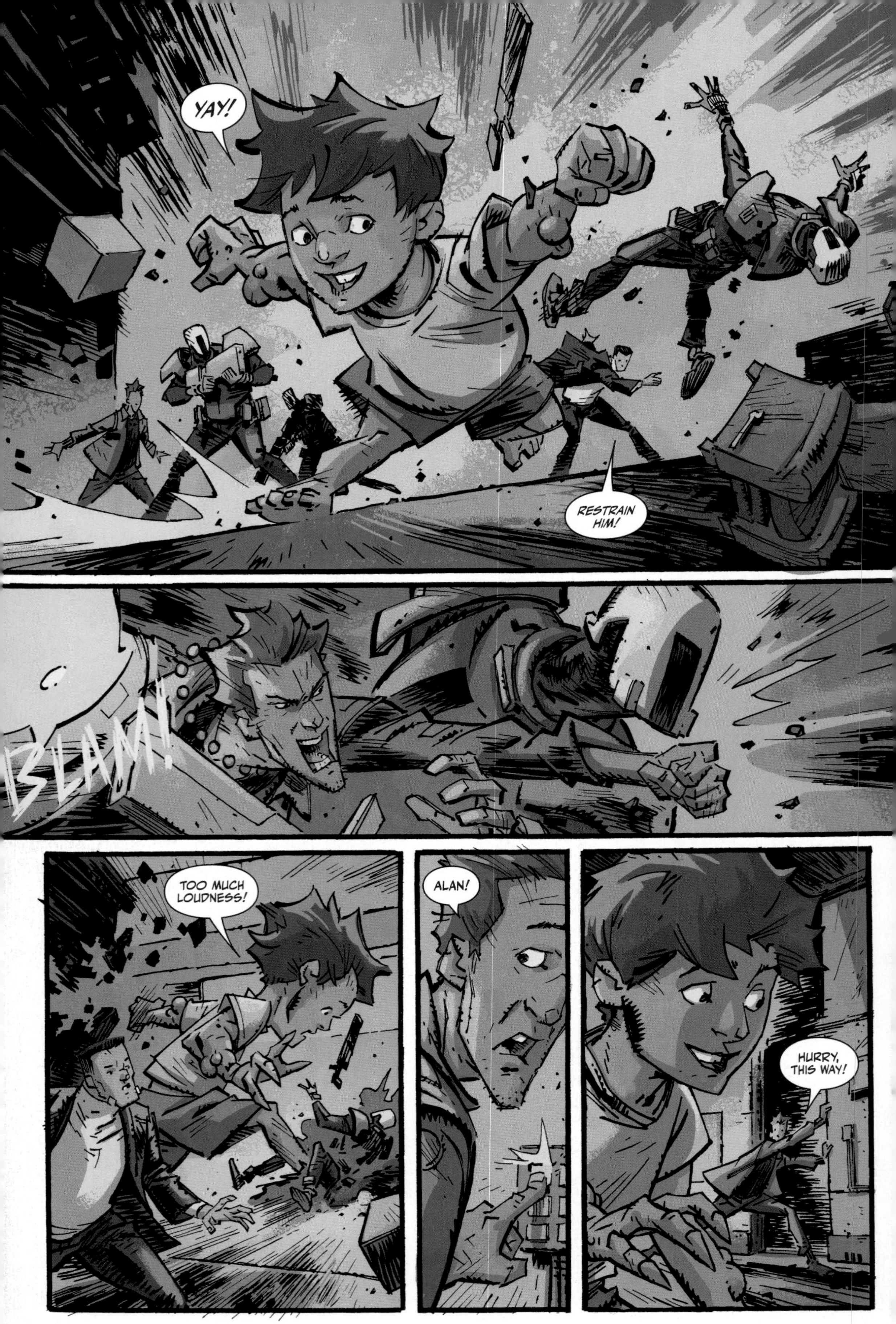
YAY!
RESTRAIN HIM!
BLAM!
TOO MUCH LOUDNESS!
ALAN!
HURRY, THIS WAY!

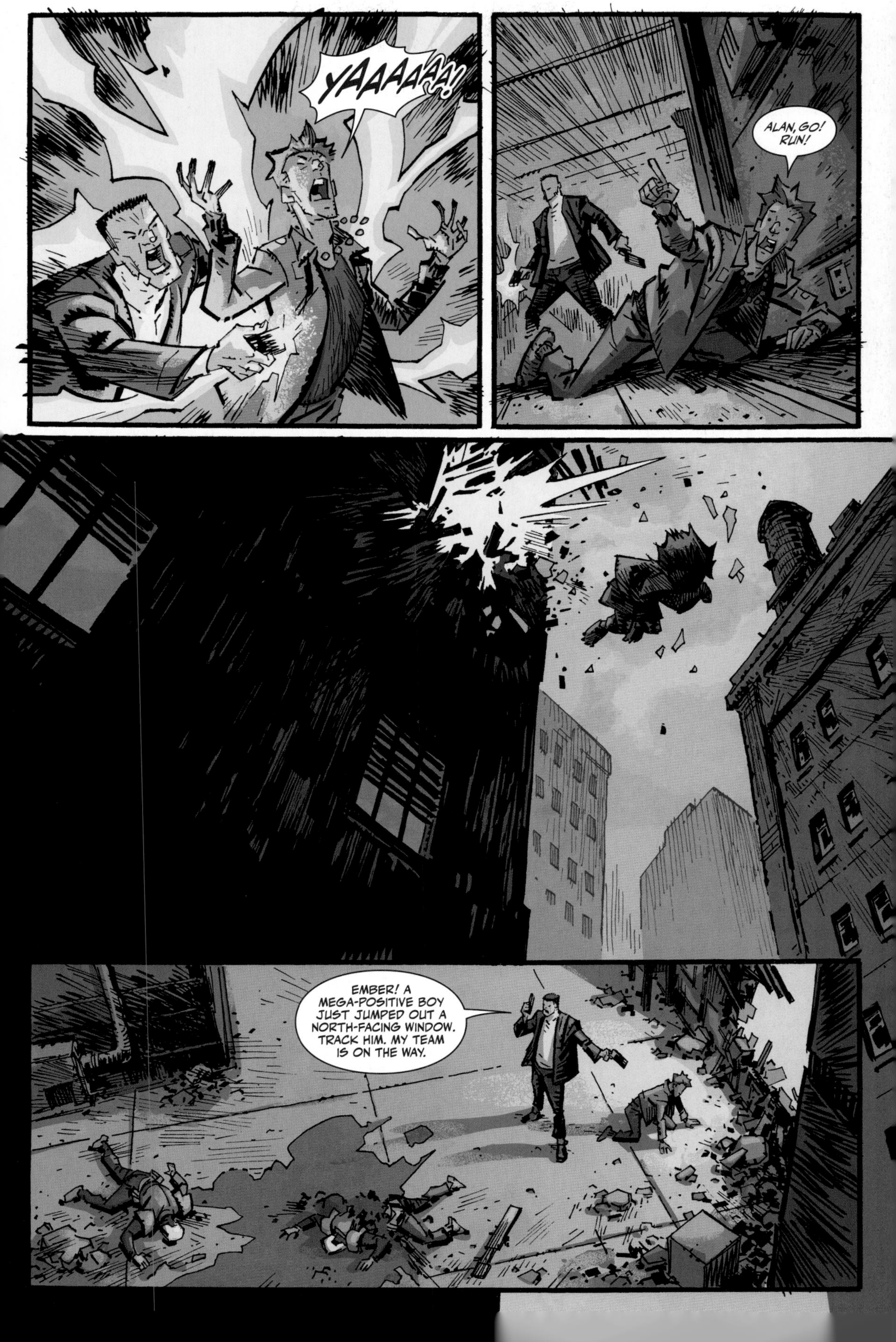
YAAAAAA!
ALAN, GO! RUN!
EMBER! A MEGA-POSITIVE BOY JUST JUMPED OUT A NORTH-FACING WINDOW. TRACK HIM. MY TEAM IS ON THE WAY.

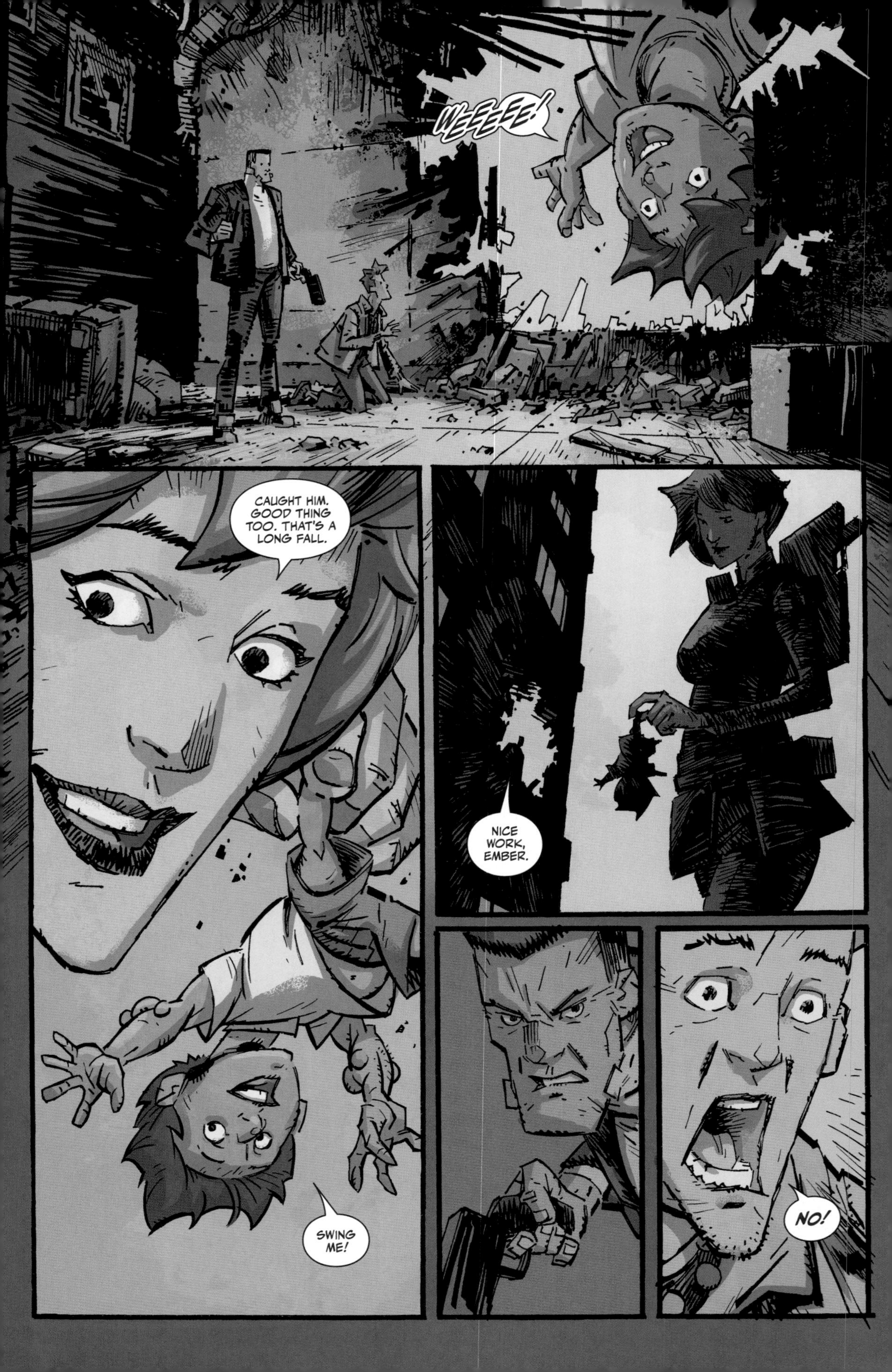
WEEEEEE!
CAUGHT HIM. GOOD THING TOO. THAT'S A LONG FALL.
SWING ME!
NICE WORK, EMBER.
NO!

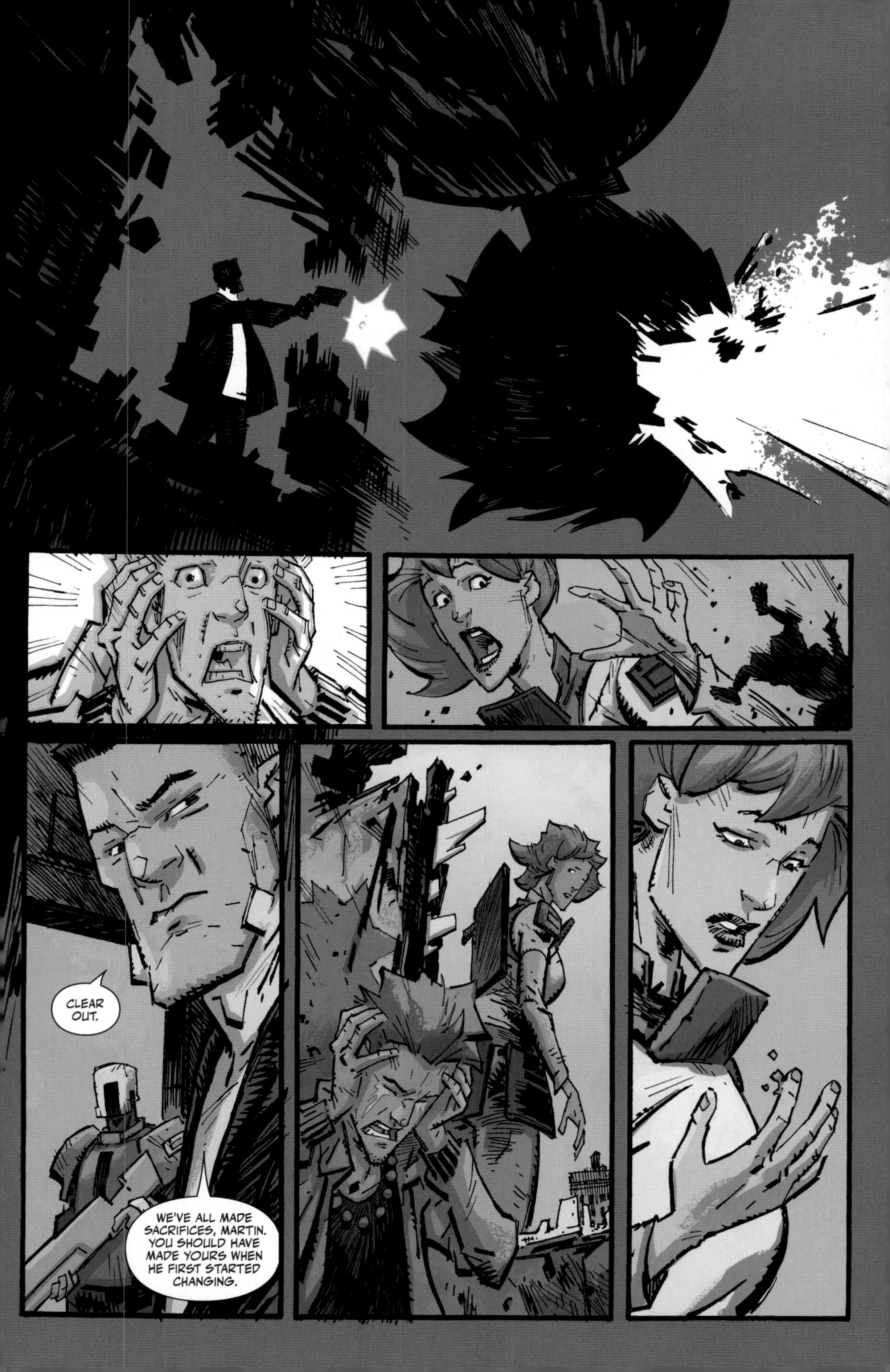
CLEAR OUT.
WE'VE ALL MADE SACRIFICES, MARTIN. YOU SHOULD HAVE MADE YOURS WHEN HE FIRST STARTED CHANGING.

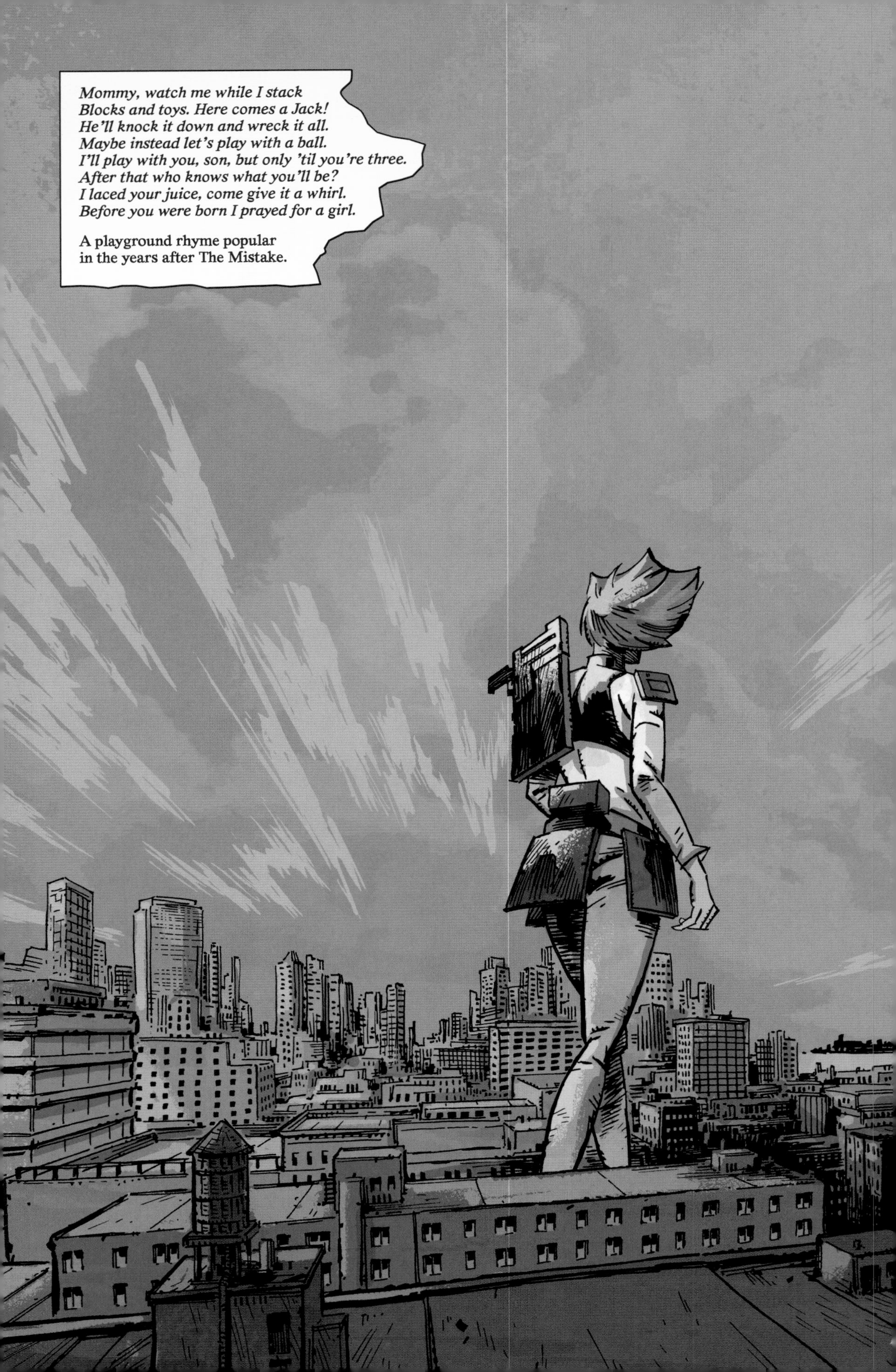
*Mommy, watch me while I stack
Blocks and toys. Here comes a Jack!
He'll knock it down and wreck it all.
Maybe instead let's play with a ball.
I'll play with you, son, but only 'til you're three.
After that who knows what you'll be?
I laced your juice, come give it a whirl.
Before you were born I prayed for a girl.*
A playground rhyme popular
in the years after The Mistake.

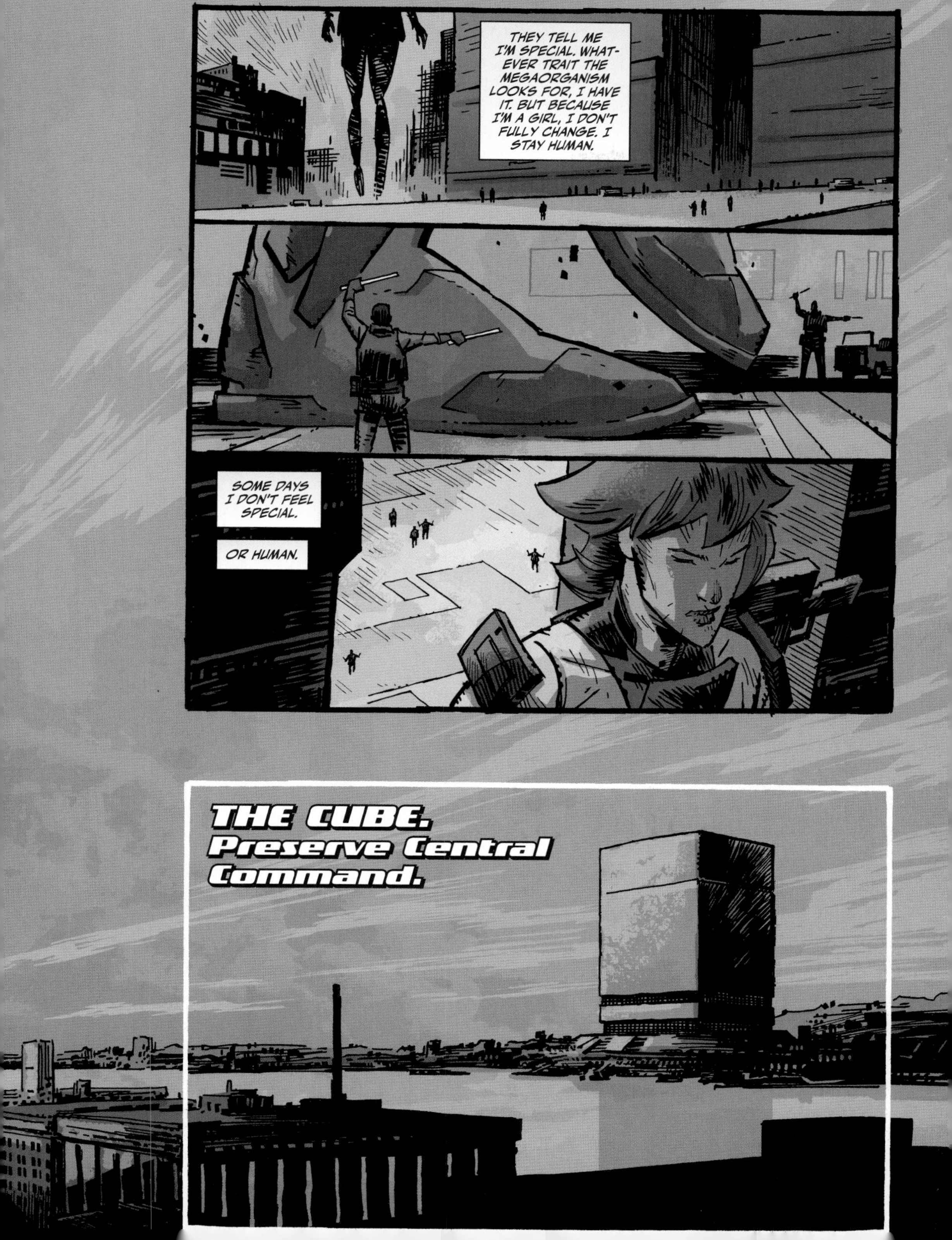

THEY TELL ME I'M SPECIAL. WHATEVER TRAIT THE MEGAORGANISM LOOKS FOR, I HAVE IT. BUT BECAUSE I'M A GIRL, I DON'T FULLY CHANGE. I STAY HUMAN.
SOME DAYS I DON'T FEEL SPECIAL.
OR HUMAN.
THE CUBE. Preserve Central Command.

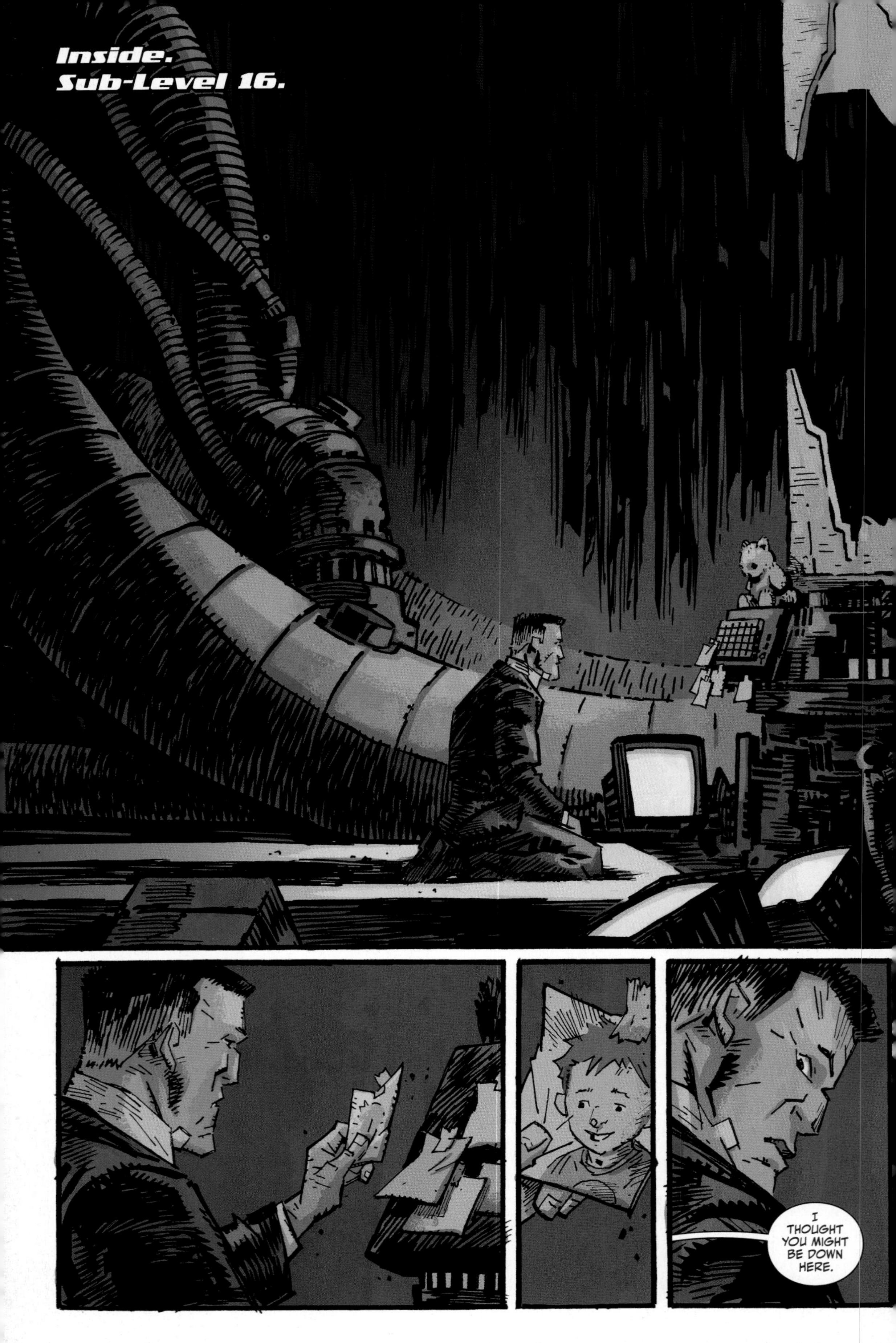
Inside.
Sub-Level 16.
I THOUGHT YOU MIGHT BE DOWN HERE.

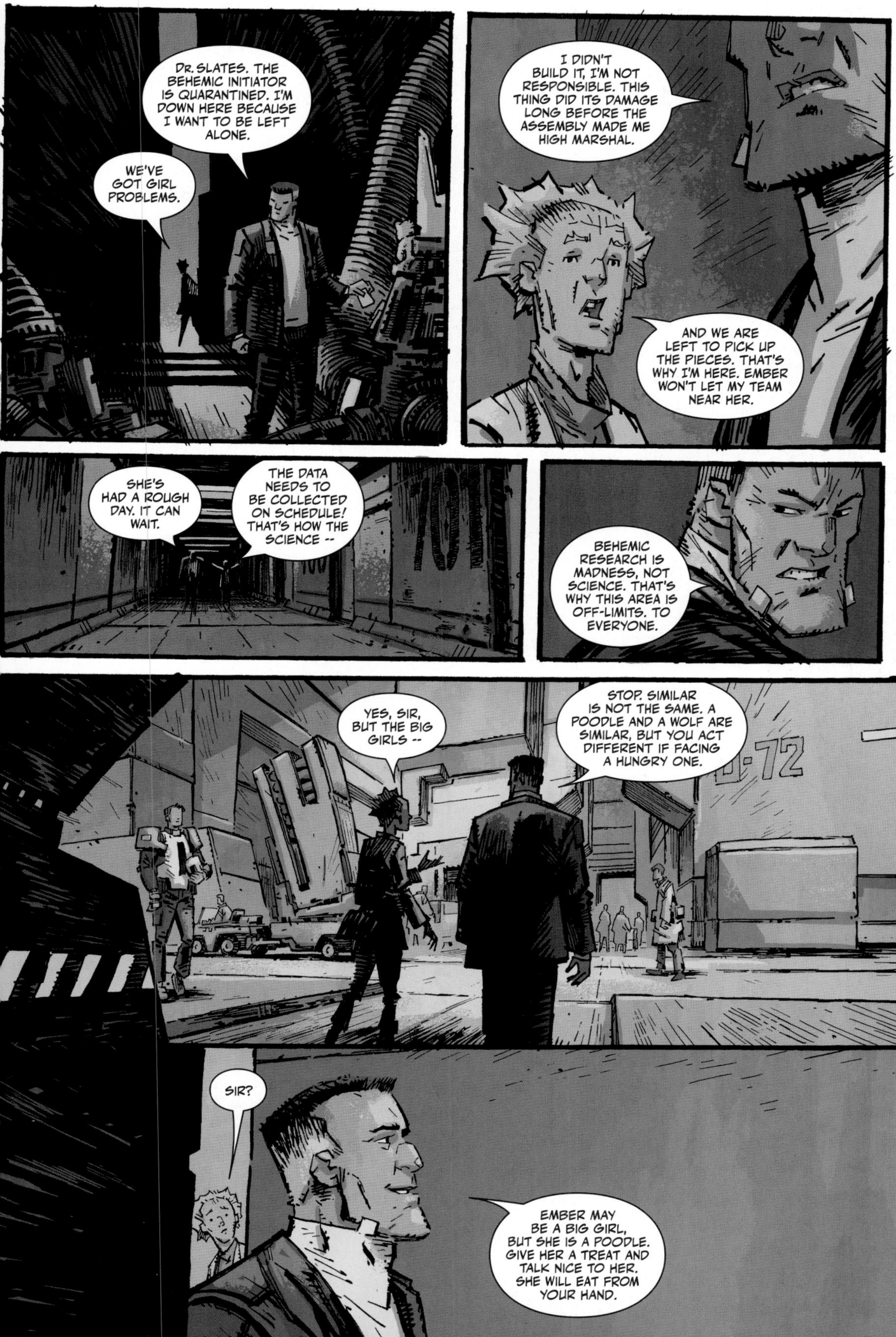
Dr. SLATES. THE BEHEMIC INITIATOR IS QUARANTINED. I'M DOWN HERE BECAUSE I WANT TO BE LEFT ALONE.
WE'VE GOT GIRL PROBLEMS.
I DIDN'T BUILD IT, I'M NOT RESPONSIBLE. THIS THING DID ITS DAMAGE LONG BEFORE THE ASSEMBLY MADE ME HIGH MARSHAL.
AND WE ARE LEFT TO PICK UP THE PIECES. THAT'S WHY I'M HERE. EMBER WON'T LET MY TEAM NEAR HER.
SHE'S HAD A ROUGH DAY. IT CAN WAIT.
THE DATA NEEDS TO BE COLLECTED ON SCHEDULE! THAT'S HOW THE SCIENCE --
BEHEMIC RESEARCH IS MADNESS, NOT SCIENCE. THAT'S WHY THIS AREA IS OFF-LIMITS. TO EVERYONE.
YES, SIR, BUT THE BIG GIRLS --
STOP. SIMILAR IS NOT THE SAME. A POODLE AND A WOLF ARE SIMILAR, BUT YOU ACT DIFFERENT IF FACING A HUNGRY ONE.
SIR?
EMBER MAY BE A BIG GIRL, BUT SHE IS A POODLE. GIVE HER A TREAT AND TALK NICE TO HER. SHE WILL EAT FROM YOUR HAND.

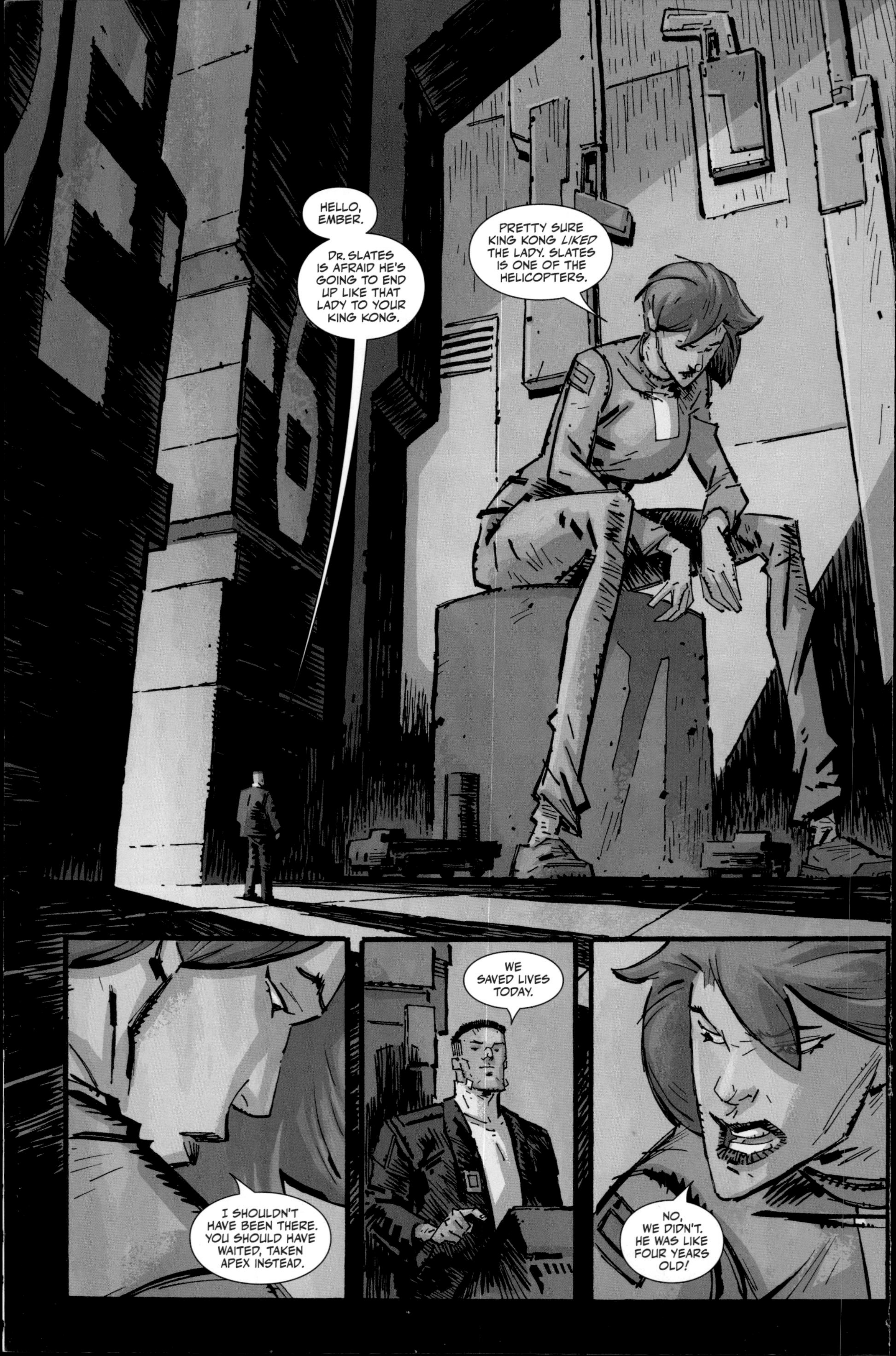
HELLO, EMBER.
DR. SLATES IS AFRAID HE'S GOING TO END UP LIKE THAT LADY TO YOUR KING KONG.
PRETTY SURE KING KONG *LIKED* THE LADY. SLATES IS ONE OF THE HELICOPTERS.
I SHOULDN'T HAVE BEEN THERE. YOU SHOULD HAVE WAITED, TAKEN APEX INSTEAD.
WE SAVED LIVES TODAY.
NO, WE DIDN'T. HE WAS LIKE FOUR YEARS OLD!

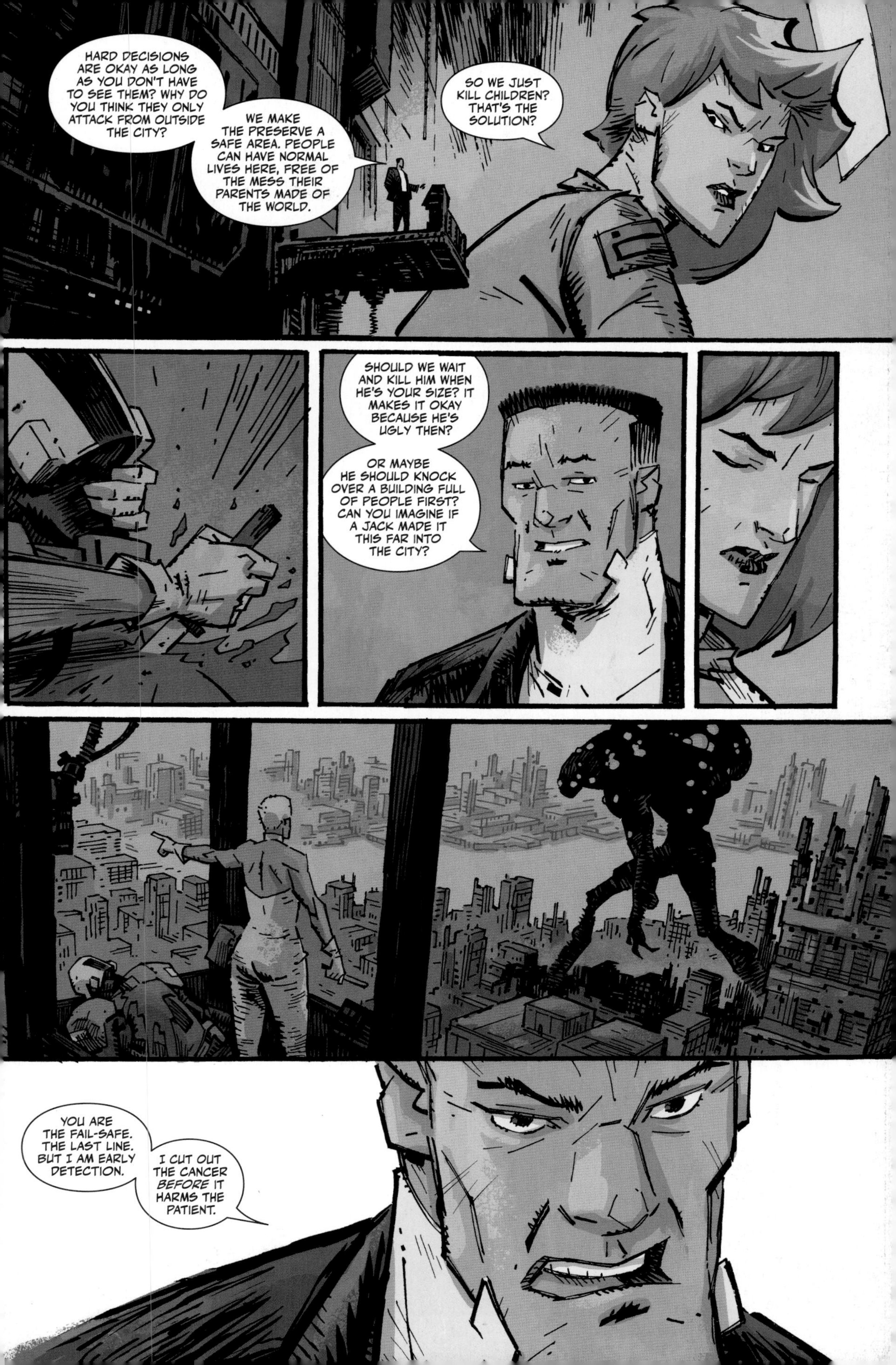
HARD DECISIONS ARE OKAY AS LONG AS YOU DON'T HAVE TO SEE THEM? WHY DO YOU THINK THEY ONLY ATTACK FROM OUTSIDE THE CITY?
WE MAKE THE PRESERVE A SAFE AREA. PEOPLE CAN HAVE NORMAL LIVES HERE, FREE OF THE MESS THEIR PARENTS MADE OF THE WORLD.
SO WE JUST KILL CHILDREN? THAT'S THE SOLUTION?
SHOULD WE WAIT AND KILL HIM WHEN HE'S YOUR SIZE? IT MAKES IT OKAY BECAUSE HE'S UGLY THEN?
OR MAYBE HE SHOULD KNOCK OVER A BUILDING FULL OF PEOPLE FIRST? CAN YOU IMAGINE IF A JACK MADE IT THIS FAR INTO THE CITY?
YOU ARE THE FAIL-SAFE. THE LAST LINE. BUT I AM EARLY DETECTION.
I CUT OUT THE CANCER *BEFORE* IT HARMS THE PATIENT.

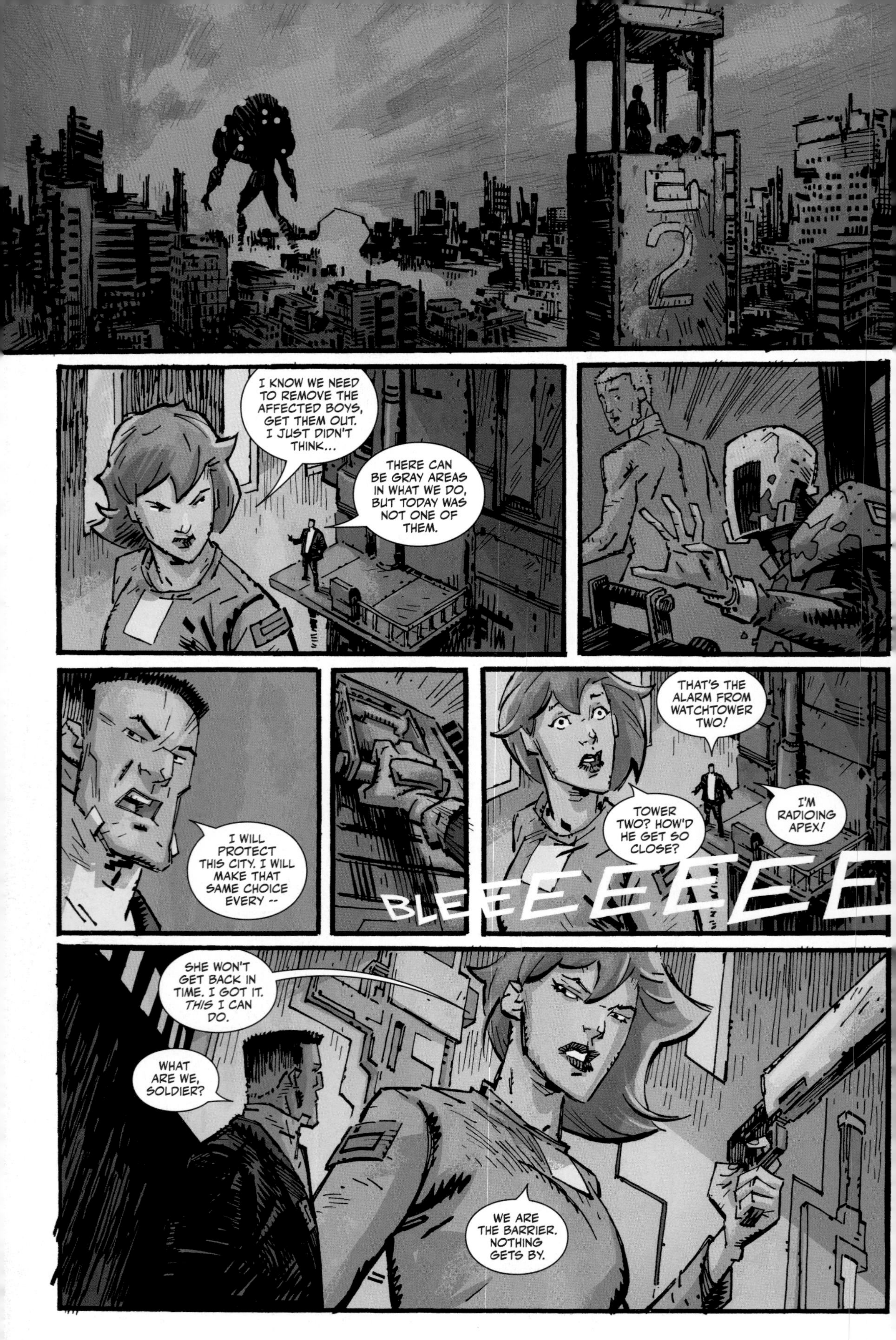
I KNOW WE NEED TO REMOVE THE AFFECTED BOYS, GET THEM OUT. I JUST DIDN'T THINK...
THERE CAN BE GRAY AREAS IN WHAT WE DO, BUT TODAY WAS NOT ONE OF THEM.
I WILL PROTECT THIS CITY. I WILL MAKE THAT SAME CHOICE EVERY --
BLEEEEEEEE
THAT'S THE ALARM FROM WATCHTOWER TWO!
TOWER TWO? HOW'D HE GET SO CLOSE?
I'M RADIOING APEX!
SHE WON'T GET BACK IN TIME. I GOT IT. *THIS* I CAN DO.
WHAT ARE WE, SOLDIER?
WE ARE THE BARRIER. NOTHING GETS BY.

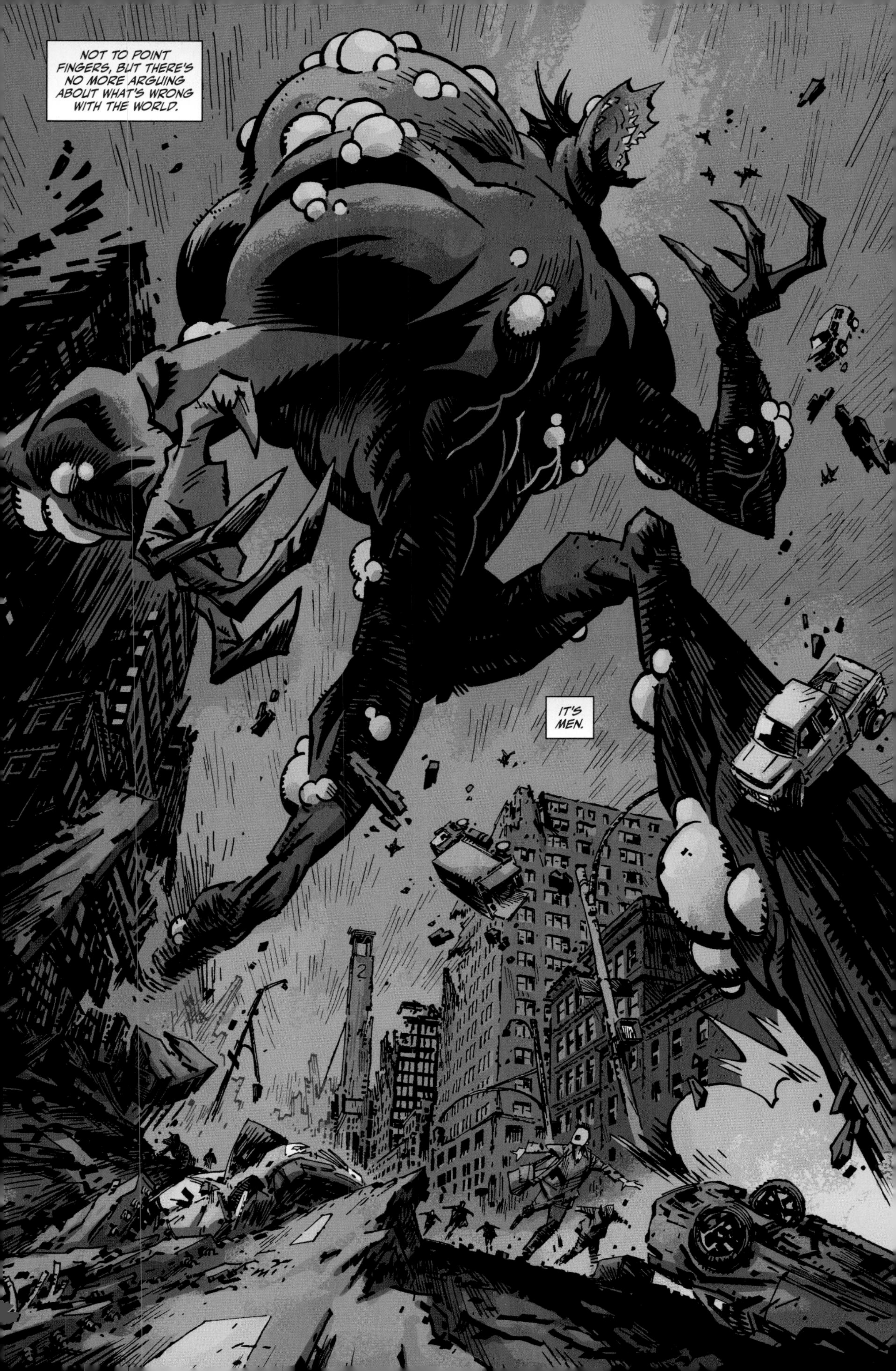
NOT TO POINT FINGERS, BUT THERE'S NO MORE ARGUING ABOUT WHAT'S WRONG WITH THE WORLD.
IT'S MEN.

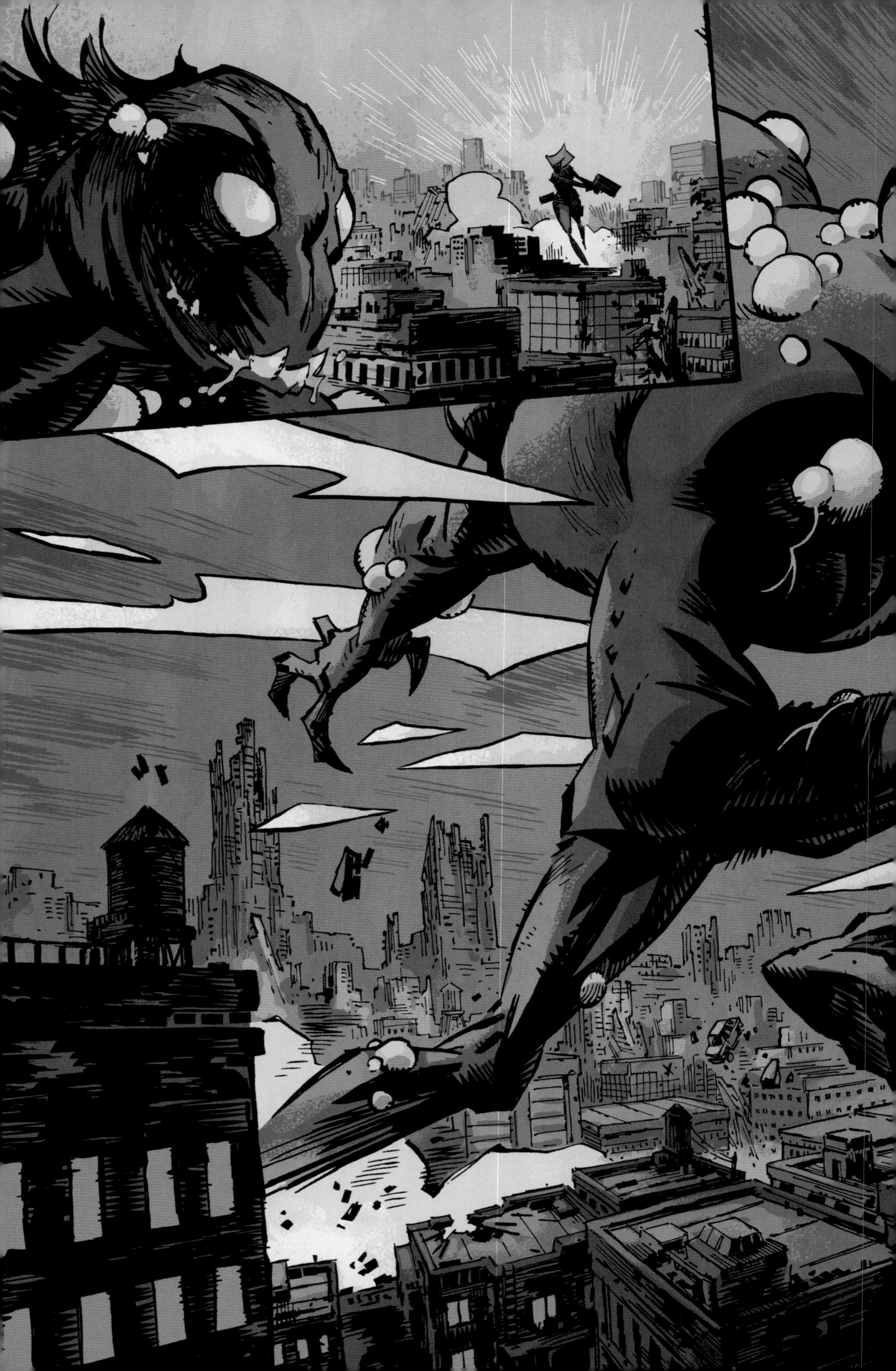

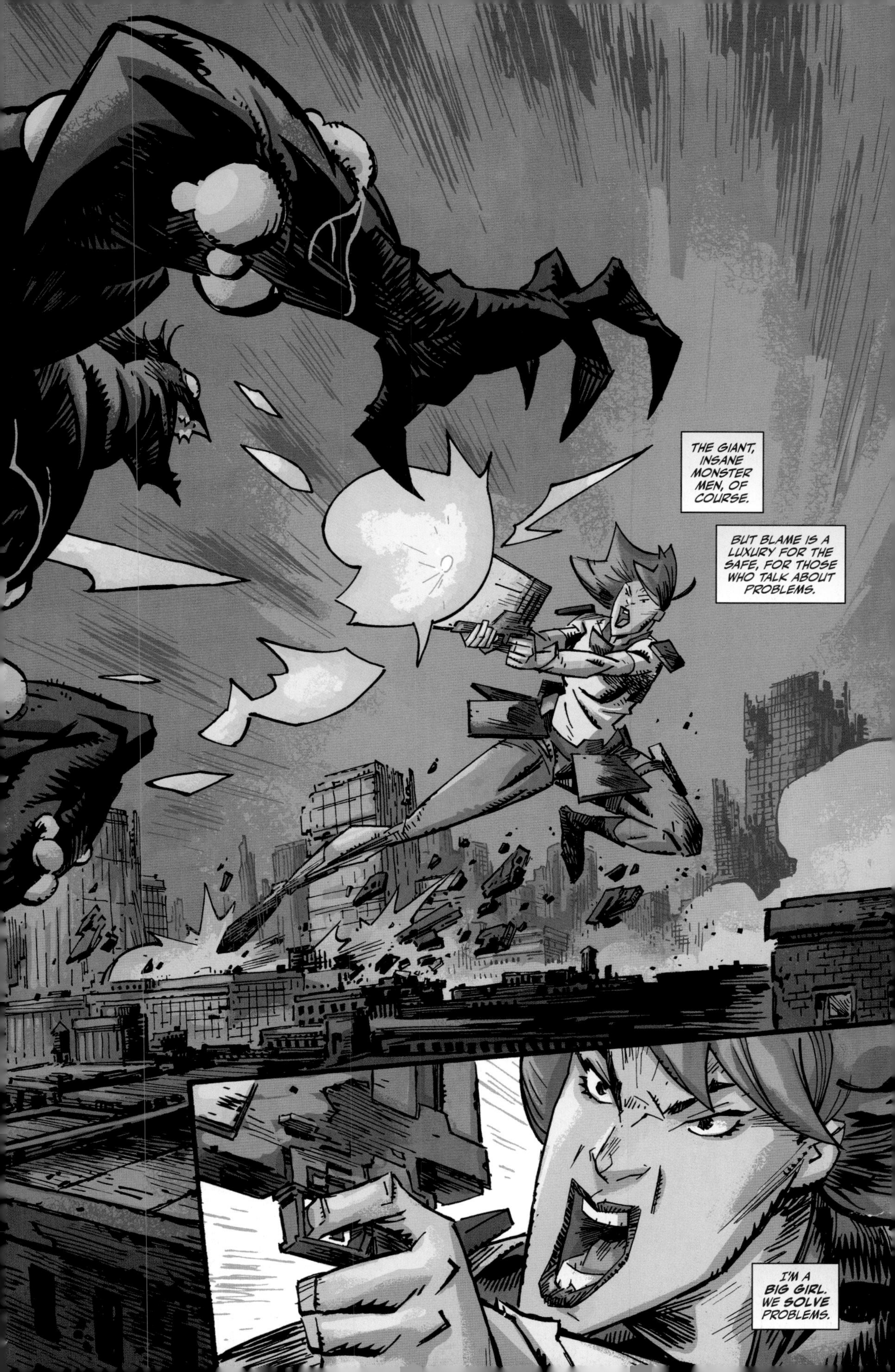
THE GIANT, INSANE MONSTER MEN, OF COURSE.
BUT BLAME IS A LUXURY FOR THE SAFE, FOR THOSE WHO TALK ABOUT PROBLEMS.
I'M A BIG GIRL. WE SOLVE PROBLEMS.

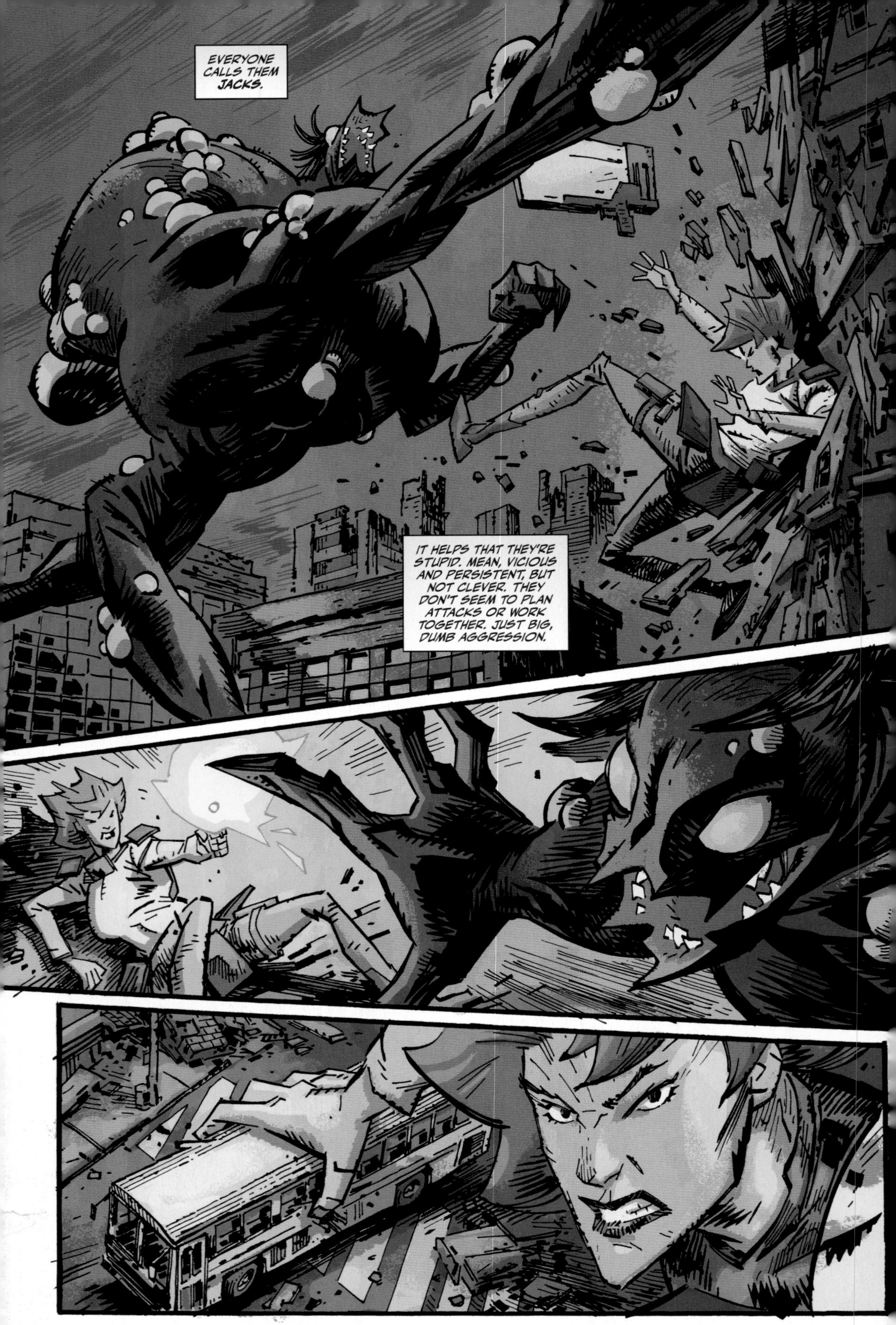
EVERYONE CALLS THEM JACKS.
IT HELPS THAT THEY'RE STUPID. MEAN, VICIOUS AND PERSISTENT, BUT NOT CLEVER. THEY DON'T SEEM TO PLAN ATTACKS OR WORK TOGETHER. JUST BIG, DUMB AGGRESSION.

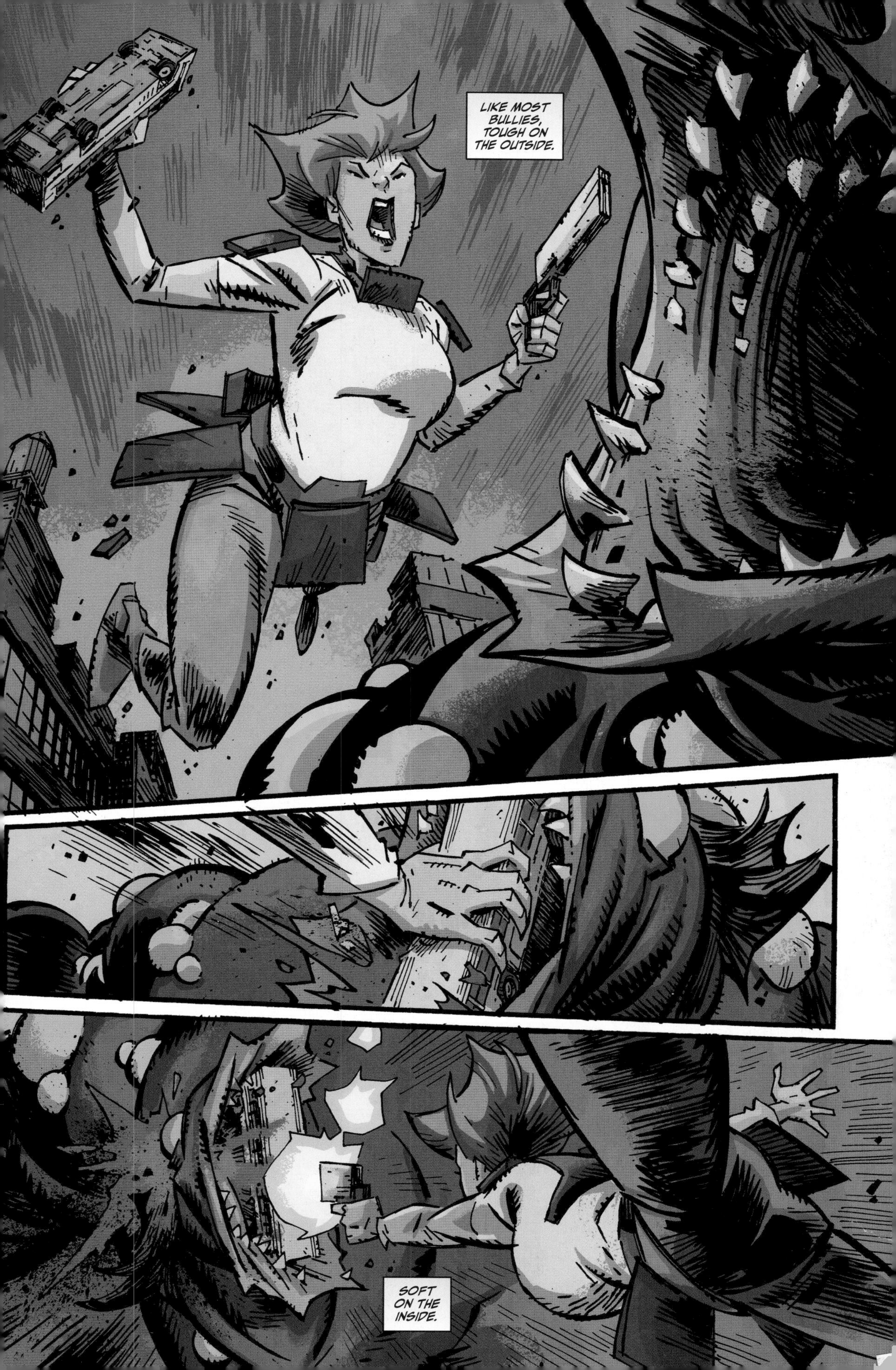
LIKE MOST BULLIES, TOUGH ON THE OUTSIDE.
SOFT ON THE INSIDE.

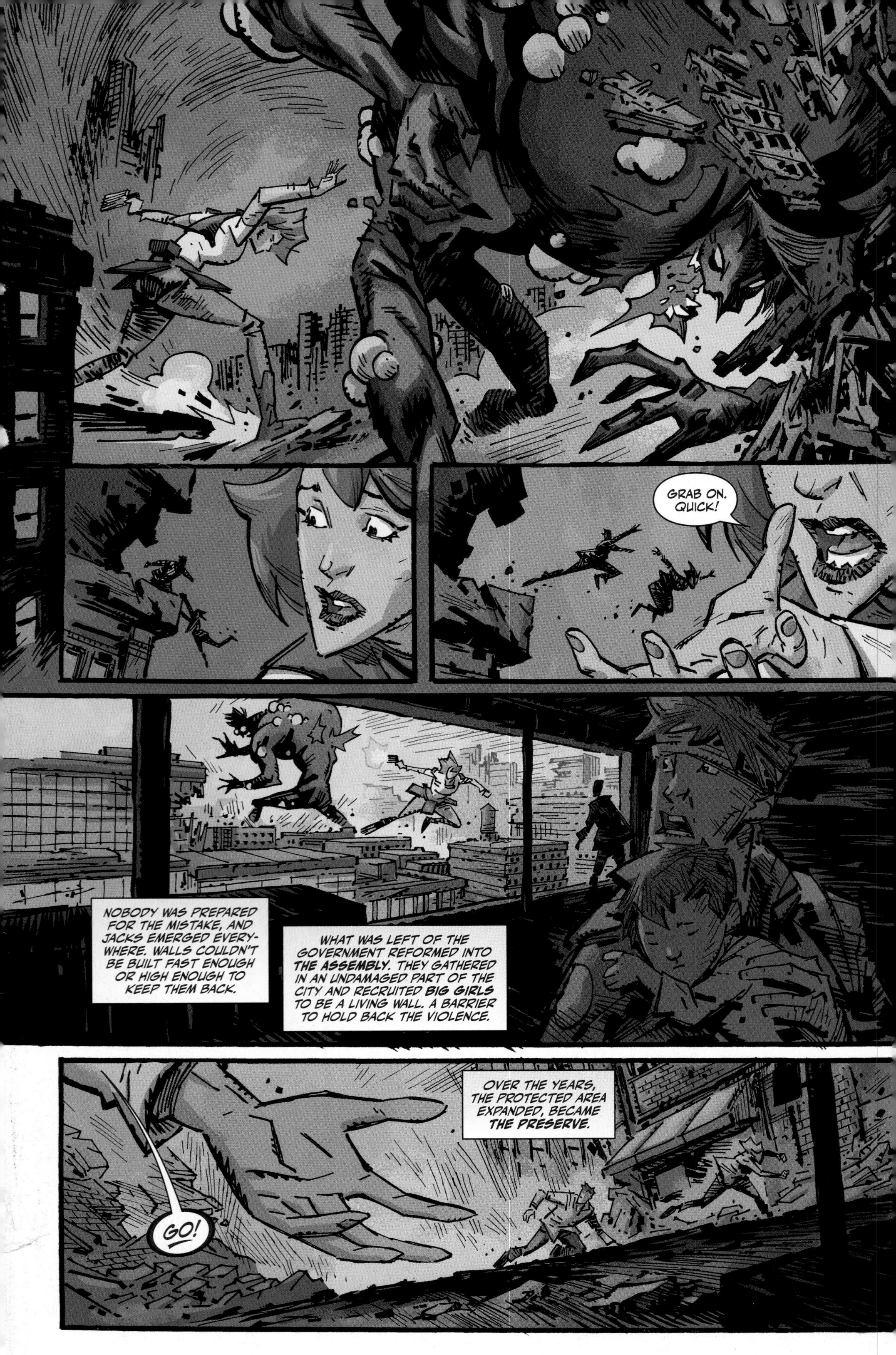
GRAB ON. QUICK!
NOBODY WAS PREPARED FOR THE MISTAKE, AND JACKS EMERGED EVERYWHERE. WALLS COULDN'T BE BUILT FAST ENOUGH OR HIGH ENOUGH TO KEEP THEM BACK.
WHAT WAS LEFT OF THE GOVERNMENT REFORMED INTO THE ASSEMBLY. THEY GATHERED IN AN UNDAMAGED PART OF THE CITY AND RECRUITED BIG GIRLS TO BE A LIVING WALL. A BARRIER TO HOLD BACK THE VIOLENCE.
OVER THE YEARS, THE PROTECTED AREA EXPANDED, BECAME THE PRESERVE.
GO!

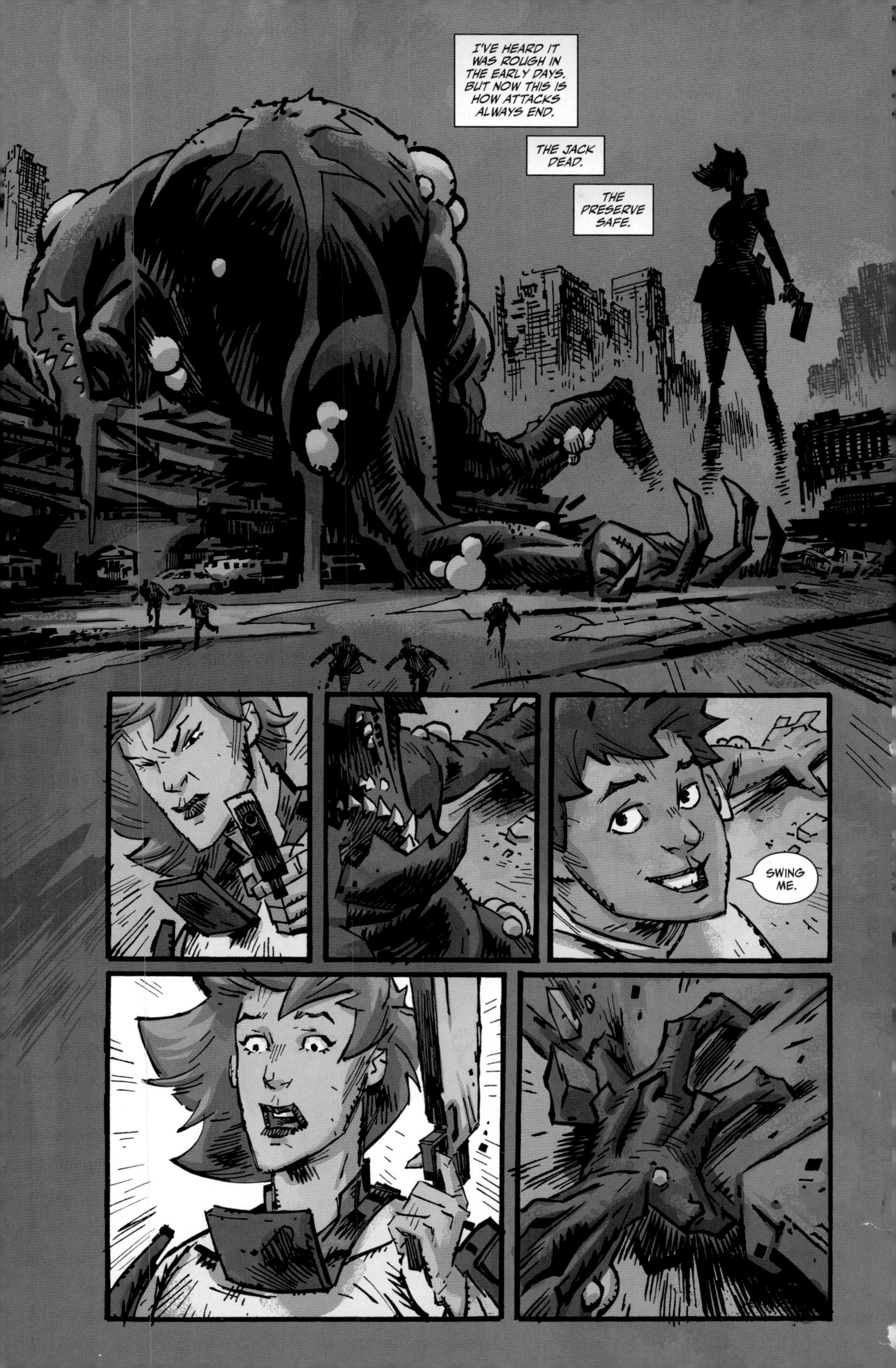
I'VE HEARD IT WAS ROUGH IN THE EARLY DAYS. BUT NOW THIS IS HOW ATTACKS ALWAYS END.
THE JACK DEAD.
THE PRESERVE SAFE.
SWING ME.

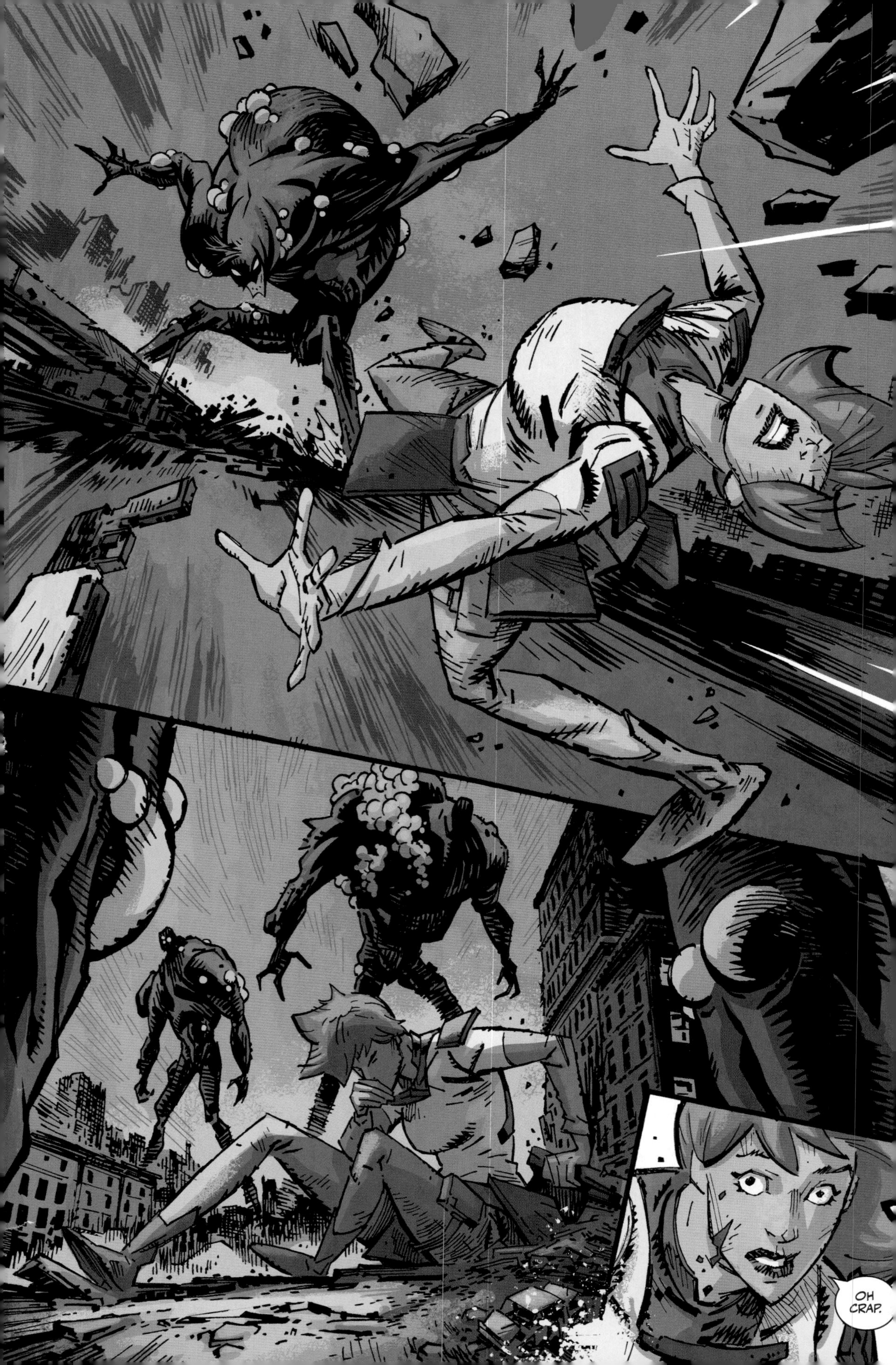
OH CRAP.

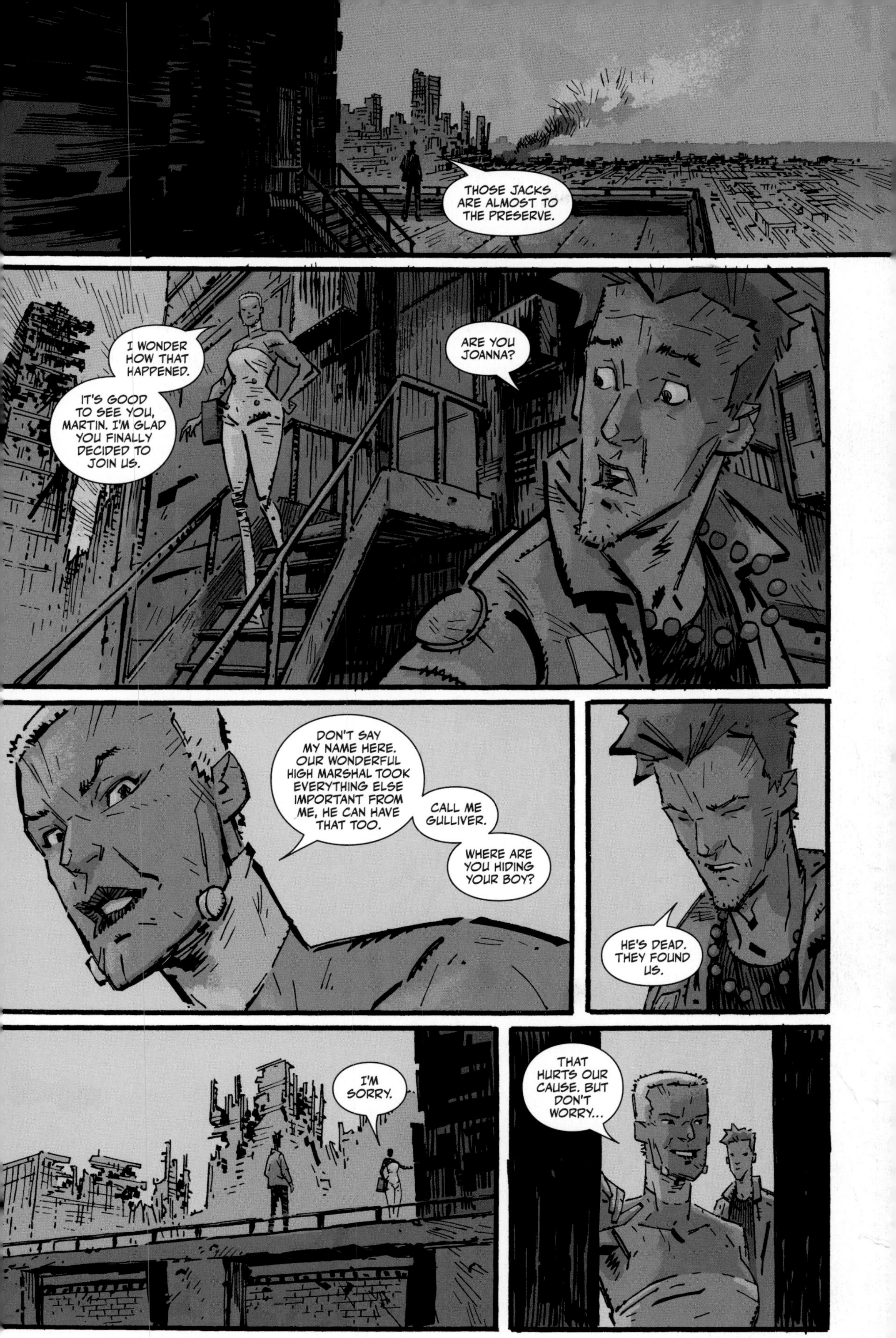
THOSE JACKS ARE ALMOST TO THE PRESERVE.
I WONDER HOW THAT HAPPENED.
IT'S GOOD TO SEE YOU, MARTIN. I'M GLAD YOU FINALLY DECIDED TO JOIN US.
ARE YOU JOANNA?
DON'T SAY MY NAME HERE. OUR WONDERFUL HIGH MARSHAL TOOK EVERYTHING ELSE IMPORTANT FROM ME, HE CAN HAVE THAT TOO.
CALL ME GULLIVER.
WHERE ARE YOU HIDING YOUR BOY?
HE'S DEAD. THEY FOUND US.
I'M SORRY.
THAT HURTS OUR CAUSE. BUT DON'T WORRY...

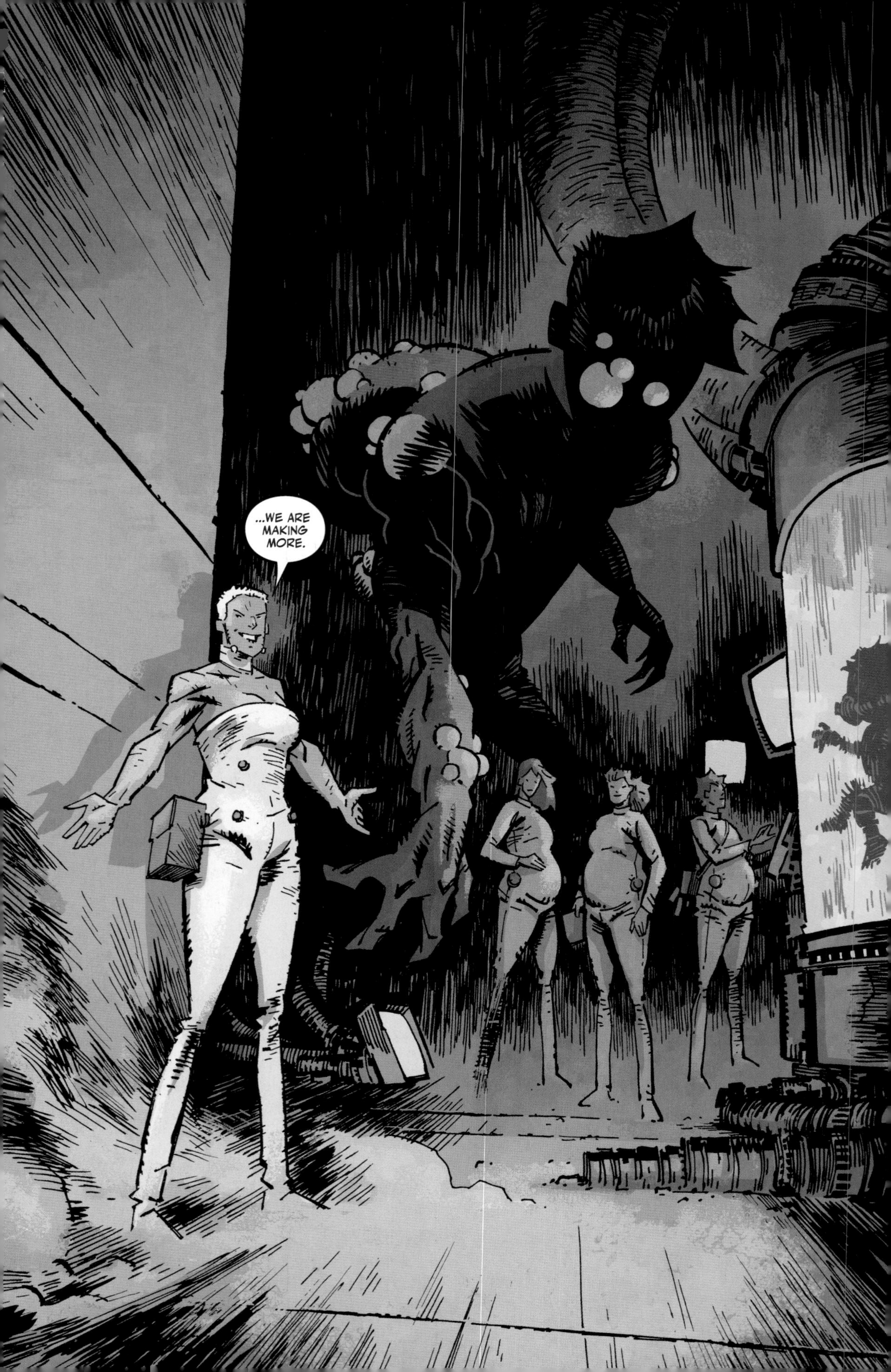
...WE ARE MAKING MORE.

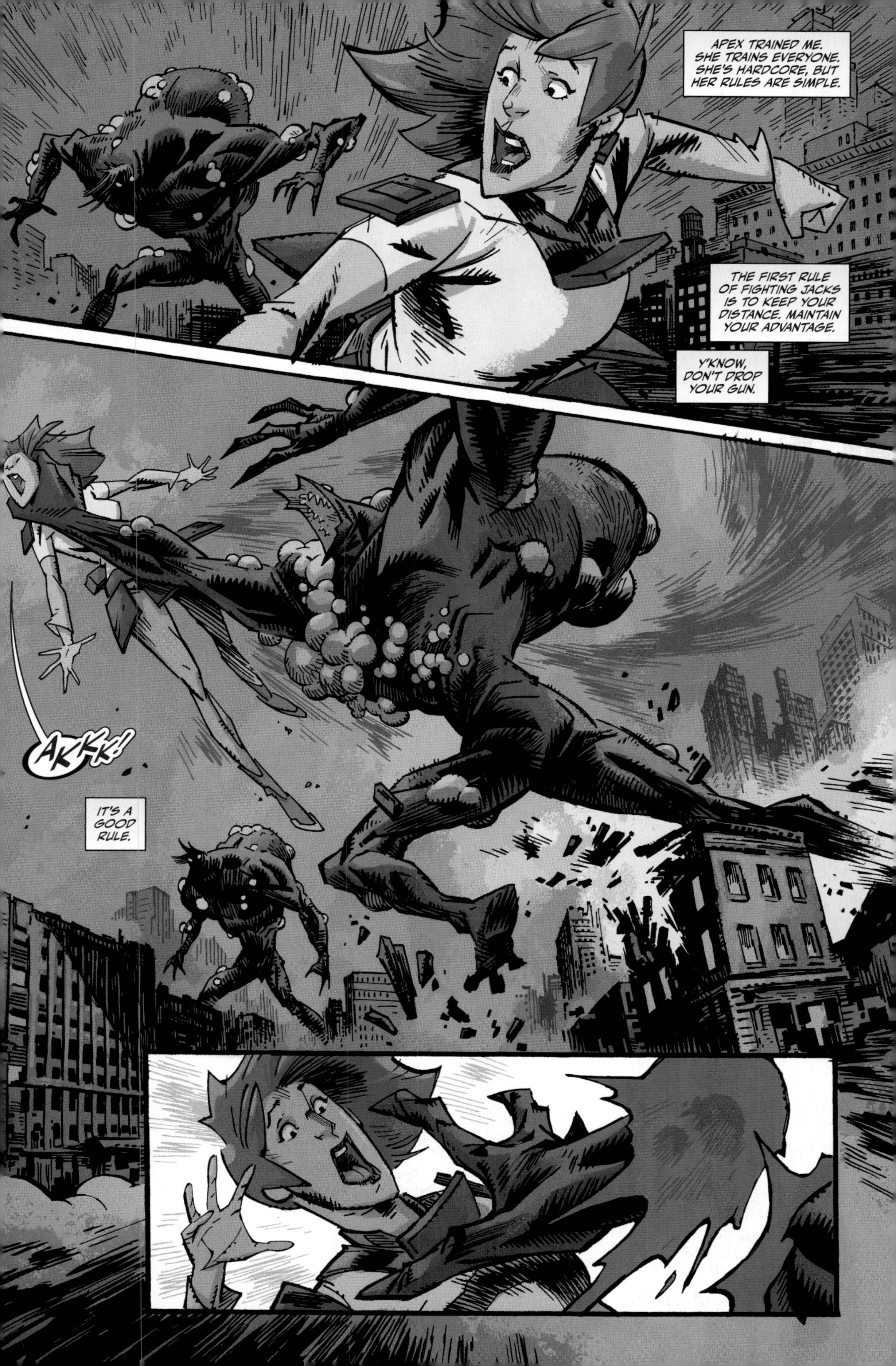
APEX TRAINED ME. SHE TRAINS EVERYONE. SHE'S HARDCORE, BUT HER RULES ARE SIMPLE.
THE FIRST RULE OF FIGHTING JACKS IS TO KEEP YOUR DISTANCE. MAINTAIN YOUR ADVANTAGE.
Y'KNOW, DON'T DROP YOUR GUN.
AKKK!
IT'S A GOOD RULE.

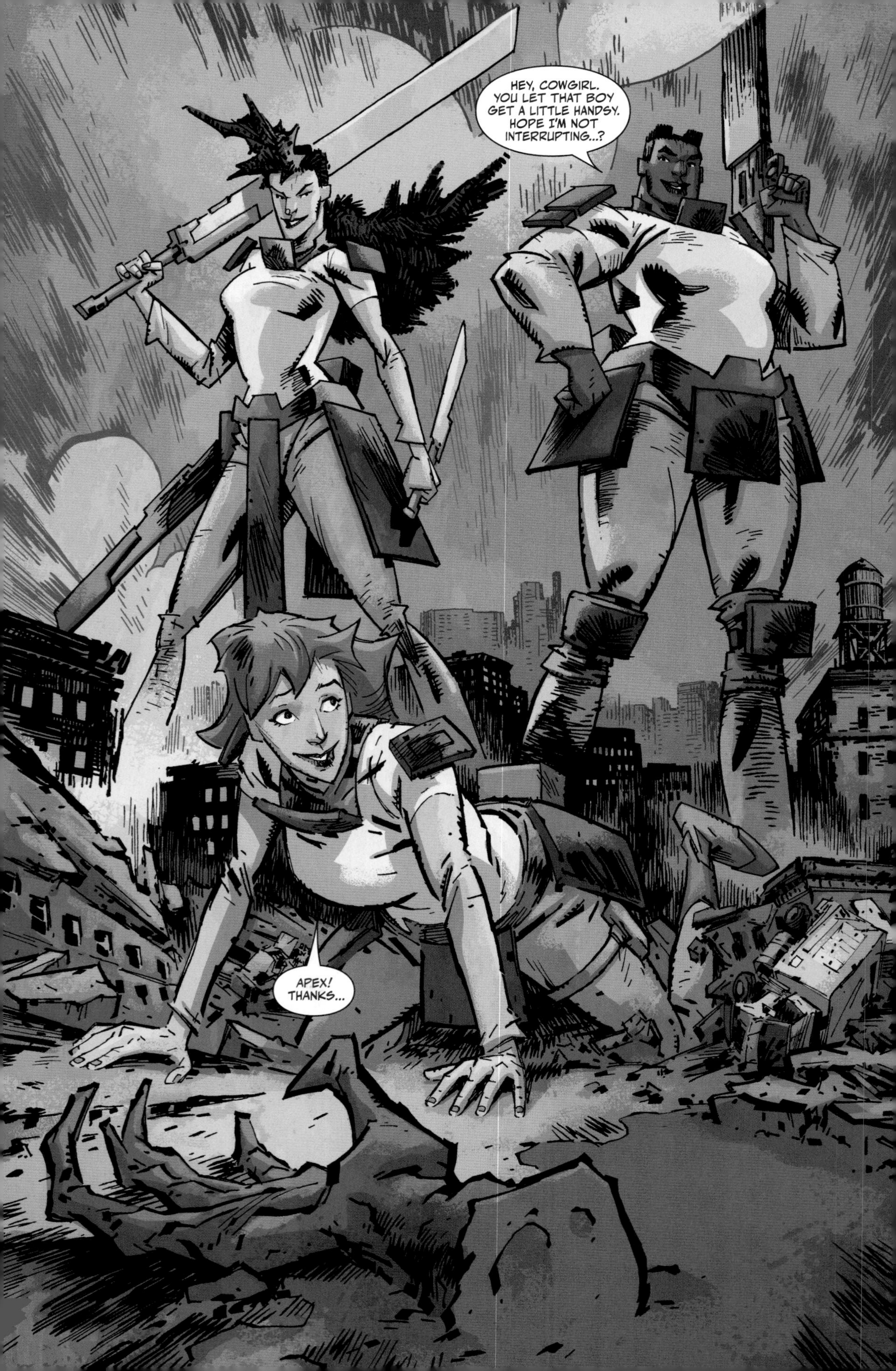
HEY, COWGIRL. YOU LET THAT BOY GET A LITTLE HANDSY. HOPE I'M NOT INTERRUPTING...?
APEX! THANKS...

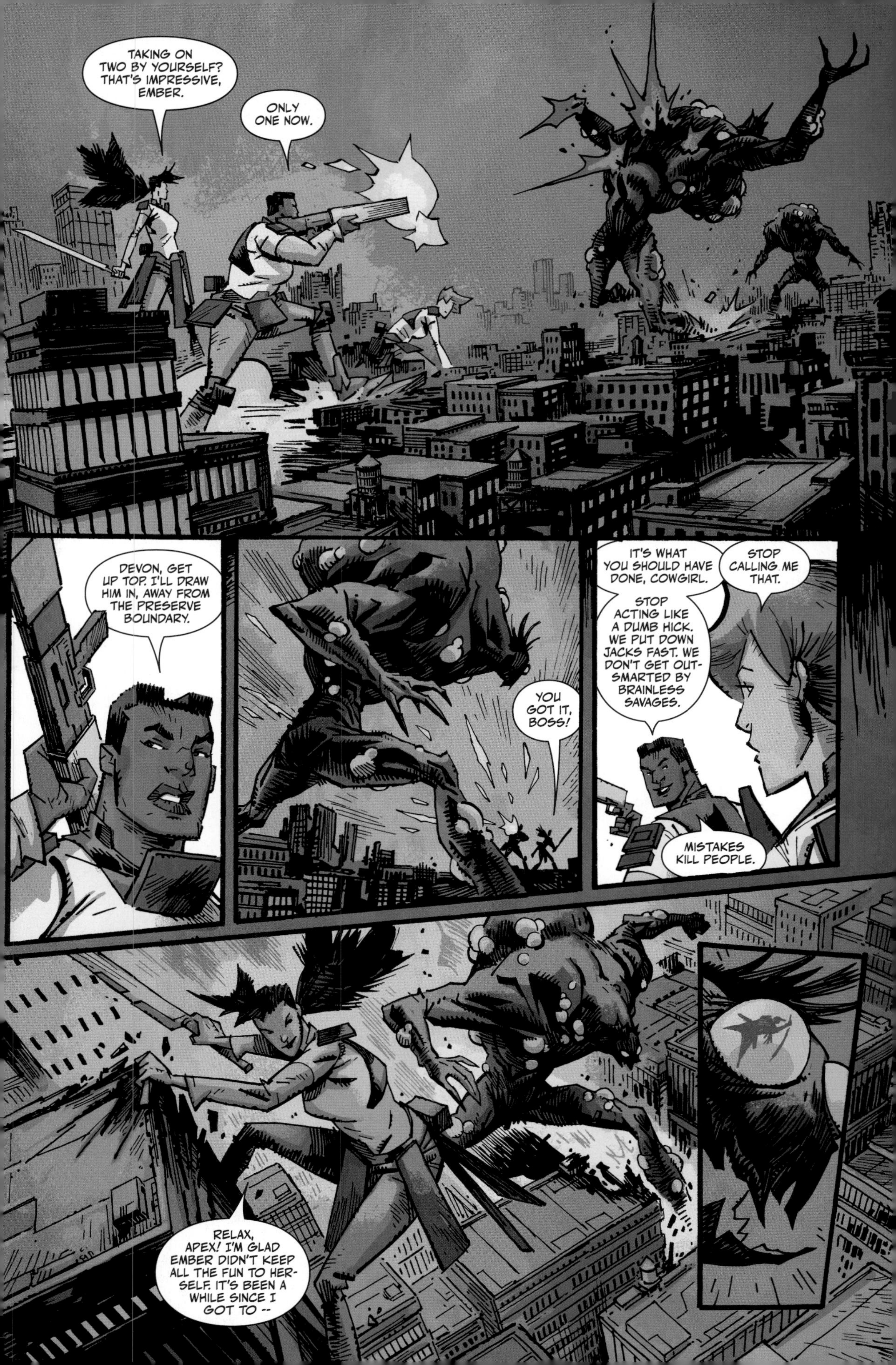
TAKING ON TWO BY YOURSELF? THAT'S IMPRESSIVE, EMBER.
ONLY ONE NOW.
DEVON, GET UP TOP. I'LL DRAW HIM IN, AWAY FROM THE PRESERVE BOUNDARY.
YOU GOT IT, BOSS!
IT'S WHAT YOU SHOULD HAVE DONE, COWGIRL.
STOP CALLING ME THAT.
STOP ACTING LIKE A DUMB HICK. WE PUT DOWN JACKS FAST. WE DON'T GET OUT-SMARTED BY BRAINLESS SAVAGES.
MISTAKES KILL PEOPLE.
RELAX, APEX! I'M GLAD EMBER DIDN'T KEEP ALL THE FUN TO HER-SELF. IT'S BEEN A WHILE SINCE I GOT TO --

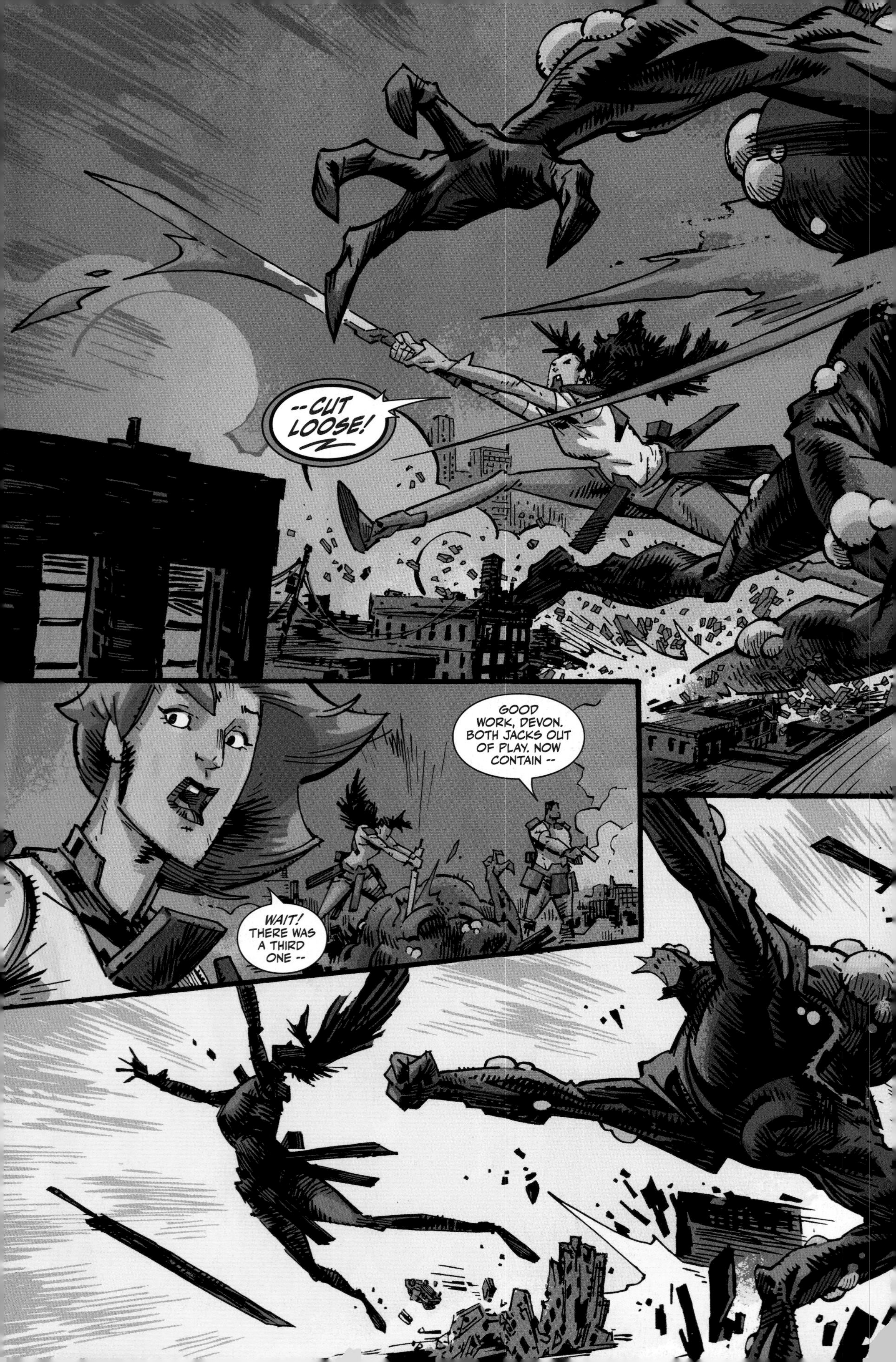
--CUT LOOSE!
GOOD WORK, DEVON. BOTH JACKS OUT OF PLAY. NOW CONTAIN --
WAIT! THERE WAS A THIRD ONE --

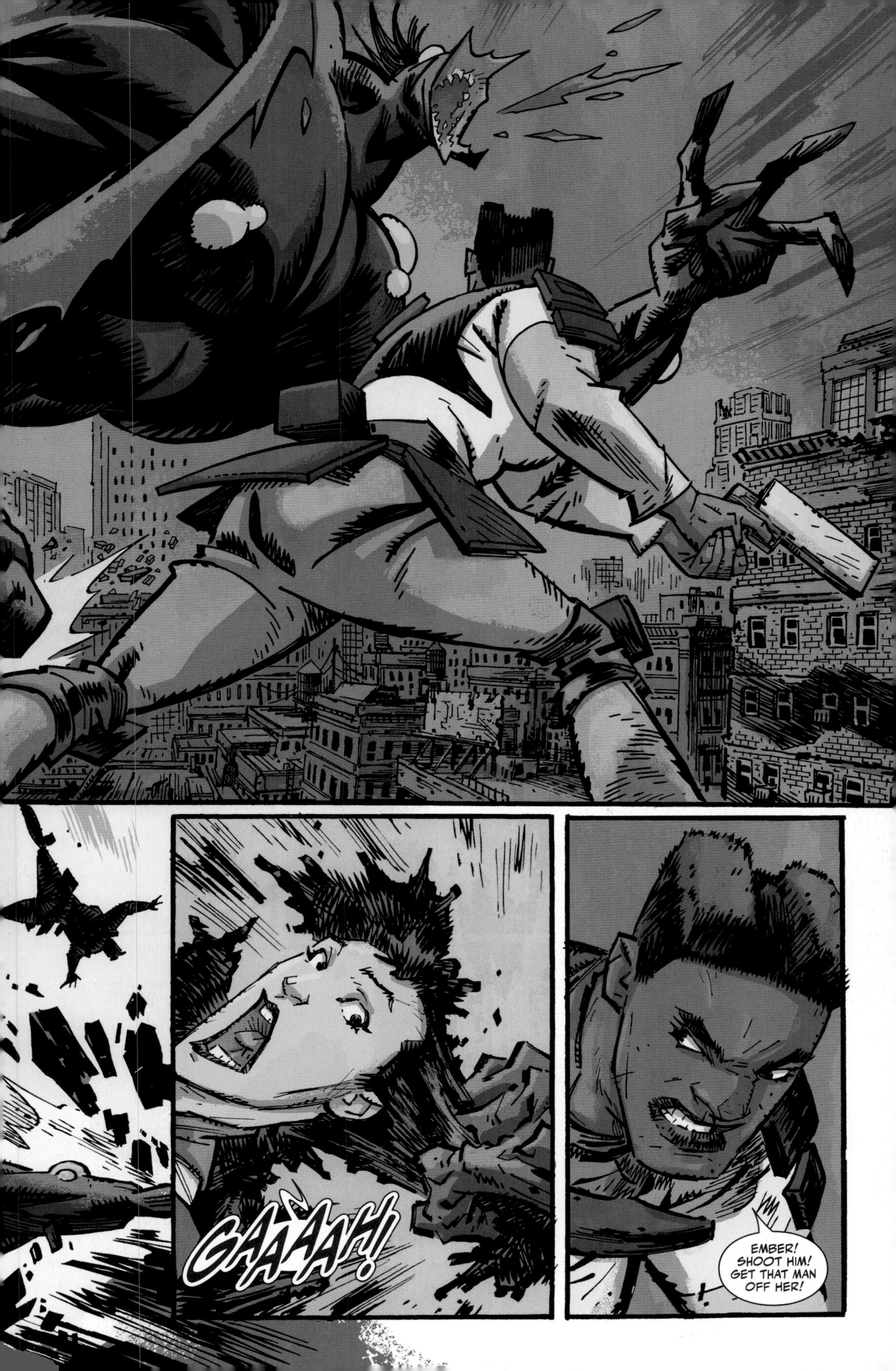

GAAAAH!
EMBER! SHOOT HIM! GET THAT MAN OFF HER!

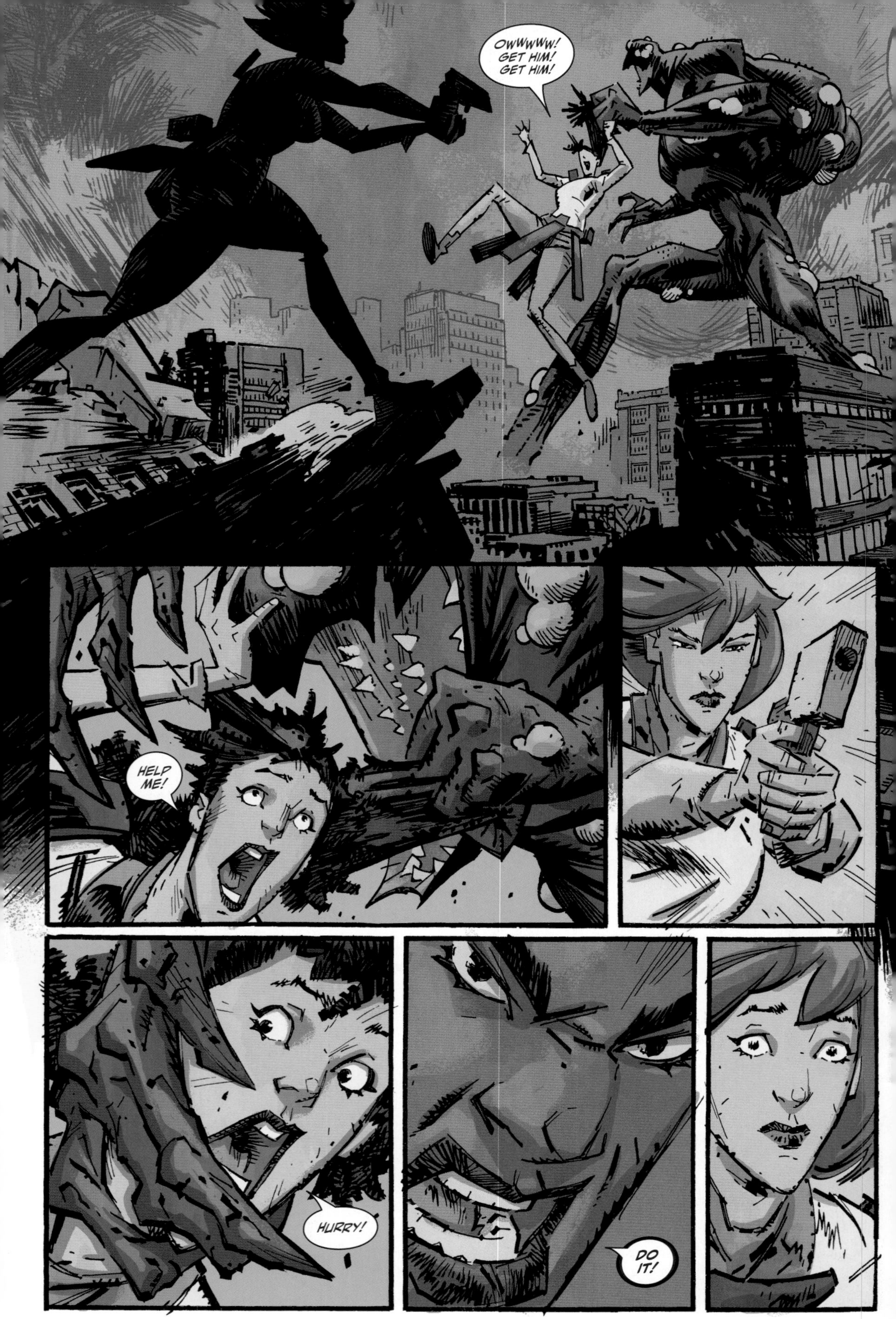
OWWWWW! GET HIM! GET HIM!
HELP ME!
HURRY!
DO IT!

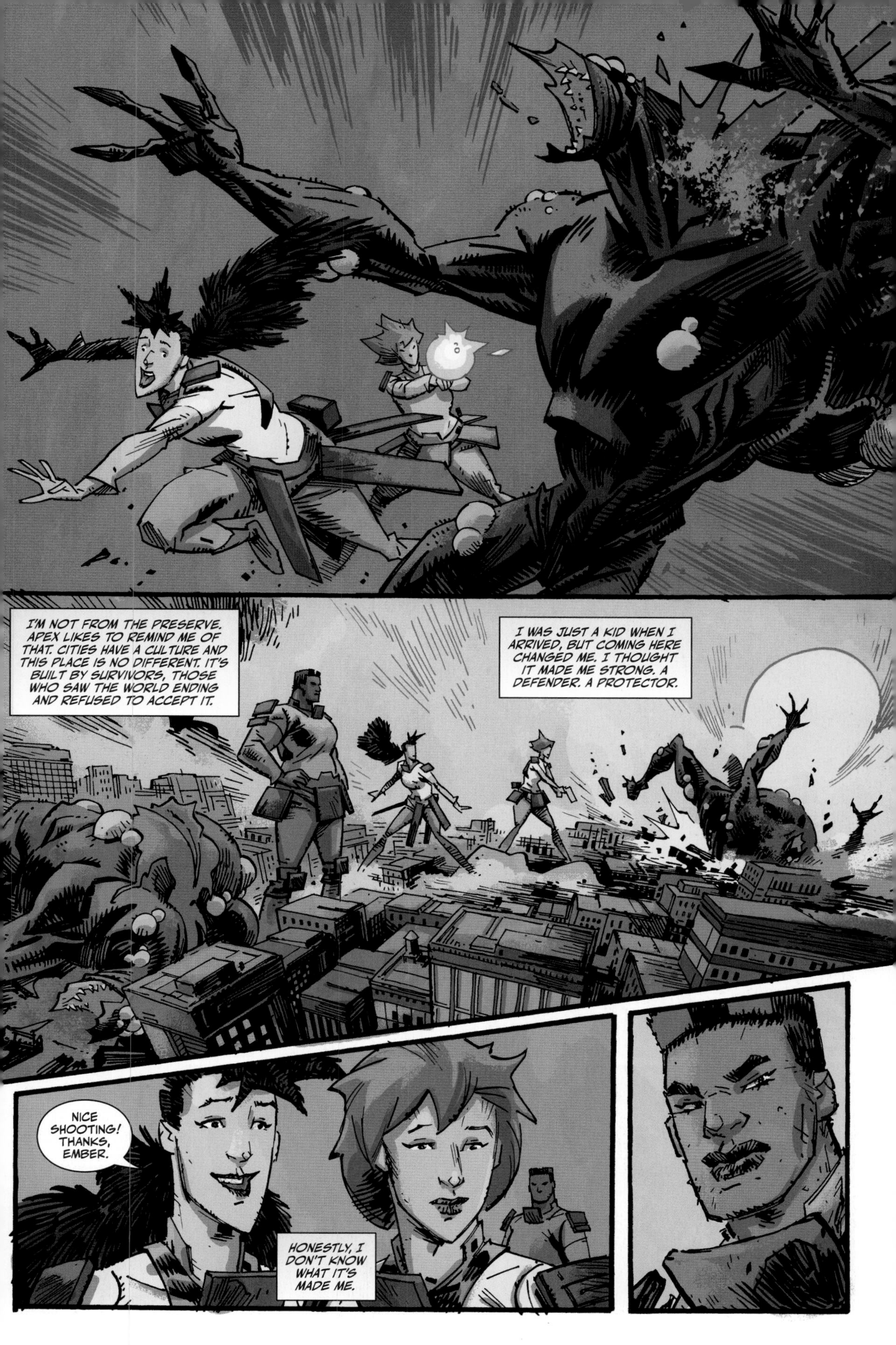
I'M NOT FROM THE PRESERVE. APEX LIKES TO REMIND ME OF THAT. CITIES HAVE A CULTURE AND THIS PLACE IS NO DIFFERENT. IT'S BUILT BY SURVIVORS, THOSE WHO SAW THE WORLD ENDING AND REFUSED TO ACCEPT IT.
I WAS JUST A KID WHEN I ARRIVED, BUT COMING HERE CHANGED ME. I THOUGHT IT MADE ME STRONG. A DEFENDER. A PROTECTOR.
NICE SHOOTING! THANKS, EMBER.
HONESTLY, I DON'T KNOW WHAT IT'S MADE ME.

PRESERVE EVERYONE

PRES EVER

A MISTAKE

PRESERVE EVERYONE

AN BARRIE

BIG G

THE PROTESTERS HAVE BEEN HERE SINCE THURSDAY. I GUESS ONE OF THE GIRLS STEPPED ON SOMETHING THEY CARE ABOUT.

BEGGARS COMPLAINING THEIR WATER ISN'T CHAMPAGNE.

RUMORS SAY THE WATCHTOWER KILLERS CAME FROM PROTEST GROUPS.

WE'RE ON TOP OF IT, SOLDIER.

MAJOR FORD, ANY REASON WHY THIS ISN'T FINISHED YET?

YOU KNOW, REMOVAL AND RECOVERY, SIR. WE'VE HAD TEAMS HERE ALL WEEK. TWO OF THE DEAD JACKS ARE ALREADY CUT AND MOVED BUT THIS THIRD ONE FELL IN A TOUGH SPOT. WILL TAKE A FEW MORE DAYS.

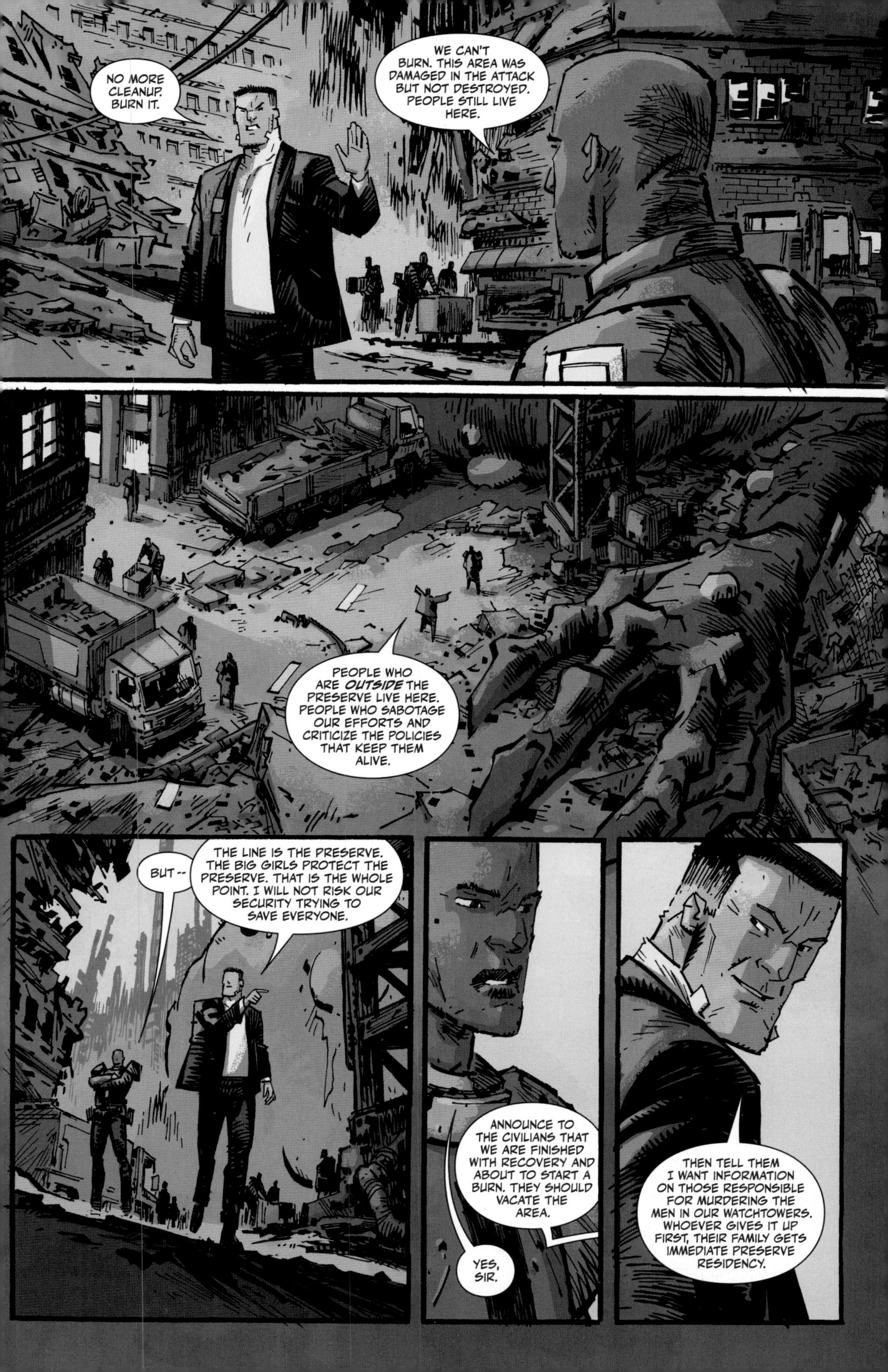
NO MORE CLEANUP. BURN IT.
WE CAN'T BURN. THIS AREA WAS DAMAGED IN THE ATTACK BUT NOT DESTROYED. PEOPLE STILL LIVE HERE.
PEOPLE WHO ARE OUTSIDE THE PRESERVE LIVE HERE. PEOPLE WHO SABOTAGE OUR EFFORTS AND CRITICIZE THE POLICIES THAT KEEP THEM ALIVE.
BUT--
THE LINE IS THE PRESERVE. THE BIG GIRLS PROTECT THE PRESERVE. THAT IS THE WHOLE POINT. I WILL NOT RISK OUR SECURITY TRYING TO SAVE EVERYONE.
ANNOUNCE TO THE CIVILIANS THAT WE ARE FINISHED WITH RECOVERY AND ABOUT TO START A BURN. THEY SHOULD VACATE THE AREA.
YES, SIR.
THEN TELL THEM I WANT INFORMATION ON THOSE RESPONSIBLE FOR MURDERING THE MEN IN OUR WATCHTOWERS. WHOEVER GIVES IT UP FIRST, THEIR FAMILY GETS IMMEDIATE PRESERVE RESIDENCY.

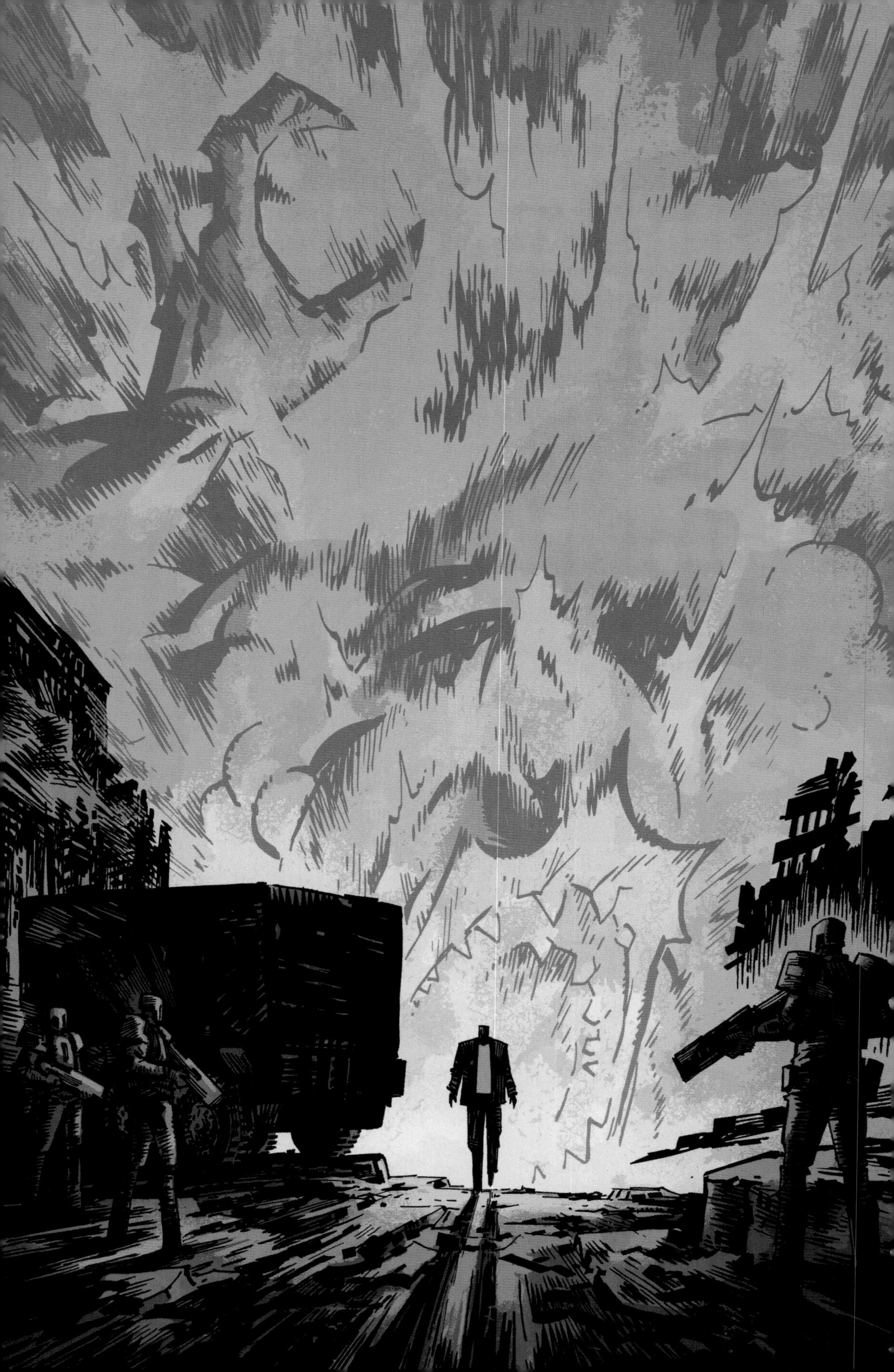

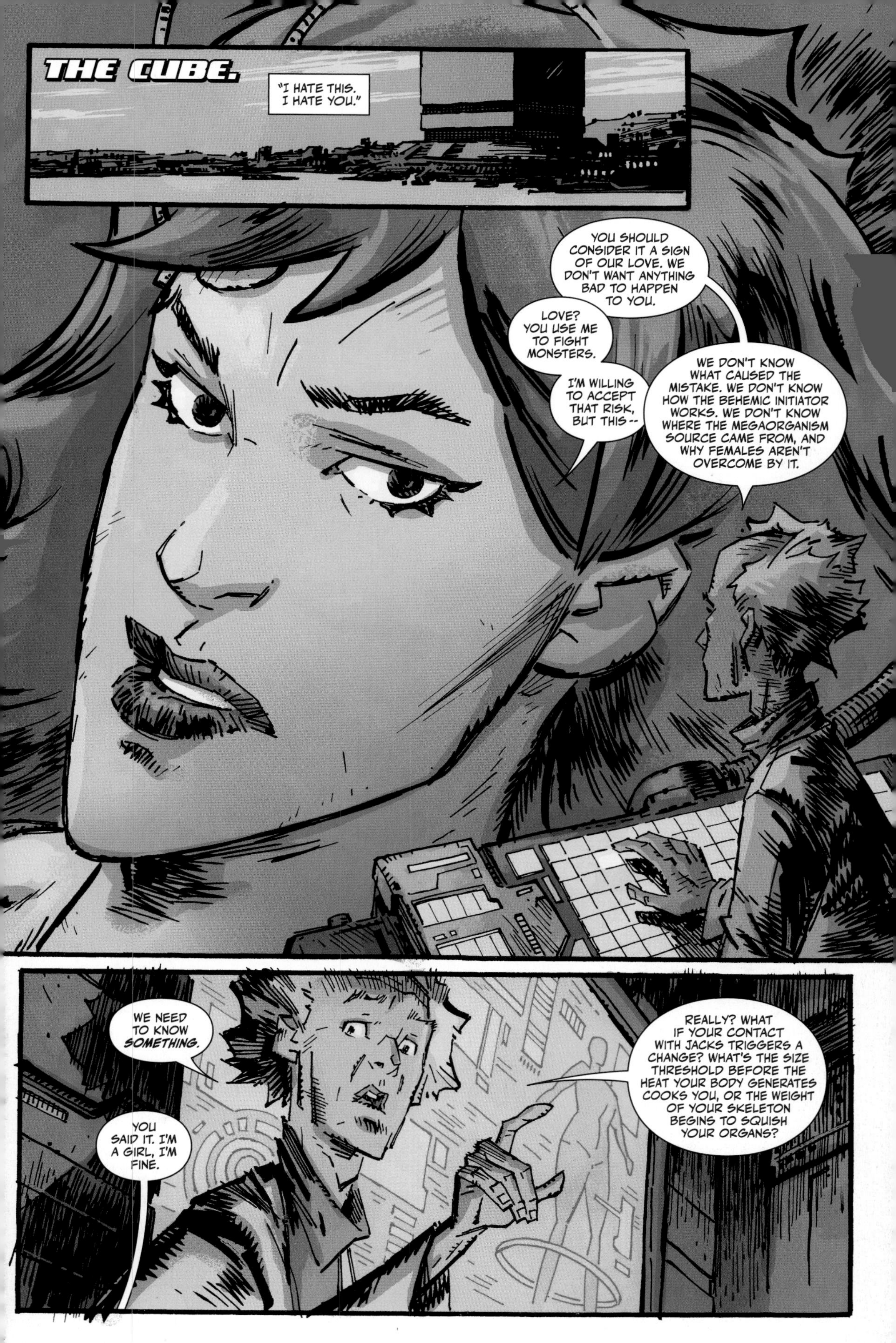
THE CUBE.
"I HATE THIS. I HATE YOU."
YOU SHOULD CONSIDER IT A SIGN OF OUR LOVE. WE DON'T WANT ANYTHING BAD TO HAPPEN TO YOU.
LOVE? YOU USE ME TO FIGHT MONSTERS.
I'M WILLING TO ACCEPT THAT RISK, BUT THIS --
WE DON'T KNOW WHAT CAUSED THE MISTAKE. WE DON'T KNOW HOW THE BEHEMIC INITIATOR WORKS. WE DON'T KNOW WHERE THE MEGAORGANISM SOURCE CAME FROM, AND WHY FEMALES AREN'T OVERCOME BY IT.
WE NEED TO KNOW *SOMETHING.*
YOU SAID IT. I'M A GIRL, I'M FINE.
REALLY? WHAT IF YOUR CONTACT WITH JACKS TRIGGERS A CHANGE? WHAT'S THE SIZE THRESHOLD BEFORE THE HEAT YOUR BODY GENERATES COOKS YOU, OR THE WEIGHT OF YOUR SKELETON BEGINS TO SQUISH YOUR ORGANS?

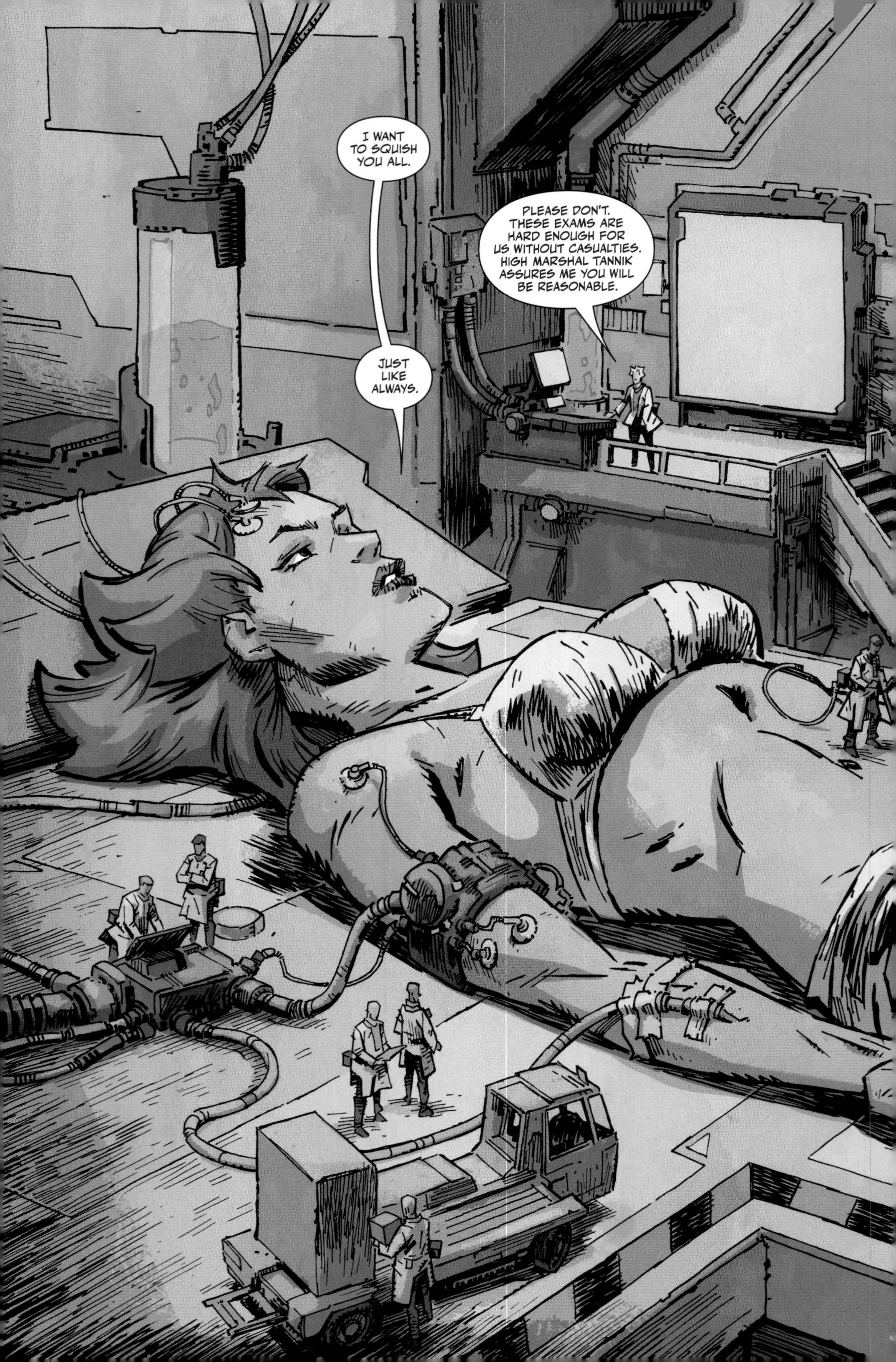
I WANT TO SQUISH YOU ALL.
JUST LIKE ALWAYS.
PLEASE DON'T. THESE EXAMS ARE HARD ENOUGH FOR US WITHOUT CASUALTIES. HIGH MARSHAL TANNIK ASSURES ME YOU WILL BE REASONABLE.

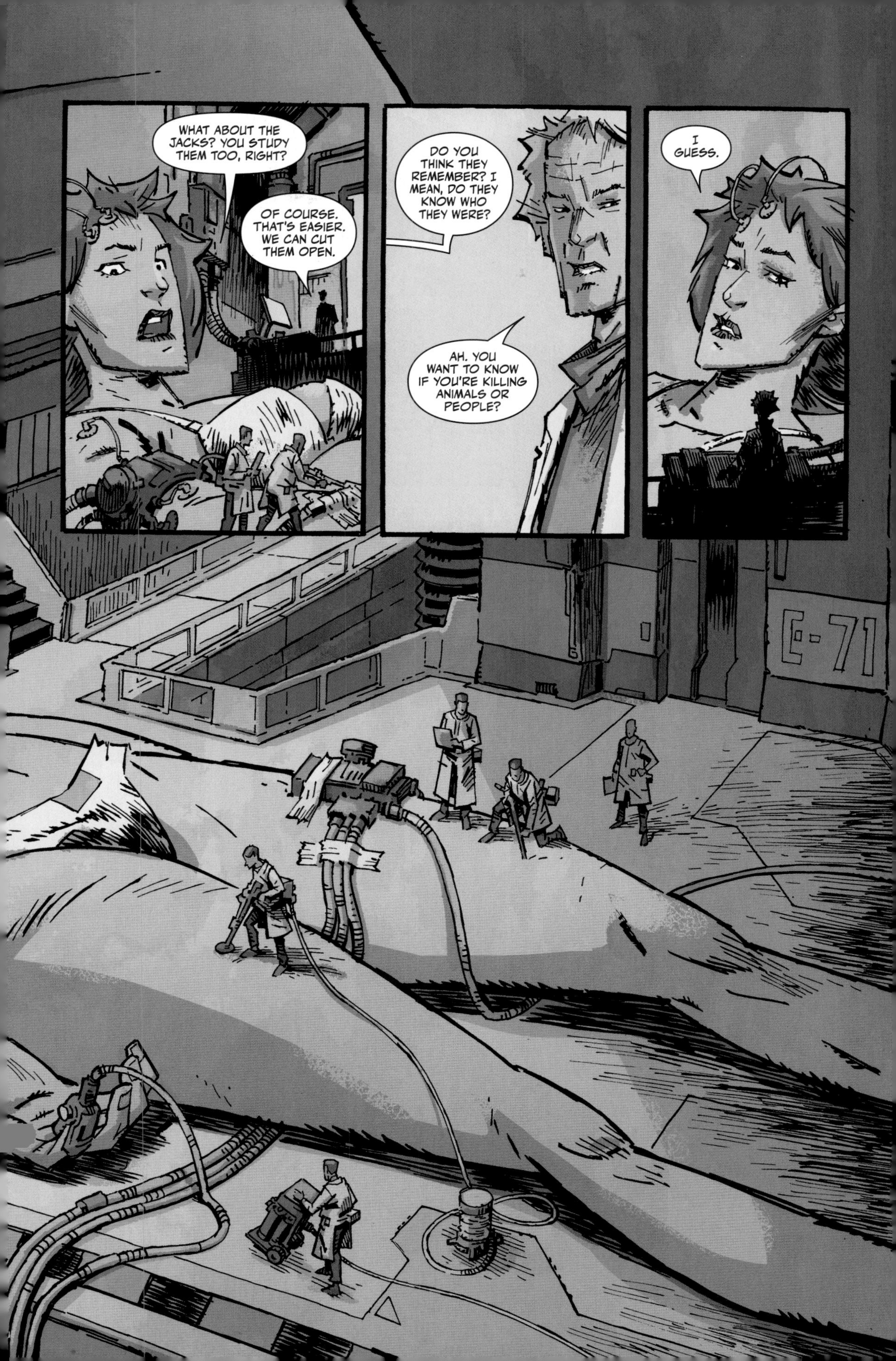
WHAT ABOUT THE JACKS? YOU STUDY THEM TOO, RIGHT?
OF COURSE. THAT'S EASIER. WE CAN CUT THEM OPEN.
DO YOU THINK THEY REMEMBER? I MEAN, DO THEY KNOW WHO THEY WERE?
AH. YOU WANT TO KNOW IF YOU'RE KILLING ANIMALS OR PEOPLE?
I GUESS.
E-71

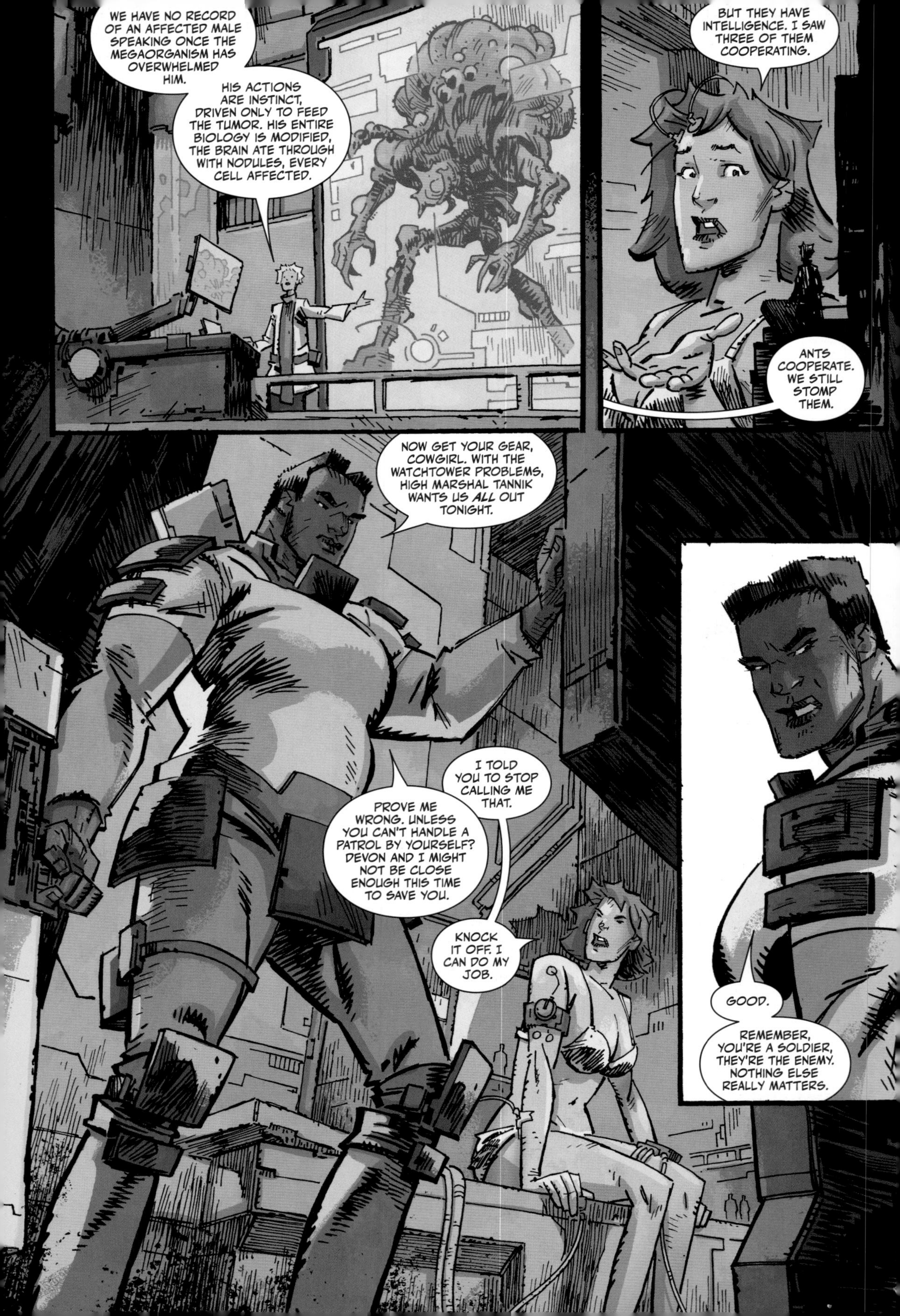
WE HAVE NO RECORD OF AN AFFECTED MALE SPEAKING ONCE THE MEGAORGANISM HAS OVERWHELMED HIM.
HIS ACTIONS ARE INSTINCT, DRIVEN ONLY TO FEED THE TUMOR. HIS ENTIRE BIOLOGY IS MODIFIED, THE BRAIN ATE THROUGH WITH NODULES, EVERY CELL AFFECTED.
BUT THEY HAVE INTELLIGENCE. I SAW THREE OF THEM COOPERATING.
ANTS COOPERATE. WE STILL STOMP THEM.
NOW GET YOUR GEAR, COWGIRL. WITH THE WATCHTOWER PROBLEMS, HIGH MARSHAL TANNIK WANTS US *ALL* OUT TONIGHT.
I TOLD YOU TO STOP CALLING ME THAT.
PROVE ME WRONG. UNLESS YOU CAN'T HANDLE A PATROL BY YOURSELF? DEVON AND I MIGHT NOT BE CLOSE ENOUGH THIS TIME TO SAVE YOU.
KNOCK IT OFF. I CAN DO MY JOB.
GOOD.
REMEMBER, YOU'RE A SOLDIER, THEY'RE THE ENEMY. NOTHING ELSE REALLY MATTERS.

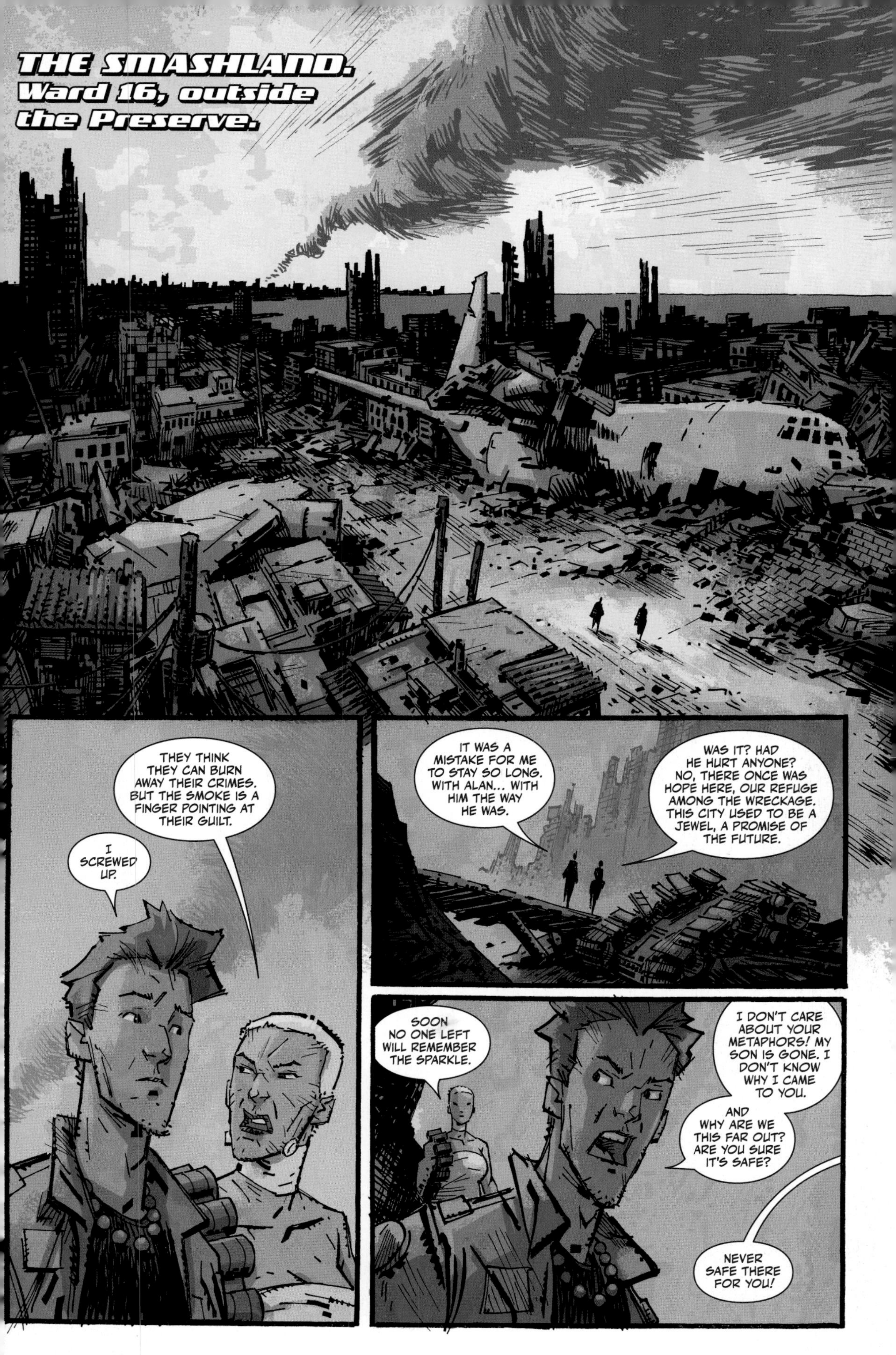
THE SMASHLAND.
Ward 16, outside the Preserve.
THEY THINK THEY CAN BURN AWAY THEIR CRIMES. BUT THE SMOKE IS A FINGER POINTING AT THEIR GUILT.
I SCREWED UP.
IT WAS A MISTAKE FOR ME TO STAY SO LONG. WITH ALAN... WITH HIM THE WAY HE WAS.
WAS IT? HAD HE HURT ANYONE? NO, THERE ONCE WAS HOPE HERE, OUR REFUGE AMONG THE WRECKAGE. THIS CITY USED TO BE A JEWEL, A PROMISE OF THE FUTURE.
SOON NO ONE LEFT WILL REMEMBER THE SPARKLE.
I DON'T CARE ABOUT YOUR METAPHORS! MY SON IS GONE. I DON'T KNOW WHY I CAME TO YOU.
AND WHY ARE WE THIS FAR OUT? ARE YOU SURE IT'S SAFE?
NEVER SAFE THERE FOR YOU!

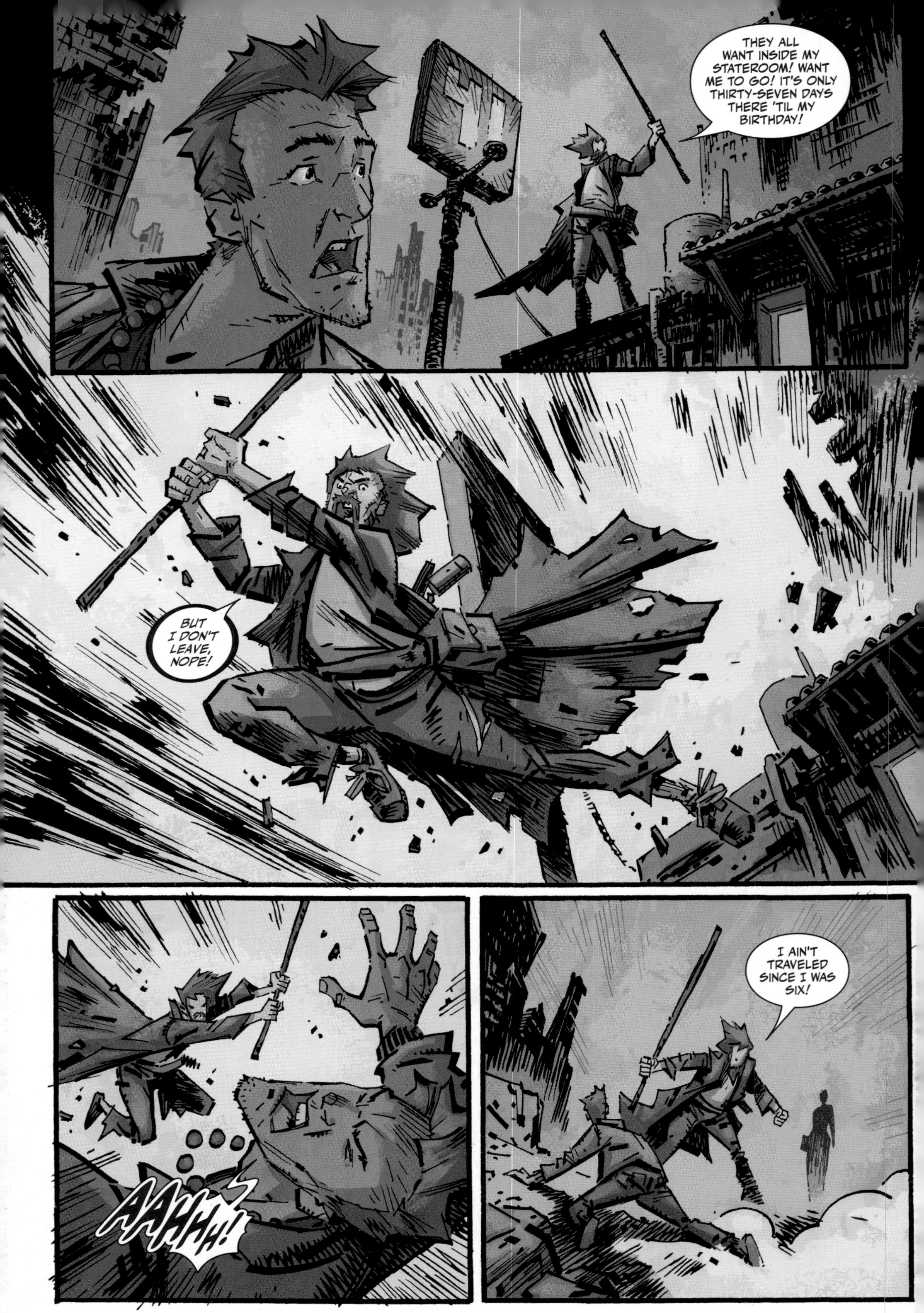
THEY ALL WANT INSIDE MY STATEROOM! WANT ME TO GO! IT'S ONLY THIRTY-SEVEN DAYS THERE 'TIL MY BIRTHDAY!
BUT I DON'T LEAVE, NOPE!
AAHHH!
I AIN'T TRAVELED SINCE I WAS SIX!

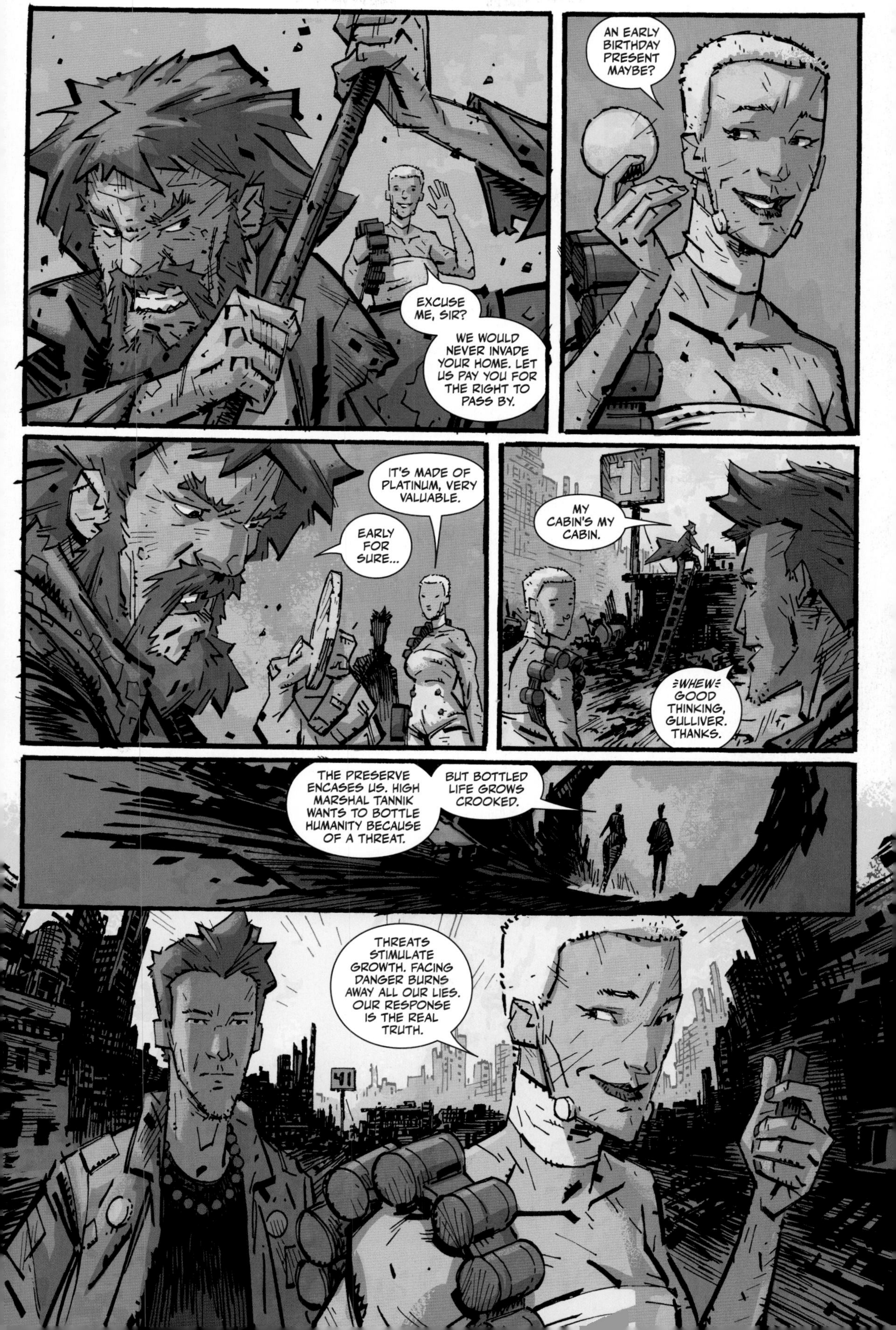
EXCUSE ME, SIR?
WE WOULD NEVER INVADE YOUR HOME. LET US PAY YOU FOR THE RIGHT TO PASS BY.
AN EARLY BIRTHDAY PRESENT MAYBE?
IT'S MADE OF PLATINUM, VERY VALUABLE.
EARLY FOR SURE...
MY CABIN'S MY CABIN.
WHEW GOOD THINKING, GULLIVER. THANKS.
THE PRESERVE ENCASES US. HIGH MARSHAL TANNIK WANTS TO BOTTLE HUMANITY BECAUSE OF A THREAT.
BUT BOTTLED LIFE GROWS CROOKED.
THREATS STIMULATE GROWTH. FACING DANGER BURNS AWAY ALL OUR LIES. OUR RESPONSE IS THE REAL TRUTH.

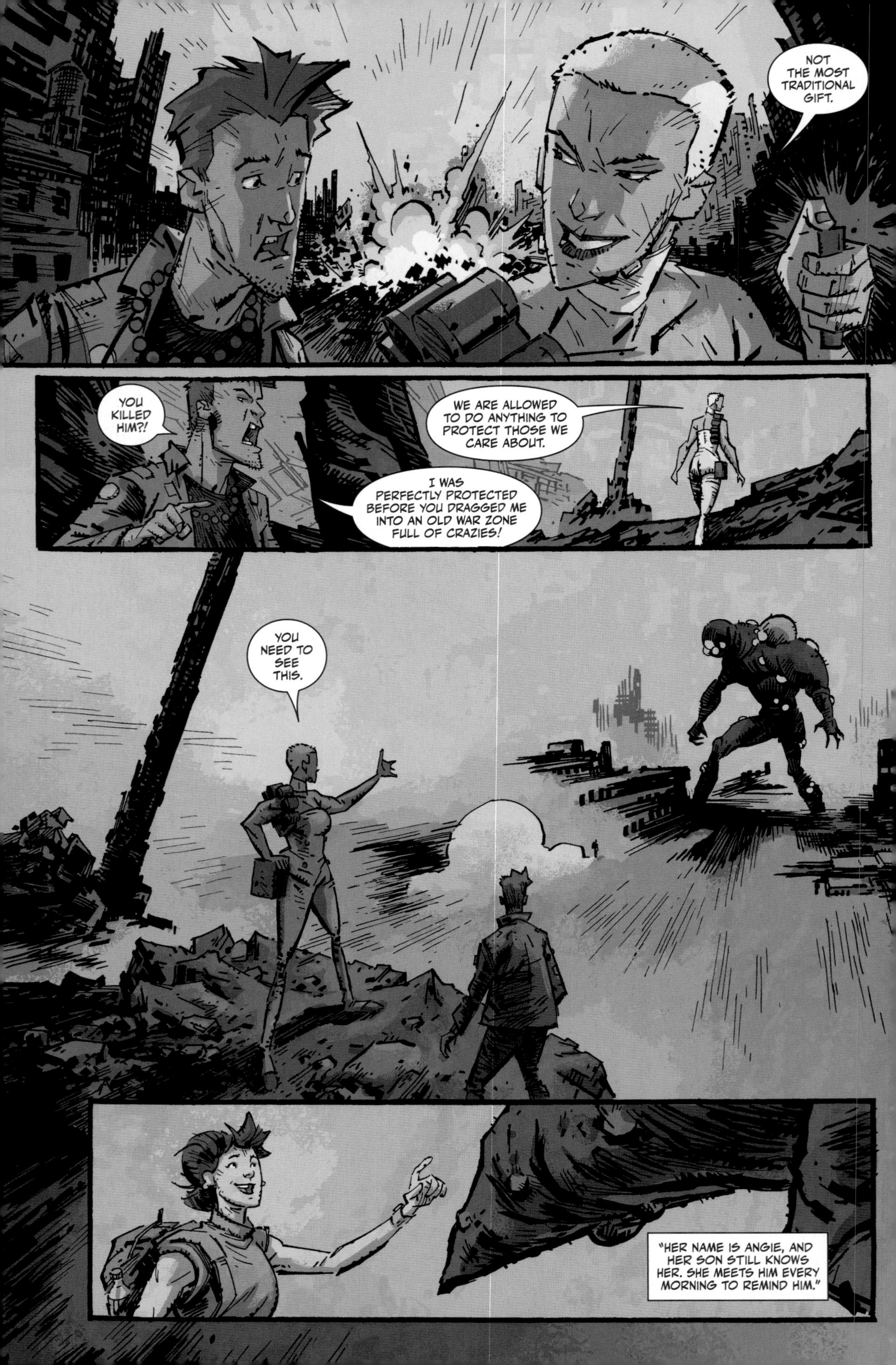
NOT THE MOST TRADITIONAL GIFT.
YOU KILLED HIM?!
WE ARE ALLOWED TO DO ANYTHING TO PROTECT THOSE WE CARE ABOUT.
I WAS PERFECTLY PROTECTED BEFORE YOU DRAGGED ME INTO AN OLD WAR ZONE FULL OF CRAZIES!
YOU NEED TO SEE THIS.
"HER NAME IS ANGIE, AND HER SON STILL KNOWS HER. SHE MEETS HIM EVERY MORNING TO REMIND HIM."

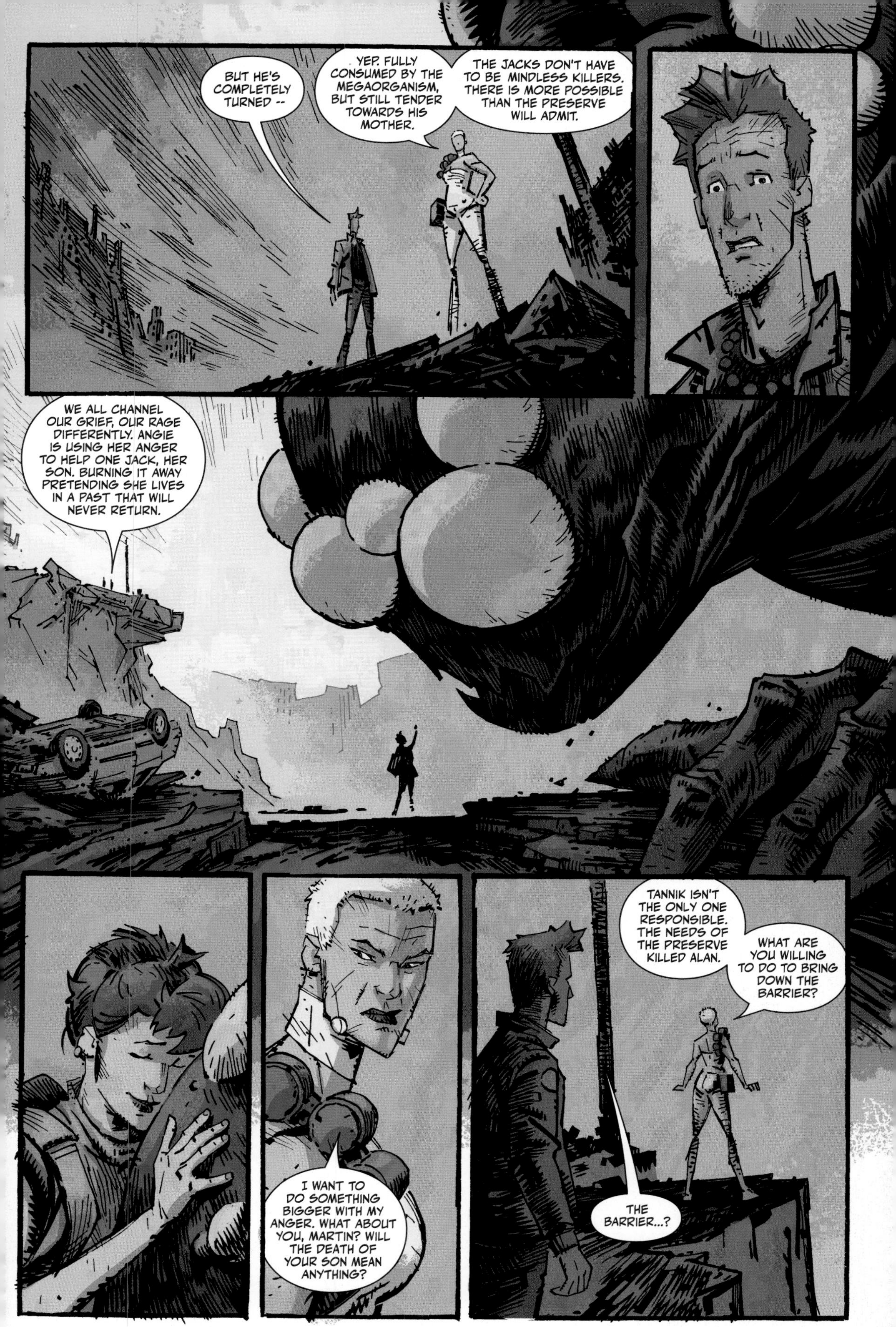

BUT HE'S COMPLETELY TURNED --
YEP. FULLY CONSUMED BY THE MEGAORGANISM, BUT STILL TENDER TOWARDS HIS MOTHER.
THE JACKS DON'T HAVE TO BE MINDLESS KILLERS. THERE IS MORE POSSIBLE THAN THE PRESERVE WILL ADMIT.
WE ALL CHANNEL OUR GRIEF, OUR RAGE DIFFERENTLY. ANGIE IS USING HER ANGER TO HELP ONE JACK, HER SON. BURNING IT AWAY PRETENDING SHE LIVES IN A PAST THAT WILL NEVER RETURN.
I WANT TO DO SOMETHING BIGGER WITH MY ANGER. WHAT ABOUT YOU, MARTIN? WILL THE DEATH OF YOUR SON MEAN ANYTHING?
TANNIK ISN'T THE ONLY ONE RESPONSIBLE. THE NEEDS OF THE PRESERVE KILLED ALAN.
WHAT ARE YOU WILLING TO DO TO BRING DOWN THE BARRIER?
THE BARRIER...?

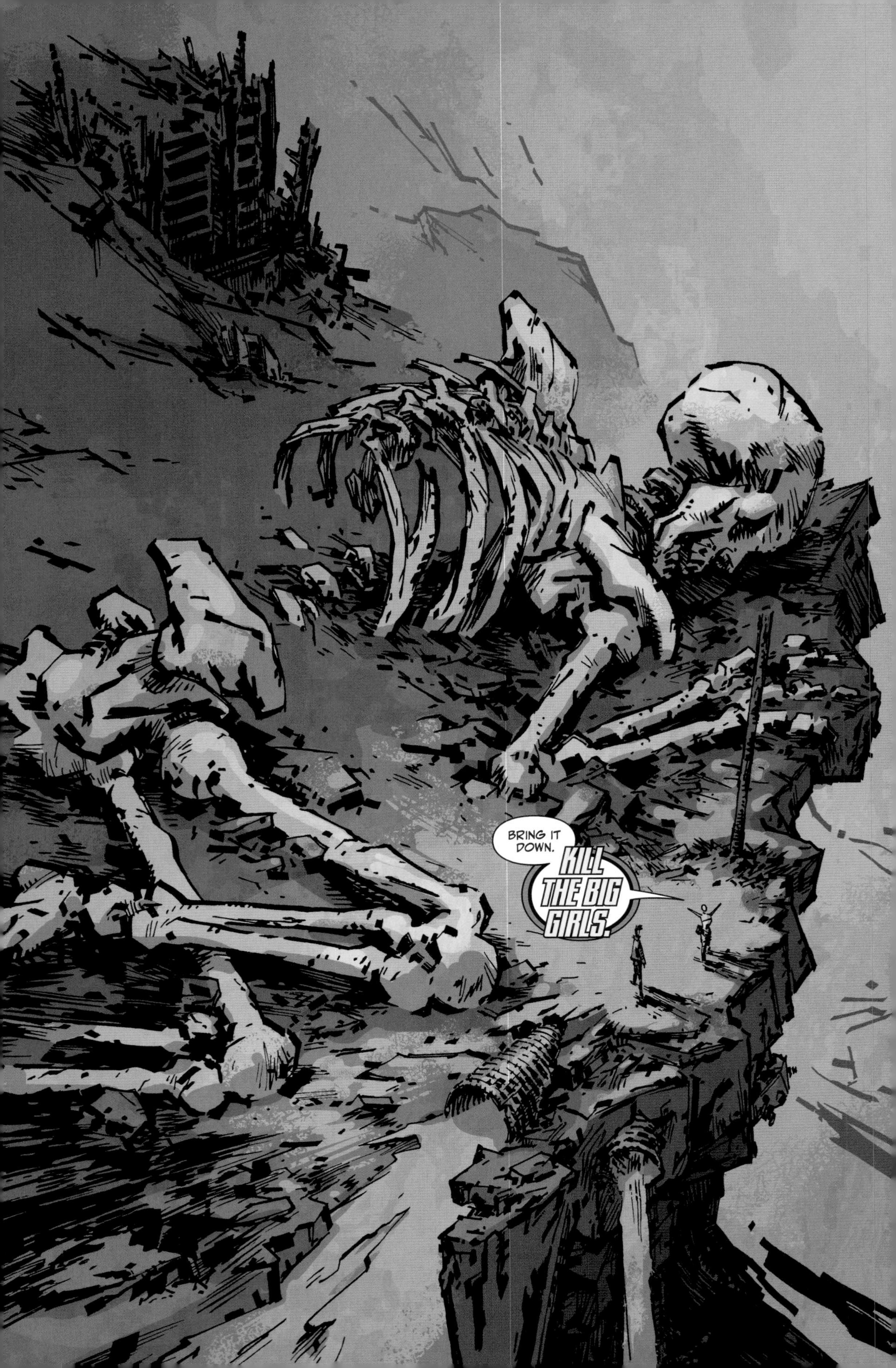
BRING IT DOWN.
KILL THE BIG GIRLS.

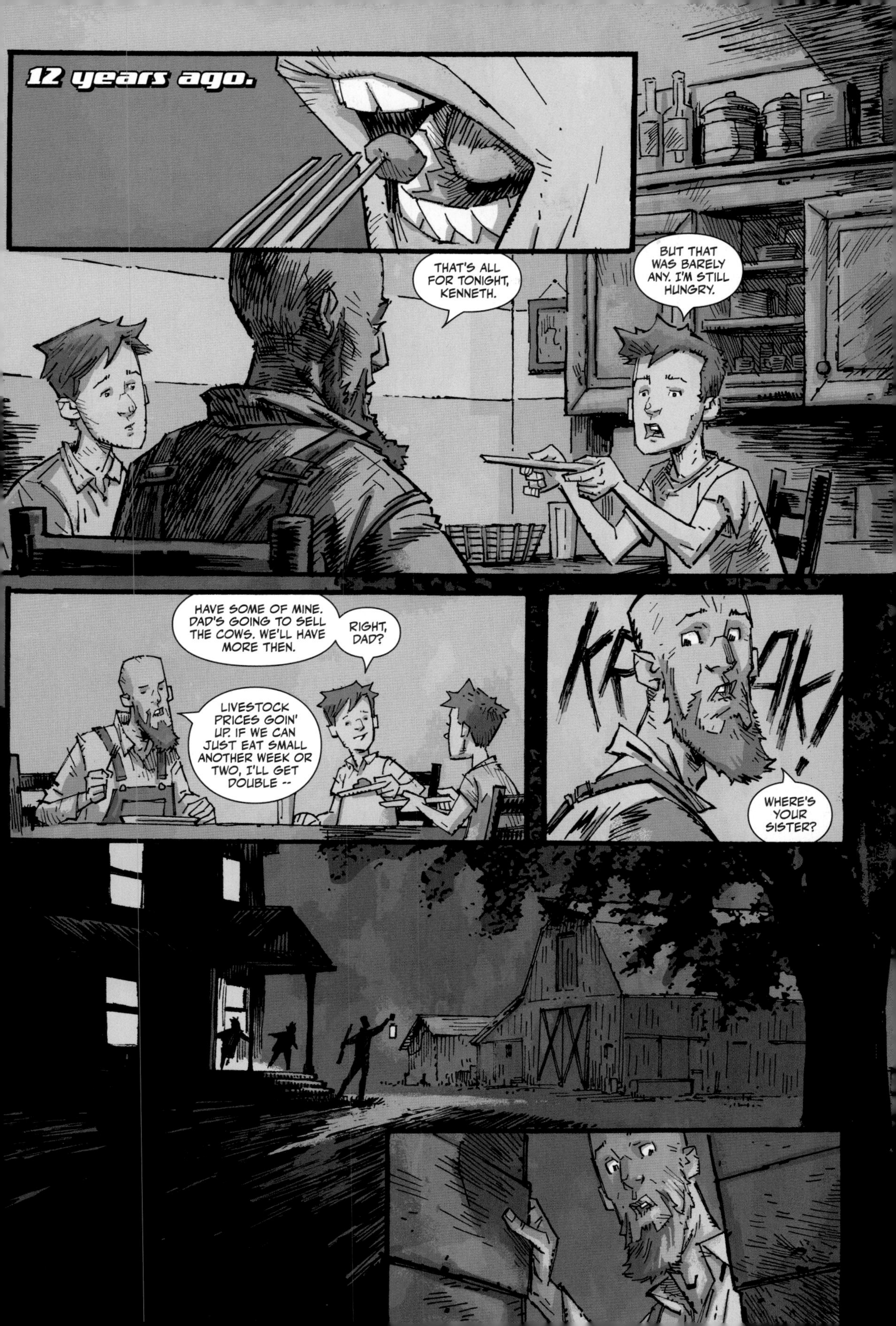
12 years ago.
THAT'S ALL FOR TONIGHT, KENNETH.
BUT THAT WAS BARELY ANY. I'M STILL HUNGRY.
HAVE SOME OF MINE. DAD'S GOING TO SELL THE COWS. WE'LL HAVE MORE THEN.
RIGHT, DAD?
LIVESTOCK PRICES GOIN' UP. IF WE CAN JUST EAT SMALL ANOTHER WEEK OR TWO, I'LL GET DOUBLE --
WHERE'S YOUR SISTER?

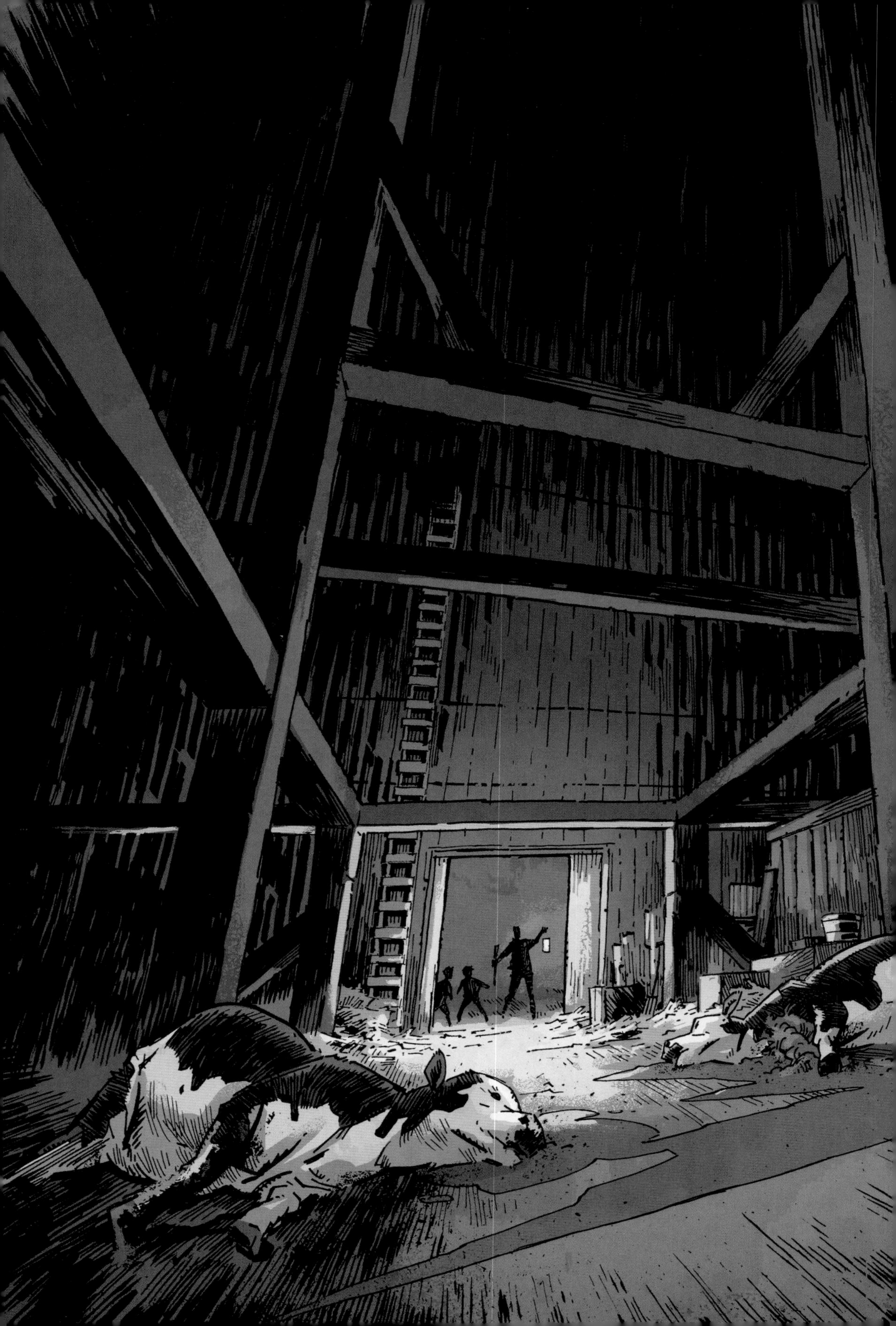

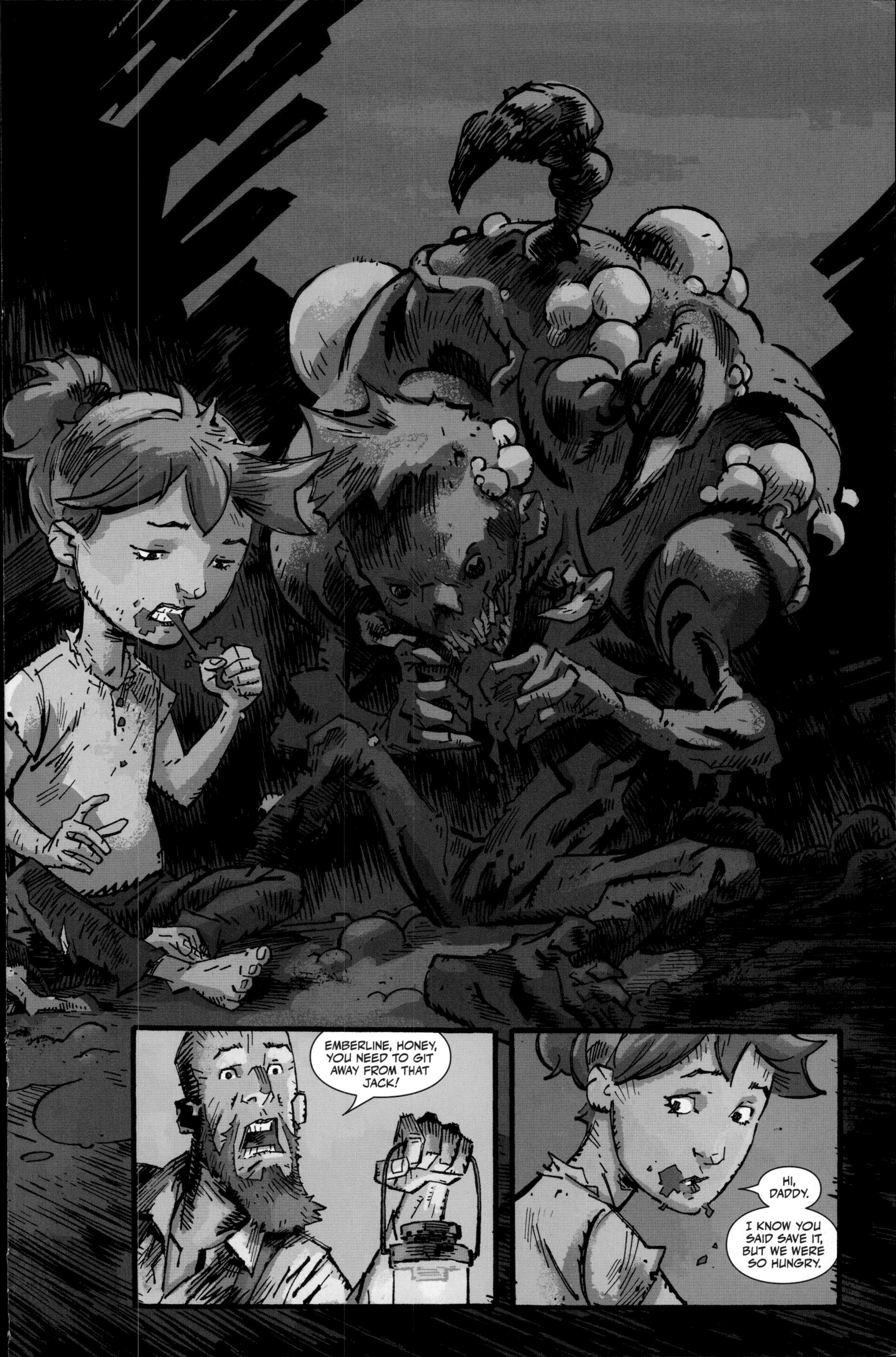
EMBERLINE, HONEY, YOU NEED TO GIT AWAY FROM THAT JACK!
HI, DADDY.
I KNOW YOU SAID SAVE IT, BUT WE WERE SO HUNGRY.

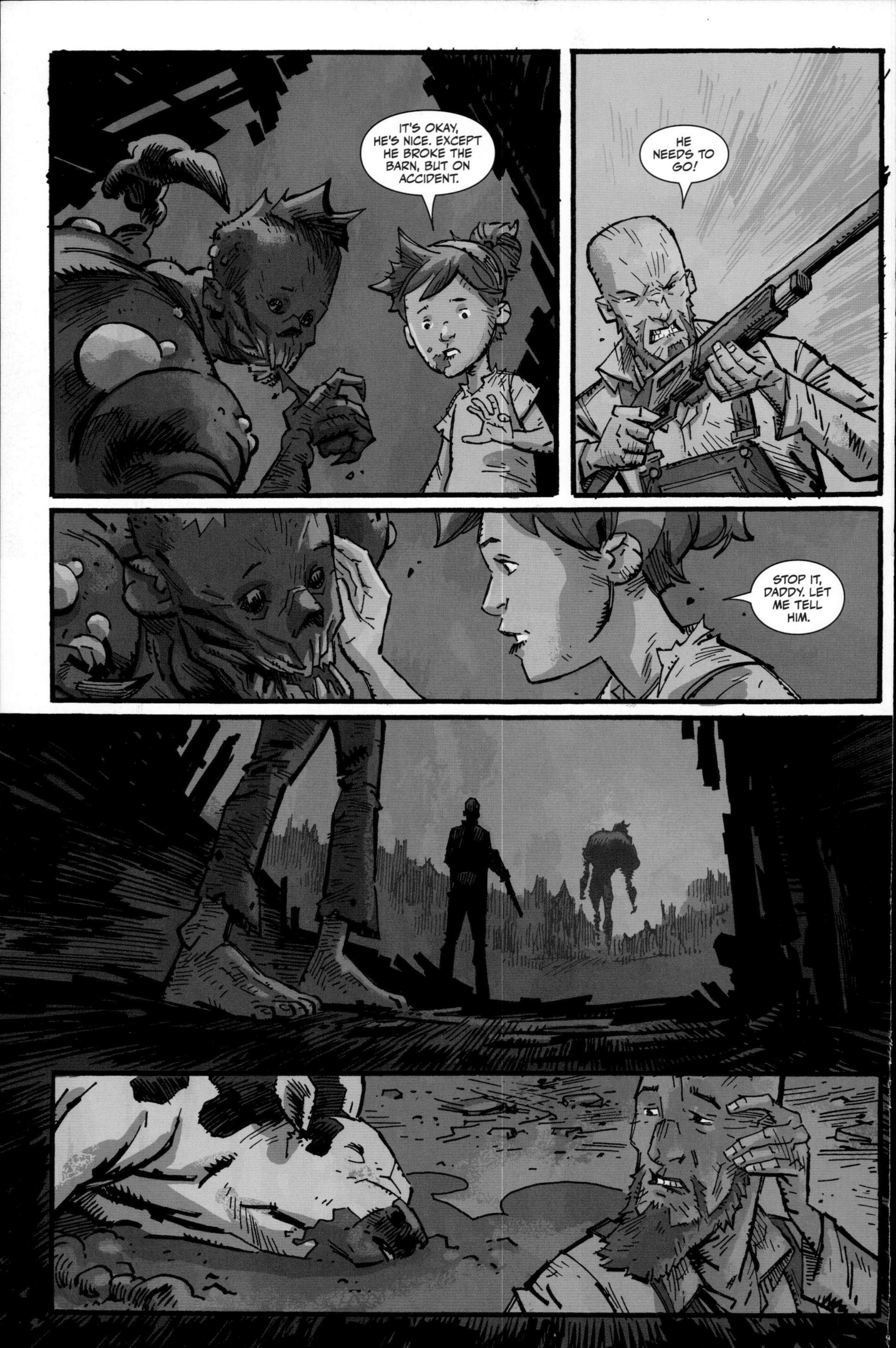

IT'S OKAY, HE'S NICE. EXCEPT HE BROKE THE BARN, BUT ON ACCIDENT.
HE NEEDS TO GO!
STOP IT, DADDY. LET ME TELL HIM.

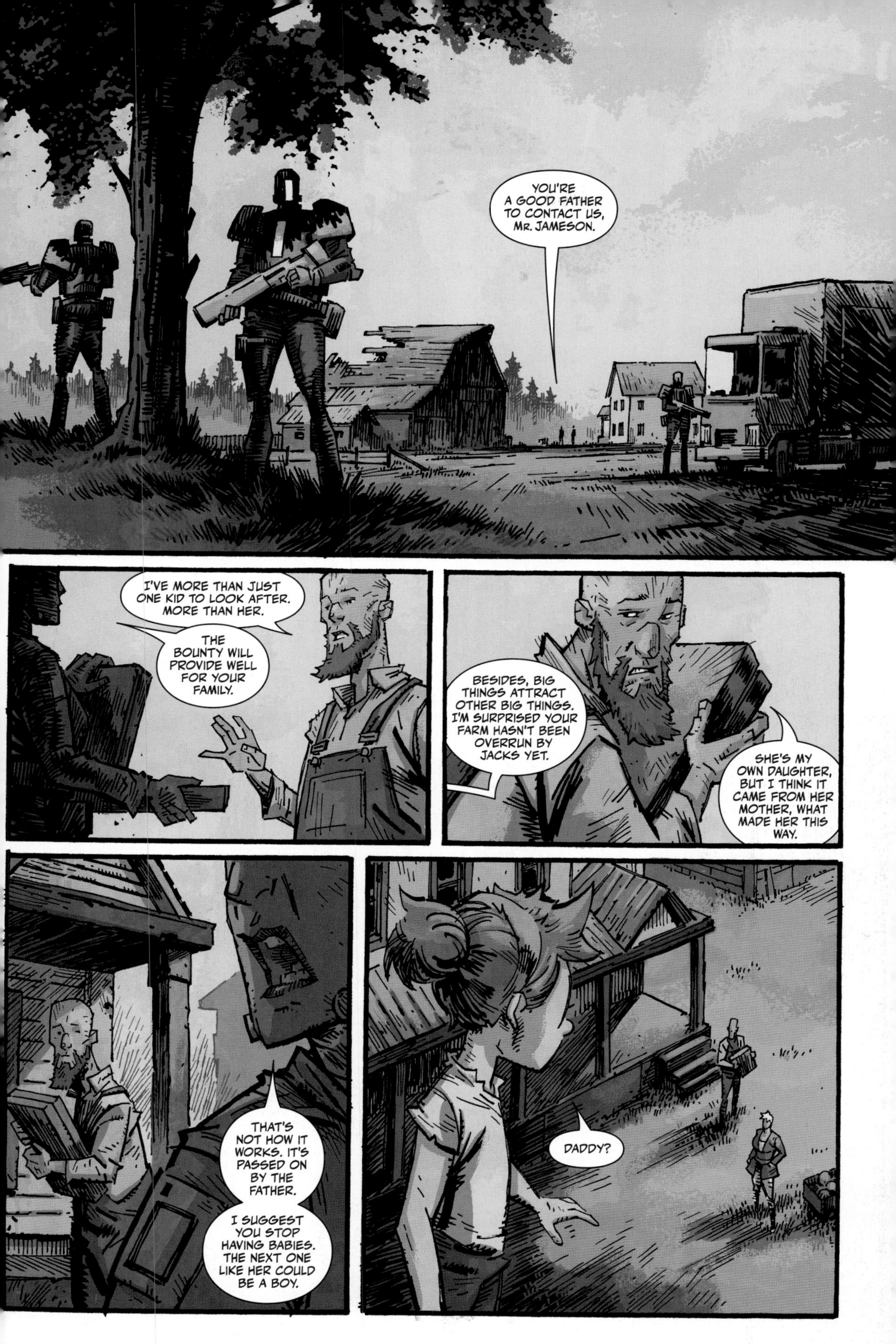
YOU'RE A GOOD FATHER TO CONTACT US, MR. JAMESON.
I'VE MORE THAN JUST ONE KID TO LOOK AFTER. MORE THAN HER.
THE BOUNTY WILL PROVIDE WELL FOR YOUR FAMILY.
BESIDES, BIG THINGS ATTRACT OTHER BIG THINGS. I'M SURPRISED YOUR FARM HASN'T BEEN OVERRUN BY JACKS YET.
SHE'S MY OWN DAUGHTER, BUT I THINK IT CAME FROM HER MOTHER, WHAT MADE HER THIS WAY.
THAT'S NOT HOW IT WORKS. IT'S PASSED ON BY THE FATHER.
I SUGGEST YOU STOP HAVING BABIES. THE NEXT ONE LIKE HER COULD BE A BOY.
DADDY?

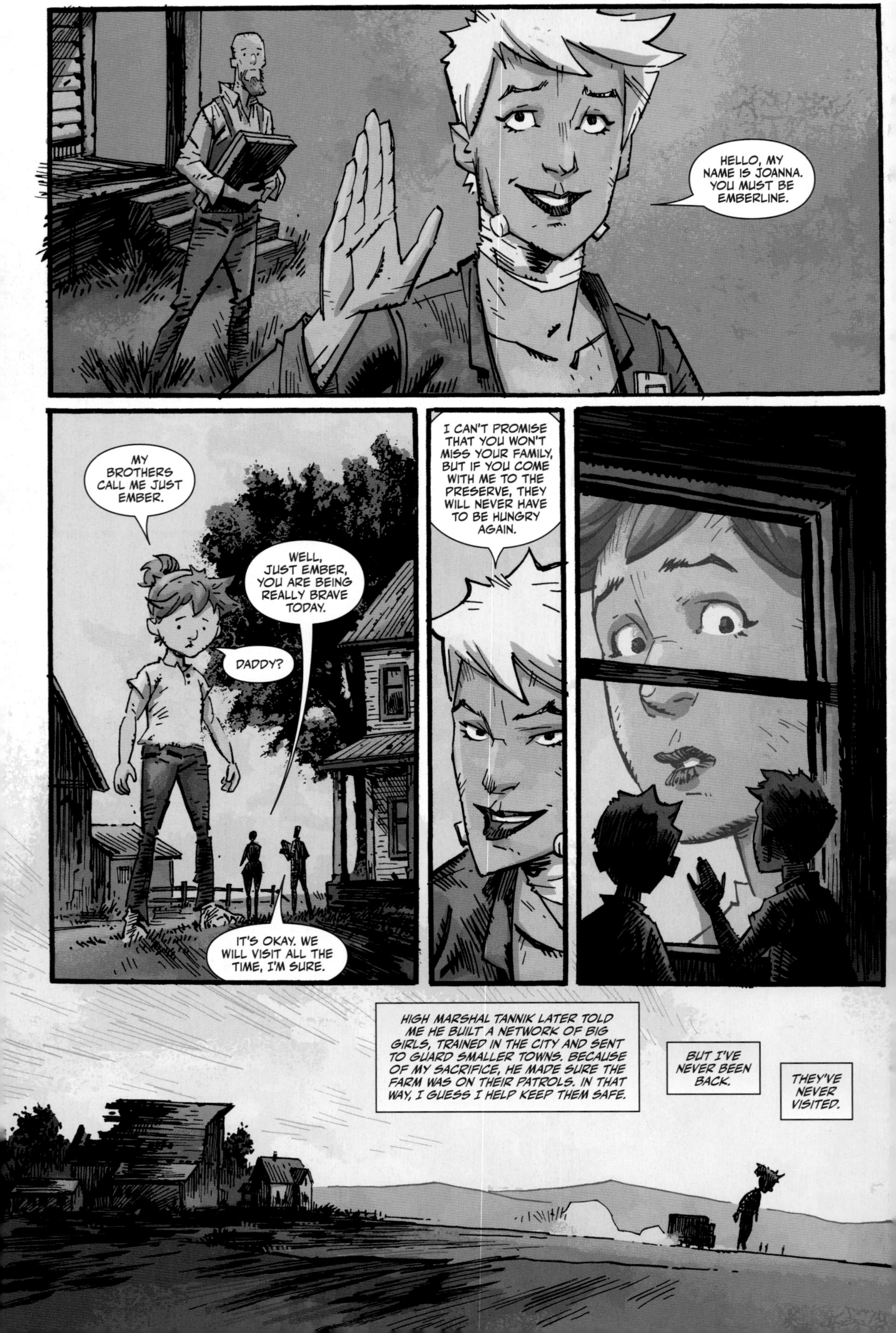
HELLO, MY NAME IS JOANNA. YOU MUST BE EMBERLINE.
MY BROTHERS CALL ME JUST EMBER.
WELL, JUST EMBER, YOU ARE BEING REALLY BRAVE TODAY.
DADDY?
IT'S OKAY. WE WILL VISIT ALL THE TIME, I'M SURE.
I CAN'T PROMISE THAT YOU WON'T MISS YOUR FAMILY, BUT IF YOU COME WITH ME TO THE PRESERVE, THEY WILL NEVER HAVE TO BE HUNGRY AGAIN.
HIGH MARSHAL TANNIK LATER TOLD ME HE BUILT A NETWORK OF BIG GIRLS, TRAINED IN THE CITY AND SENT TO GUARD SMALLER TOWNS. BECAUSE OF MY SACRIFICE, HE MADE SURE THE FARM WAS ON THEIR PATROLS. IN THAT WAY, I GUESS I HELP KEEP THEM SAFE.
BUT I'VE NEVER BEEN BACK.
THEY'VE NEVER VISITED.

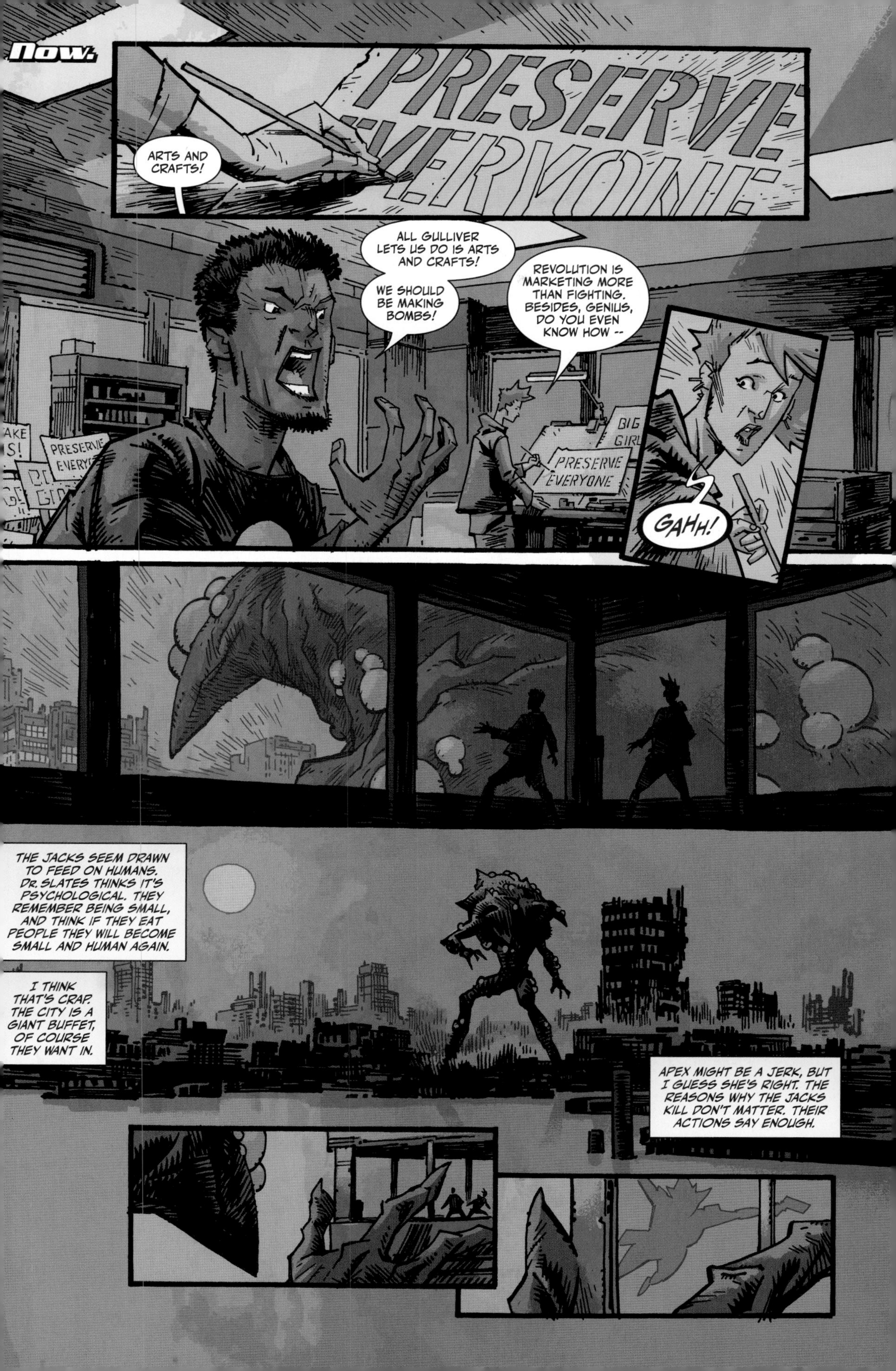

Now.
PRESERVE EVERYONE
ARTS AND CRAFTS!
ALL GULLIVER LETS US DO IS ARTS AND CRAFTS!
WE SHOULD BE MAKING BOMBS!
REVOLUTION IS MARKETING MORE THAN FIGHTING. BESIDES, GENIUS, DO YOU EVEN KNOW HOW --
PRESERVE EVERYONE
BIG GIRL
GAHH!
THE JACKS SEEM DRAWN TO FEED ON HUMANS. Dr. SLATES THINKS IT'S PSYCHOLOGICAL. THEY REMEMBER BEING SMALL, AND THINK IF THEY EAT PEOPLE THEY WILL BECOME SMALL AND HUMAN AGAIN.
I THINK THAT'S CRAP. THE CITY IS A GIANT BUFFET, OF COURSE THEY WANT IN.
APEX MIGHT BE A JERK, BUT I GUESS SHE'S RIGHT. THE REASONS WHY THE JACKS KILL DON'T MATTER. THEIR ACTIONS SAY ENOUGH.

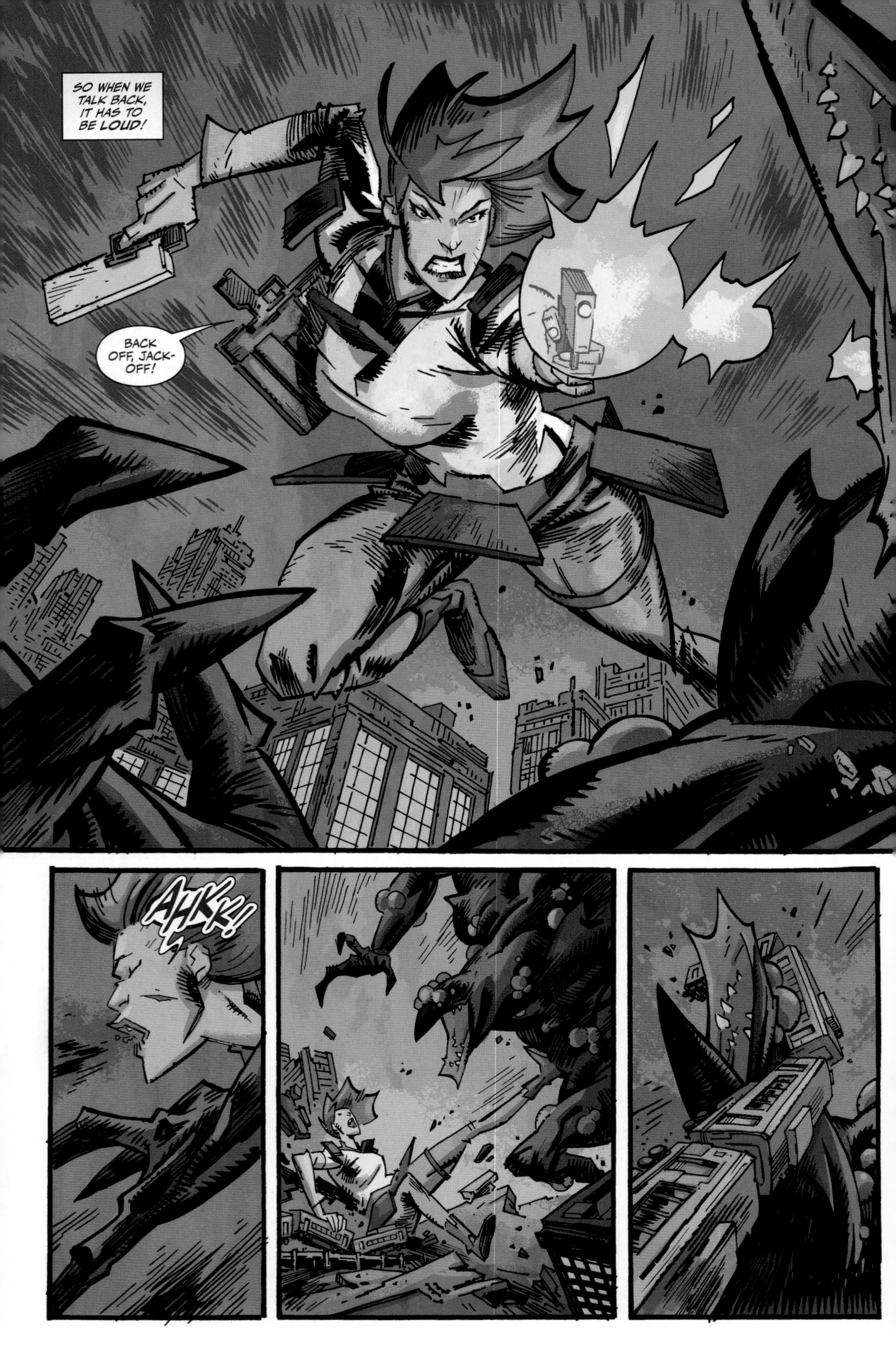
SO WHEN WE TALK BACK, IT HAS TO BE LOUD!
BACK OFF, JACK-OFF!
AHKK!

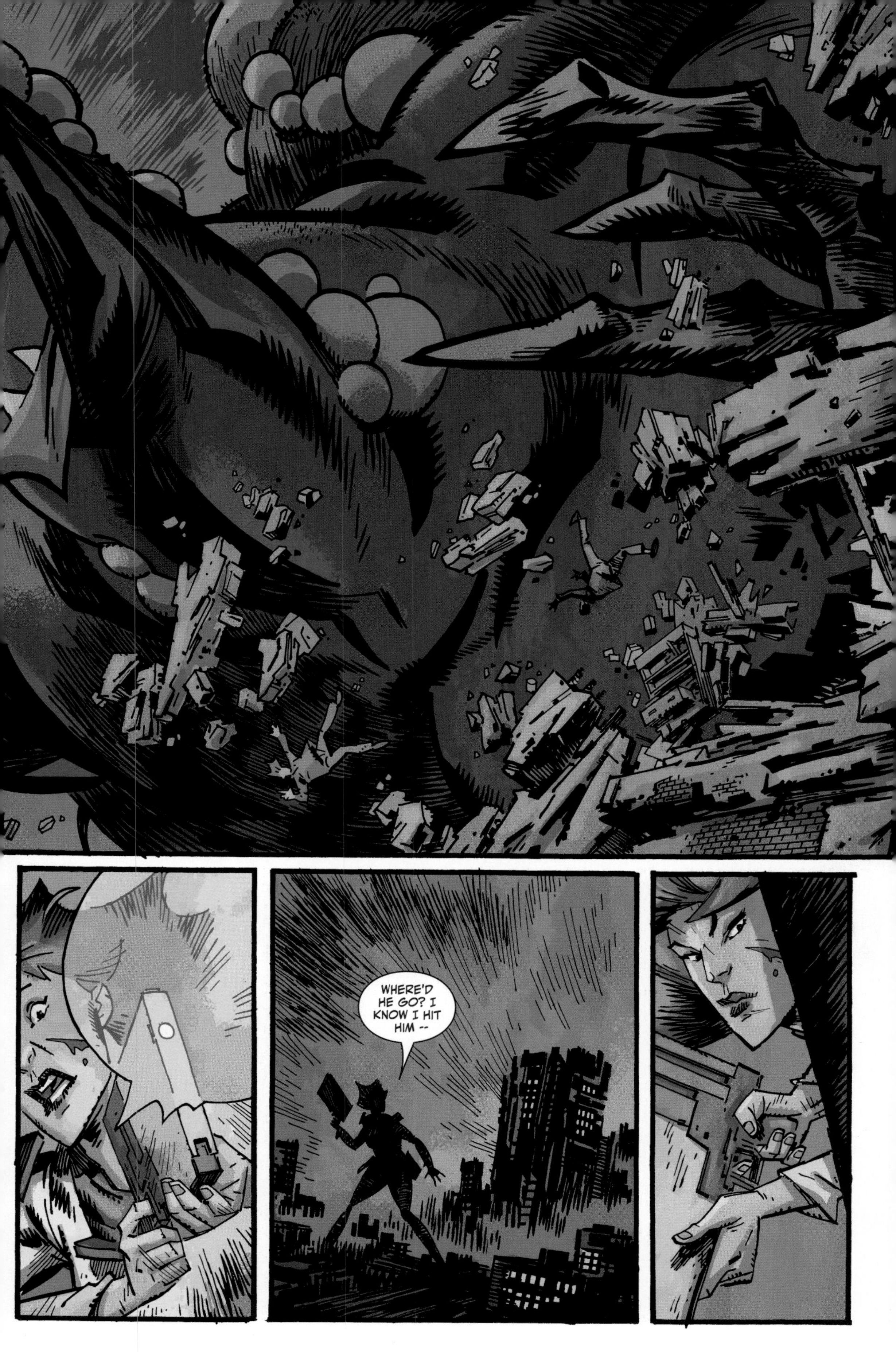
WHERE'D HE GO? I KNOW I HIT HIM --

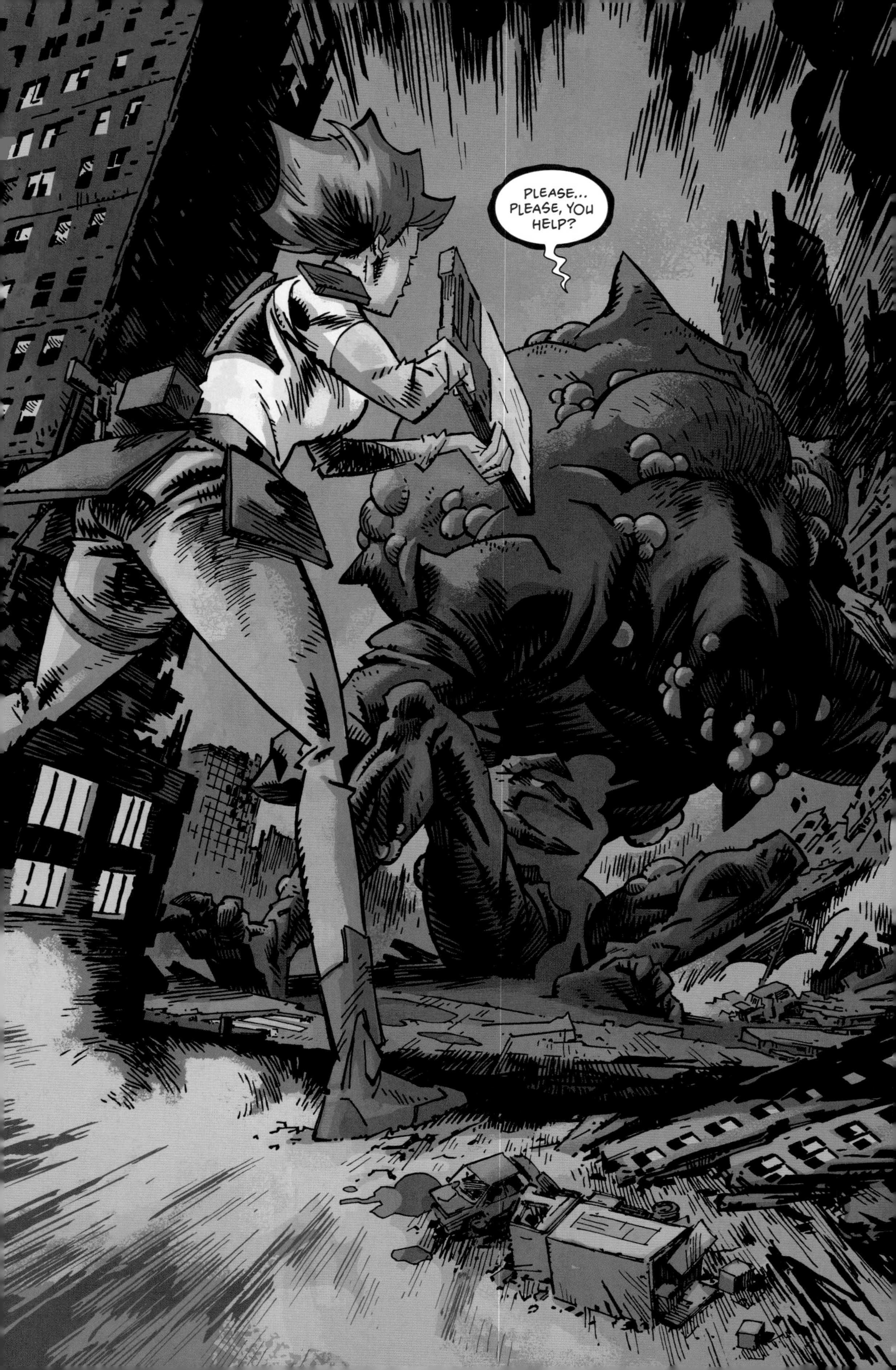
PLEASE... PLEASE, YOU HELP?

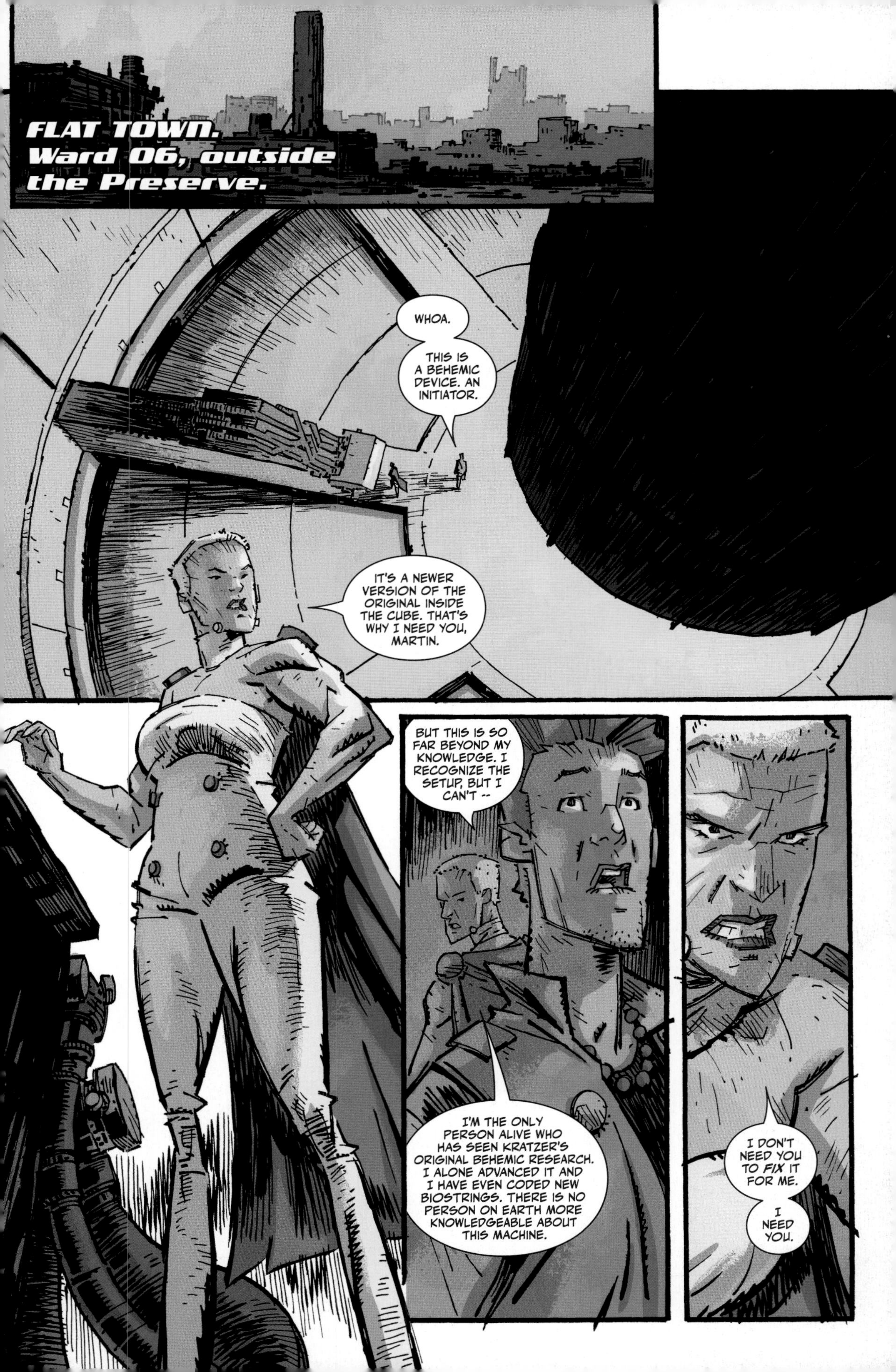

FLAT TOWN. Ward 06, outside the Preserve.
WHOA.
THIS IS A BEHEMIC DEVICE. AN INITIATOR.
IT'S A NEWER VERSION OF THE ORIGINAL INSIDE THE CUBE. THAT'S WHY I NEED YOU, MARTIN.
BUT THIS IS SO FAR BEYOND MY KNOWLEDGE. I RECOGNIZE THE SETUP, BUT I CAN'T --
I'M THE ONLY PERSON ALIVE WHO HAS SEEN KRATZER'S ORIGINAL BEHEMIC RESEARCH. I ALONE ADVANCED IT AND I HAVE EVEN CODED NEW BIOSTRINGS. THERE IS NO PERSON ON EARTH MORE KNOWLEDGEABLE ABOUT THIS MACHINE.
I DON'T NEED YOU TO *FIX* IT FOR ME.
I NEED YOU.

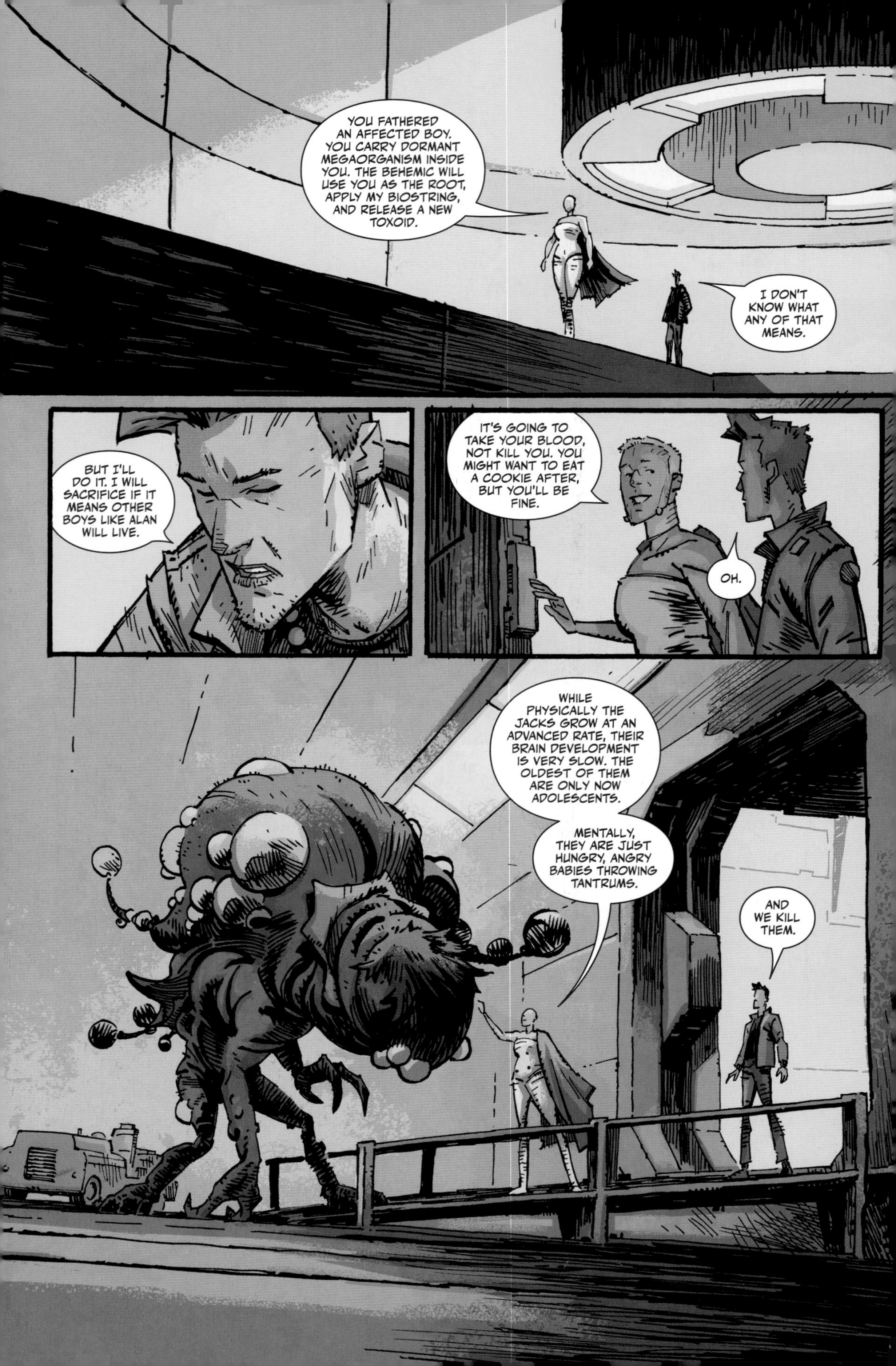
YOU FATHERED AN AFFECTED BOY. YOU CARRY DORMANT MEGAORGANISM INSIDE YOU. THE BEHEMIC WILL USE YOU AS THE ROOT, APPLY MY BIOSTRING, AND RELEASE A NEW TOXOID.
I DON'T KNOW WHAT ANY OF THAT MEANS.
BUT I'LL DO IT. I WILL SACRIFICE IF IT MEANS OTHER BOYS LIKE ALAN WILL LIVE.
IT'S GOING TO TAKE YOUR BLOOD, NOT KILL YOU. YOU MIGHT WANT TO EAT A COOKIE AFTER, BUT YOU'LL BE FINE.
OH.
WHILE PHYSICALLY THE JACKS GROW AT AN ADVANCED RATE, THEIR BRAIN DEVELOPMENT IS VERY SLOW. THE OLDEST OF THEM ARE ONLY NOW ADOLESCENTS.
MENTALLY, THEY ARE JUST HUNGRY, ANGRY BABIES THROWING TANTRUMS.
AND WE KILL THEM.

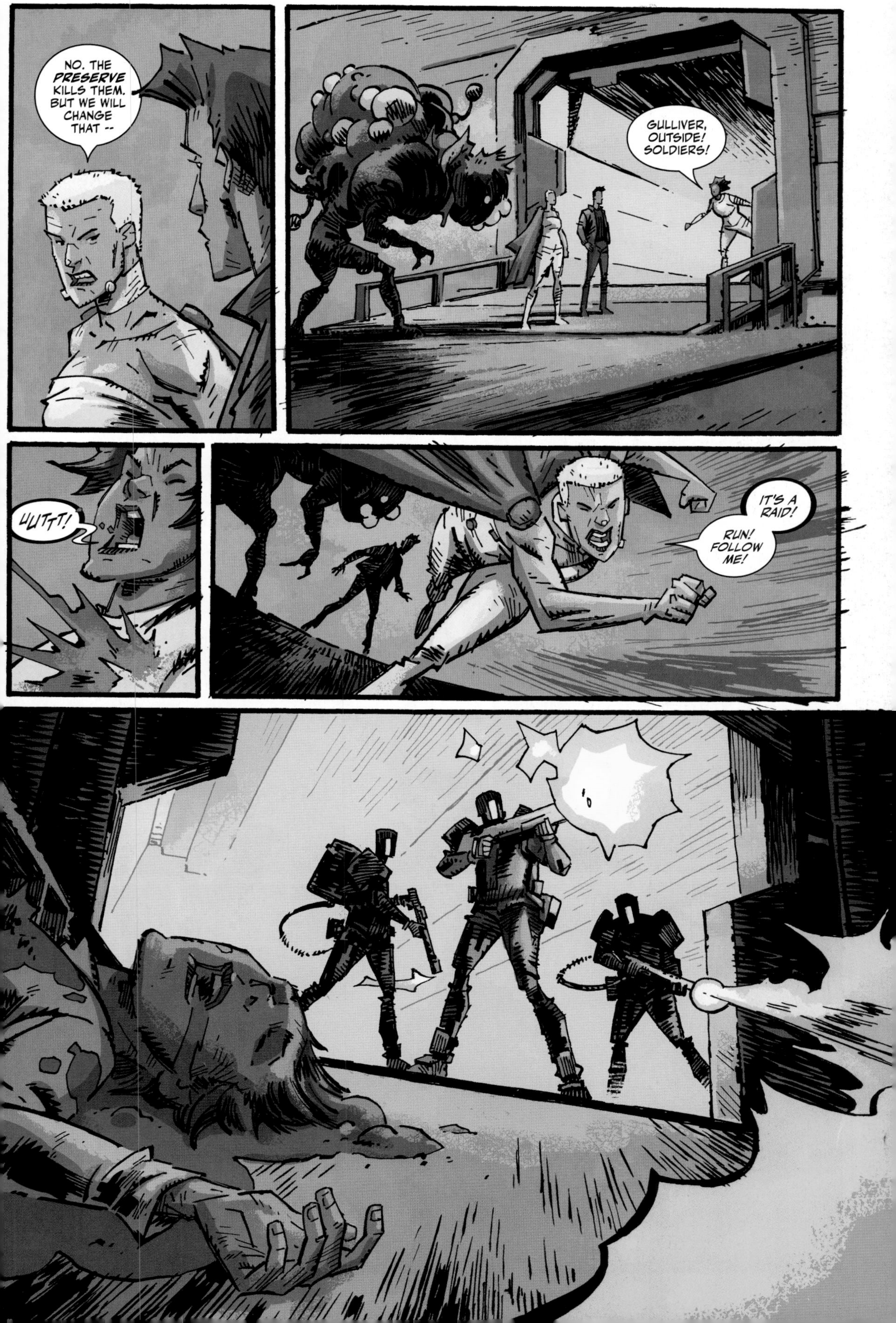
NO. THE *PRESERVE* KILLS THEM. BUT WE WILL CHANGE THAT --
GULLIVER, OUTSIDE! SOLDIERS!
UUTTT!
IT'S A RAID!
RUN! FOLLOW ME!

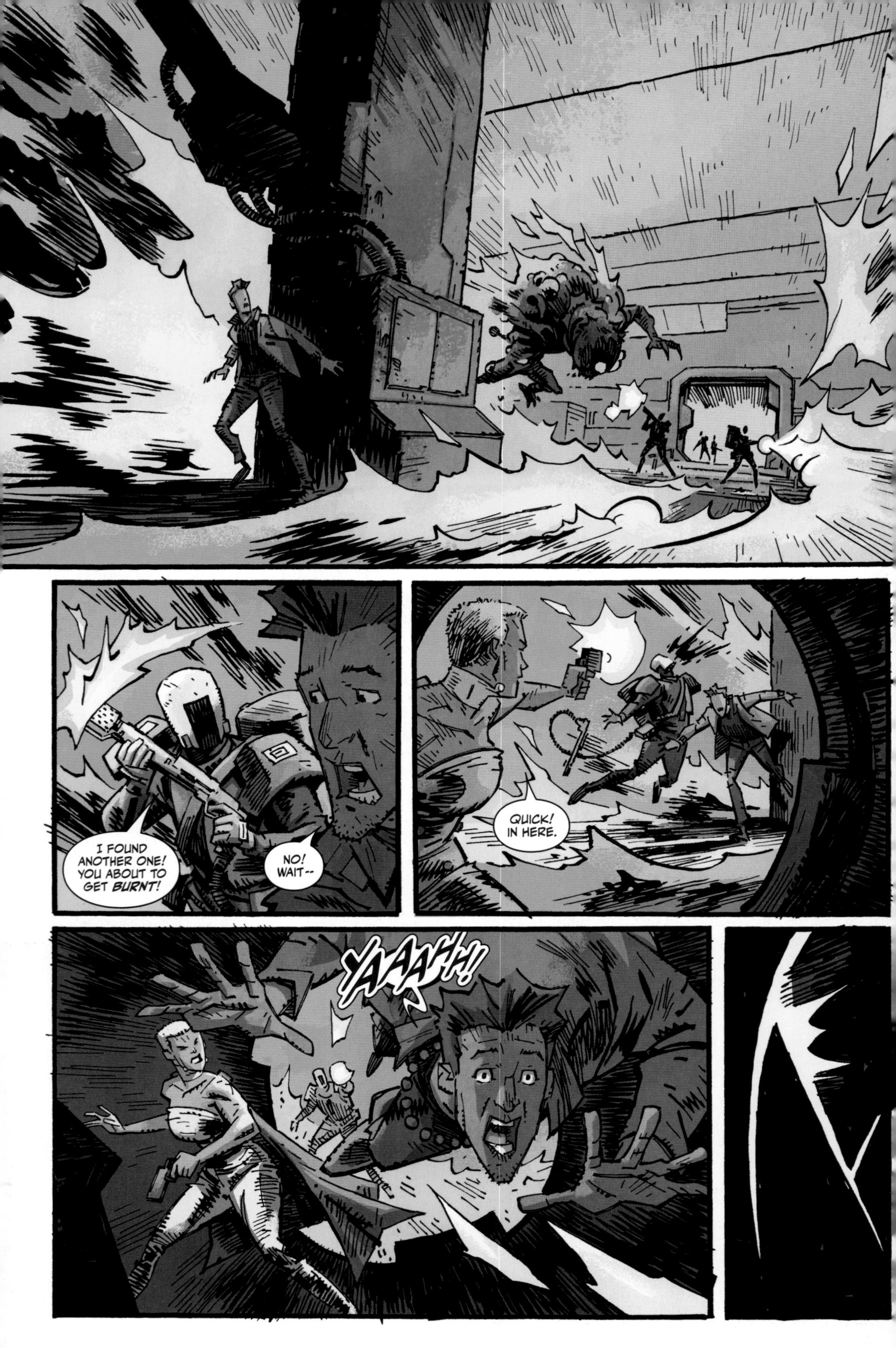
I FOUND ANOTHER ONE! YOU ABOUT TO GET BURNT!
NO! WAIT--
QUICK! IN HERE.
YAAAHH!

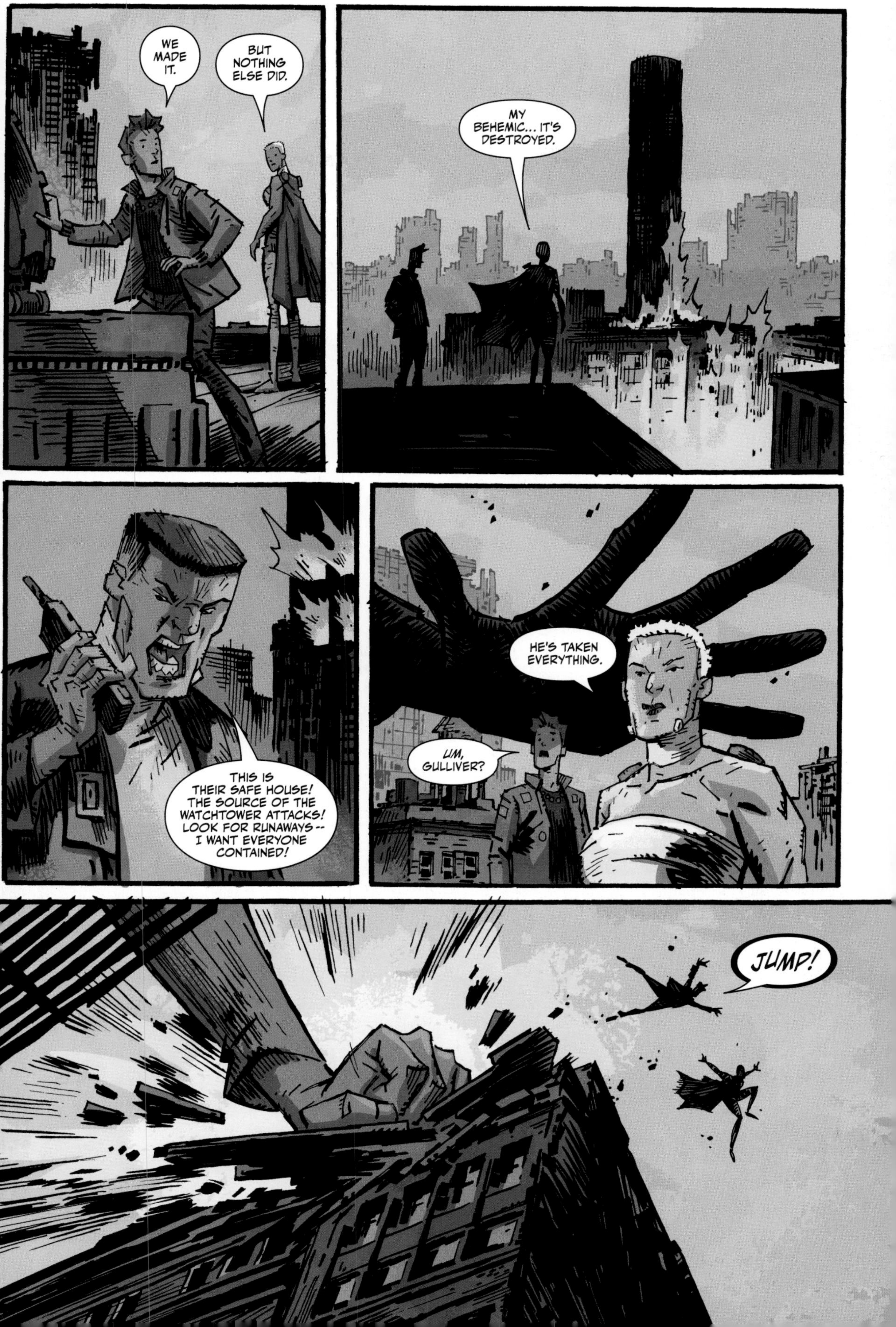
WE MADE IT.
BUT NOTHING ELSE DID.
MY BEHEMIC... IT'S DESTROYED.
THIS IS THEIR SAFE HOUSE! THE SOURCE OF THE WATCHTOWER ATTACKS! LOOK FOR RUNAWAYS -- I WANT EVERYONE CONTAINED!
HE'S TAKEN EVERYTHING.
UM, GULLIVER?
JUMP!

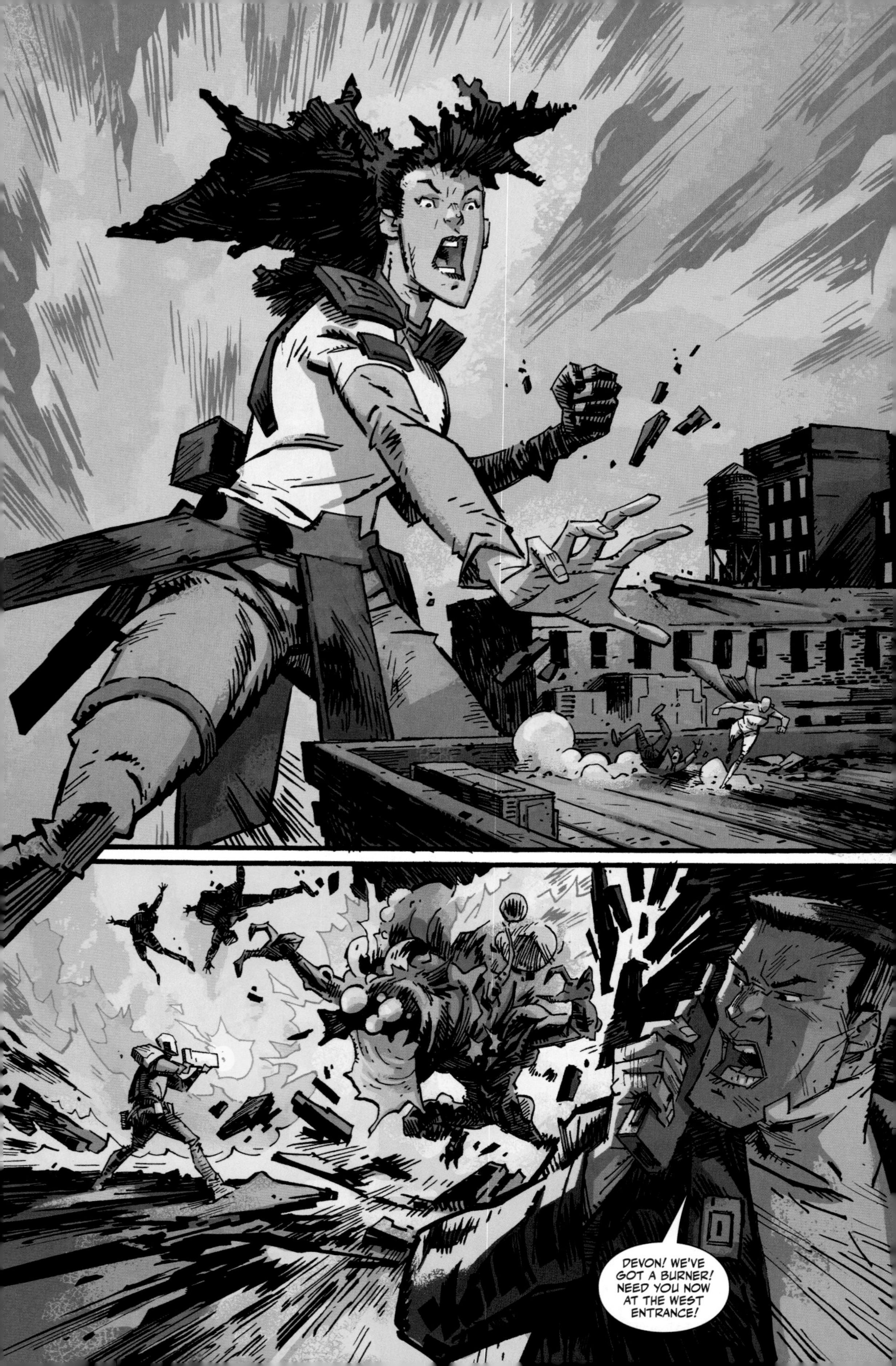
DEVON! WE'VE GOT A BURNER! NEED YOU NOW AT THE WEST ENTRANCE!

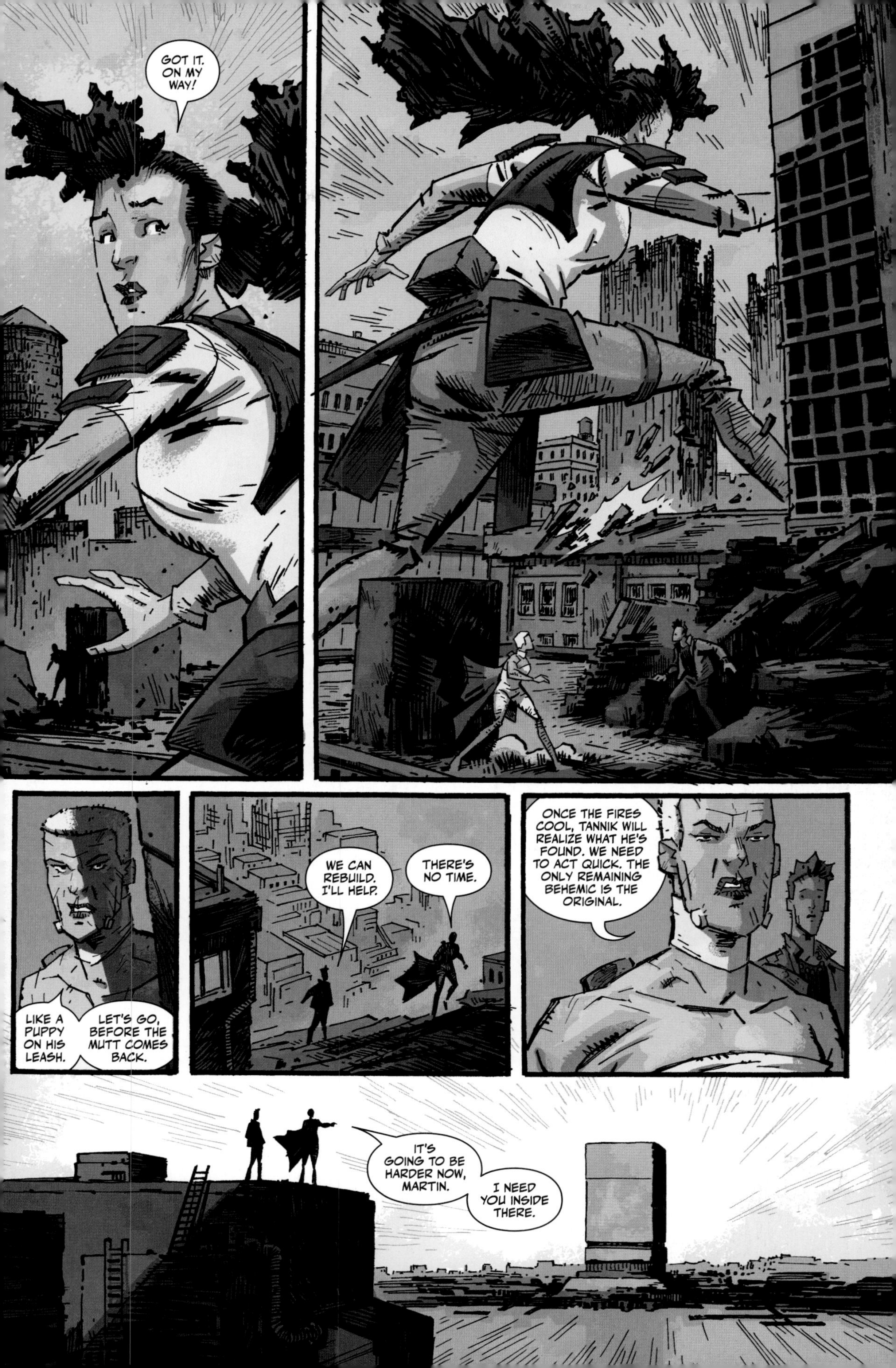
GOT IT. ON MY WAY!
LIKE A PUPPY ON HIS LEASH.
LET'S GO, BEFORE THE MUTT COMES BACK.
WE CAN REBUILD. I'LL HELP.
THERE'S NO TIME.
ONCE THE FIRES COOL, TANNIK WILL REALIZE WHAT HE'S FOUND. WE NEED TO ACT QUICK. THE ONLY REMAINING BEHEMIC IS THE ORIGINAL.
IT'S GOING TO BE HARDER NOW, MARTIN.
I NEED YOU INSIDE THERE.

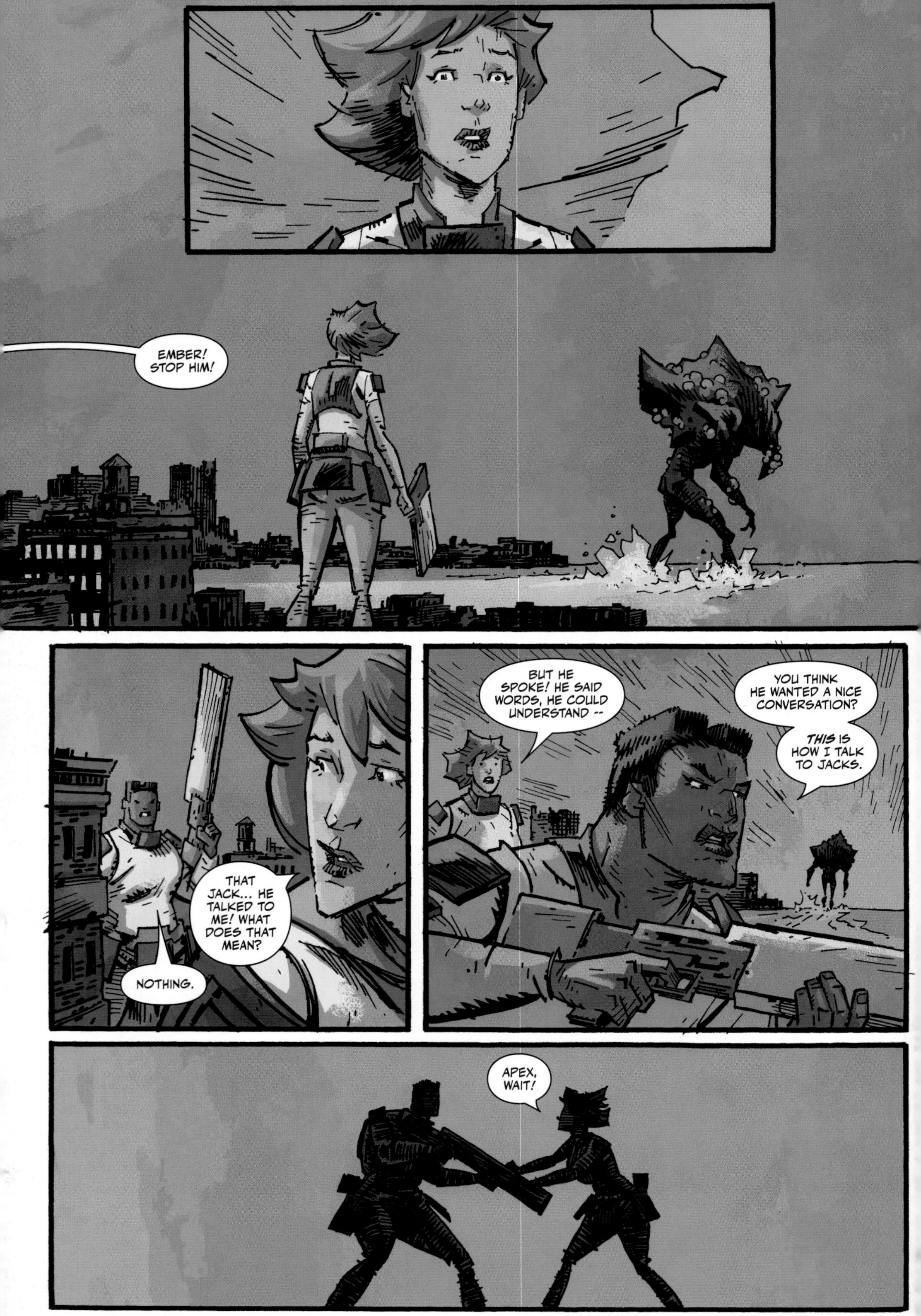
EMBER! STOP HIM!
THAT JACK... HE TALKED TO ME! WHAT DOES THAT MEAN?
NOTHING.
BUT HE SPOKE! HE SAID WORDS, HE COULD UNDERSTAND --
YOU THINK HE WANTED A NICE CONVERSATION?
THIS IS HOW I TALK TO JACKS.
APEX, WAIT!

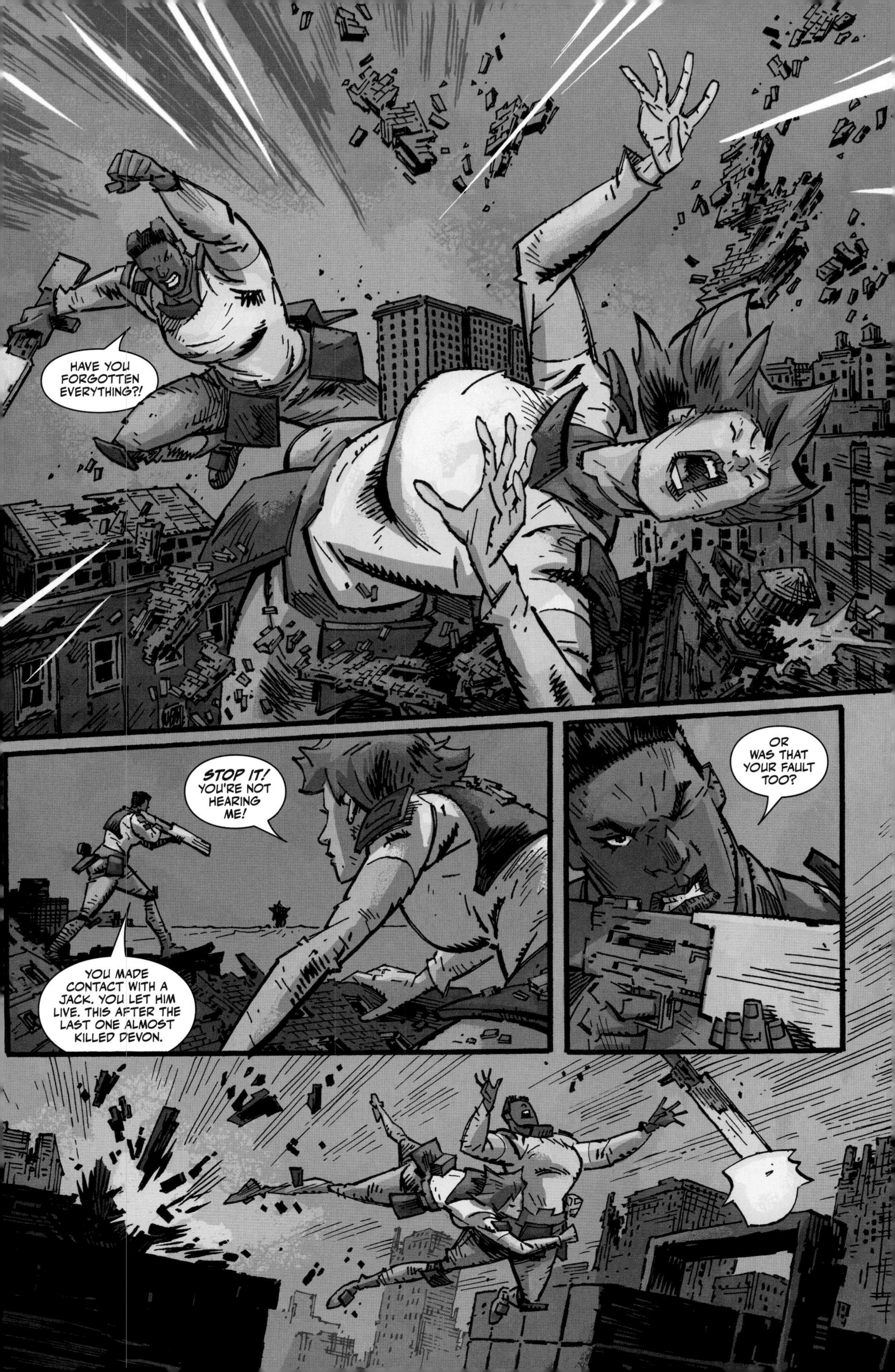
HAVE YOU FORGOTTEN EVERYTHING?!
STOP IT! YOU'RE NOT HEARING ME!
YOU MADE CONTACT WITH A JACK. YOU LET HIM LIVE. THIS AFTER THE LAST ONE ALMOST KILLED DEVON.
OR WAS THAT YOUR FAULT TOO?

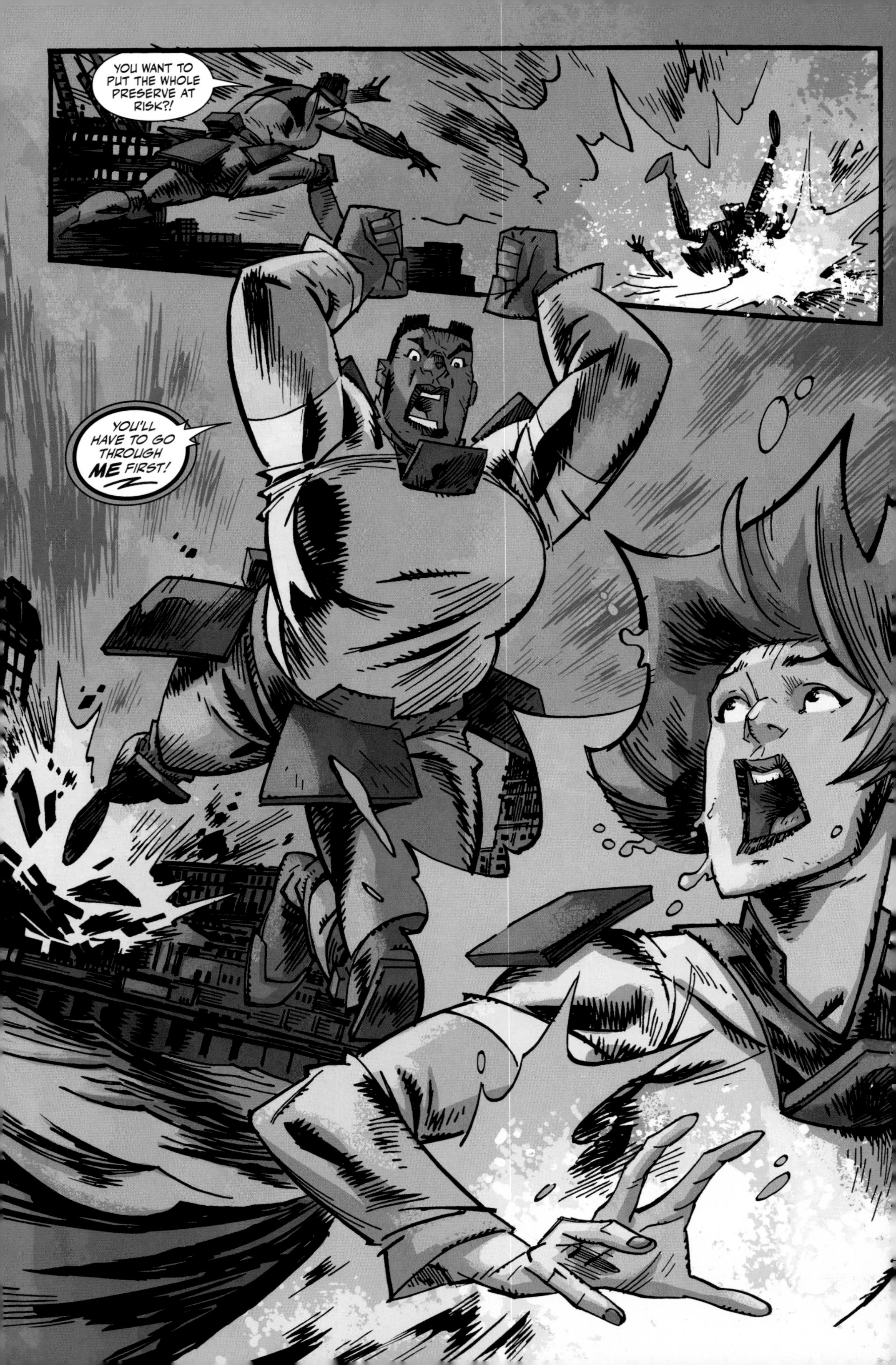
YOU WANT TO PUT THE WHOLE PRESERVE AT RISK?!
YOU'LL HAVE TO GO THROUGH ME FIRST!

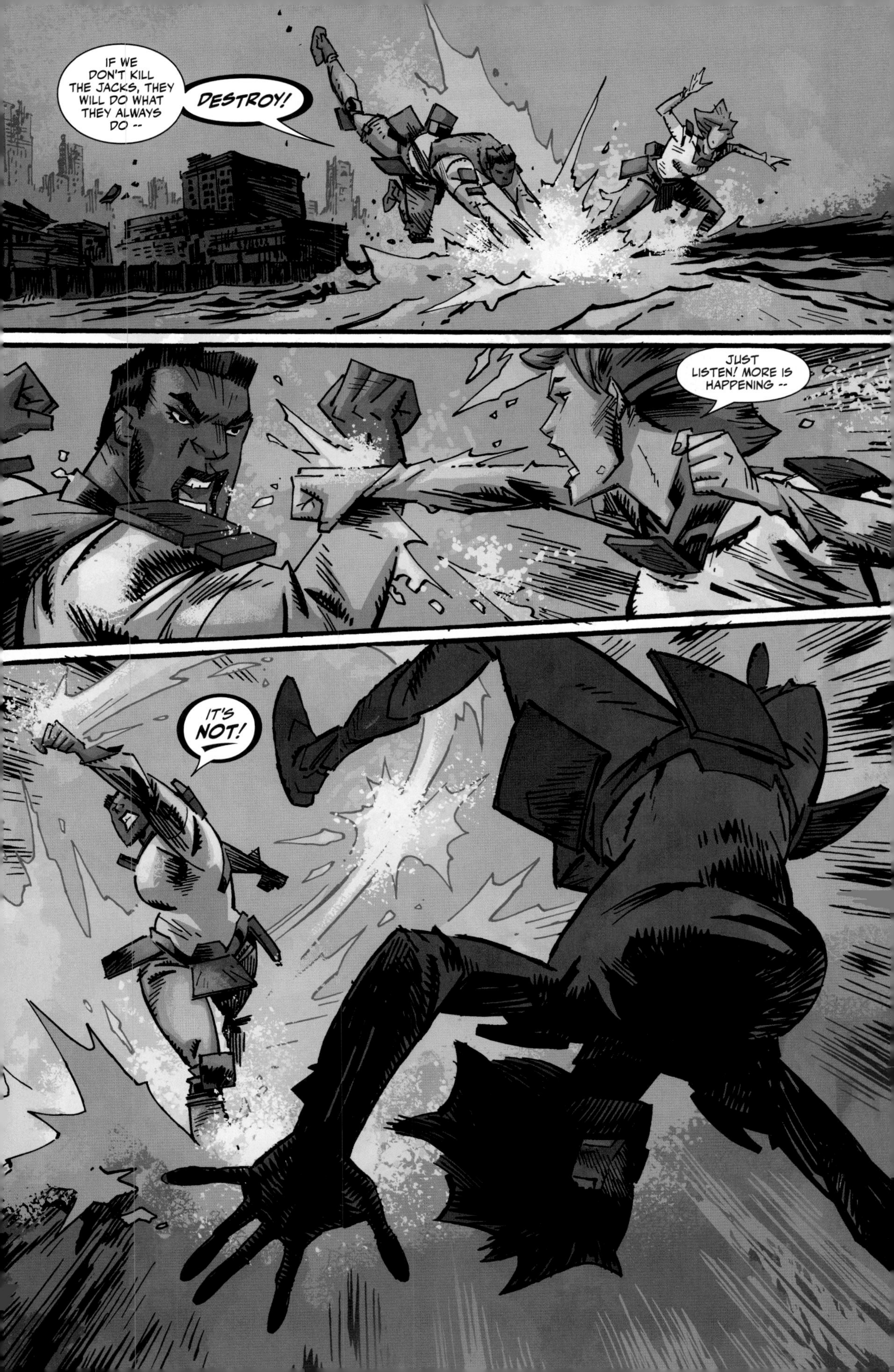
IF WE DON'T KILL THE JACKS, THEY WILL DO WHAT THEY ALWAYS DO --
DESTROY!
JUST LISTEN! MORE IS HAPPENING --
IT'S NOT!

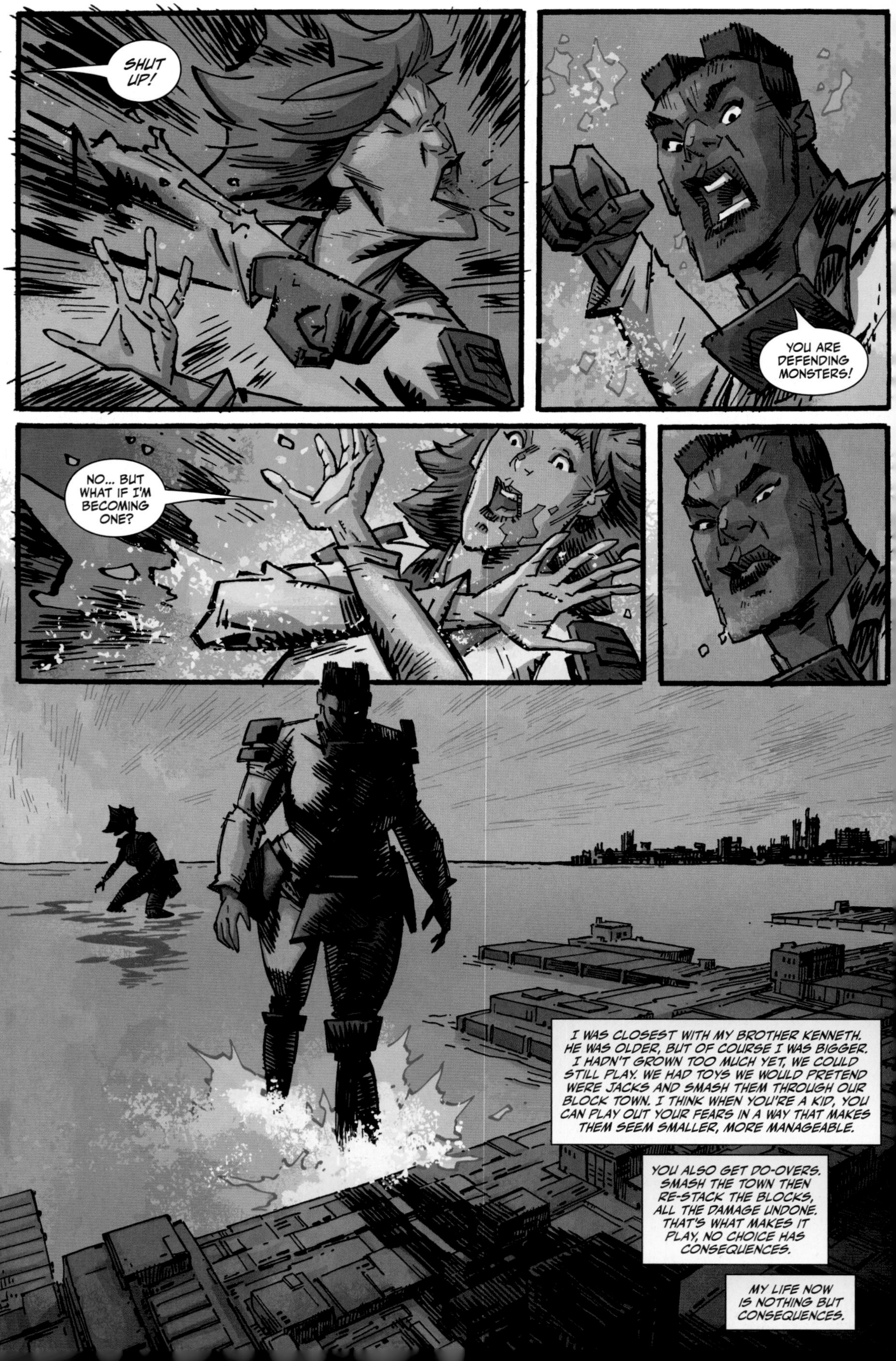
SHUT UP!
YOU ARE DEFENDING MONSTERS!
NO... BUT WHAT IF I'M BECOMING ONE?
I WAS CLOSEST WITH MY BROTHER KENNETH. HE WAS OLDER, BUT OF COURSE I WAS BIGGER. I HADN'T GROWN TOO MUCH YET, WE COULD STILL PLAY. WE HAD TOYS WE WOULD PRETEND WERE JACKS AND SMASH THEM THROUGH OUR BLOCK TOWN. I THINK WHEN YOU'RE A KID, YOU CAN PLAY OUT YOUR FEARS IN A WAY THAT MAKES THEM SEEM SMALLER, MORE MANAGEABLE.
YOU ALSO GET DO-OVERS. SMASH THE TOWN THEN RE-STACK THE BLOCKS, ALL THE DAMAGE UNDONE. THAT'S WHAT MAKES IT PLAY, NO CHOICE HAS CONSEQUENCES.
MY LIFE NOW IS NOTHING BUT CONSEQUENCES.

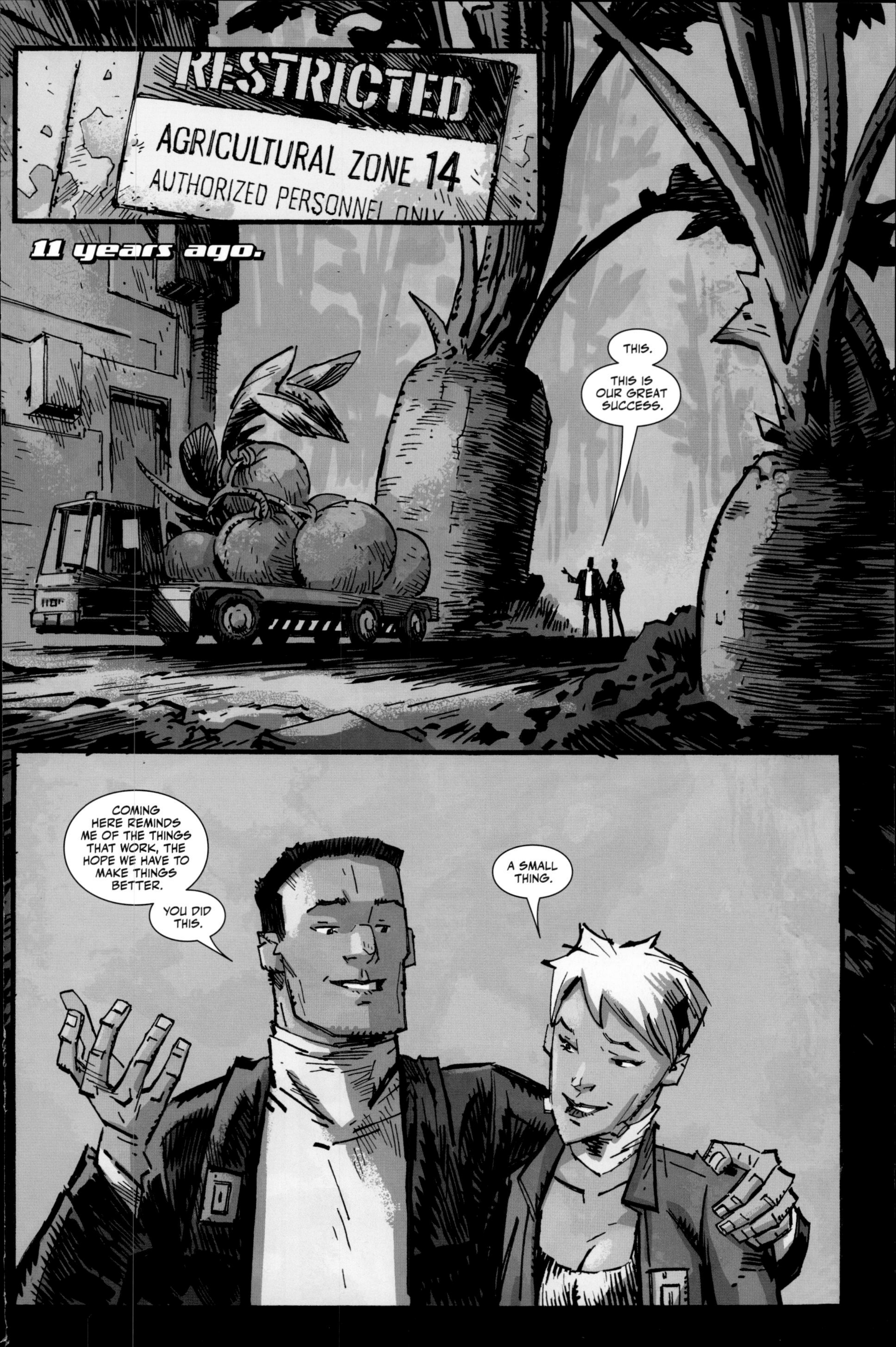
RESTRICTED
AGRICULTURAL ZONE 14
AUTHORIZED PERSONNEL ONLY
11 years ago.
THIS.
THIS IS OUR GREAT SUCCESS.
COMING HERE REMINDS ME OF THE THINGS THAT WORK, THE HOPE WE HAVE TO MAKE THINGS BETTER.
YOU DID THIS.
A SMALL THING.

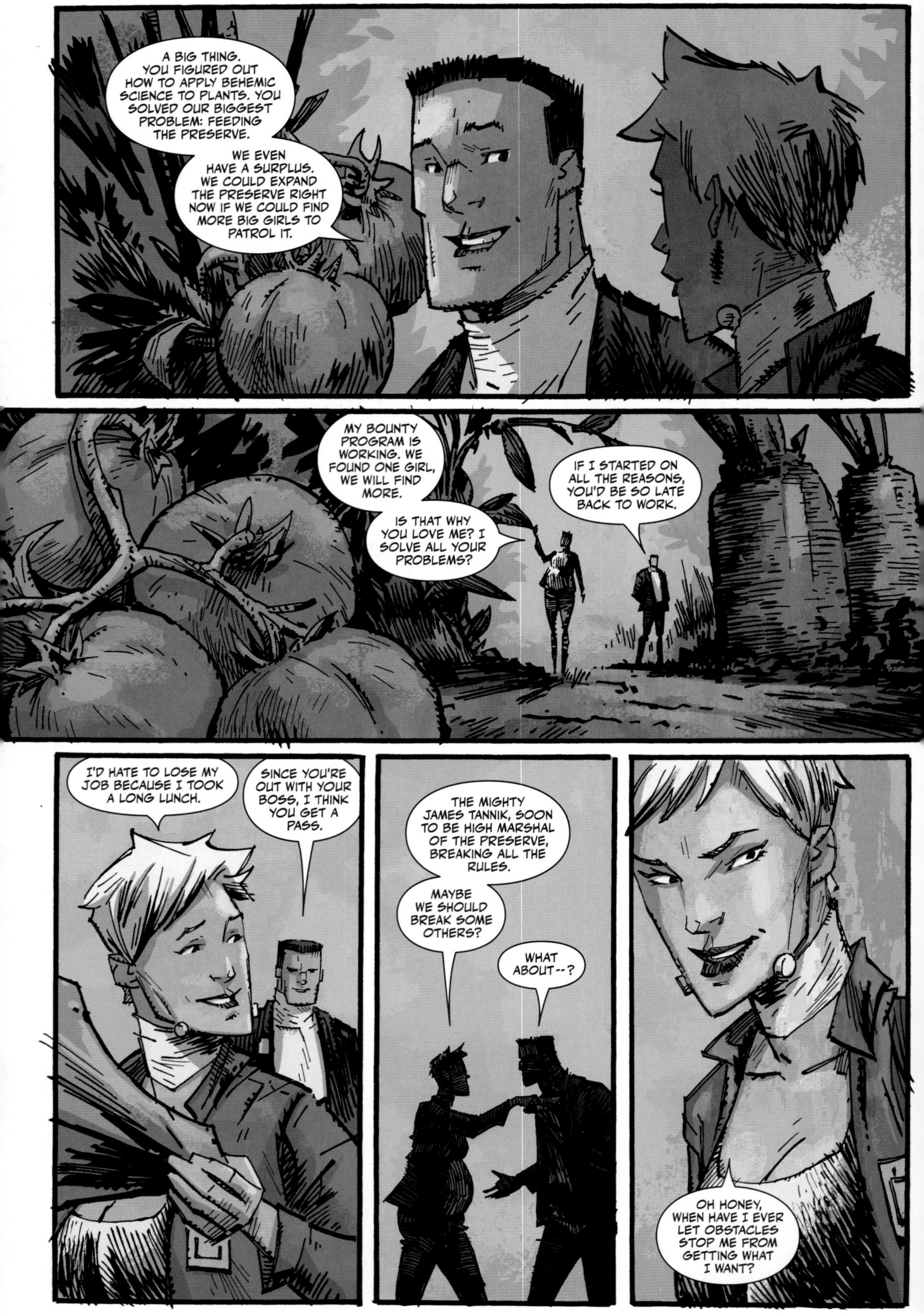
A BIG THING. YOU FIGURED OUT HOW TO APPLY BEHEMIC SCIENCE TO PLANTS. YOU SOLVED OUR BIGGEST PROBLEM: FEEDING THE PRESERVE.
WE EVEN HAVE A SURPLUS. WE COULD EXPAND THE PRESERVE RIGHT NOW IF WE COULD FIND MORE BIG GIRLS TO PATROL IT.
MY BOUNTY PROGRAM IS WORKING. WE FOUND ONE GIRL, WE WILL FIND MORE.
IS THAT WHY YOU LOVE ME? I SOLVE ALL YOUR PROBLEMS?
IF I STARTED ON ALL THE REASONS, YOU'D BE SO LATE BACK TO WORK.
I'D HATE TO LOSE MY JOB BECAUSE I TOOK A LONG LUNCH.
SINCE YOU'RE OUT WITH YOUR BOSS, I THINK YOU GET A PASS.
THE MIGHTY JAMES TANNIK, SOON TO BE HIGH MARSHAL OF THE PRESERVE, BREAKING ALL THE RULES.
MAYBE WE SHOULD BREAK SOME OTHERS?
WHAT ABOUT--?
OH HONEY, WHEN HAVE I EVER LET OBSTACLES STOP ME FROM GETTING WHAT I WANT?

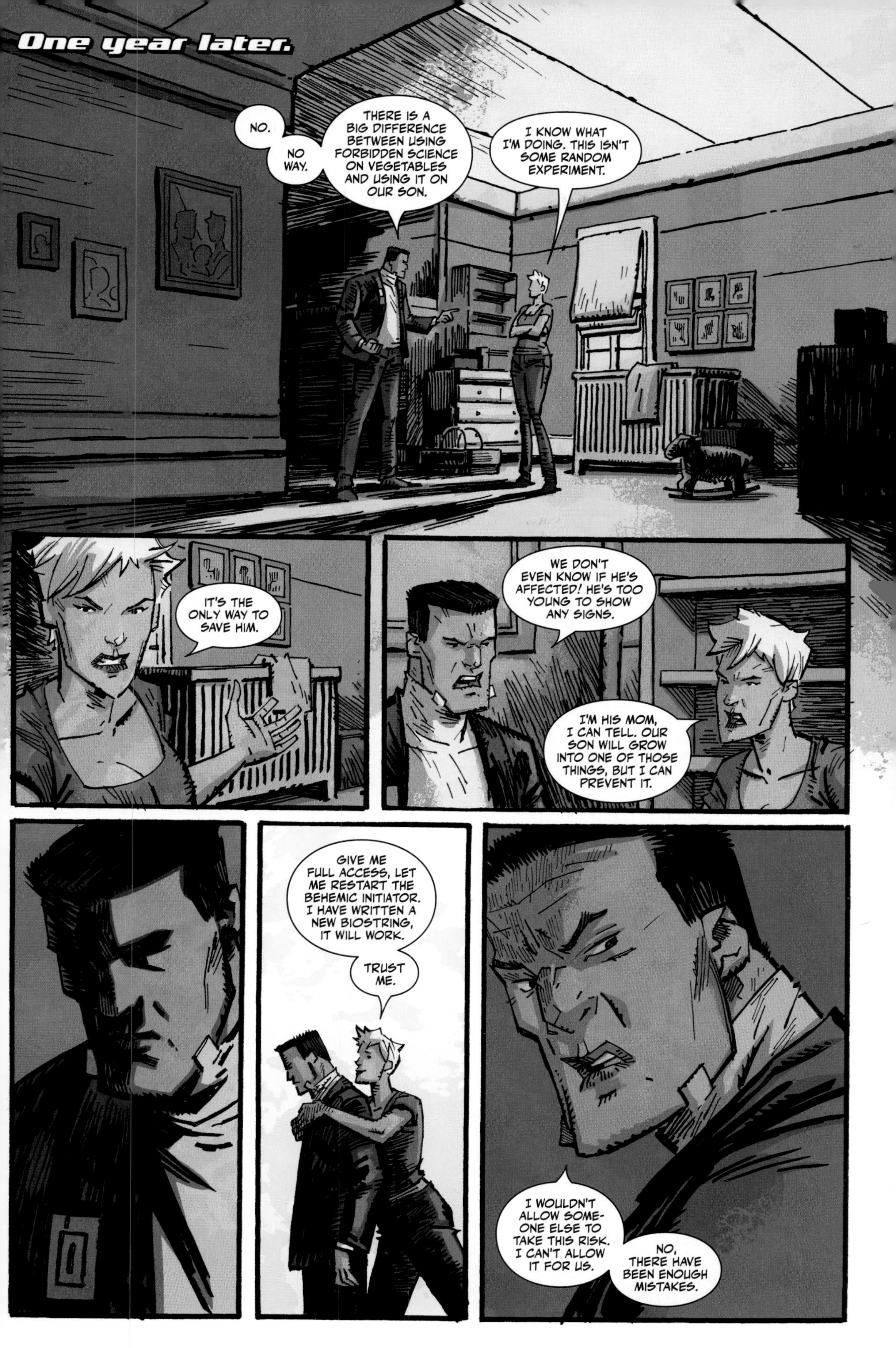
One year later.
NO.
NO WAY.
THERE IS A BIG DIFFERENCE BETWEEN USING FORBIDDEN SCIENCE ON VEGETABLES AND USING IT ON OUR SON.
I KNOW WHAT I'M DOING. THIS ISN'T SOME RANDOM EXPERIMENT.
IT'S THE ONLY WAY TO SAVE HIM.
WE DON'T EVEN KNOW IF HE'S AFFECTED! HE'S TOO YOUNG TO SHOW ANY SIGNS.
I'M HIS MOM, I CAN TELL. OUR SON WILL GROW INTO ONE OF THOSE THINGS, BUT I CAN PREVENT IT.
GIVE ME FULL ACCESS, LET ME RESTART THE BEHEMIC INITIATOR. I HAVE WRITTEN A NEW BIOSTRING, IT WILL WORK.
TRUST ME.
I WOULDN'T ALLOW SOME-ONE ELSE TO TAKE THIS RISK. I CAN'T ALLOW IT FOR US.
NO, THERE HAVE BEEN ENOUGH MISTAKES.

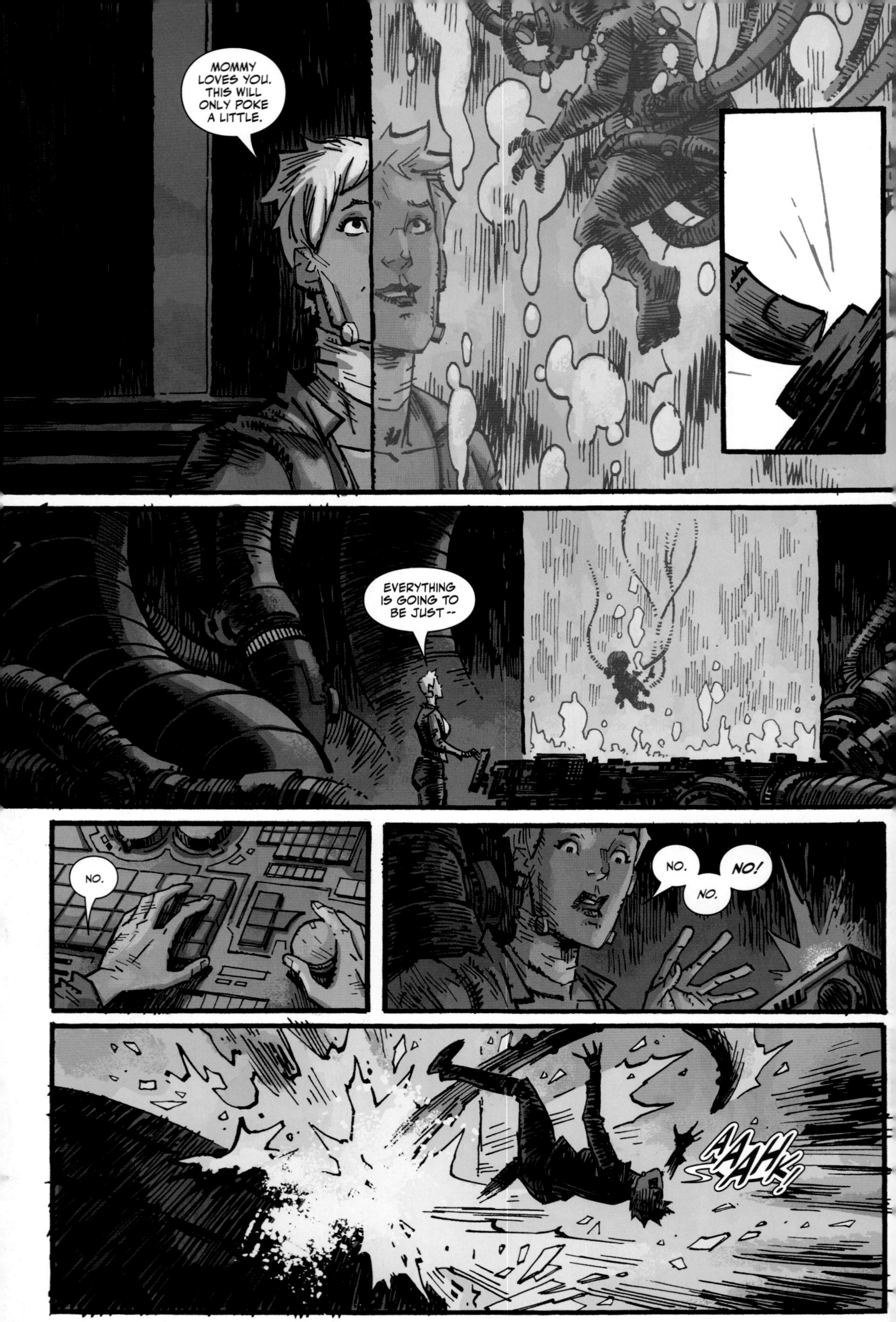
MOMMY LOVES YOU. THIS WILL ONLY POKE A LITTLE.
EVERYTHING IS GOING TO BE JUST --
NO.
NO.
NO.
NO!
AAAHK!

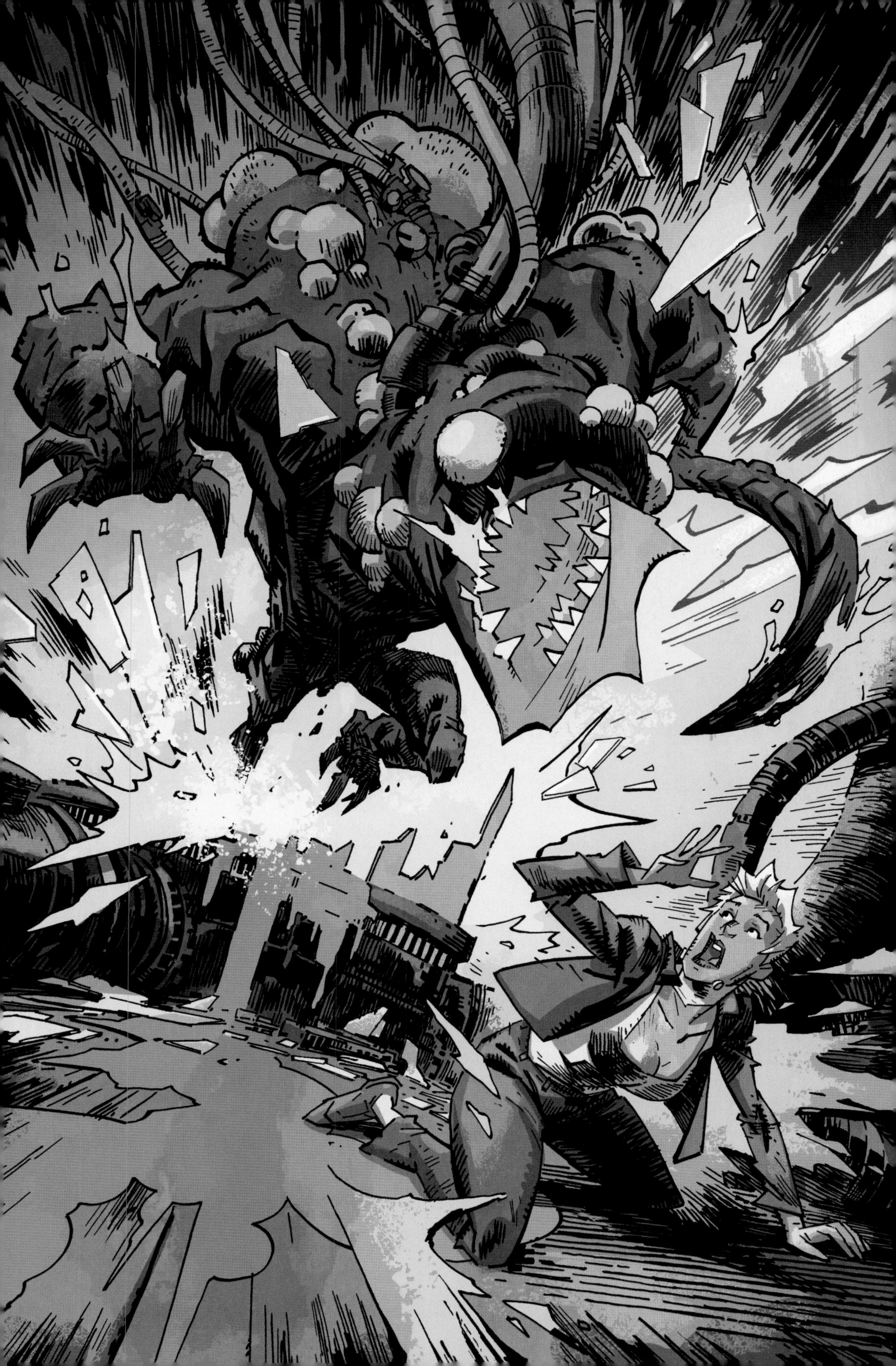

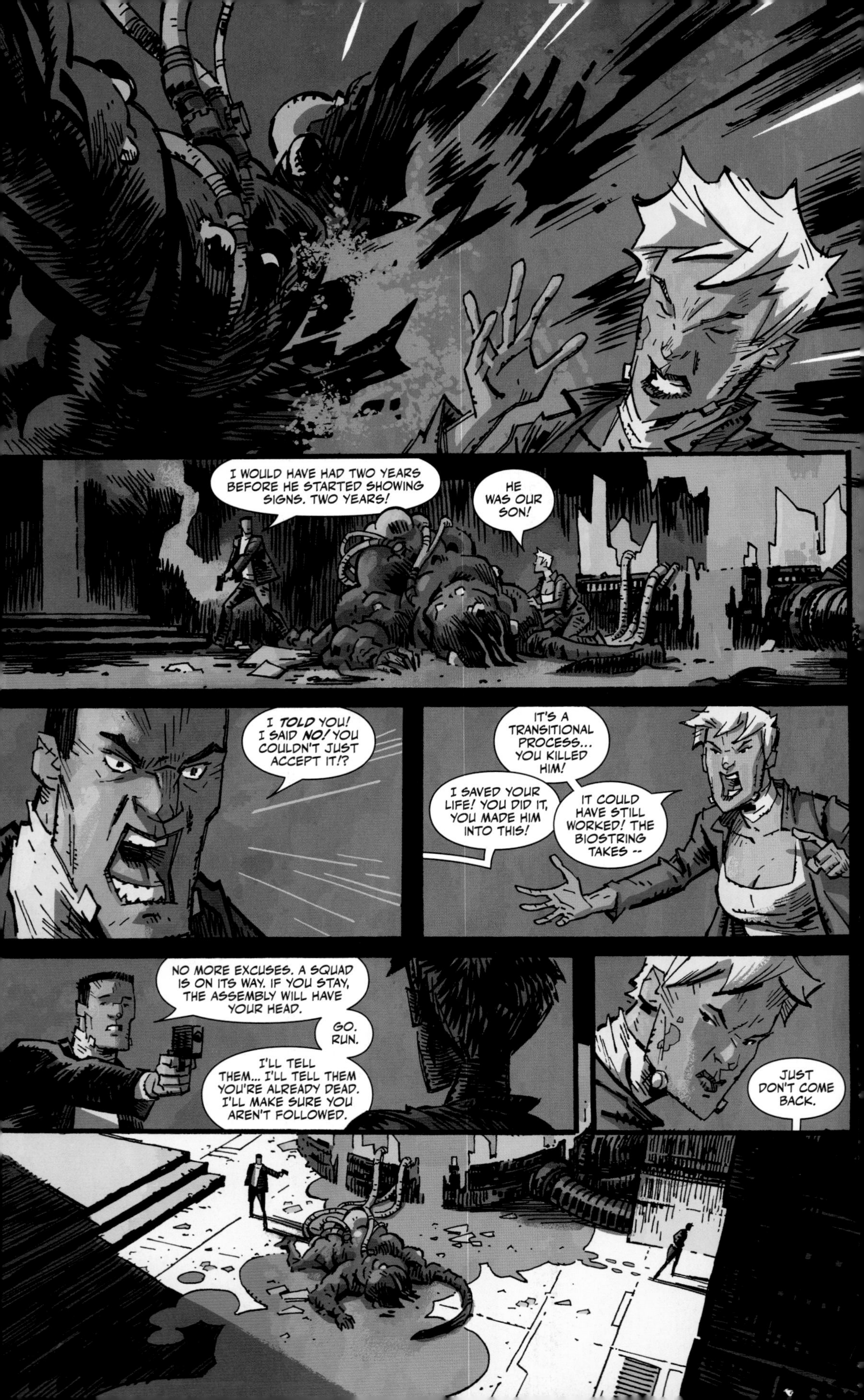
I WOULD HAVE HAD TWO YEARS BEFORE HE STARTED SHOWING SIGNS. TWO YEARS!
HE WAS OUR SON!
I TOLD YOU! I SAID NO! YOU COULDN'T JUST ACCEPT IT!?
IT'S A TRANSITIONAL PROCESS... YOU KILLED HIM!
I SAVED YOUR LIFE! YOU DID IT, YOU MADE HIM INTO THIS!
IT COULD HAVE STILL WORKED! THE BIOSTRING TAKES --
NO MORE EXCUSES. A SQUAD IS ON ITS WAY. IF YOU STAY, THE ASSEMBLY WILL HAVE YOUR HEAD.
GO. RUN.
I'LL TELL THEM... I'LL TELL THEM YOU'RE ALREADY DEAD. I'LL MAKE SURE YOU AREN'T FOLLOWED.
JUST DON'T COME BACK.

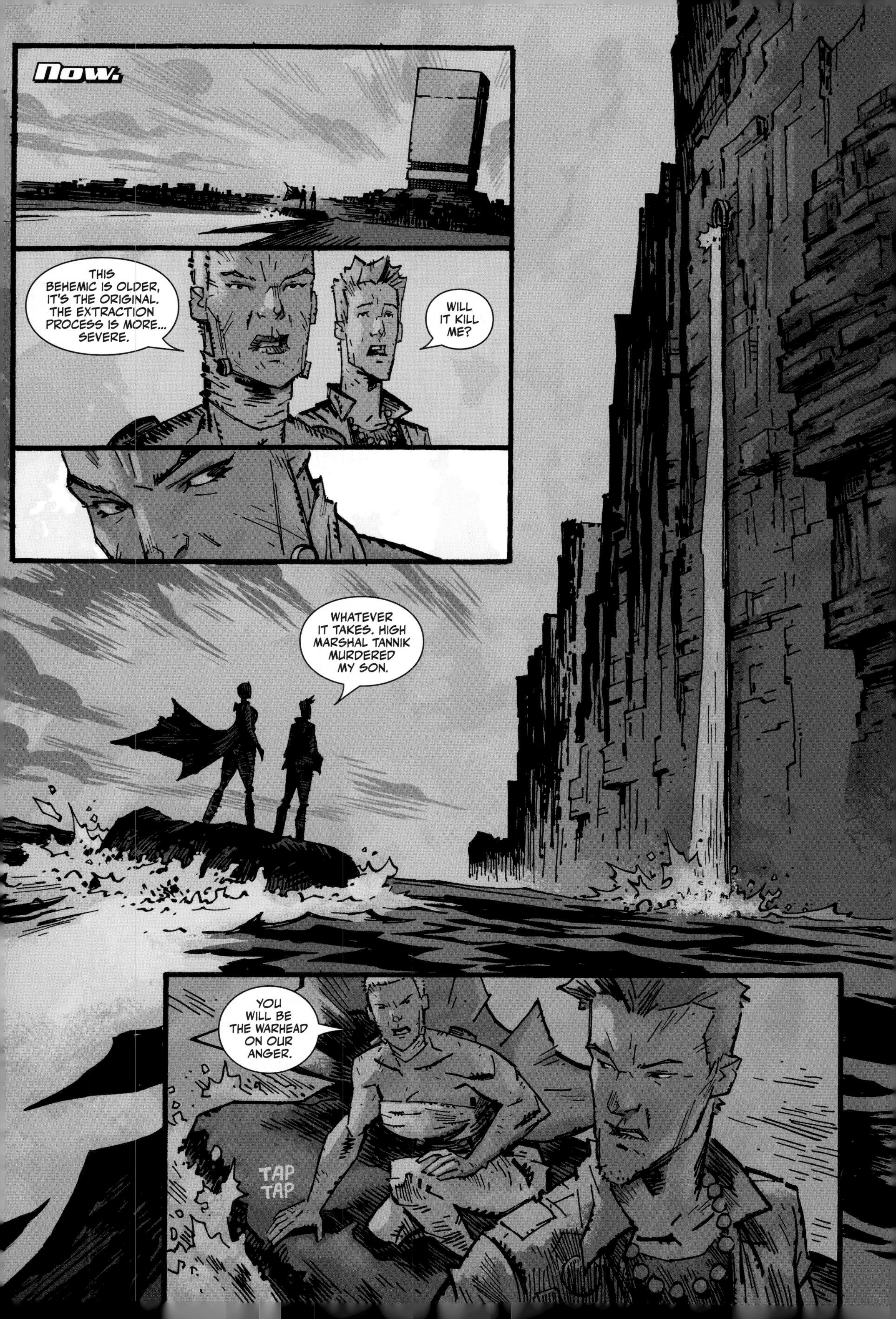
Now.
THIS BEHEMIC IS OLDER, IT'S THE ORIGINAL. THE EXTRACTION PROCESS IS MORE... SEVERE.
WILL IT KILL ME?
WHATEVER IT TAKES. HIGH MARSHAL TANNIK MURDERED MY SON.
YOU WILL BE THE WARHEAD ON OUR ANGER.
TAP TAP

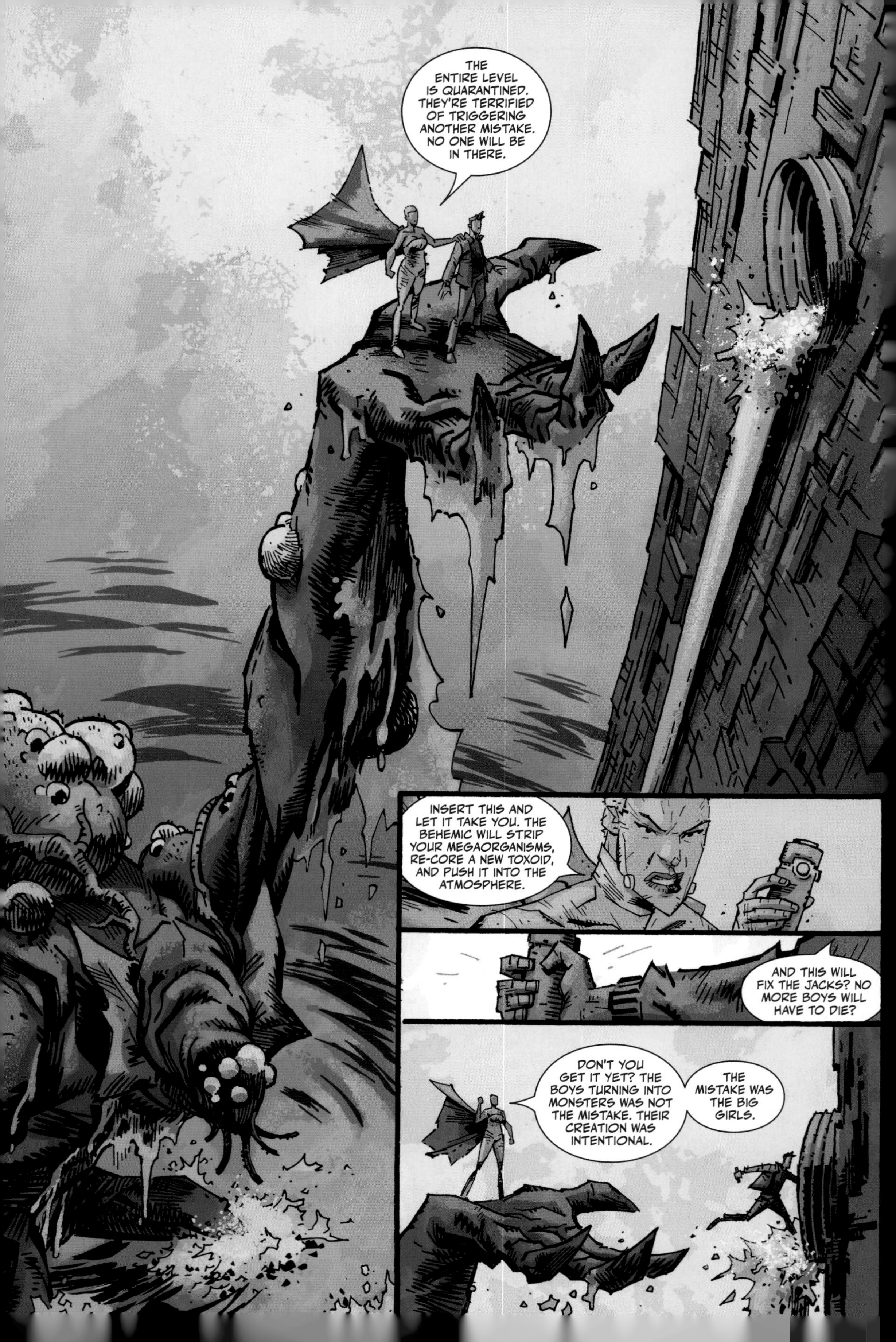
THE ENTIRE LEVEL IS QUARANTINED. THEY'RE TERRIFIED OF TRIGGERING ANOTHER MISTAKE. NO ONE WILL BE IN THERE.
INSERT THIS AND LET IT TAKE YOU. THE BEHEMIC WILL STRIP YOUR MEGAORGANISMS, RE-CORE A NEW TOXOID, AND PUSH IT INTO THE ATMOSPHERE.
AND THIS WILL FIX THE JACKS? NO MORE BOYS WILL HAVE TO DIE?
DON'T YOU GET IT YET? THE BOYS TURNING INTO MONSTERS WAS NOT THE MISTAKE. THEIR CREATION WAS INTENTIONAL.
THE MISTAKE WAS THE BIG GIRLS.

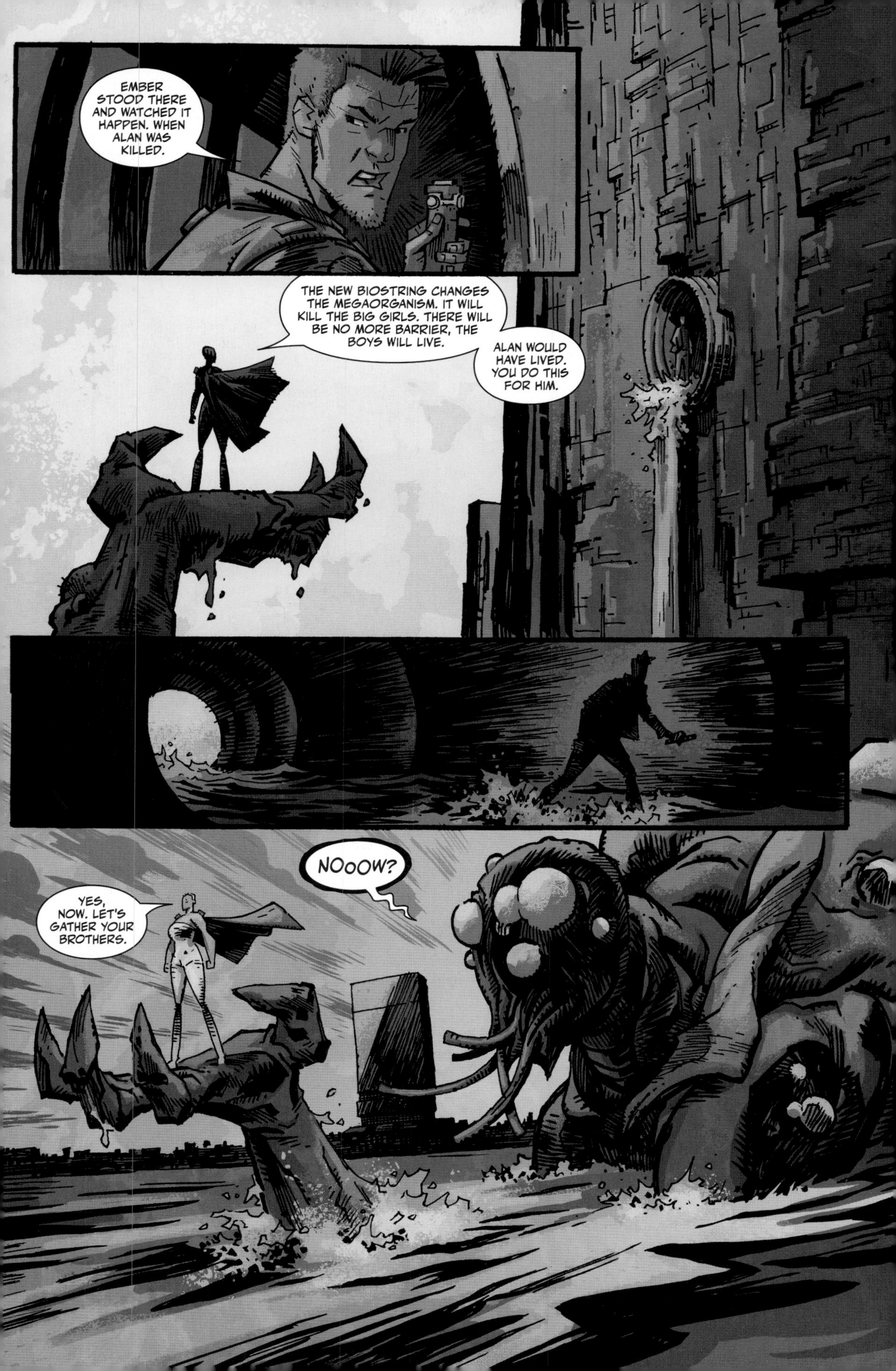
EMBER STOOD THERE AND WATCHED IT HAPPEN. WHEN ALAN WAS KILLED.
THE NEW BIOSTRING CHANGES THE MEGAORGANISM. IT WILL KILL THE BIG GIRLS. THERE WILL BE NO MORE BARRIER, THE BOYS WILL LIVE.
ALAN WOULD HAVE LIVED. YOU DO THIS FOR HIM.
NOOOW?
YES, NOW. LET'S GATHER YOUR BROTHERS.

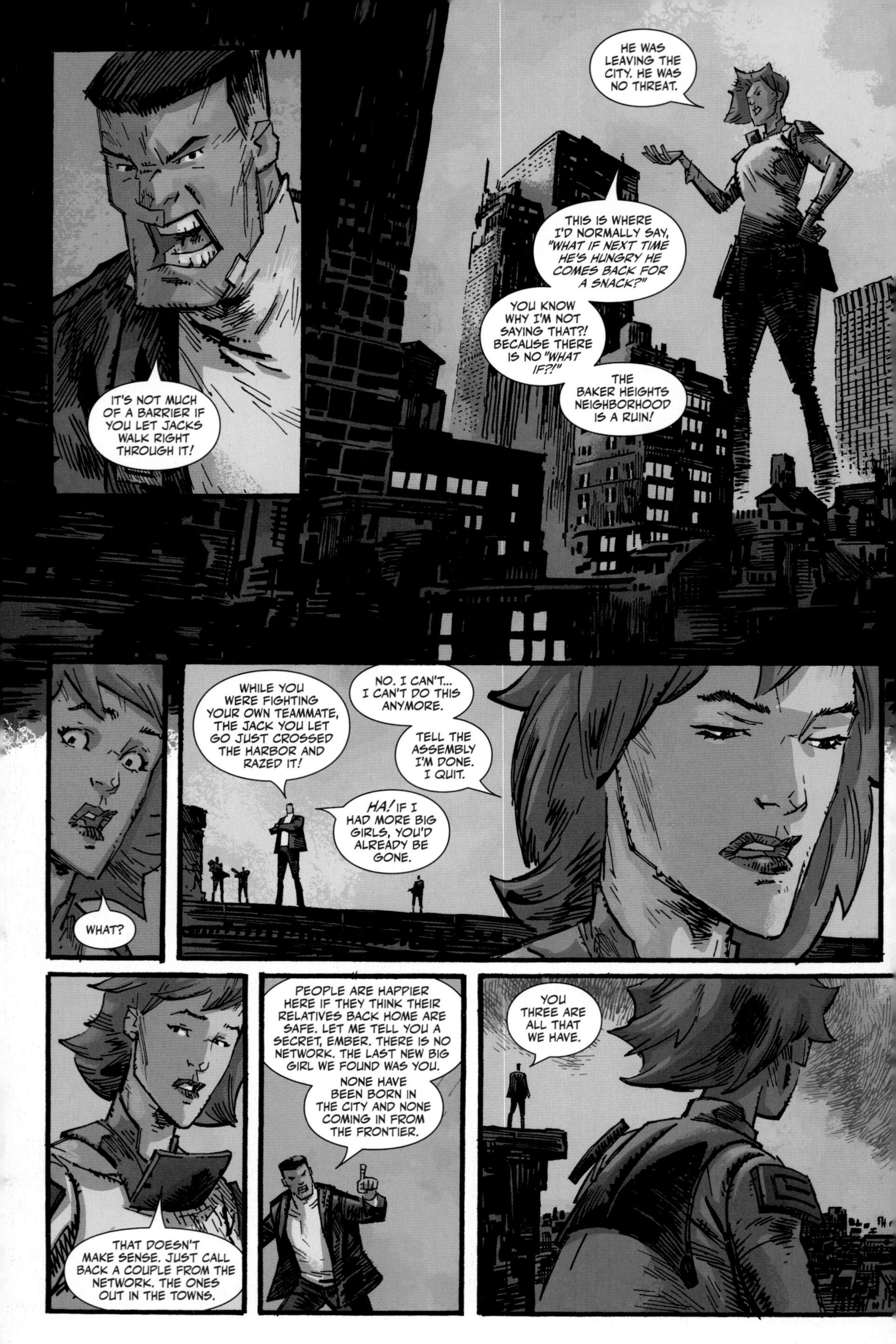
IT'S NOT MUCH OF A BARRIER IF YOU LET JACKS WALK RIGHT THROUGH IT!
HE WAS LEAVING THE CITY. HE WAS NO THREAT.
THIS IS WHERE I'D NORMALLY SAY, "WHAT IF NEXT TIME HE'S HUNGRY HE COMES BACK FOR A SNACK?"
YOU KNOW WHY I'M NOT SAYING THAT?! BECAUSE THERE IS NO "WHAT IF?!"
THE BAKER HEIGHTS NEIGHBORHOOD IS A RUIN!
WHILE YOU WERE FIGHTING YOUR OWN TEAMMATE, THE JACK YOU LET GO JUST CROSSED THE HARBOR AND RAZED IT!
WHAT?
NO. I CAN'T... I CAN'T DO THIS ANYMORE.
TELL THE ASSEMBLY I'M DONE. I QUIT.
HA! IF I HAD MORE BIG GIRLS, YOU'D ALREADY BE GONE.
THAT DOESN'T MAKE SENSE. JUST CALL BACK A COUPLE FROM THE NETWORK. THE ONES OUT IN THE TOWNS.
PEOPLE ARE HAPPIER HERE IF THEY THINK THEIR RELATIVES BACK HOME ARE SAFE. LET ME TELL YOU A SECRET, EMBER. THERE IS NO NETWORK. THE LAST NEW BIG GIRL WE FOUND WAS YOU.
NONE HAVE BEEN BORN IN THE CITY AND NONE COMING IN FROM THE FRONTIER.
YOU THREE ARE ALL THAT WE HAVE.

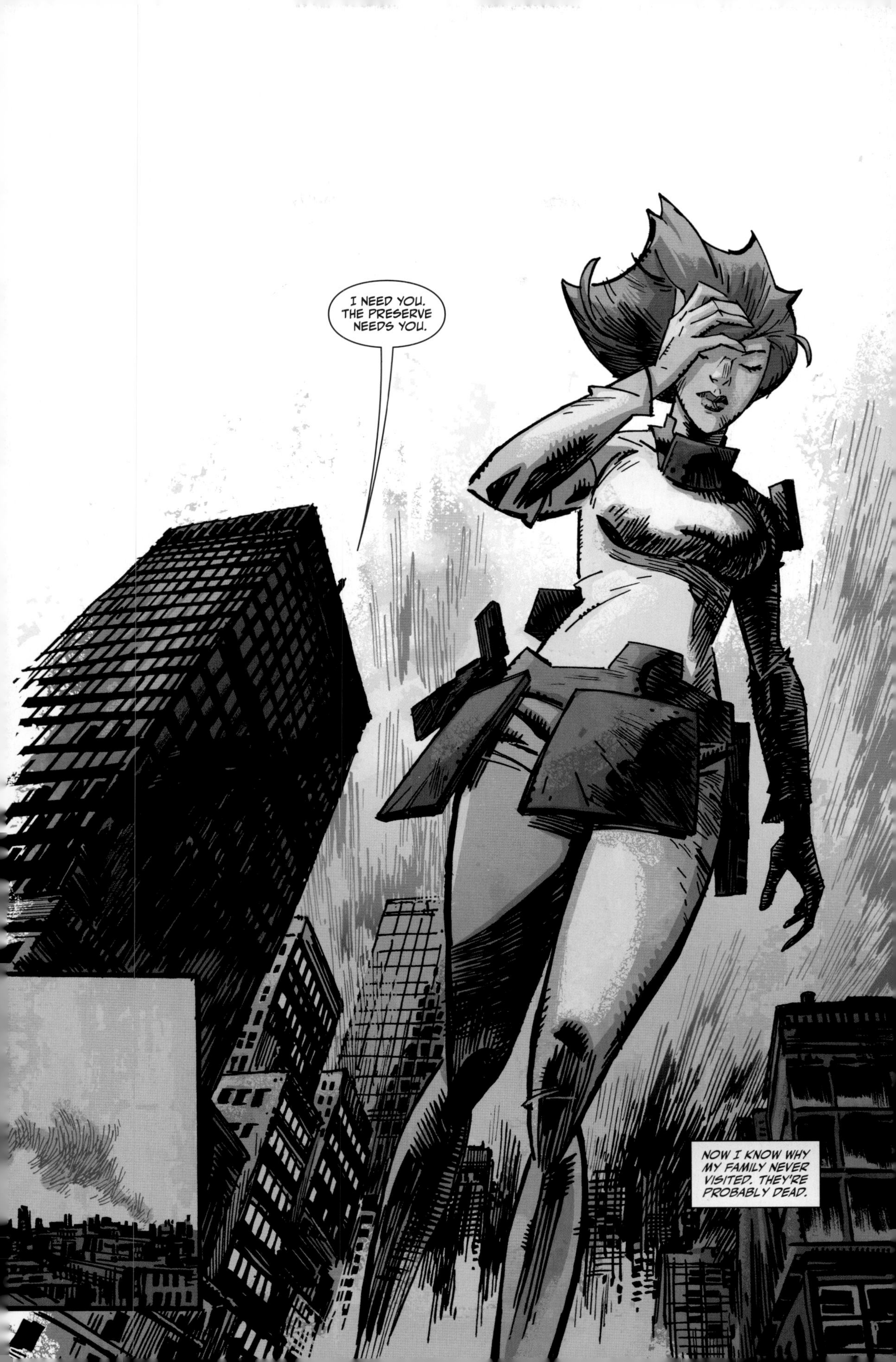
I NEED YOU. THE PRESERVE NEEDS YOU.
NOW I KNOW WHY MY FAMILY NEVER VISITED. THEY'RE PROBABLY DEAD.

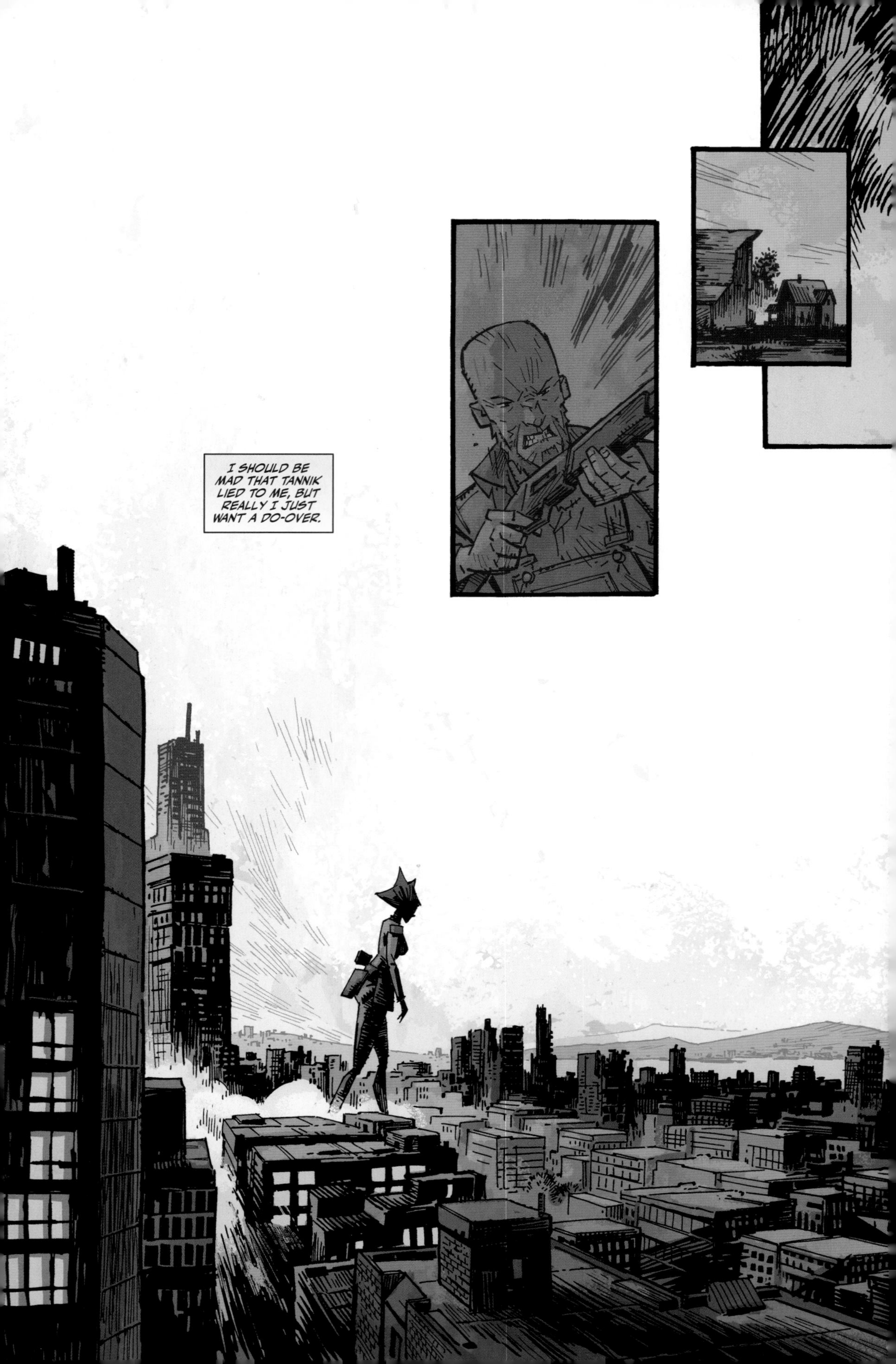
I SHOULD BE MAD THAT TANNIK LIED TO ME, BUT REALLY I JUST WANT A DO-OVER.

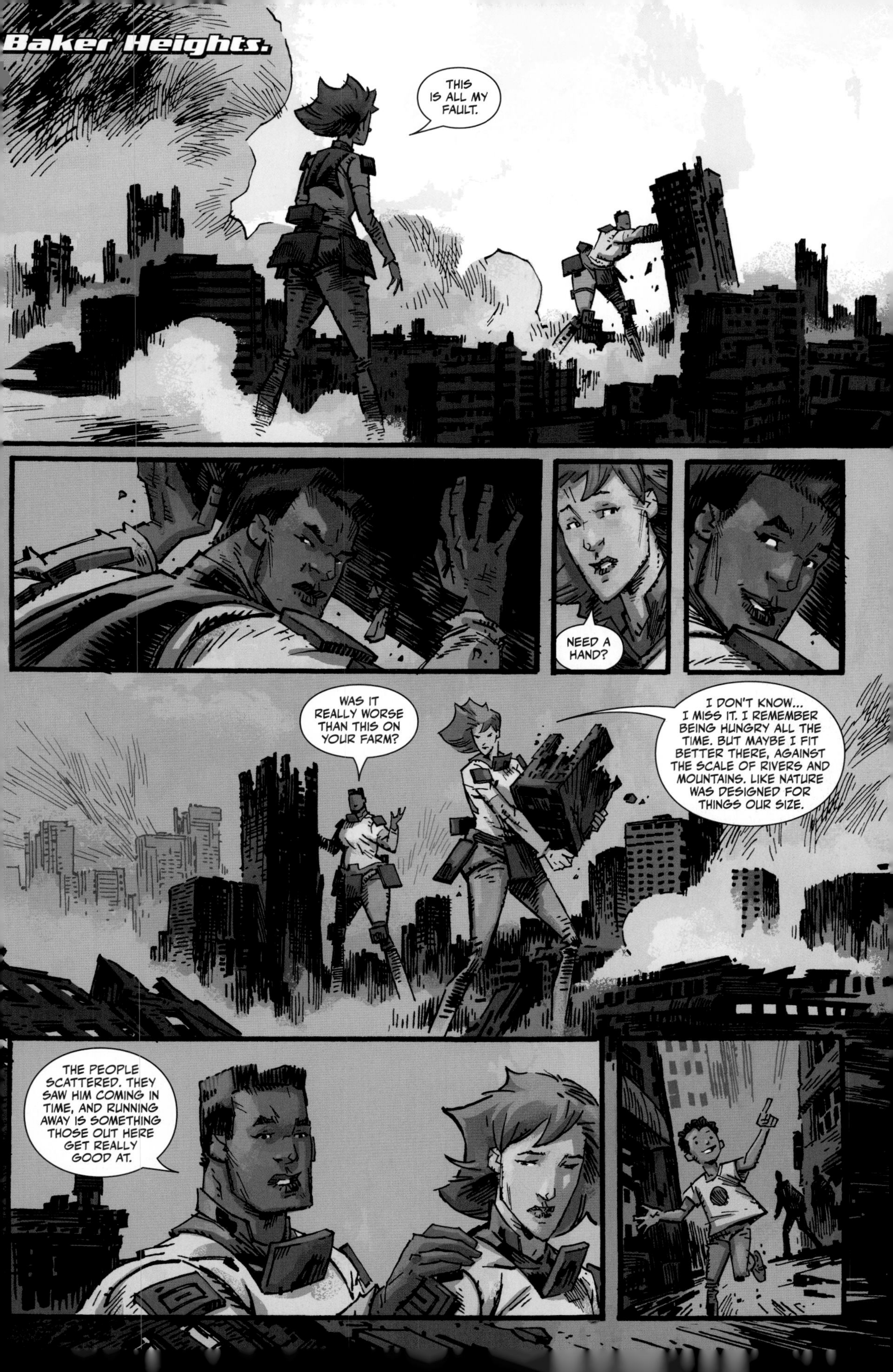
Baker Heights.
THIS IS ALL MY FAULT.
NEED A HAND?
WAS IT REALLY WORSE THAN THIS ON YOUR FARM?
I DON'T KNOW... I MISS IT. I REMEMBER BEING HUNGRY ALL THE TIME. BUT MAYBE I FIT BETTER THERE, AGAINST THE SCALE OF RIVERS AND MOUNTAINS. LIKE NATURE WAS DESIGNED FOR THINGS OUR SIZE.
THE PEOPLE SCATTERED. THEY SAW HIM COMING IN TIME, AND RUNNING AWAY IS SOMETHING THOSE OUT HERE GET REALLY GOOD AT.

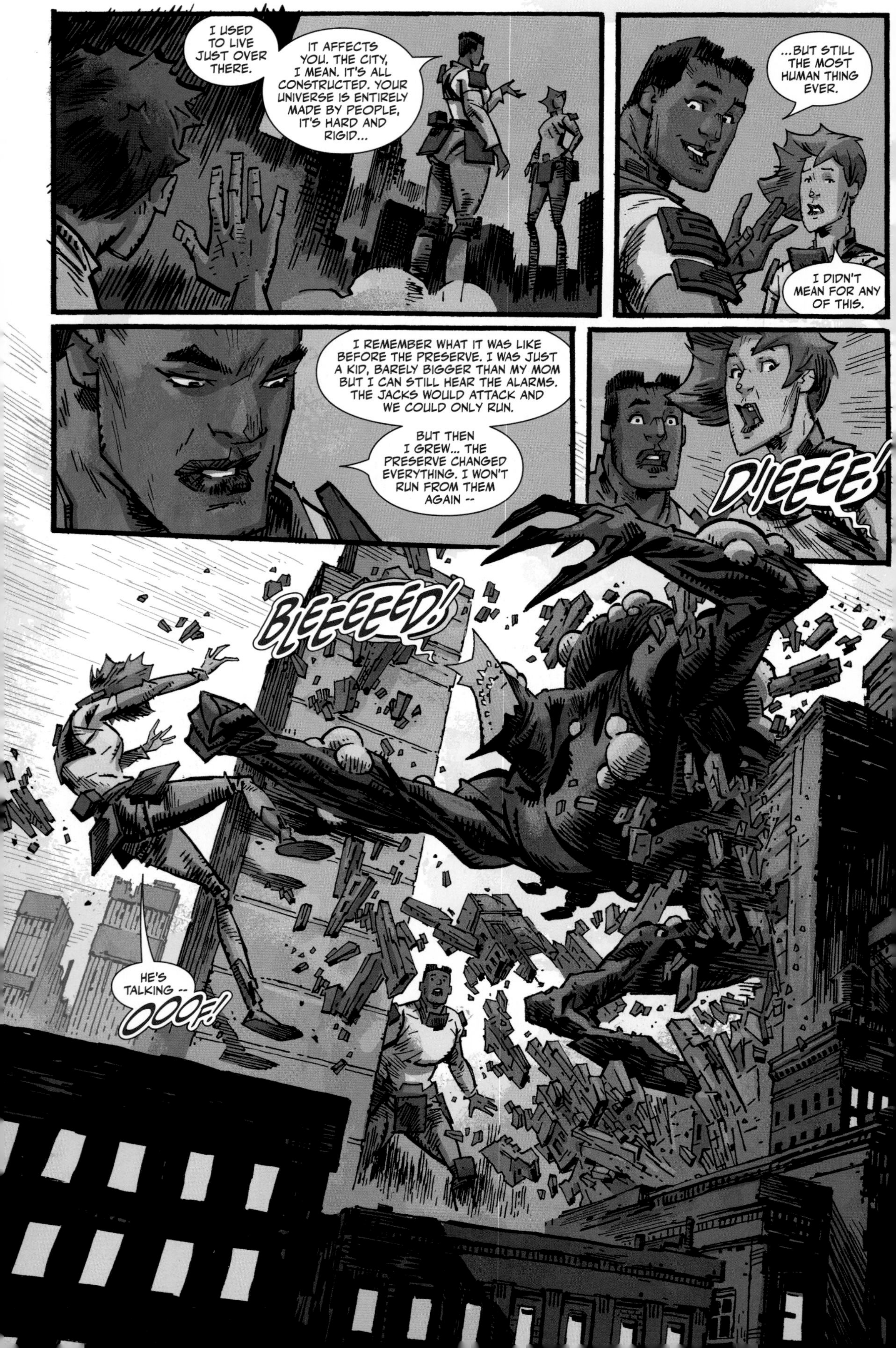
I USED TO LIVE JUST OVER THERE.
IT AFFECTS YOU. THE CITY, I MEAN. IT'S ALL CONSTRUCTED. YOUR UNIVERSE IS ENTIRELY MADE BY PEOPLE, IT'S HARD AND RIGID...
...BUT STILL THE MOST HUMAN THING EVER.
I DIDN'T MEAN FOR ANY OF THIS.
I REMEMBER WHAT IT WAS LIKE BEFORE THE PRESERVE. I WAS JUST A KID, BARELY BIGGER THAN MY MOM BUT I CAN STILL HEAR THE ALARMS. THE JACKS WOULD ATTACK AND WE COULD ONLY RUN.
BUT THEN I GREW... THE PRESERVE CHANGED EVERYTHING. I WON'T RUN FROM THEM AGAIN --
DIEEEEE!
BLEEEEEED!
HE'S TALKING --
OOOF!

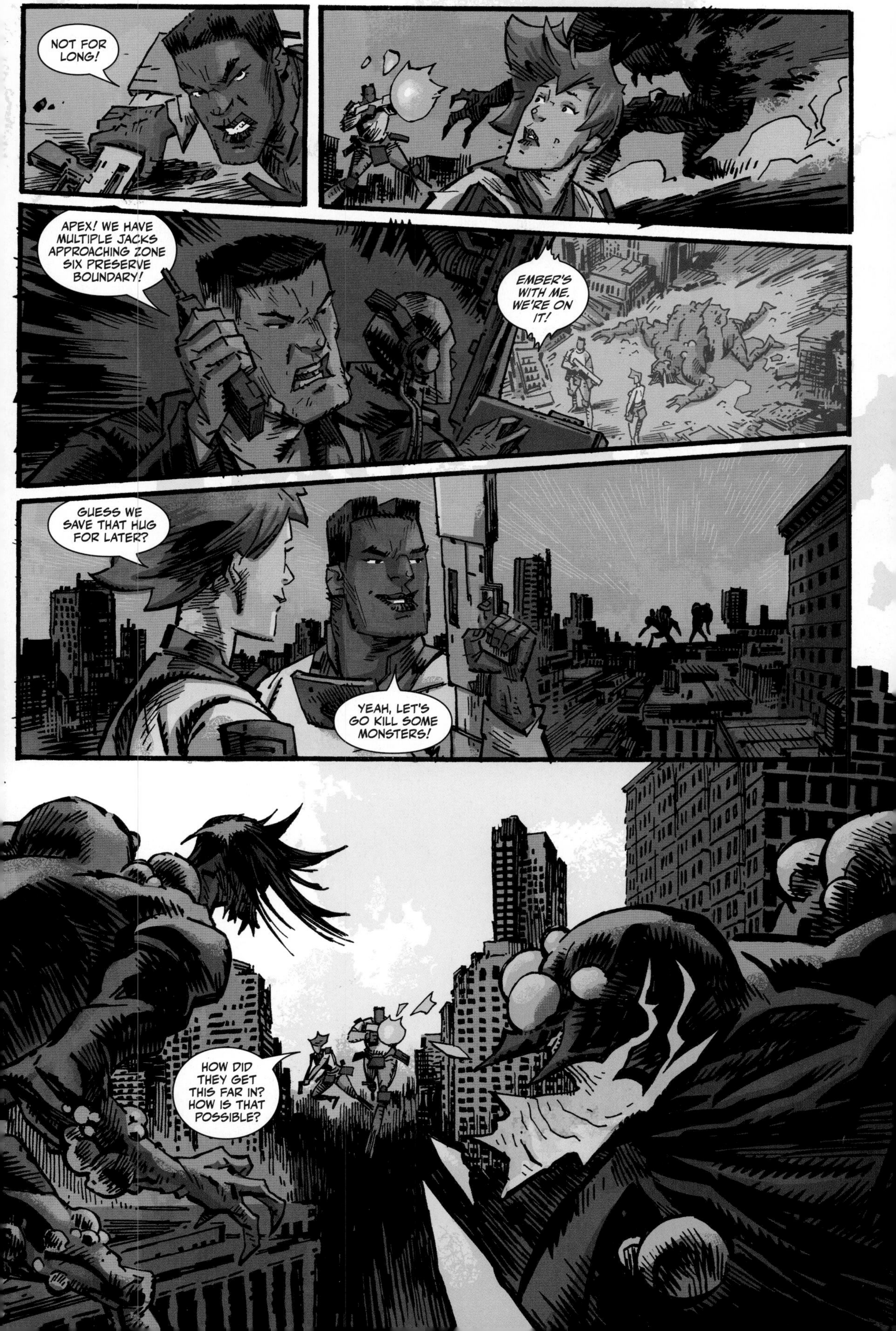
NOT FOR LONG!
APEX! WE HAVE MULTIPLE JACKS APPROACHING ZONE SIX PRESERVE BOUNDARY!
EMBER'S WITH ME. WE'RE ON IT!
GUESS WE SAVE THAT HUG FOR LATER?
YEAH, LET'S GO KILL SOME MONSTERS!
HOW DID THEY GET THIS FAR IN? HOW IS THAT POSSIBLE?

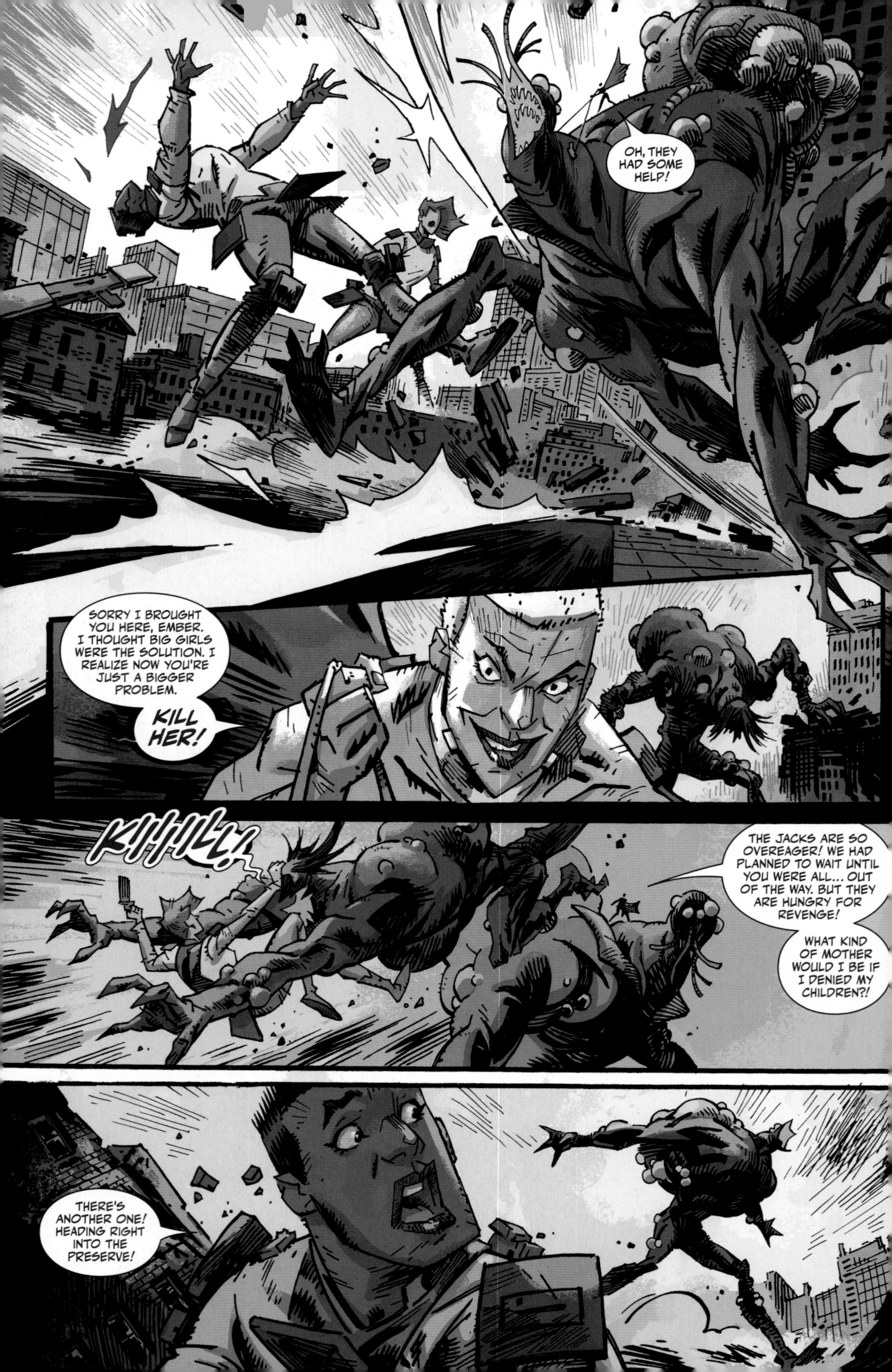
OH, THEY HAD SOME HELP!
SORRY I BROUGHT YOU HERE, EMBER. I THOUGHT BIG GIRLS WERE THE SOLUTION. I REALIZE NOW YOU'RE JUST A BIGGER PROBLEM.
KILL HER!
KIIIILL!
THE JACKS ARE SO OVEREAGER! WE HAD PLANNED TO WAIT UNTIL YOU WERE ALL... OUT OF THE WAY. BUT THEY ARE HUNGRY FOR REVENGE!
WHAT KIND OF MOTHER WOULD I BE IF I DENIED MY CHILDREN?!
THERE'S ANOTHER ONE! HEADING RIGHT INTO THE PRESERVE!

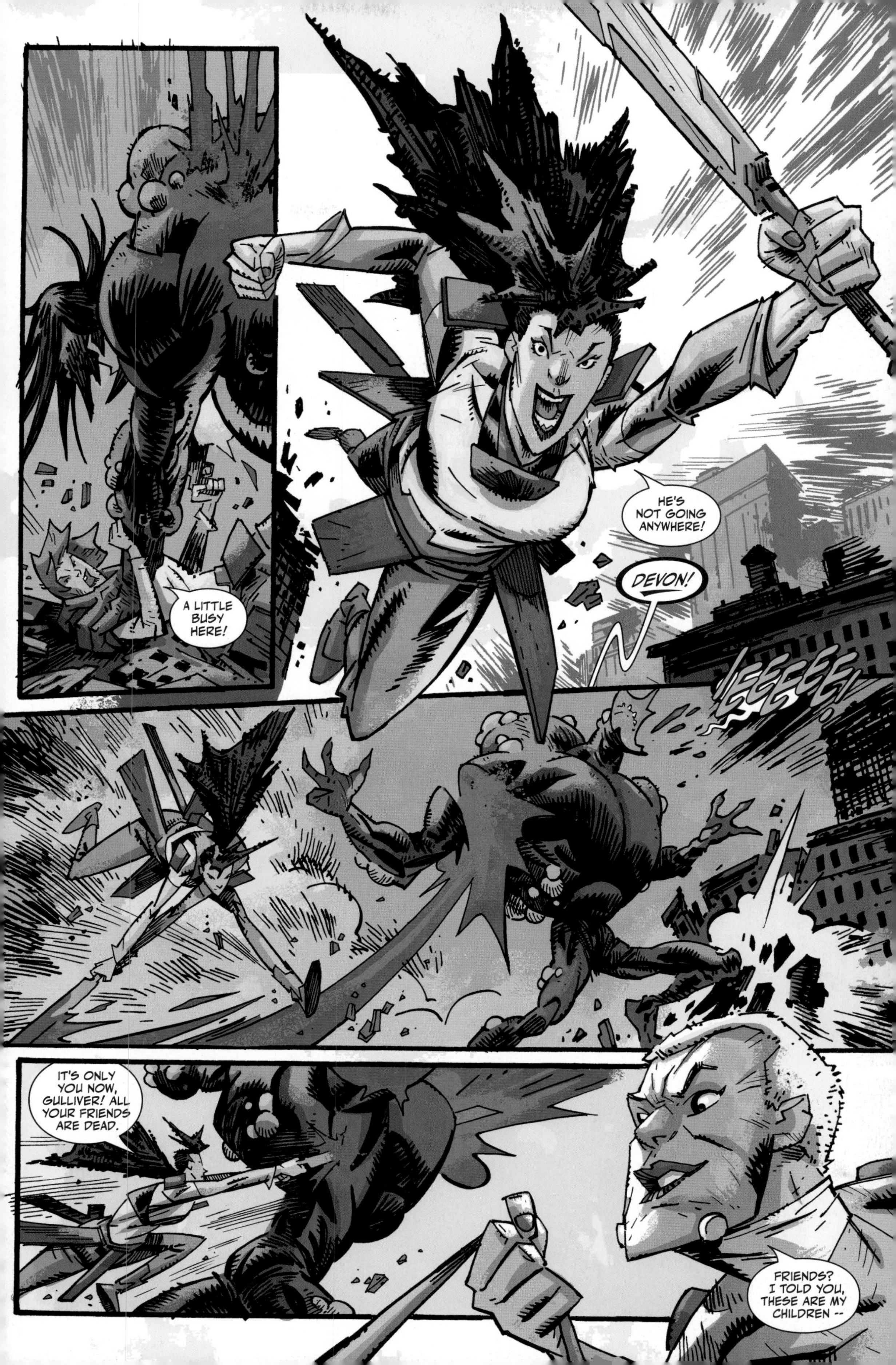

A LITTLE BUSY HERE!
HE'S NOT GOING ANYWHERE!
DEVON!
IEEEEE!
IT'S ONLY YOU NOW, GULLIVER! ALL YOUR FRIENDS ARE DEAD.
FRIENDS? I TOLD YOU, THESE ARE MY CHILDREN --

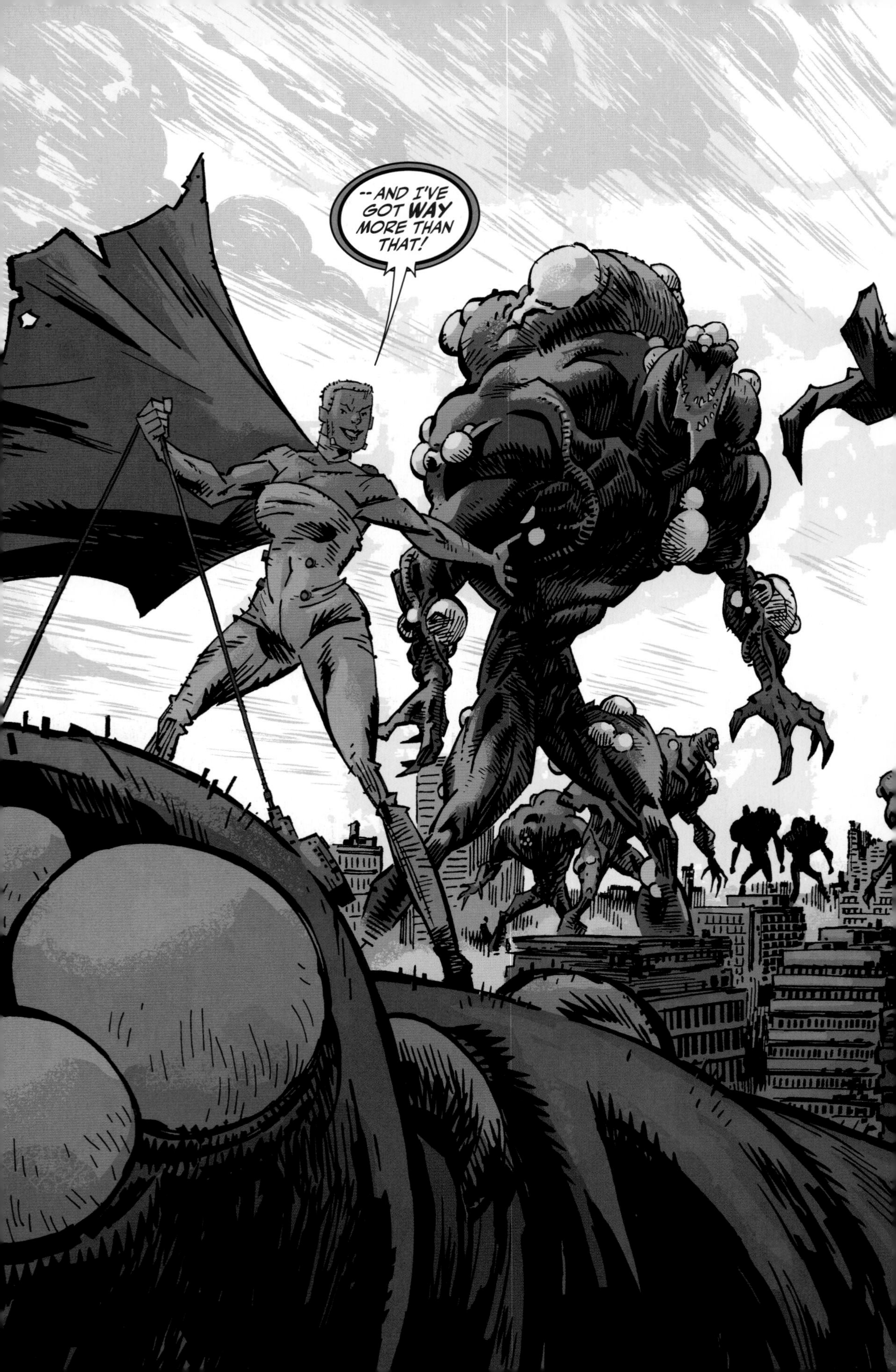
--AND I'VE GOT WAY MORE THAN THAT!

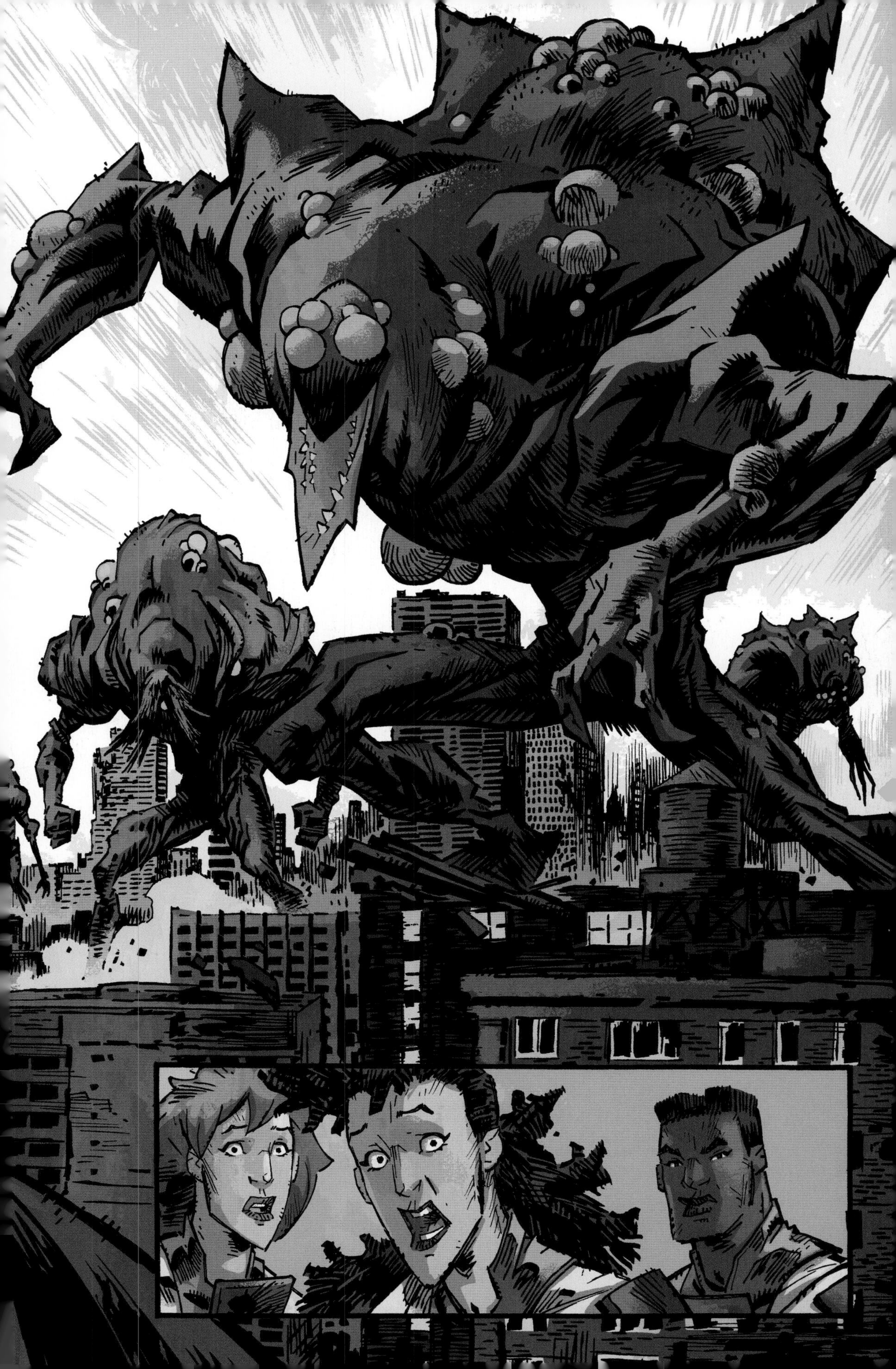

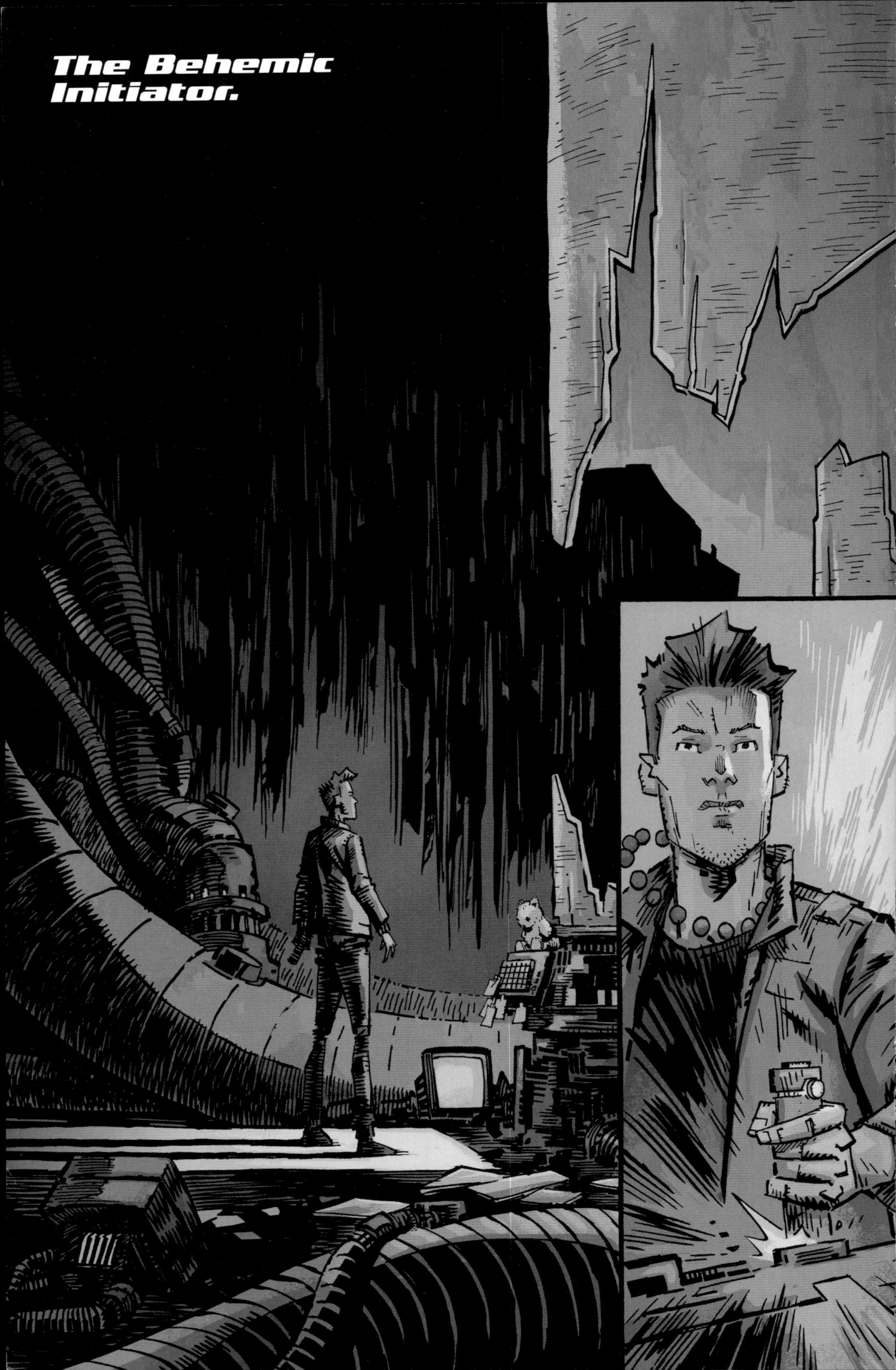
The Behemic Initiator.

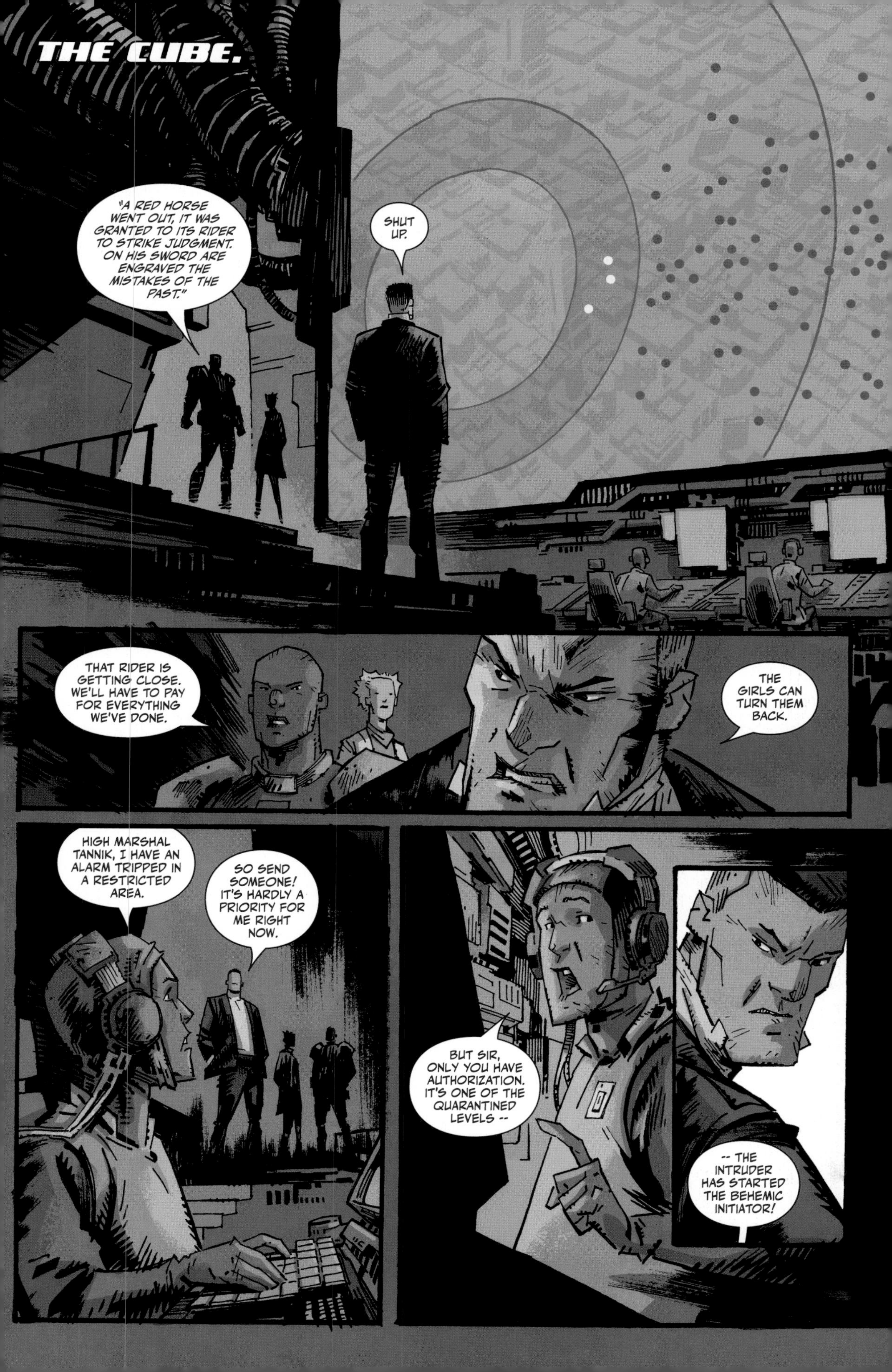
THE CUBE.
"A RED HORSE WENT OUT, IT WAS GRANTED TO ITS RIDER TO STRIKE JUDGMENT. ON HIS SWORD ARE ENGRAVED THE MISTAKES OF THE PAST."
SHUT UP.
THAT RIDER IS GETTING CLOSE. WE'LL HAVE TO PAY FOR EVERYTHING WE'VE DONE.
THE GIRLS CAN TURN THEM BACK.
HIGH MARSHAL TANNIK, I HAVE AN ALARM TRIPPED IN A RESTRICTED AREA.
SO SEND SOMEONE! IT'S HARDLY A PRIORITY FOR ME RIGHT NOW.
BUT SIR, ONLY YOU HAVE AUTHORIZATION. IT'S ONE OF THE QUARANTINED LEVELS --
-- THE INTRUDER HAS STARTED THE BEHEMIC INITIATOR!

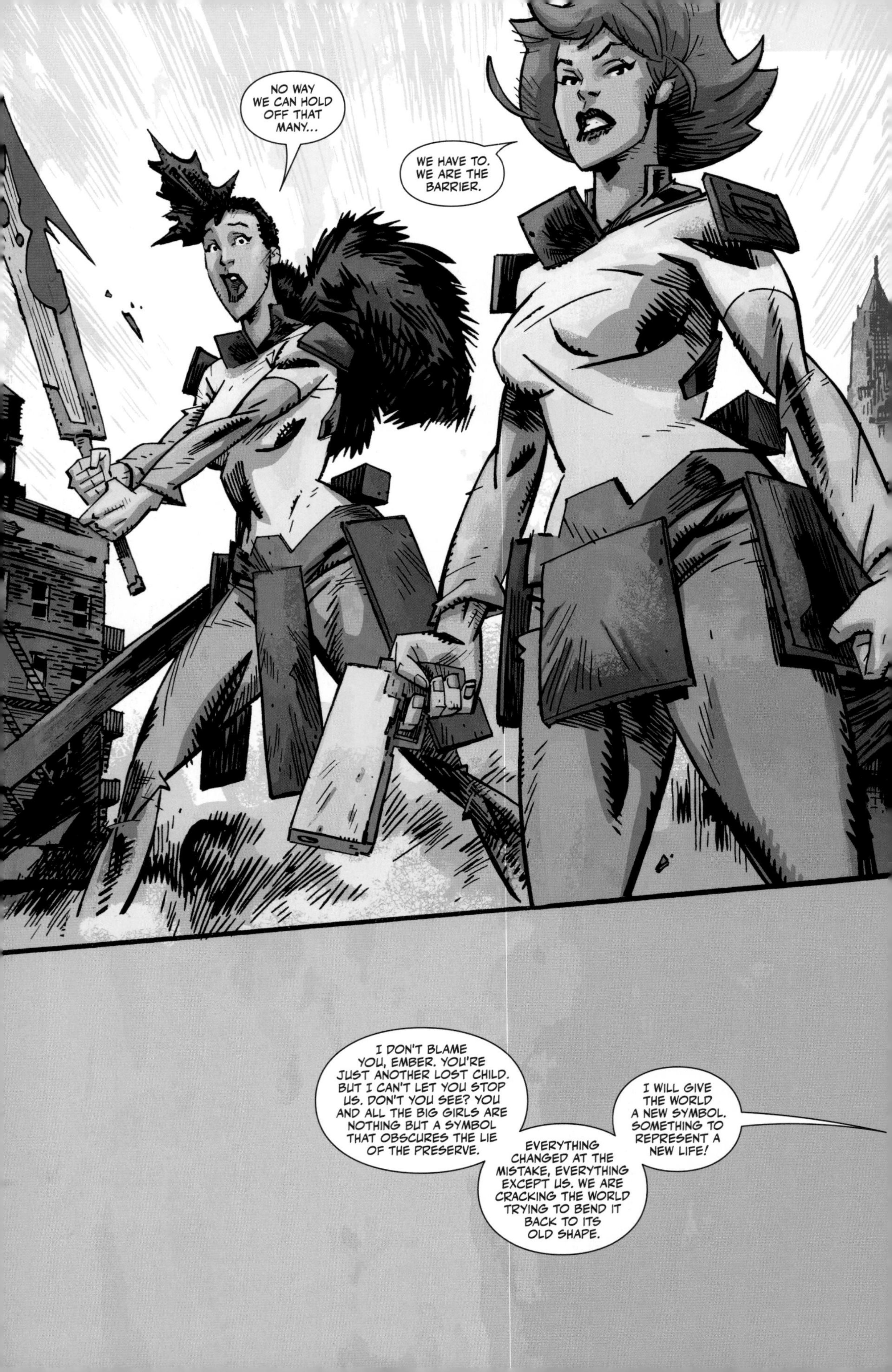
NO WAY WE CAN HOLD OFF THAT MANY...
WE HAVE TO. WE ARE THE BARRIER.
I DON'T BLAME YOU, EMBER. YOU'RE JUST ANOTHER LOST CHILD. BUT I CAN'T LET YOU STOP US. DON'T YOU SEE? YOU AND ALL THE BIG GIRLS ARE NOTHING BUT A SYMBOL THAT OBSCURES THE LIE OF THE PRESERVE.
EVERYTHING CHANGED AT THE MISTAKE, EVERYTHING EXCEPT US. WE ARE CRACKING THE WORLD TRYING TO BEND IT BACK TO ITS OLD SHAPE.
I WILL GIVE THE WORLD A NEW SYMBOL. SOMETHING TO REPRESENT A NEW LIFE!

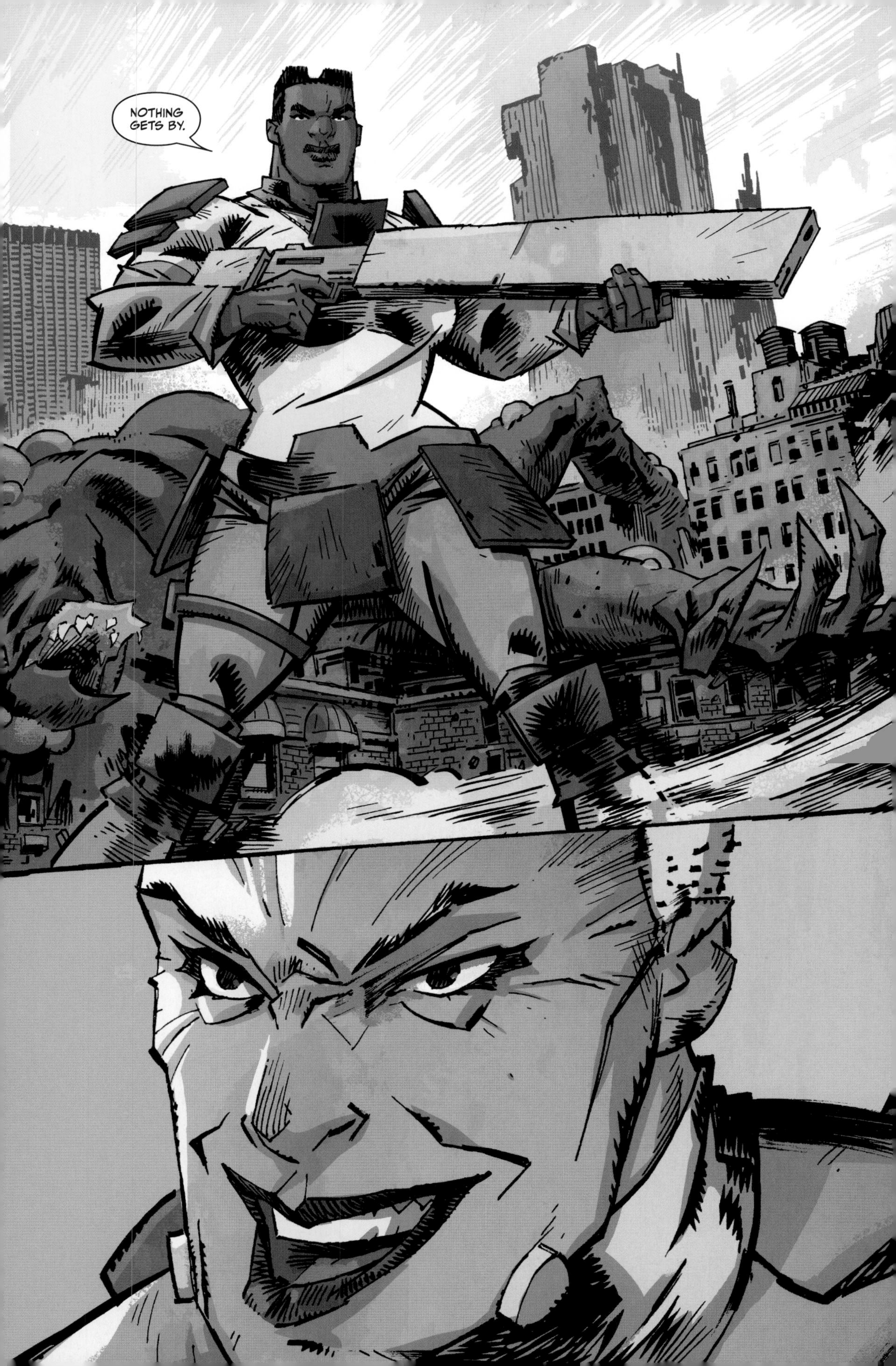
NOTHING GETS BY.

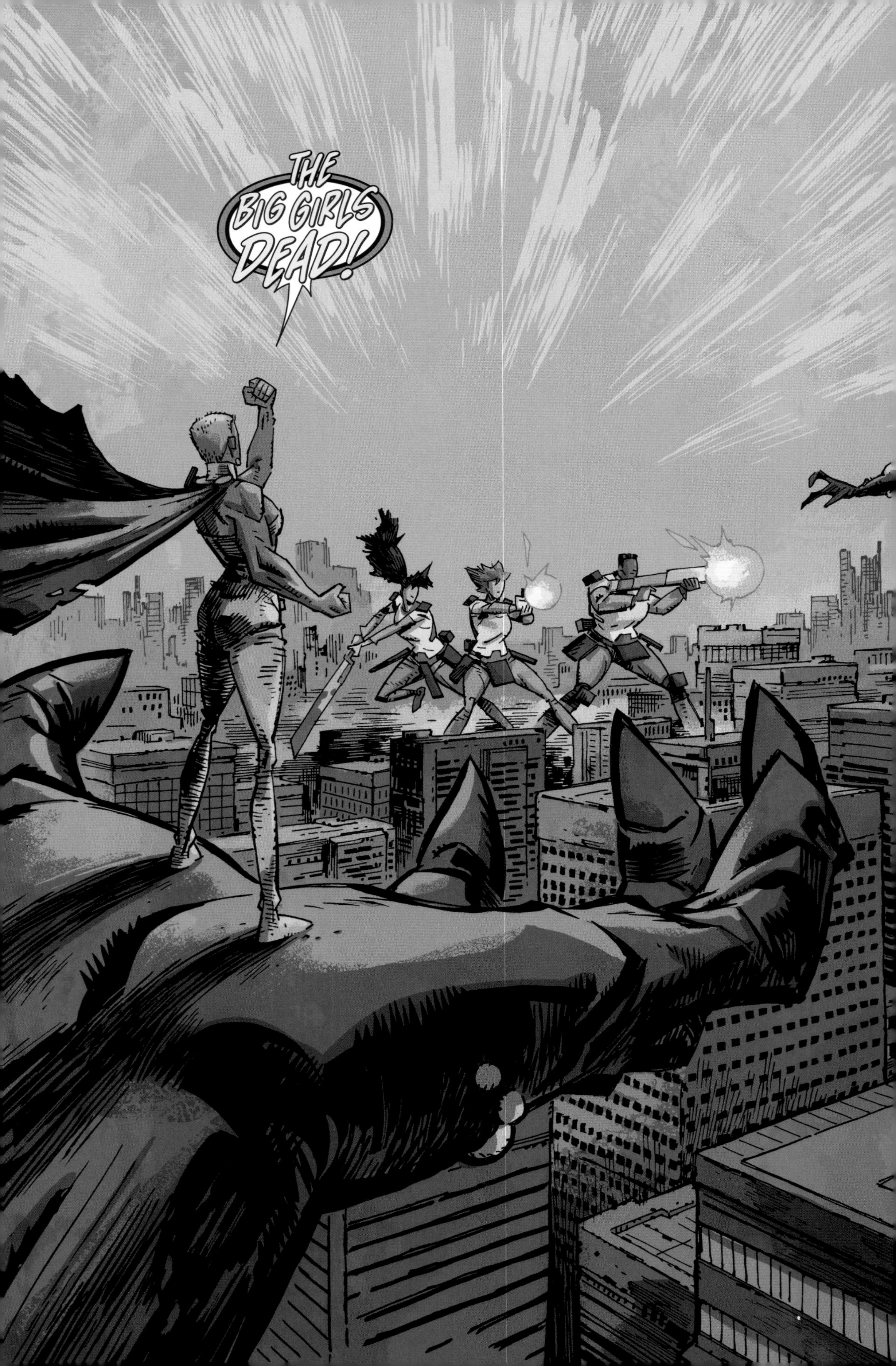
THE BIG GIRLS DEAD!

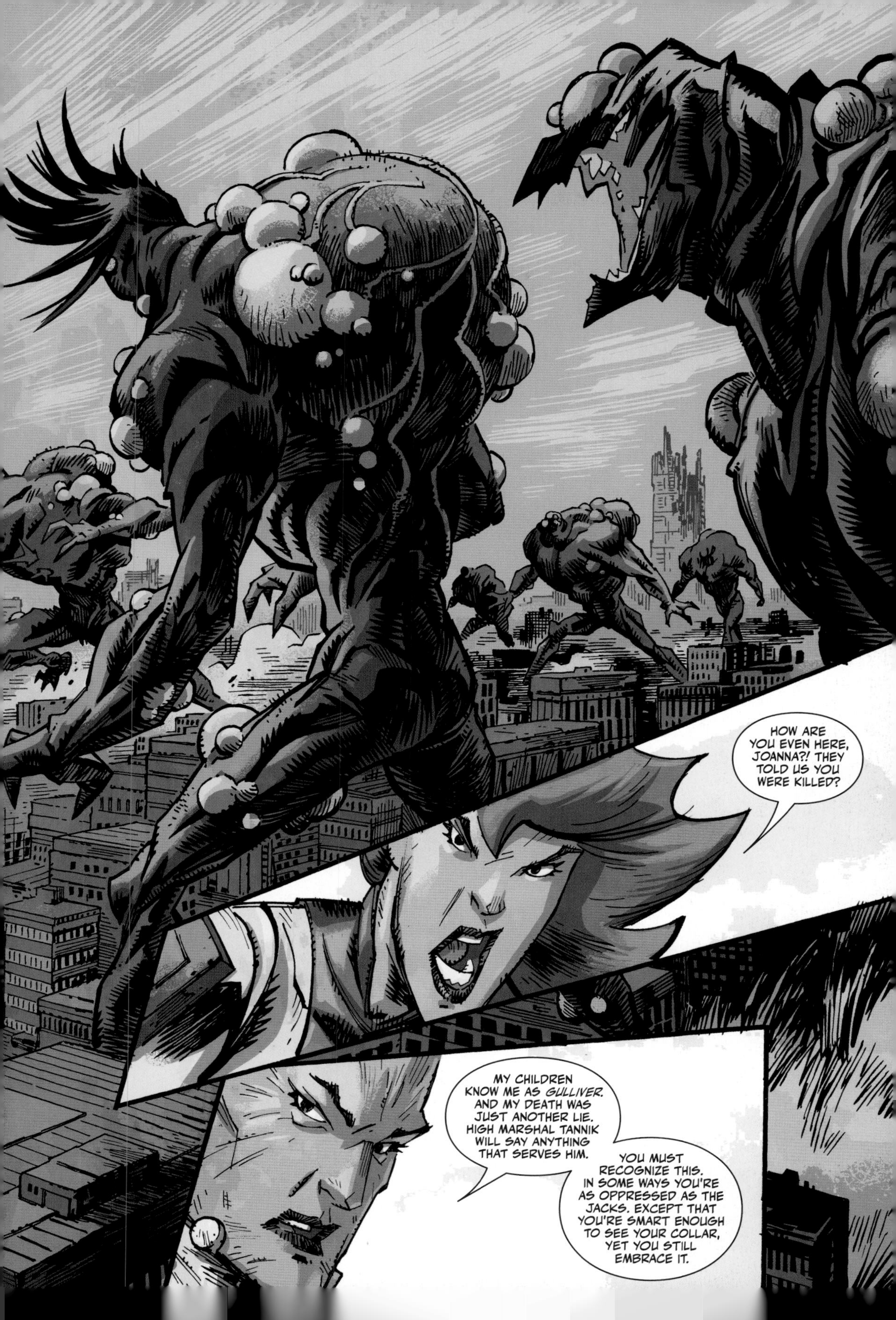
HOW ARE YOU EVEN HERE, JOANNA?! THEY TOLD US YOU WERE KILLED?
MY CHILDREN KNOW ME AS *GULLIVER*. AND MY DEATH WAS JUST ANOTHER LIE. HIGH MARSHAL TANNIK WILL SAY ANYTHING THAT SERVES HIM.
YOU MUST RECOGNIZE THIS. IN SOME WAYS YOU'RE AS OPPRESSED AS THE JACKS. EXCEPT THAT YOU'RE SMART ENOUGH TO SEE YOUR COLLAR, YET YOU STILL EMBRACE IT.

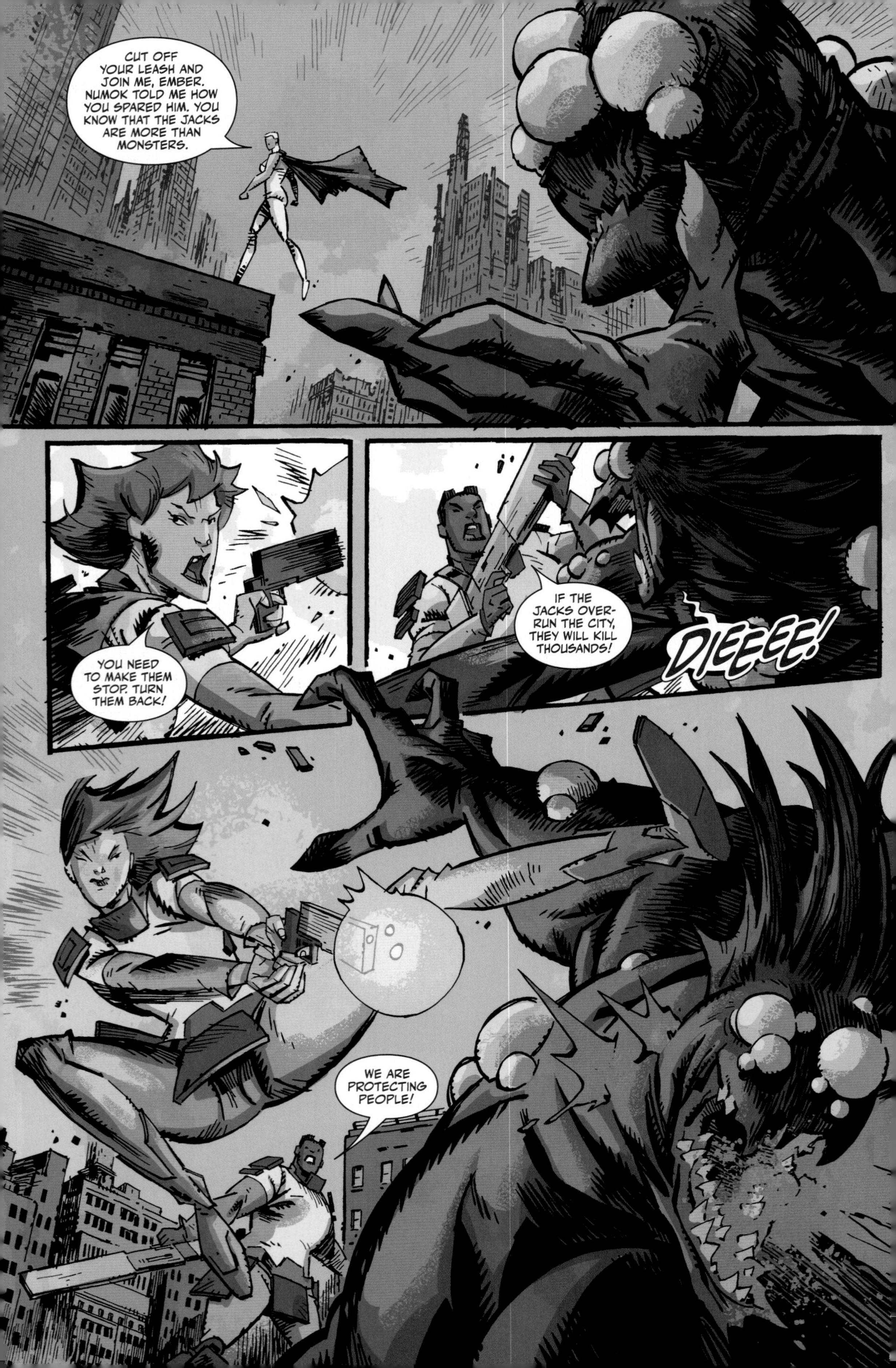
CUT OFF YOUR LEASH AND JOIN ME, EMBER. NUMOK TOLD ME HOW YOU SPARED HIM. YOU KNOW THAT THE JACKS ARE MORE THAN MONSTERS.
YOU NEED TO MAKE THEM STOP. TURN THEM BACK!
IF THE JACKS OVER-RUN THE CITY, THEY WILL KILL THOUSANDS!
DIEEEE!
WE ARE PROTECTING PEOPLE!

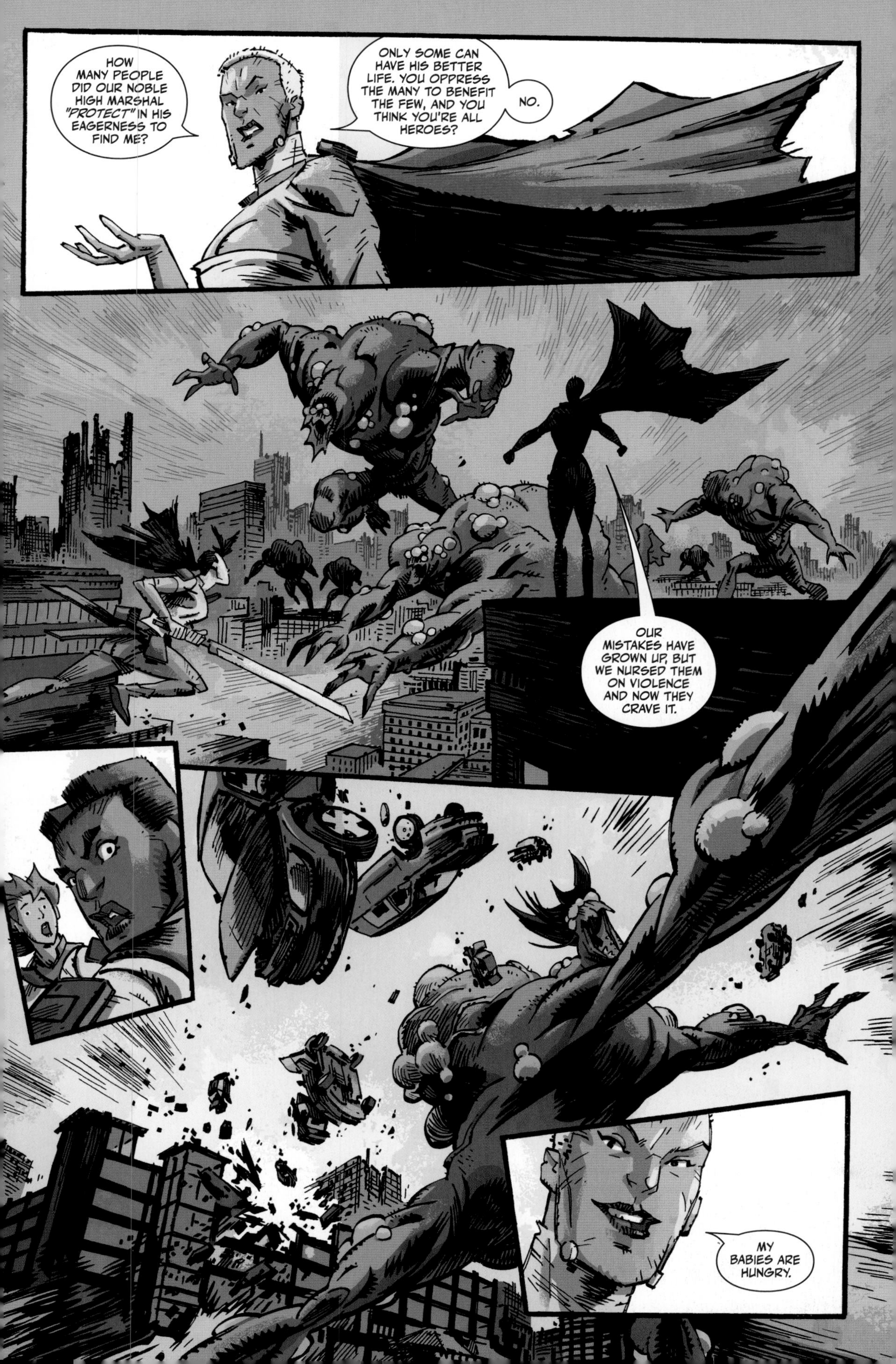
HOW MANY PEOPLE DID OUR NOBLE HIGH MARSHAL "PROTECT" IN HIS EAGERNESS TO FIND ME?
ONLY SOME CAN HAVE HIS BETTER LIFE. YOU OPPRESS THE MANY TO BENEFIT THE FEW, AND YOU THINK YOU'RE ALL HEROES?
NO.
OUR MISTAKES HAVE GROWN UP, BUT WE NURSED THEM ON VIOLENCE AND NOW THEY CRAVE IT.
MY BABIES ARE HUNGRY.

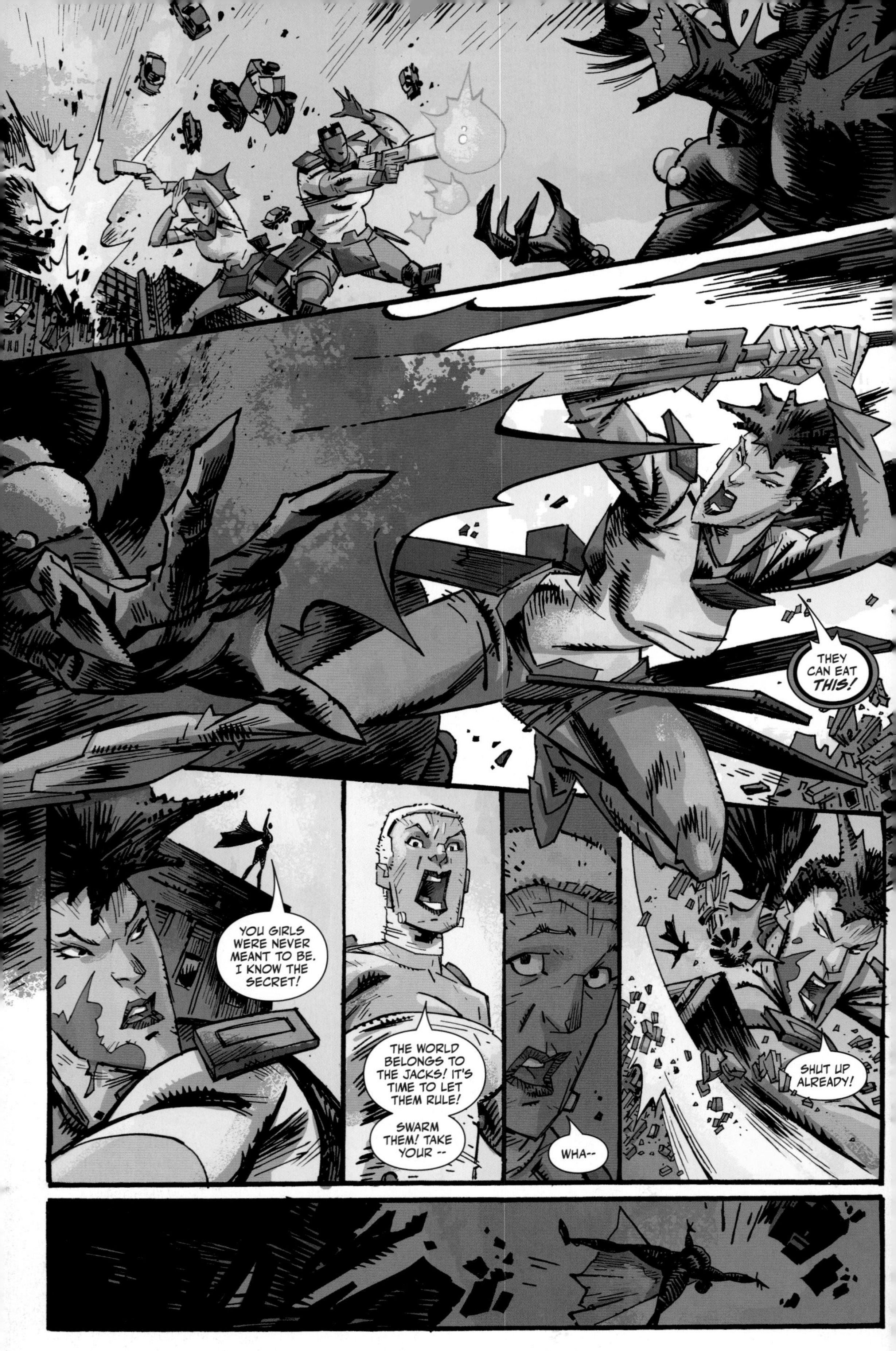
THEY CAN EAT THIS!
YOU GIRLS WERE NEVER MEANT TO BE. I KNOW THE SECRET!
THE WORLD BELONGS TO THE JACKS! IT'S TIME TO LET THEM RULE!
SWARM THEM! TAKE YOUR --
WHA--
SHUT UP ALREADY!

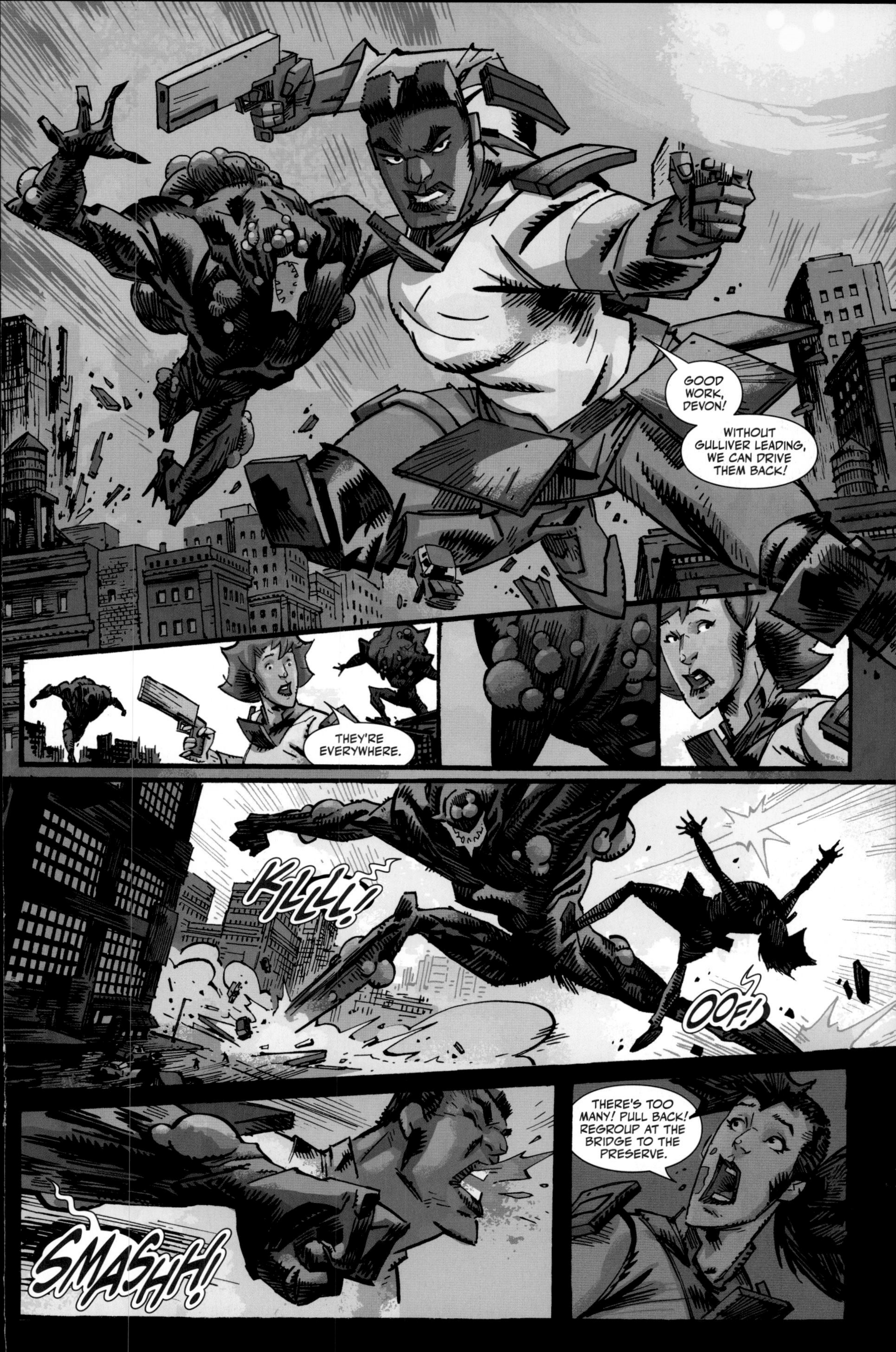
GOOD WORK, DEVON!
WITHOUT GULLIVER LEADING, WE CAN DRIVE THEM BACK!
THEY'RE EVERYWHERE.
KILLL!
OOF!
SMASHH!
THERE'S TOO MANY! PULL BACK! REGROUP AT THE BRIDGE TO THE PRESERVE.

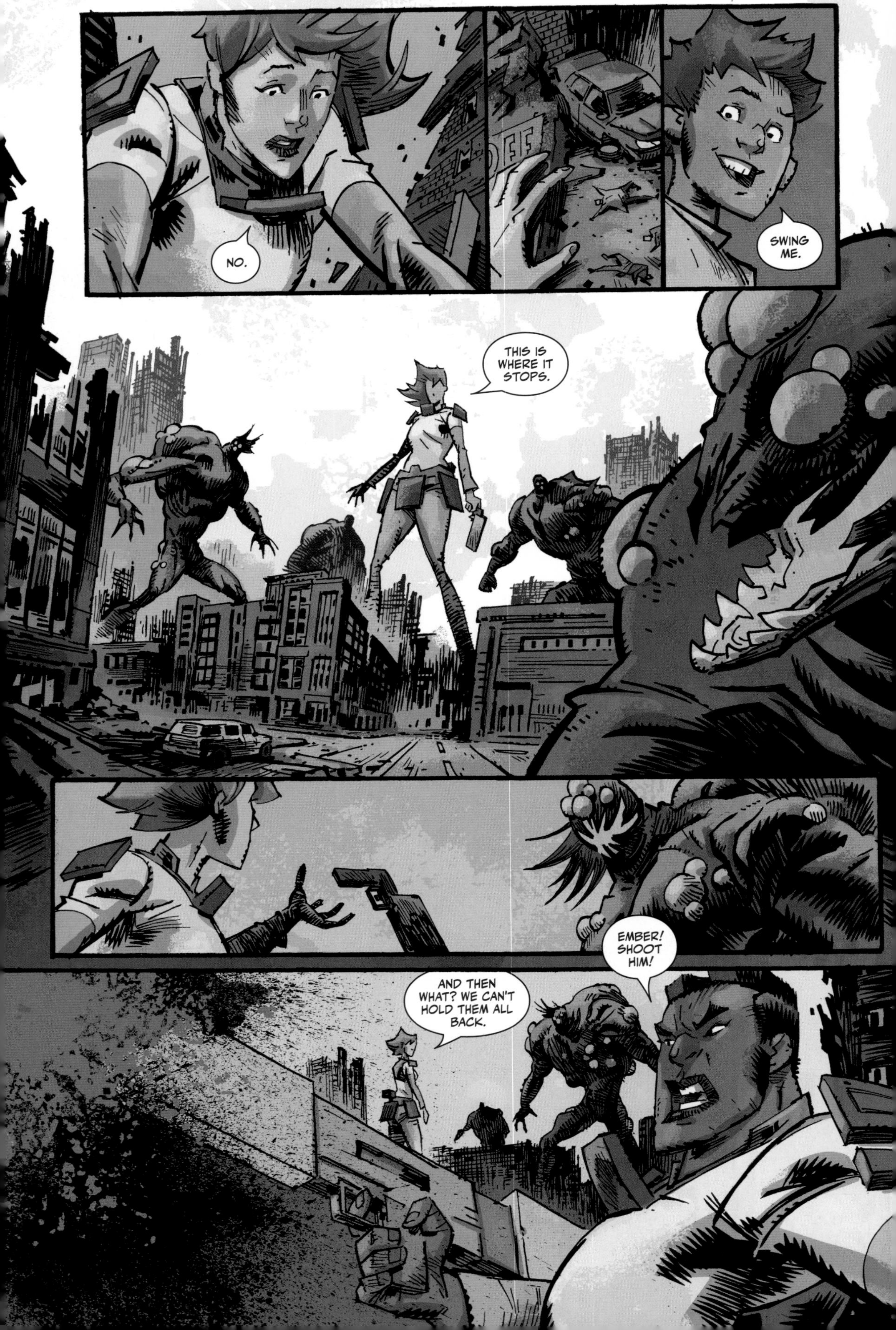
NO.
SWING ME.
THIS IS WHERE IT STOPS.
EMBER! SHOOT HIM!
AND THEN WHAT? WE CAN'T HOLD THEM ALL BACK.

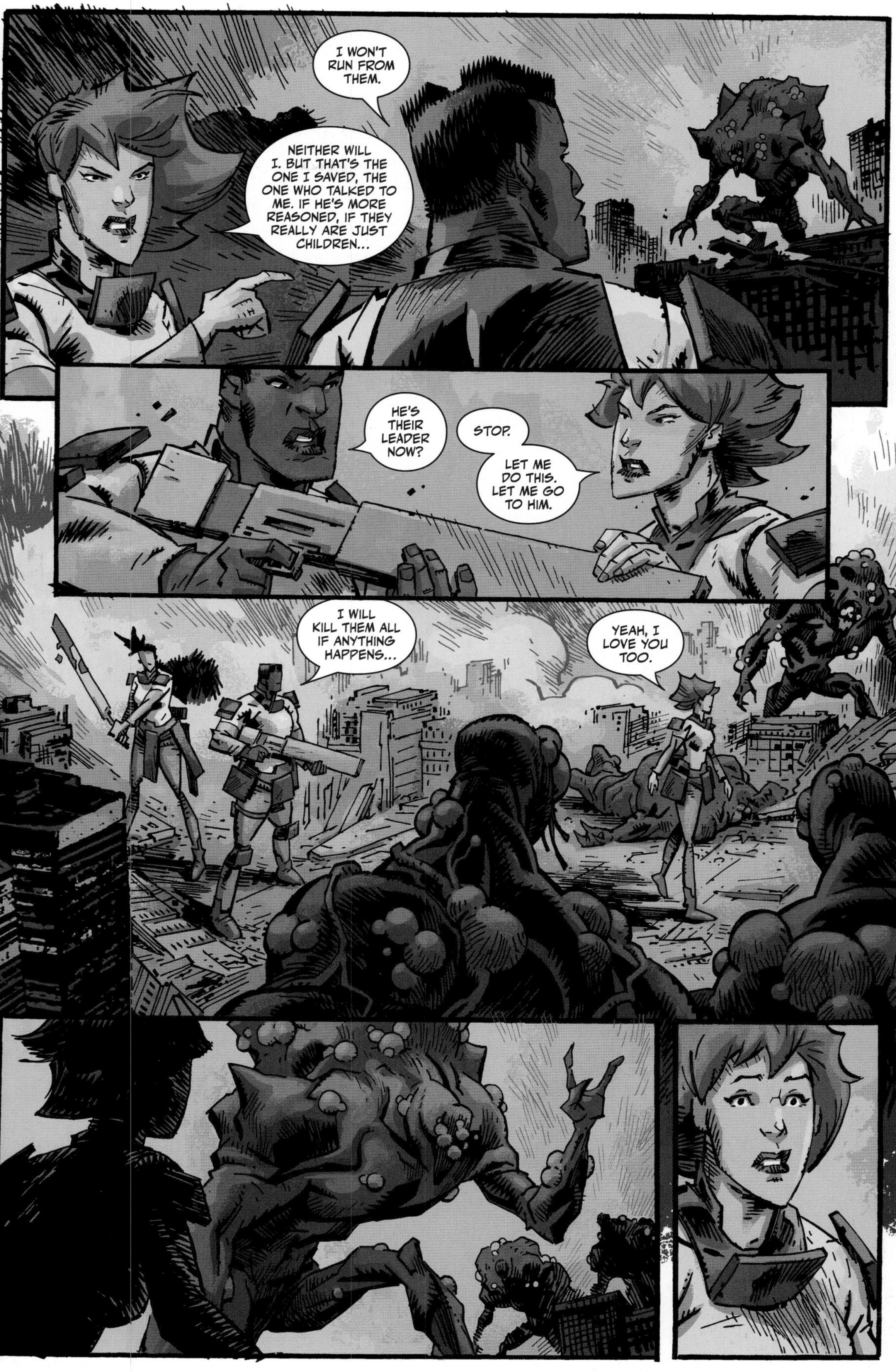
I WON'T RUN FROM THEM.
NEITHER WILL I. BUT THAT'S THE ONE I SAVED, THE ONE WHO TALKED TO ME. IF HE'S MORE REASONED, IF THEY REALLY ARE JUST CHILDREN...
HE'S THEIR LEADER NOW?
STOP.
LET ME DO THIS. LET ME GO TO HIM.
I WILL KILL THEM ALL IF ANYTHING HAPPENS...
YEAH, I LOVE YOU TOO.

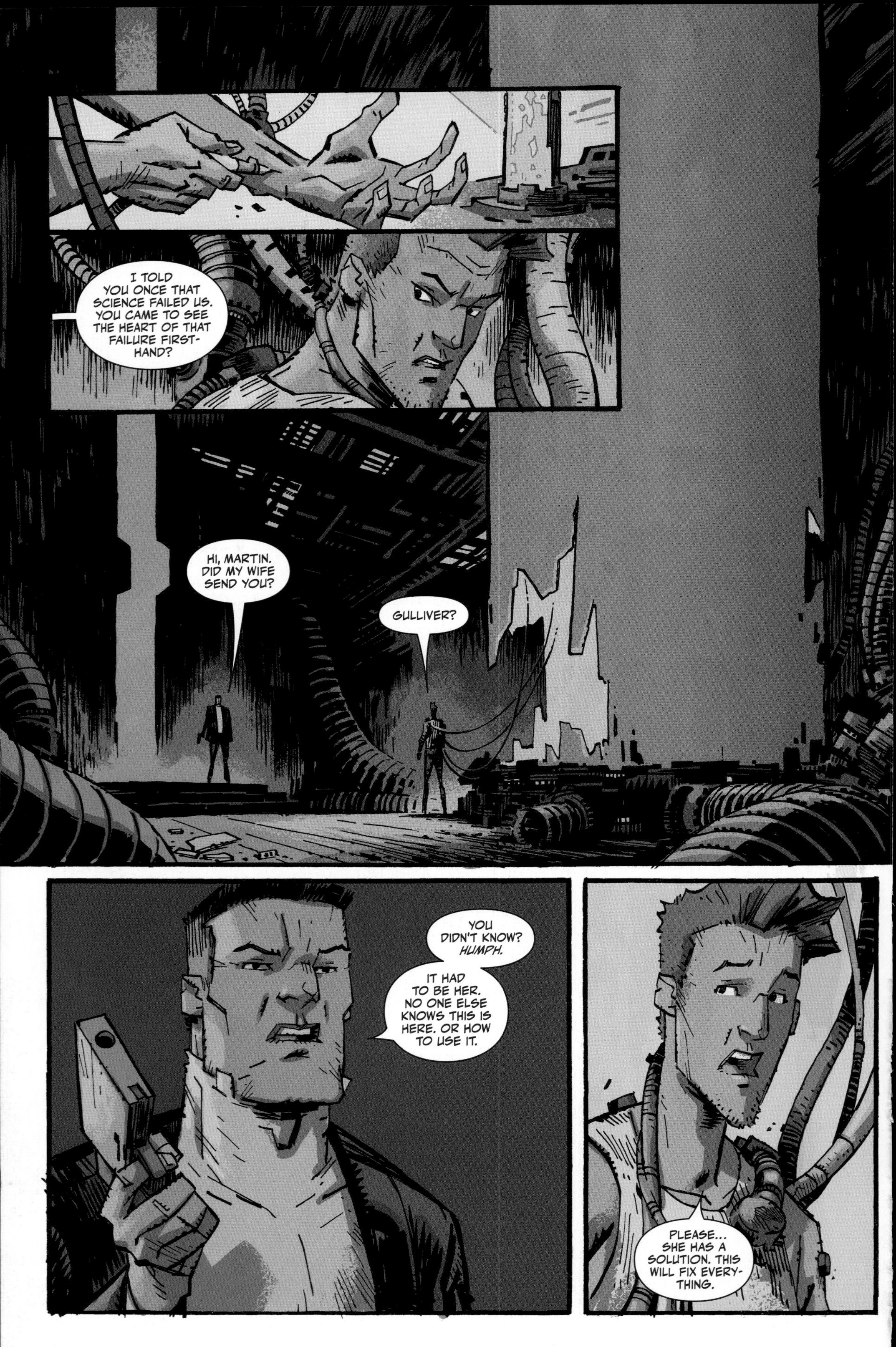
I TOLD YOU ONCE THAT SCIENCE FAILED US. YOU CAME TO SEE THE HEART OF THAT FAILURE FIRST-HAND?
HI, MARTIN. DID MY WIFE SEND YOU?
GULLIVER?
YOU DIDN'T KNOW? *HUMPH.*
IT HAD TO BE HER. NO ONE ELSE KNOWS THIS IS HERE. OR HOW TO USE IT.
PLEASE... SHE HAS A SOLUTION. THIS WILL FIX EVERY-THING.

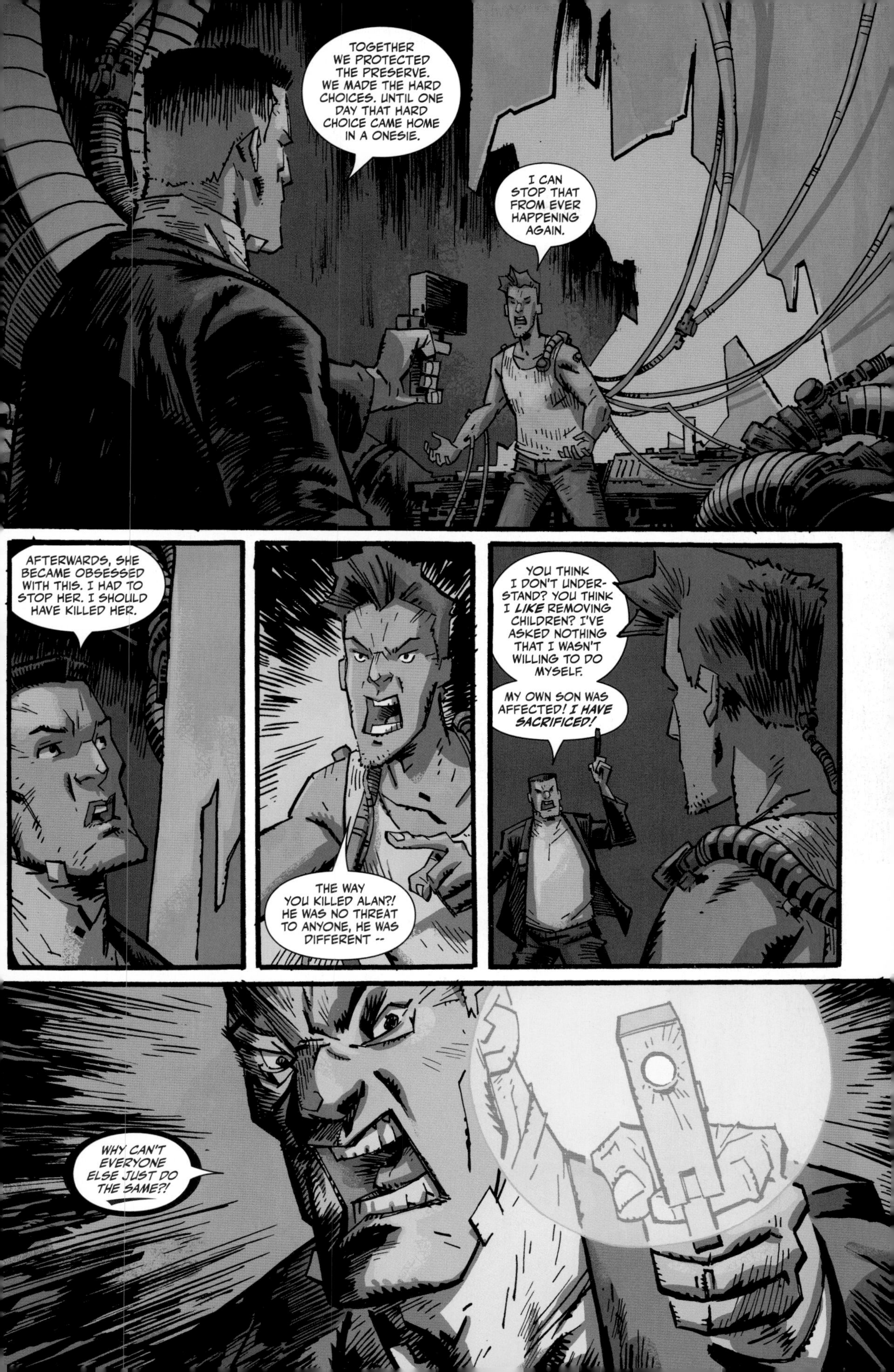

TOGETHER WE PROTECTED THE PRESERVE. WE MADE THE HARD CHOICES. UNTIL ONE DAY THAT HARD CHOICE CAME HOME IN A ONESIE.
I CAN STOP THAT FROM EVER HAPPENING AGAIN.
AFTERWARDS, SHE BECAME OBSESSED WITH THIS. I HAD TO STOP HER. I SHOULD HAVE KILLED HER.
THE WAY YOU KILLED ALAN?! HE WAS NO THREAT TO ANYONE, HE WAS DIFFERENT --
YOU THINK I DON'T UNDERSTAND? YOU THINK I *LIKE* REMOVING CHILDREN? I'VE ASKED NOTHING THAT I WASN'T WILLING TO DO MYSELF.
MY OWN SON WAS AFFECTED! ***I HAVE SACRIFICED!***
WHY CAN'T EVERYONE ELSE JUST DO THE SAME?!

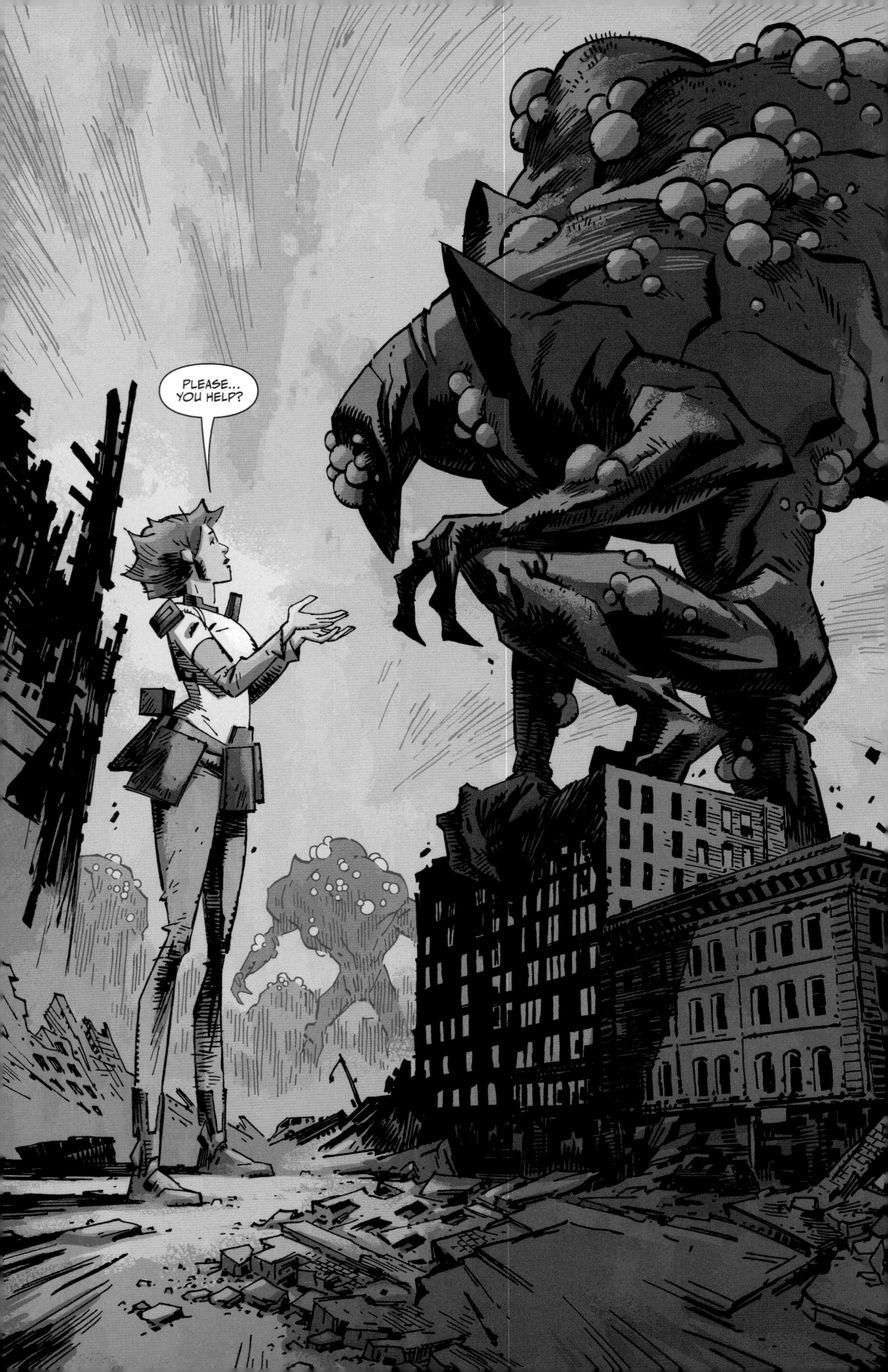
PLEASE...
YOU HELP?

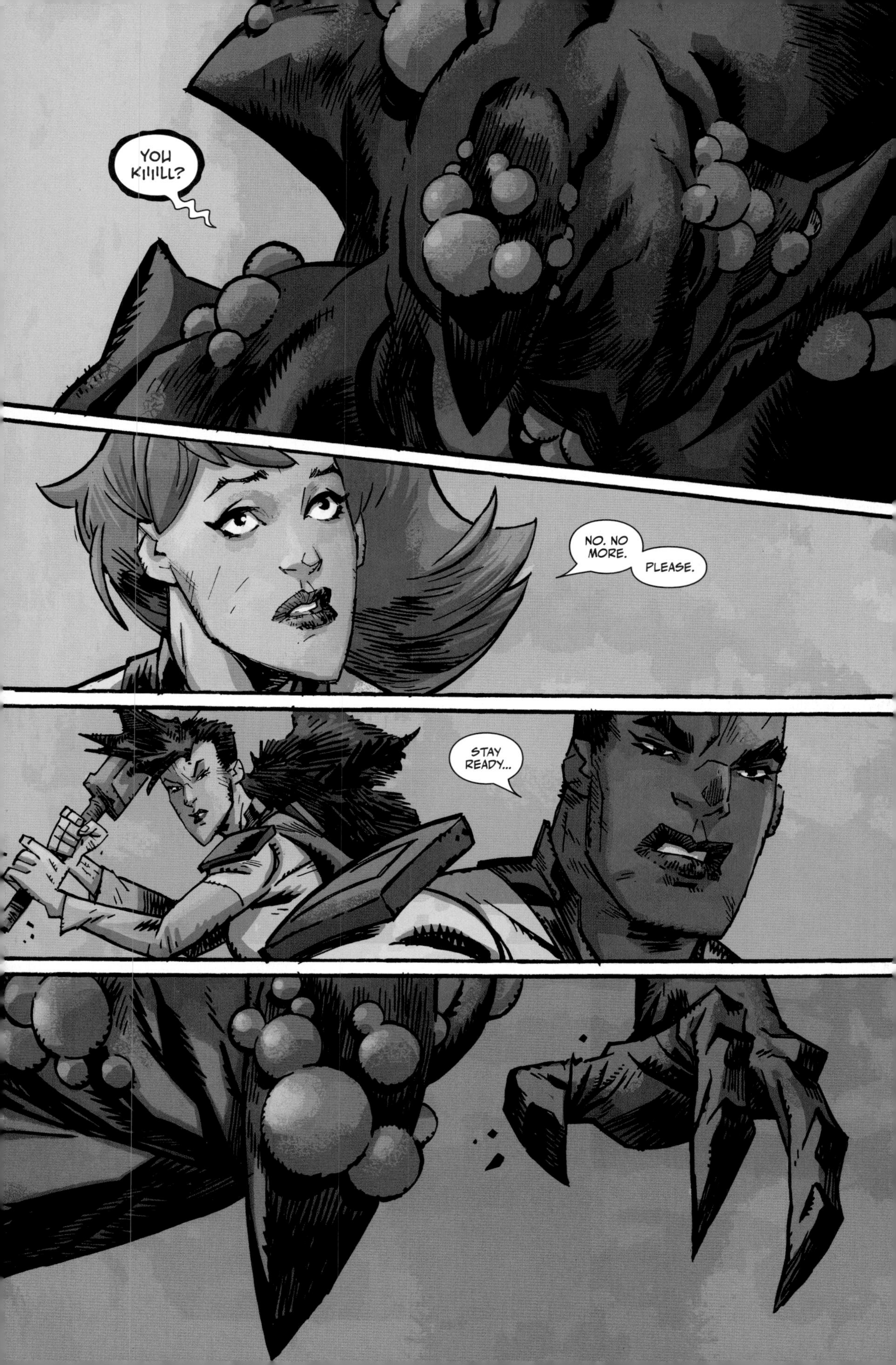
YOU KIIIILL?
NO. NO MORE.
PLEASE.
STAY READY...

I HELP. PLEASE.

WHAT JUST HAPPENED?

I THINK EMBER SAVED US ALL.

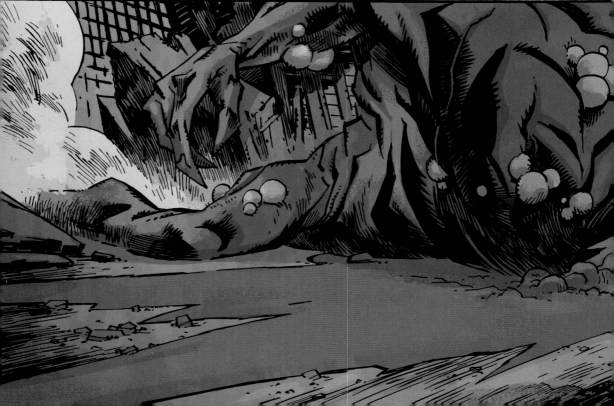

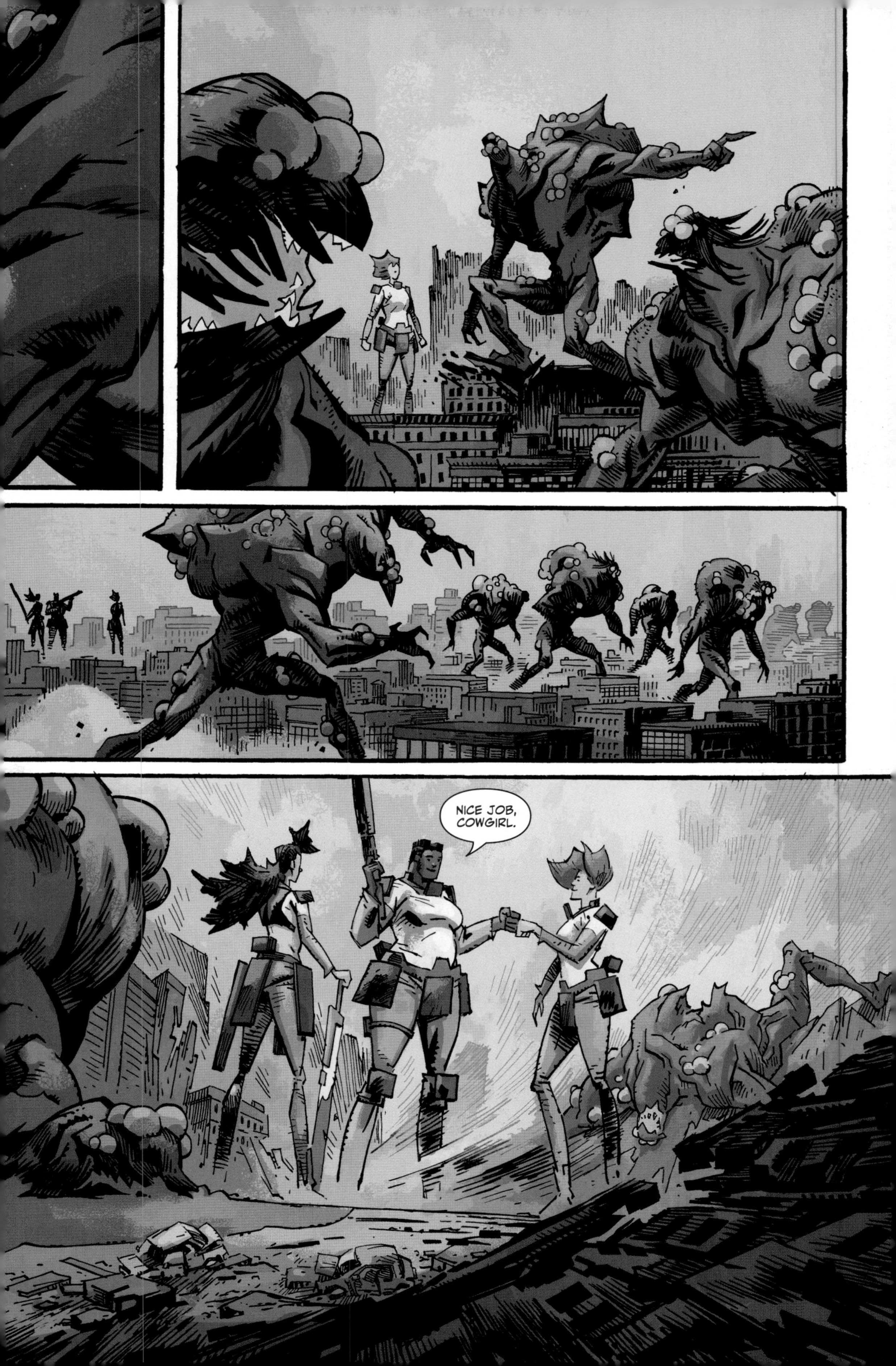
NICE JOB, COWGIRL.

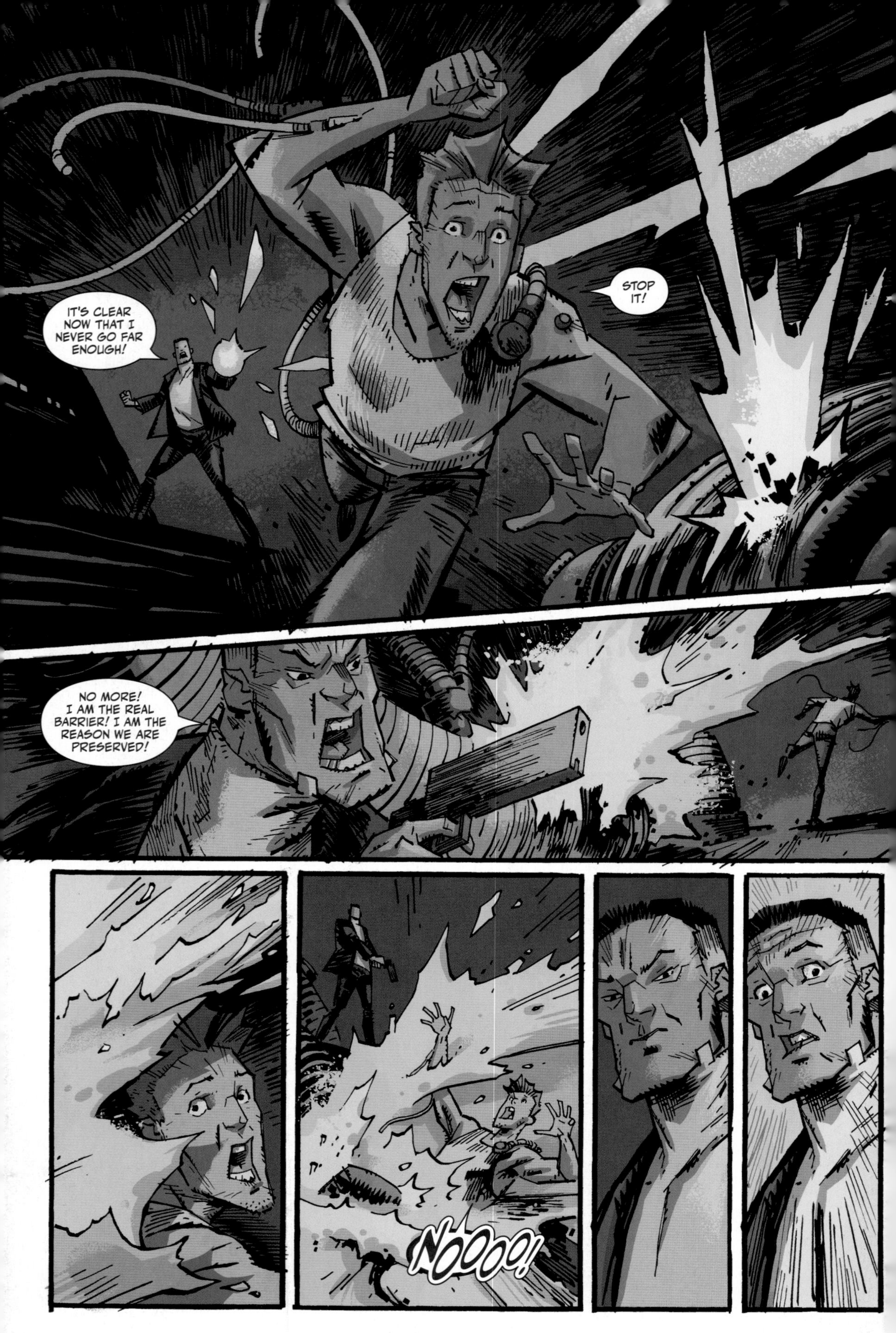
IT'S CLEAR NOW THAT I NEVER GO FAR ENOUGH!
STOP IT!
NO MORE! I AM THE REAL BARRIER! I AM THE REASON WE ARE PRESERVED!
NOOOO!

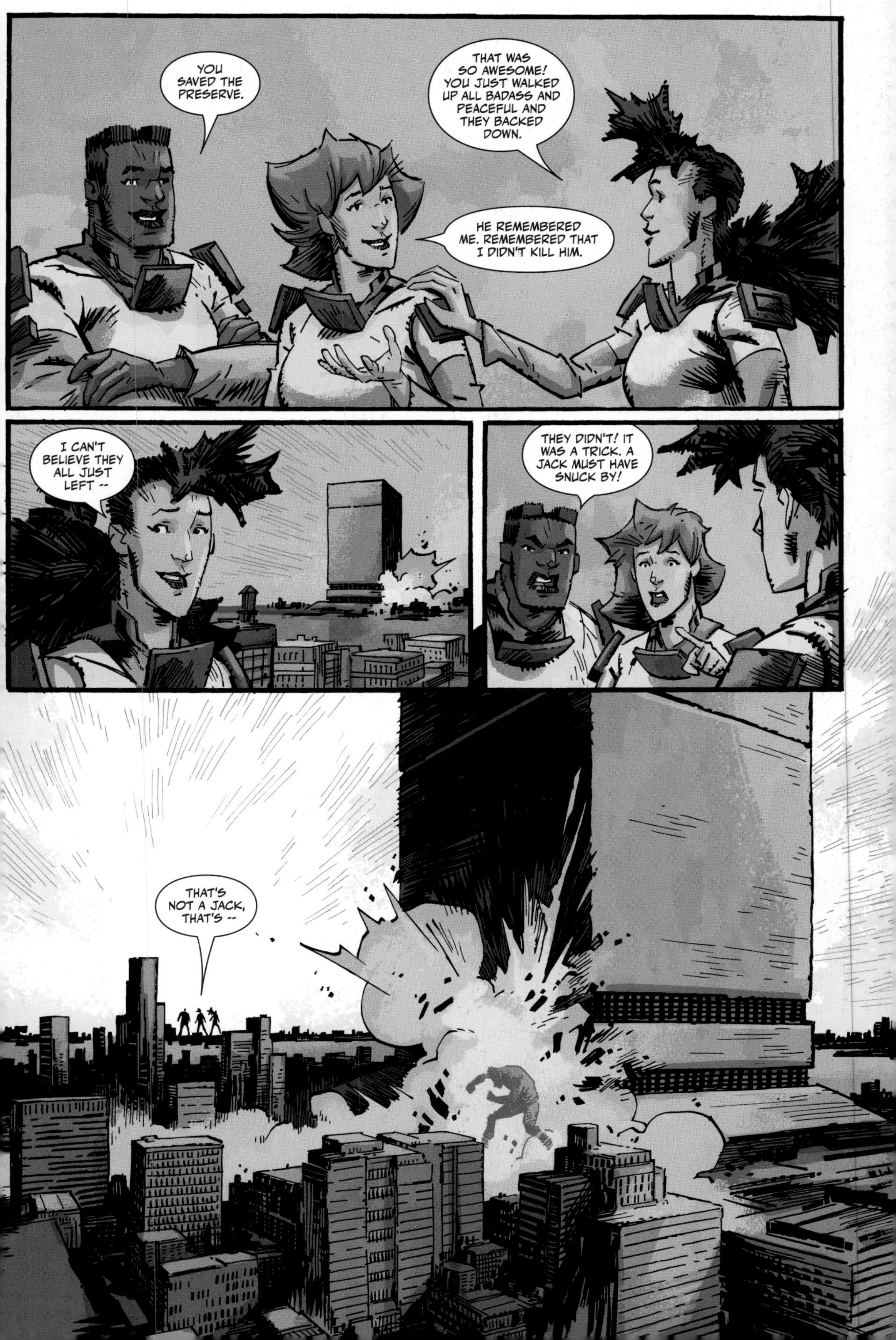
YOU SAVED THE PRESERVE.
THAT WAS SO AWESOME! YOU JUST WALKED UP ALL BADASS AND PEACEFUL AND THEY BACKED DOWN.
HE REMEMBERED ME. REMEMBERED THAT I DIDN'T KILL HIM.
I CAN'T BELIEVE THEY ALL JUST LEFT --
THEY DIDN'T! IT WAS A TRICK. A JACK MUST HAVE SNUCK BY!
THAT'S NOT A JACK, THAT'S --

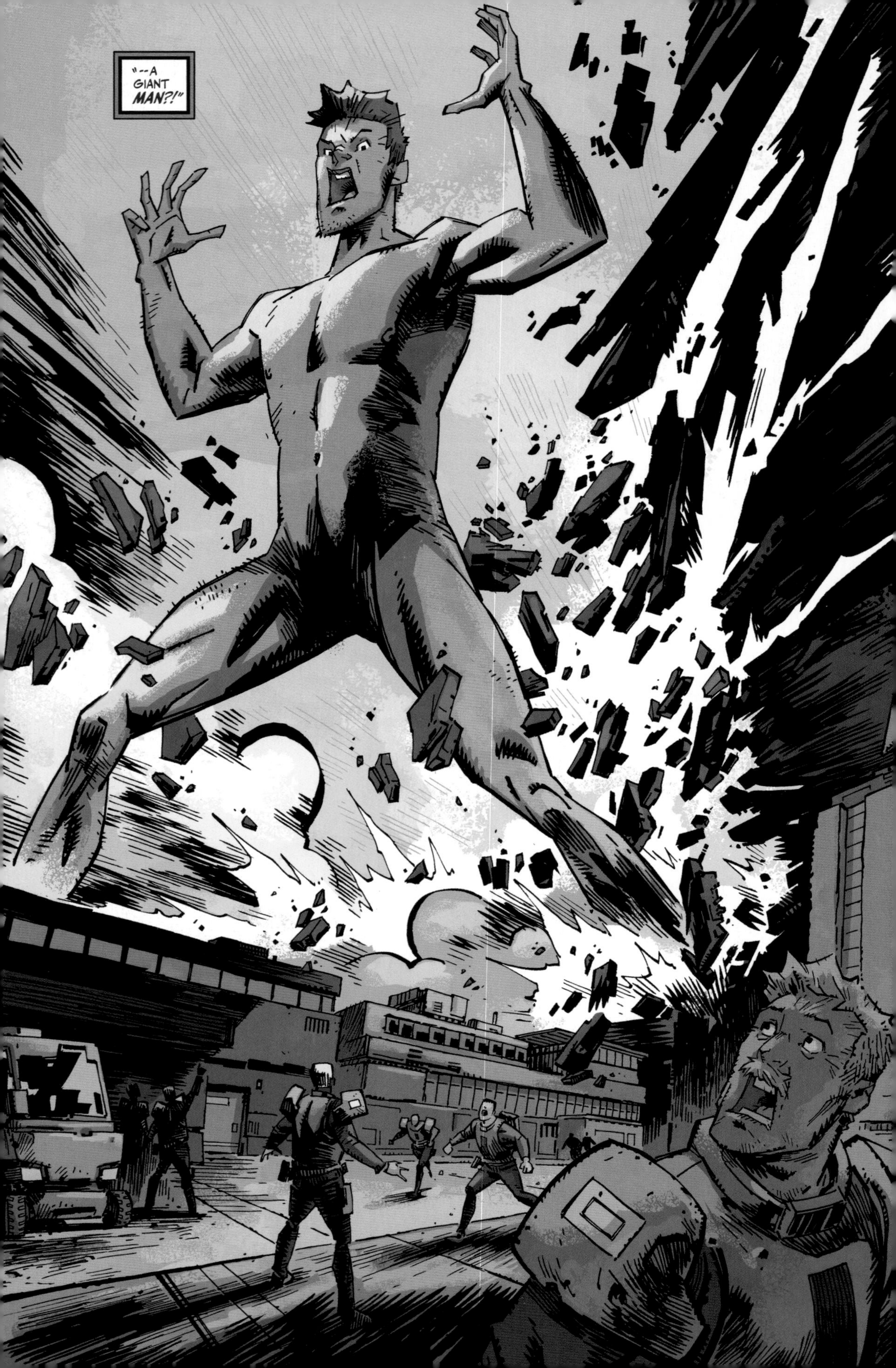
"--A GIANT MAN?!"

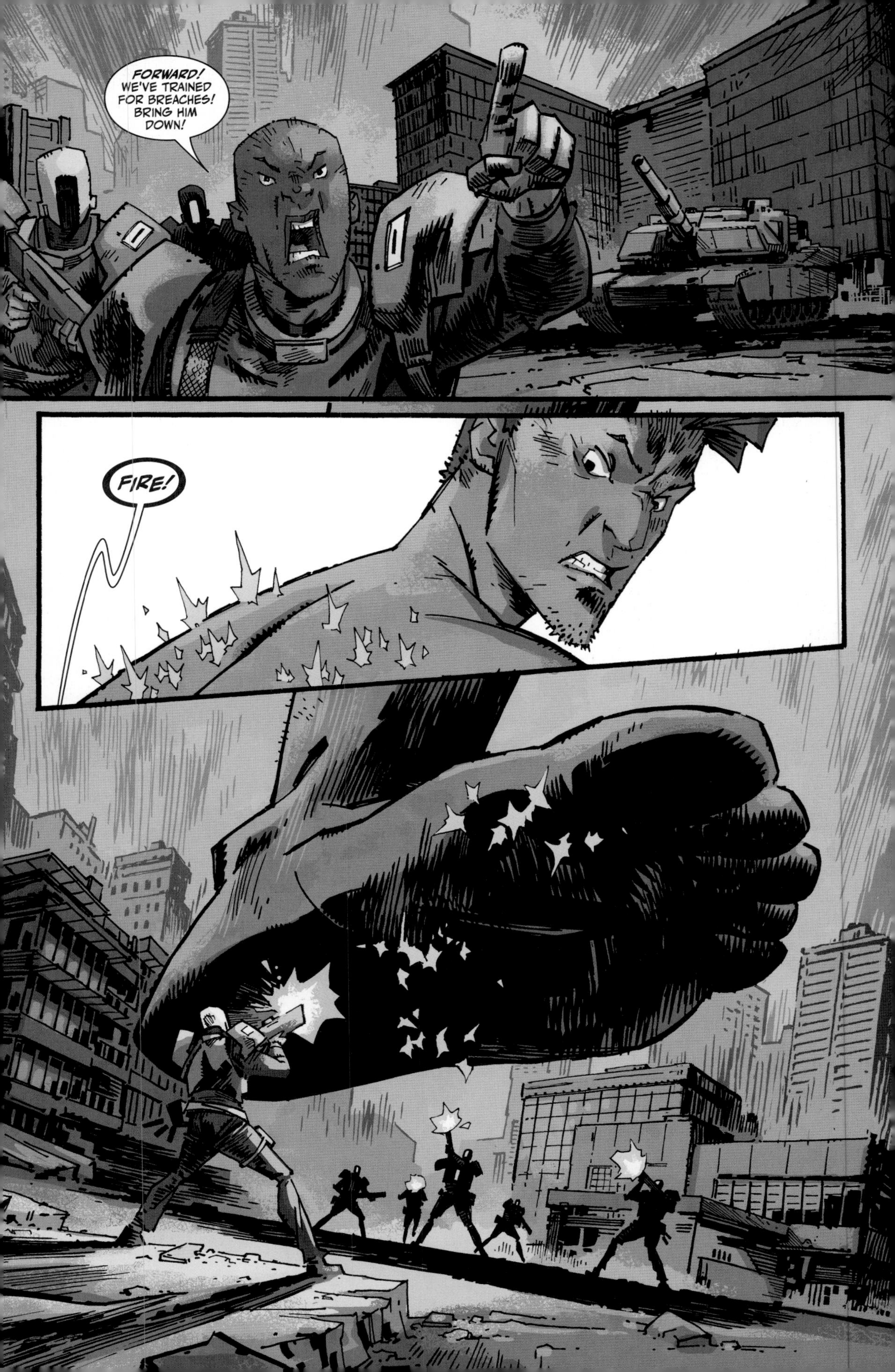
FORWARD! WE'VE TRAINED FOR BREACHES! BRING HIM DOWN!
FIRE!

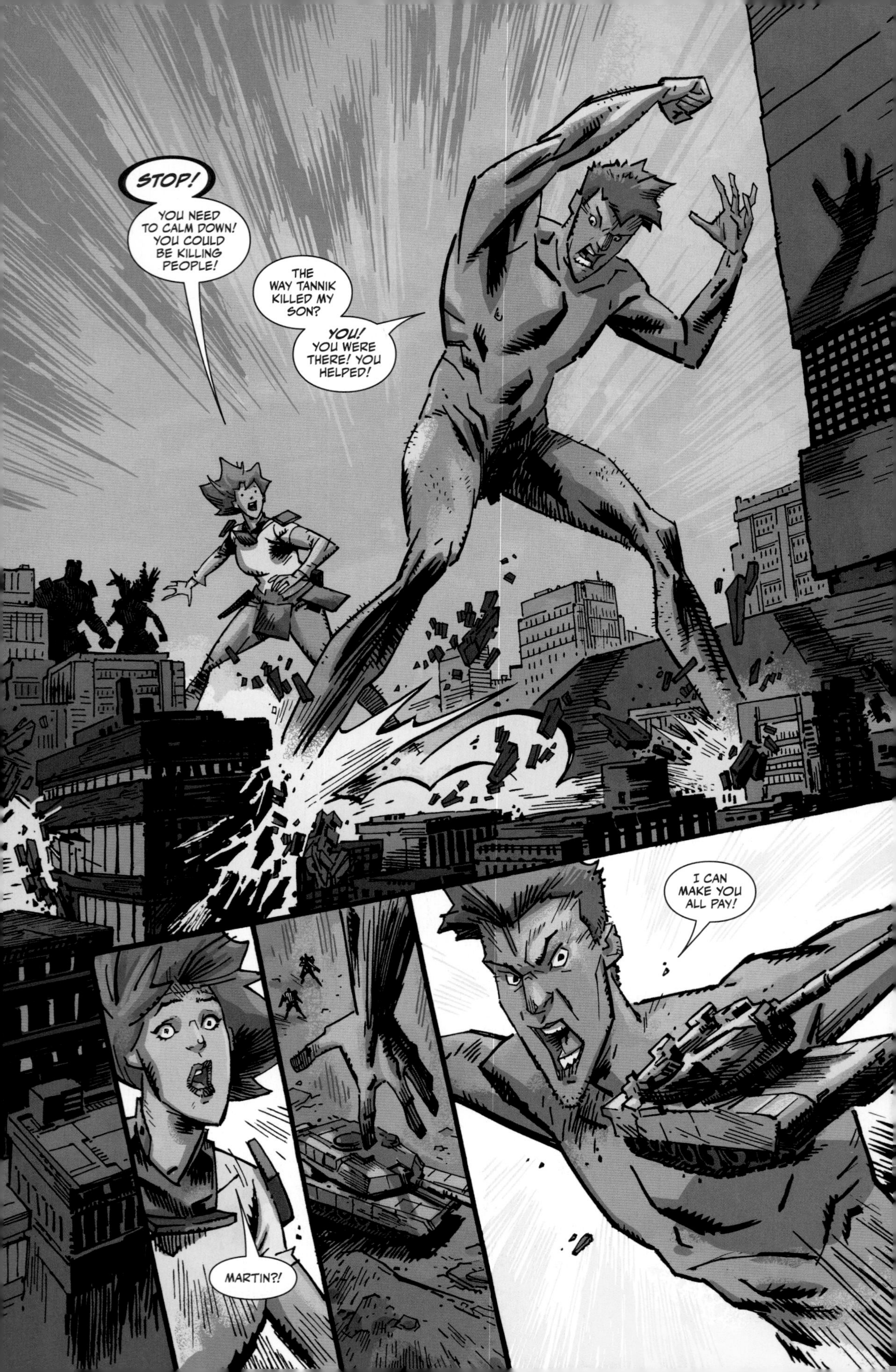
STOP!
YOU NEED TO CALM DOWN! YOU COULD BE KILLING PEOPLE!
THE WAY TANNIK KILLED MY SON?
YOU! YOU WERE THERE! YOU HELPED!
MARTIN?!
I CAN MAKE YOU ALL PAY!

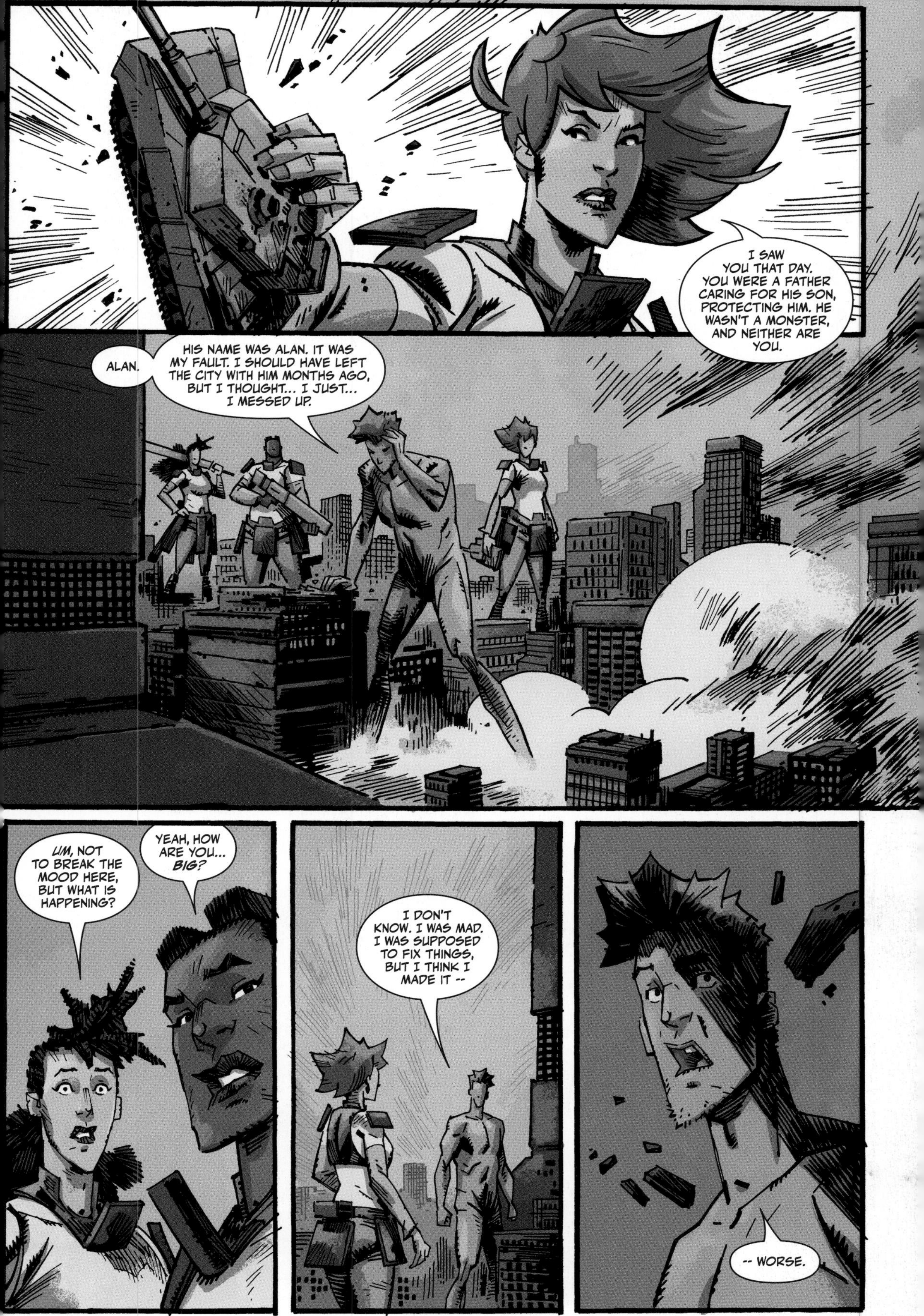
I SAW YOU THAT DAY. YOU WERE A FATHER CARING FOR HIS SON, PROTECTING HIM. HE WASN'T A MONSTER, AND NEITHER ARE YOU.
ALAN.
HIS NAME WAS ALAN. IT WAS MY FAULT. I SHOULD HAVE LEFT THE CITY WITH HIM MONTHS AGO, BUT I THOUGHT... I JUST... I MESSED UP.
UM, NOT TO BREAK THE MOOD HERE, BUT WHAT IS HAPPENING?
YEAH, HOW ARE YOU... BIG?
I DON'T KNOW. I WAS MAD. I WAS SUPPOSED TO FIX THINGS, BUT I THINK I MADE IT --
-- WORSE.

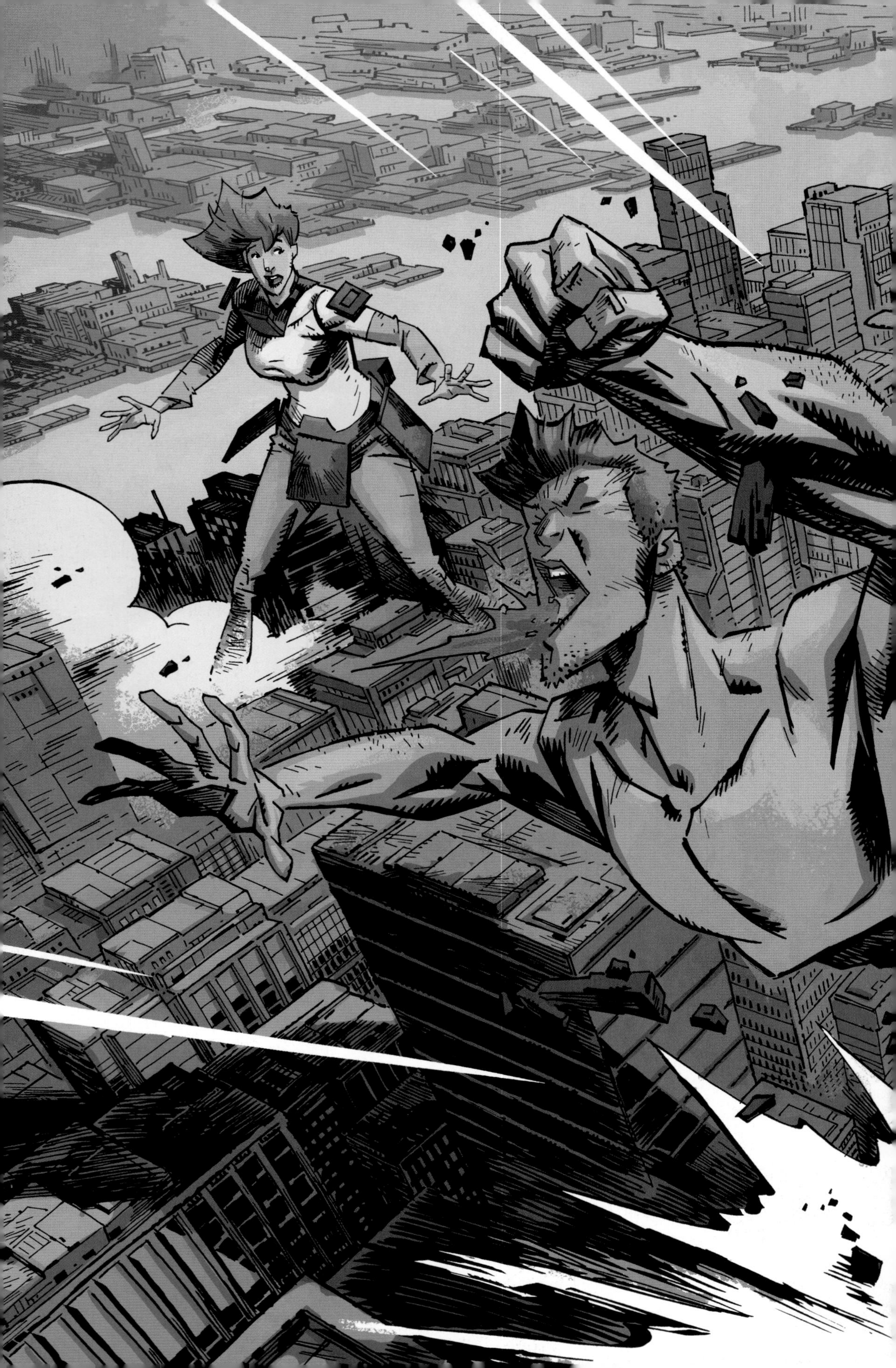

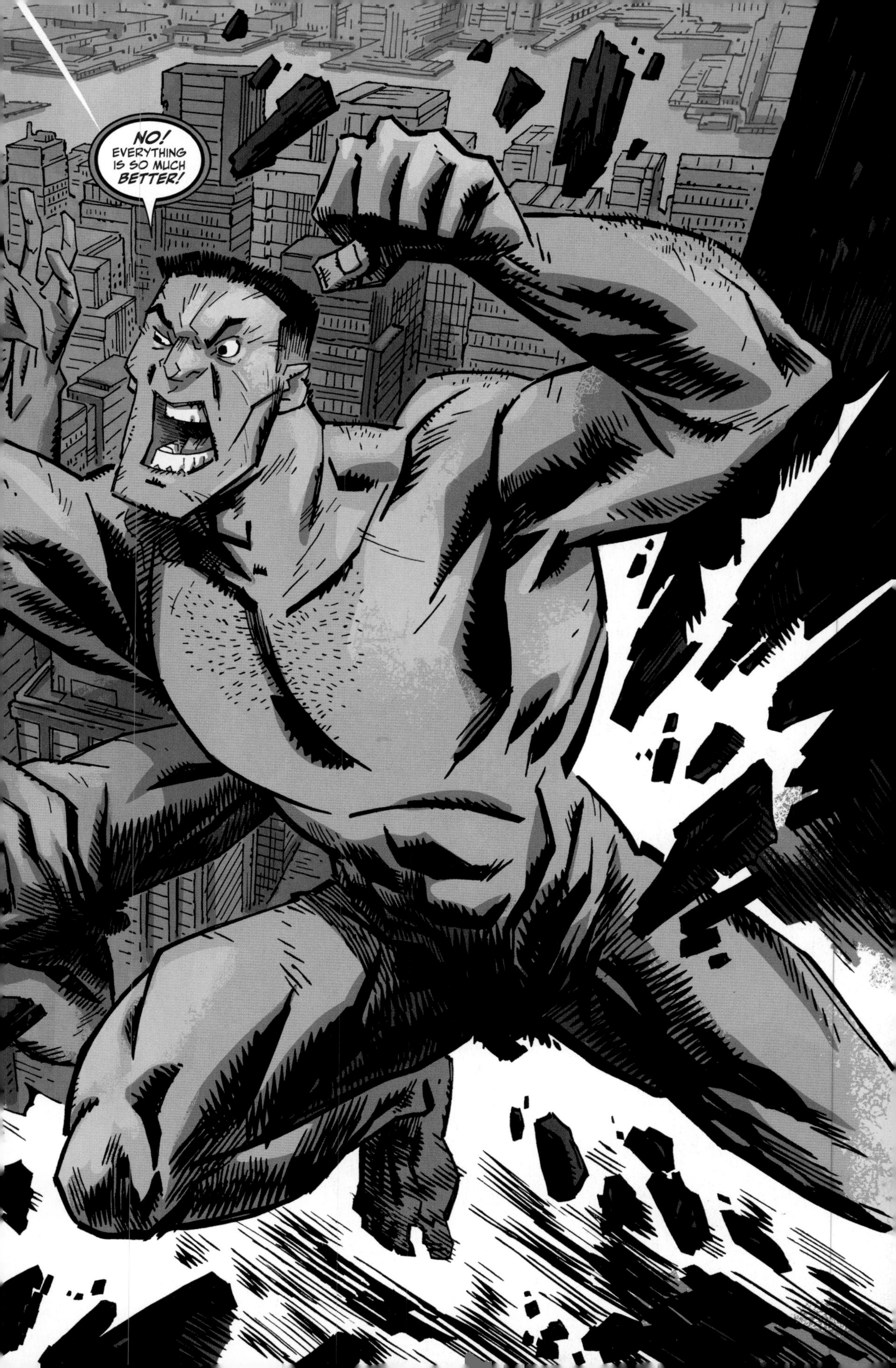
NO! EVERYTHING IS SO MUCH BETTER!

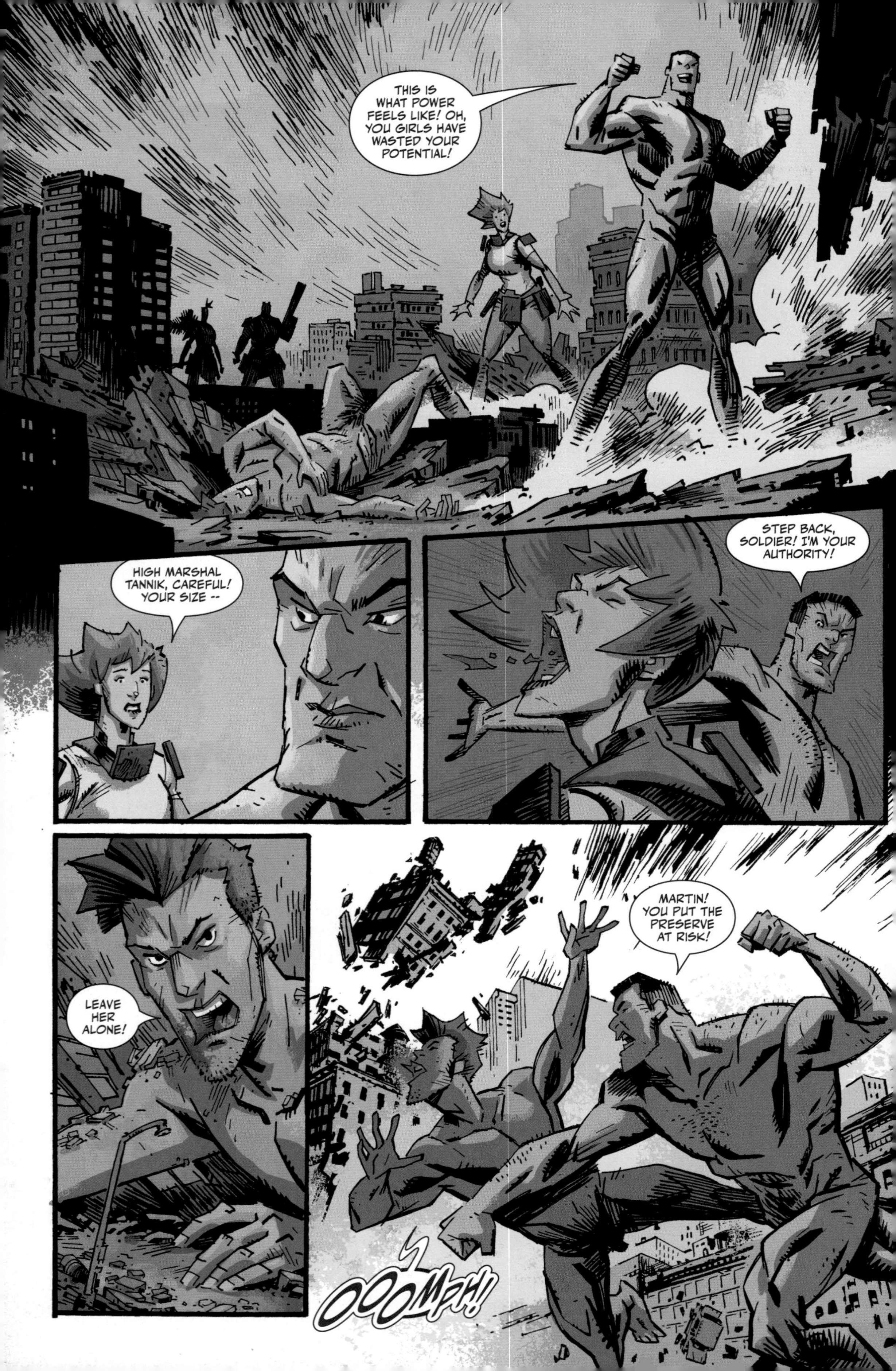
THIS IS WHAT POWER FEELS LIKE! OH, YOU GIRLS HAVE WASTED YOUR POTENTIAL!
HIGH MARSHAL TANNIK, CAREFUL! YOUR SIZE --
STEP BACK, SOLDIER! I'M YOUR AUTHORITY!
LEAVE HER ALONE!
MARTIN! YOU PUT THE PRESERVE AT RISK!
OOOMPH!!

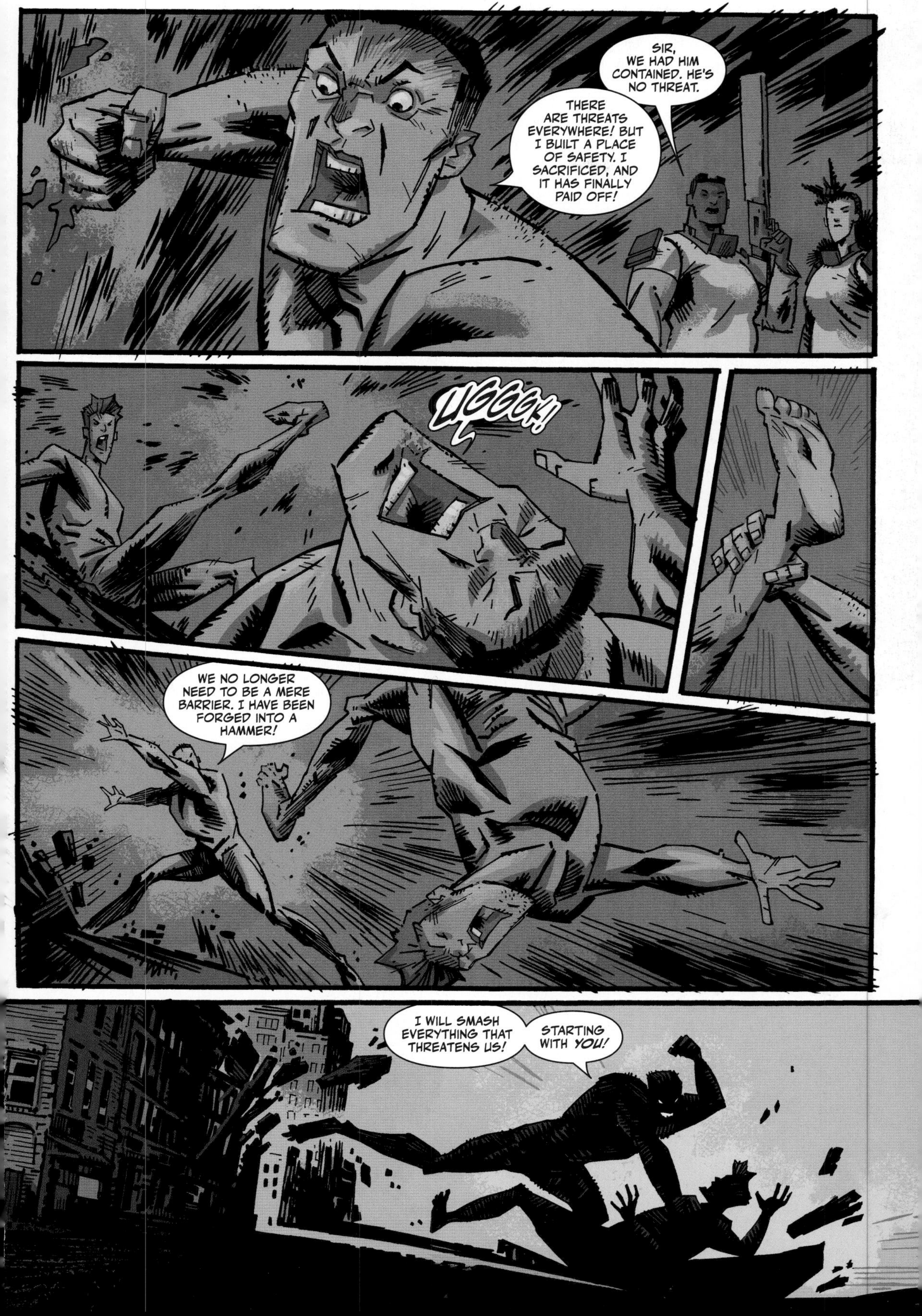
SIR, WE HAD HIM CONTAINED. HE'S NO THREAT.
THERE ARE THREATS EVERYWHERE! BUT I BUILT A PLACE OF SAFETY. I SACRIFICED, AND IT HAS FINALLY PAID OFF!
UGGG!
WE NO LONGER NEED TO BE A MERE BARRIER. I HAVE BEEN FORGED INTO A HAMMER!
I WILL SMASH EVERYTHING THAT THREATENS US!
STARTING WITH YOU!

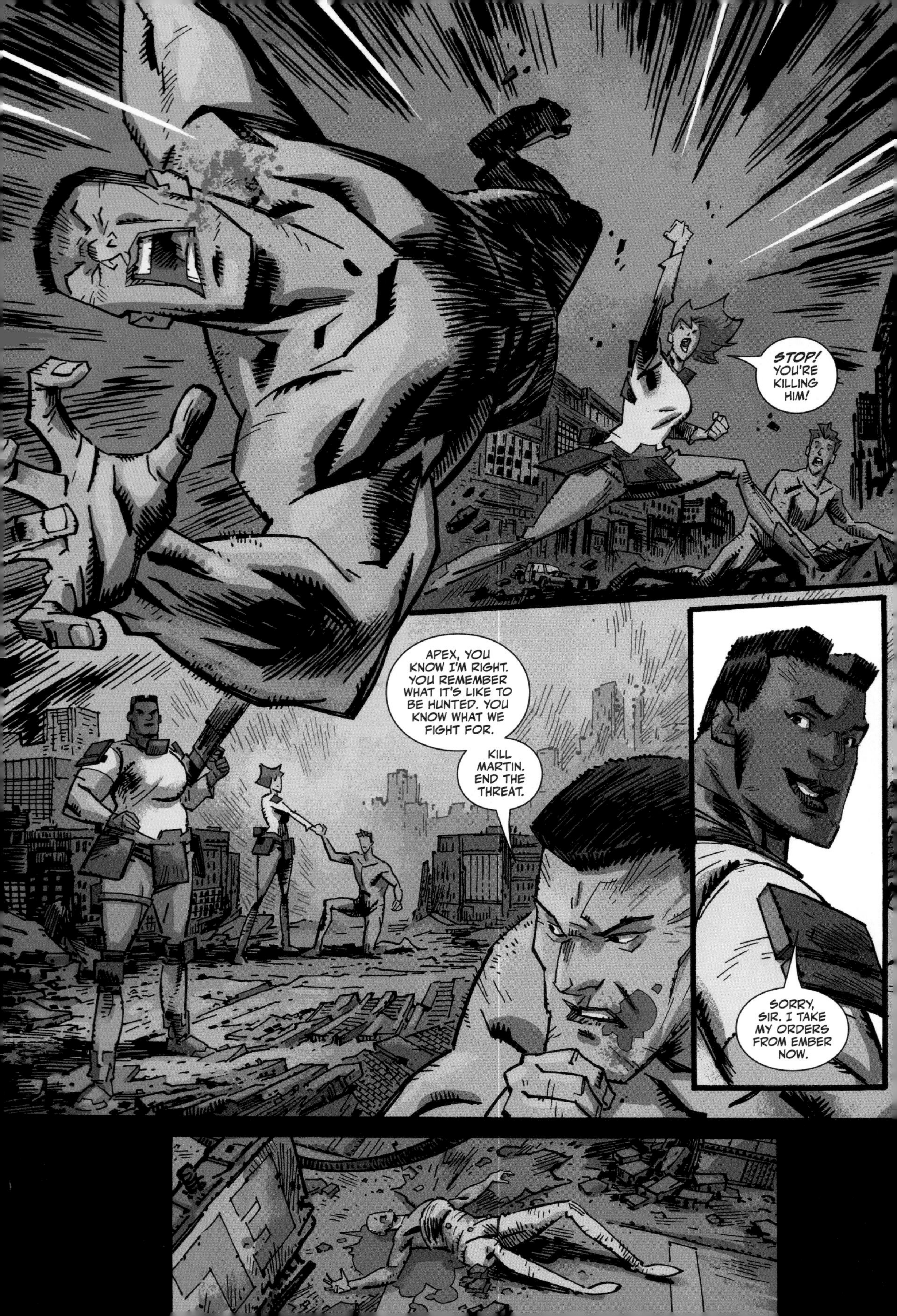
STOP! YOU'RE KILLING HIM!
APEX, YOU KNOW I'M RIGHT. YOU REMEMBER WHAT IT'S LIKE TO BE HUNTED. YOU KNOW WHAT WE FIGHT FOR.
KILL MARTIN. END THE THREAT.
SORRY, SIR. I TAKE MY ORDERS FROM EMBER NOW.

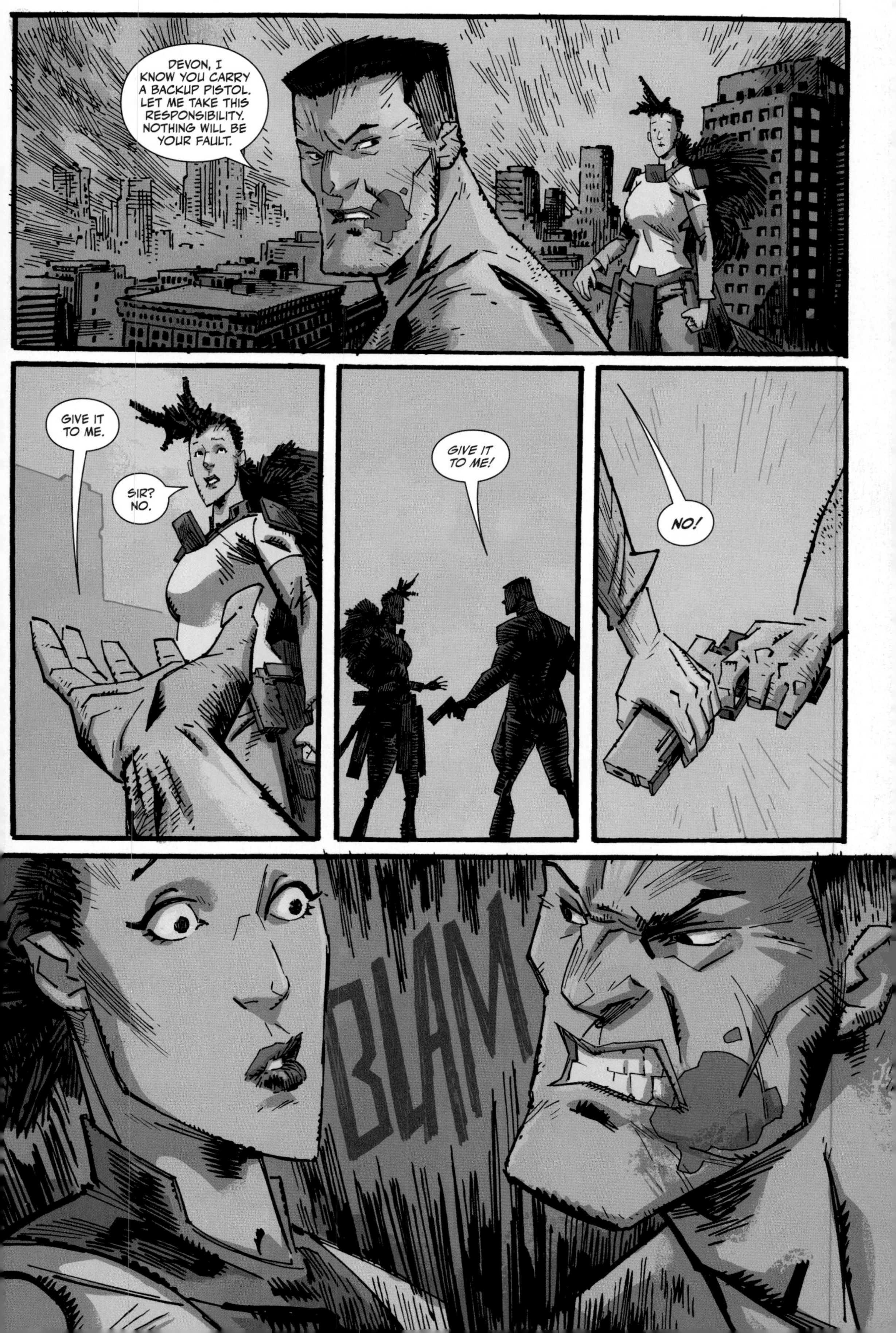
DEVON, I KNOW YOU CARRY A BACKUP PISTOL. LET ME TAKE THIS RESPONSIBILITY. NOTHING WILL BE YOUR FAULT.
GIVE IT TO ME.
SIR? NO.
GIVE IT TO ME!
NO!
BLAM

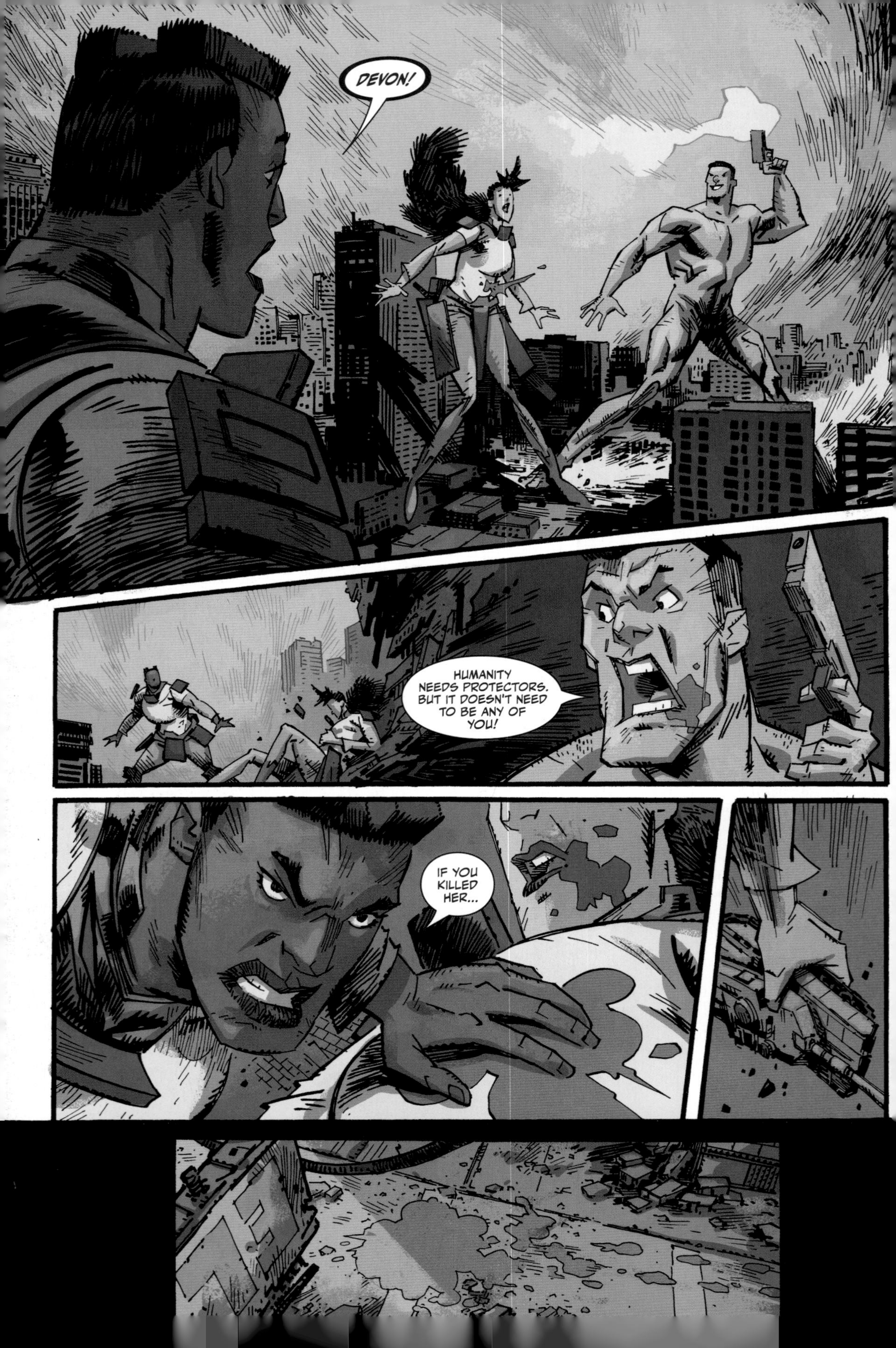
DEVON!
HUMANITY NEEDS PROTECTORS. BUT IT DOESN'T NEED TO BE ANY OF YOU!
IF YOU KILLED HER...

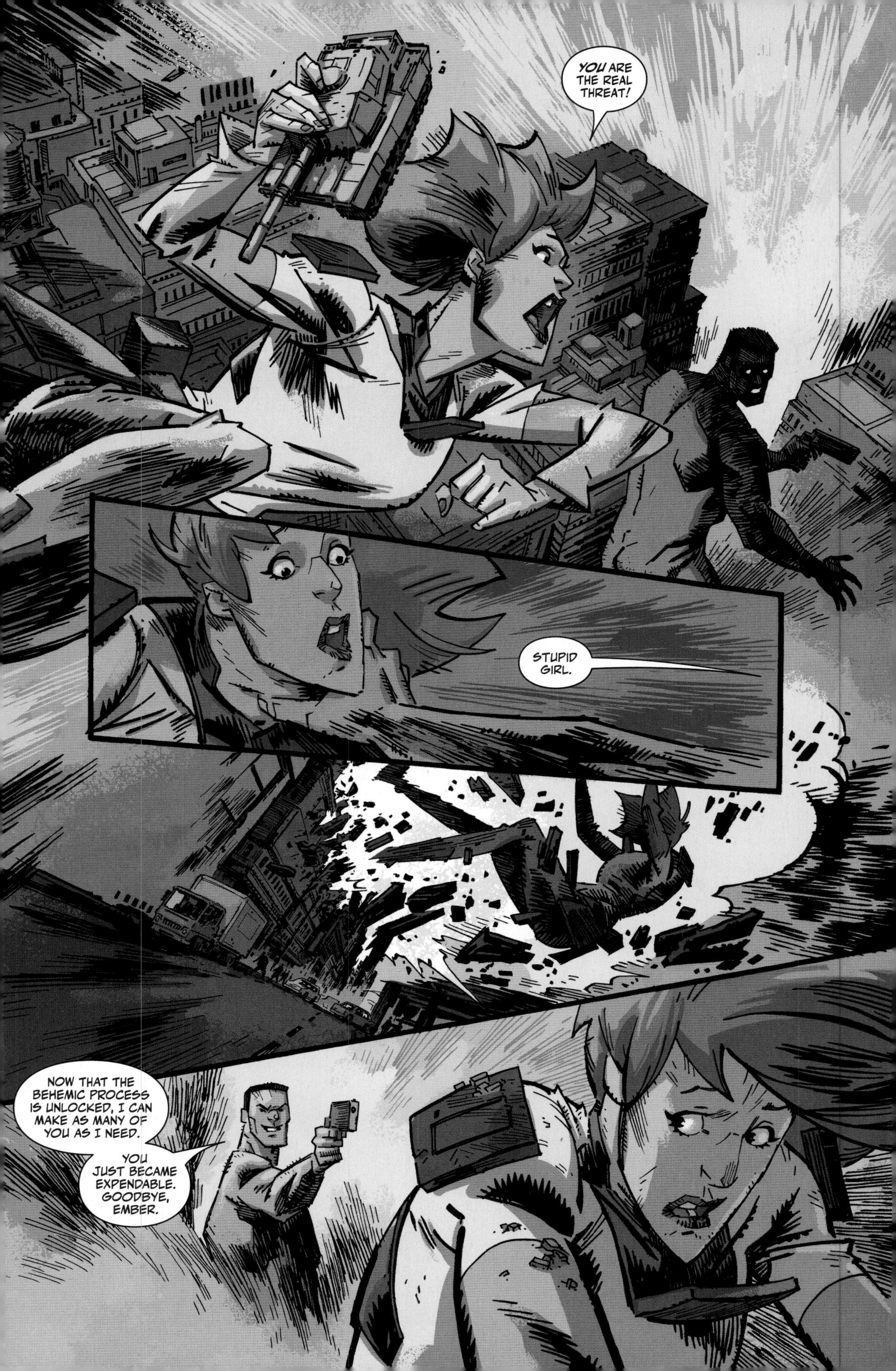
YOU ARE THE REAL THREAT!
STUPID GIRL.
NOW THAT THE BEHEMIC PROCESS IS UNLOCKED, I CAN MAKE AS MANY OF YOU AS I NEED.
YOU JUST BECAME EXPENDABLE. GOODBYE, EMBER.

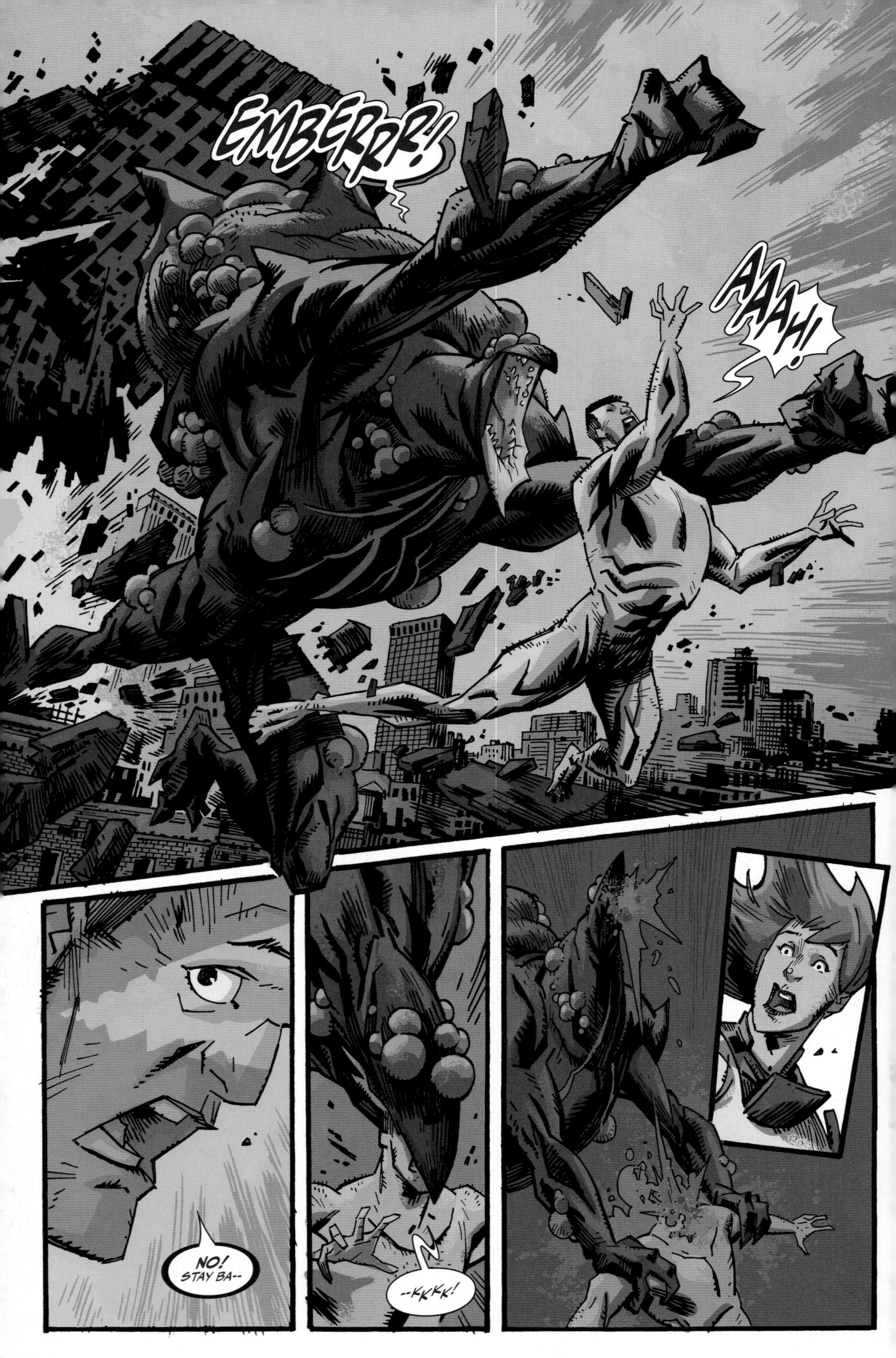
EMBERRR!
AAAH!
NO! STAY BA--
--KKKK!

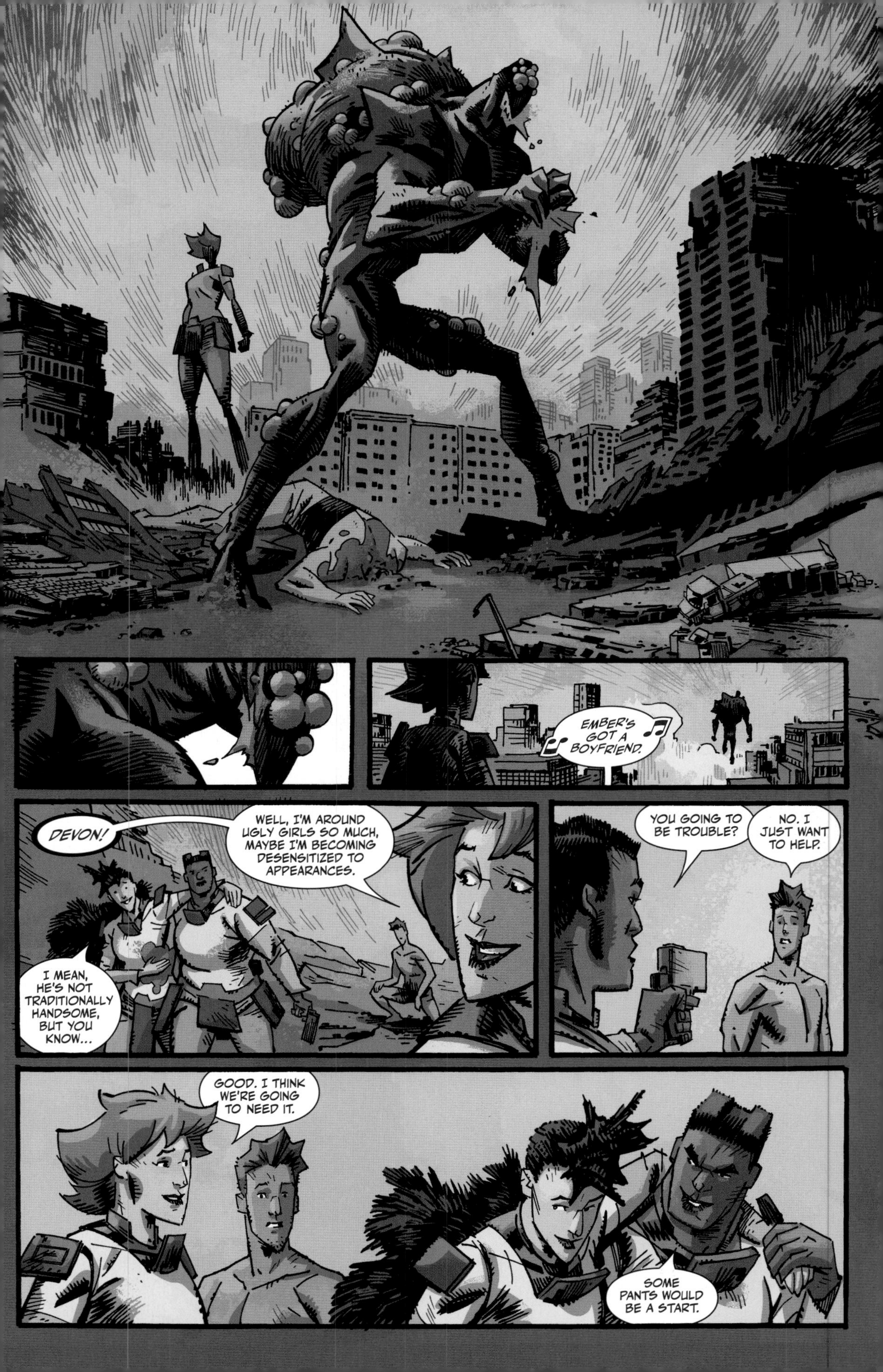
EMBER'S GOT A BOYFRIEND.
DEVON!
WELL, I'M AROUND UGLY GIRLS SO MUCH, MAYBE I'M BECOMING DESENSITIZED TO APPEARANCES.
I MEAN, HE'S NOT TRADITIONALLY HANDSOME, BUT YOU KNOW...
YOU GOING TO BE TROUBLE?
NO. I JUST WANT TO HELP.
GOOD. I THINK WE'RE GOING TO NEED IT.
SOME PANTS WOULD BE A START.

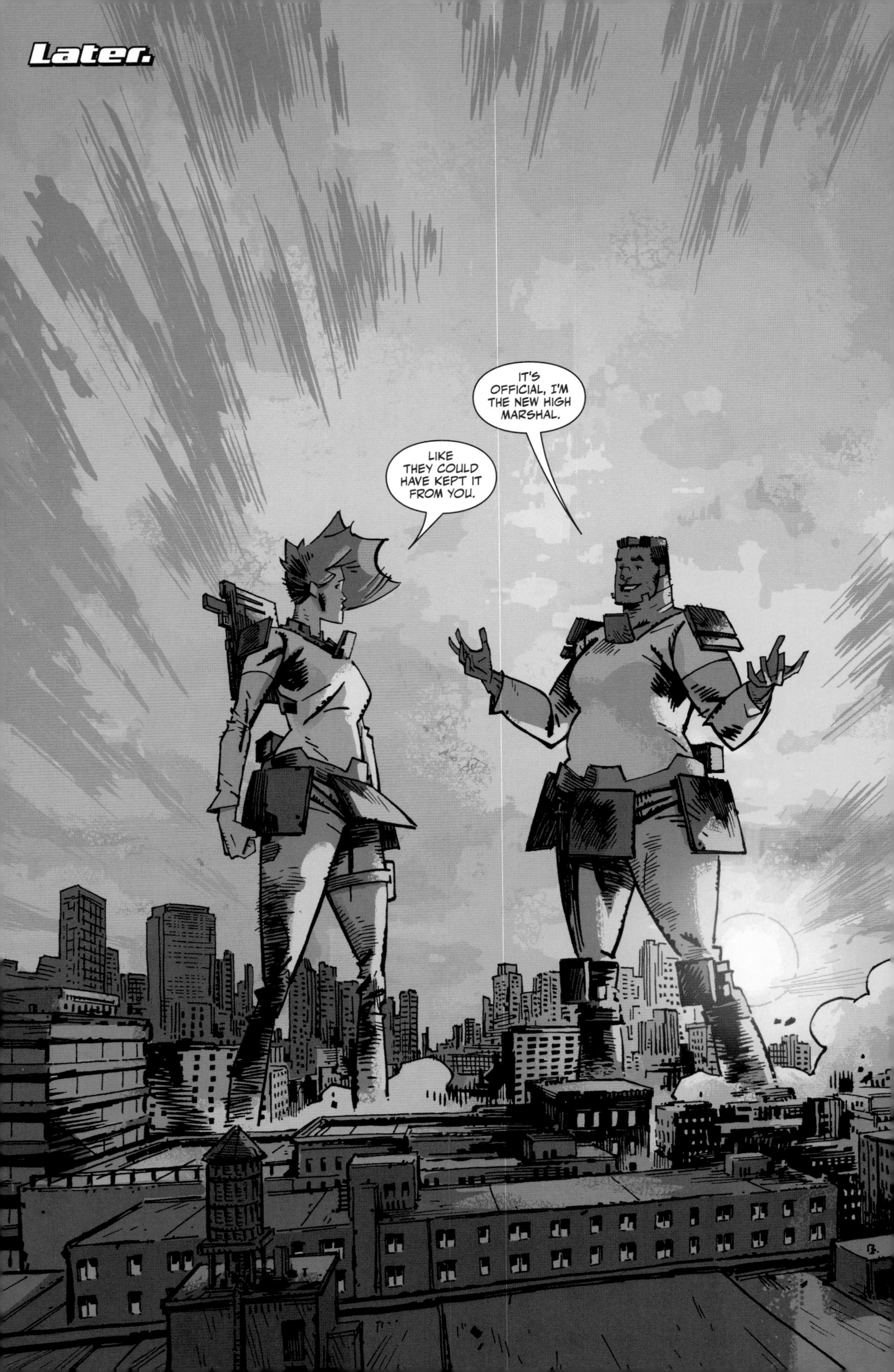
Later.
IT'S OFFICIAL, I'M THE NEW HIGH MARSHAL.
LIKE THEY COULD HAVE KEPT IT FROM YOU.

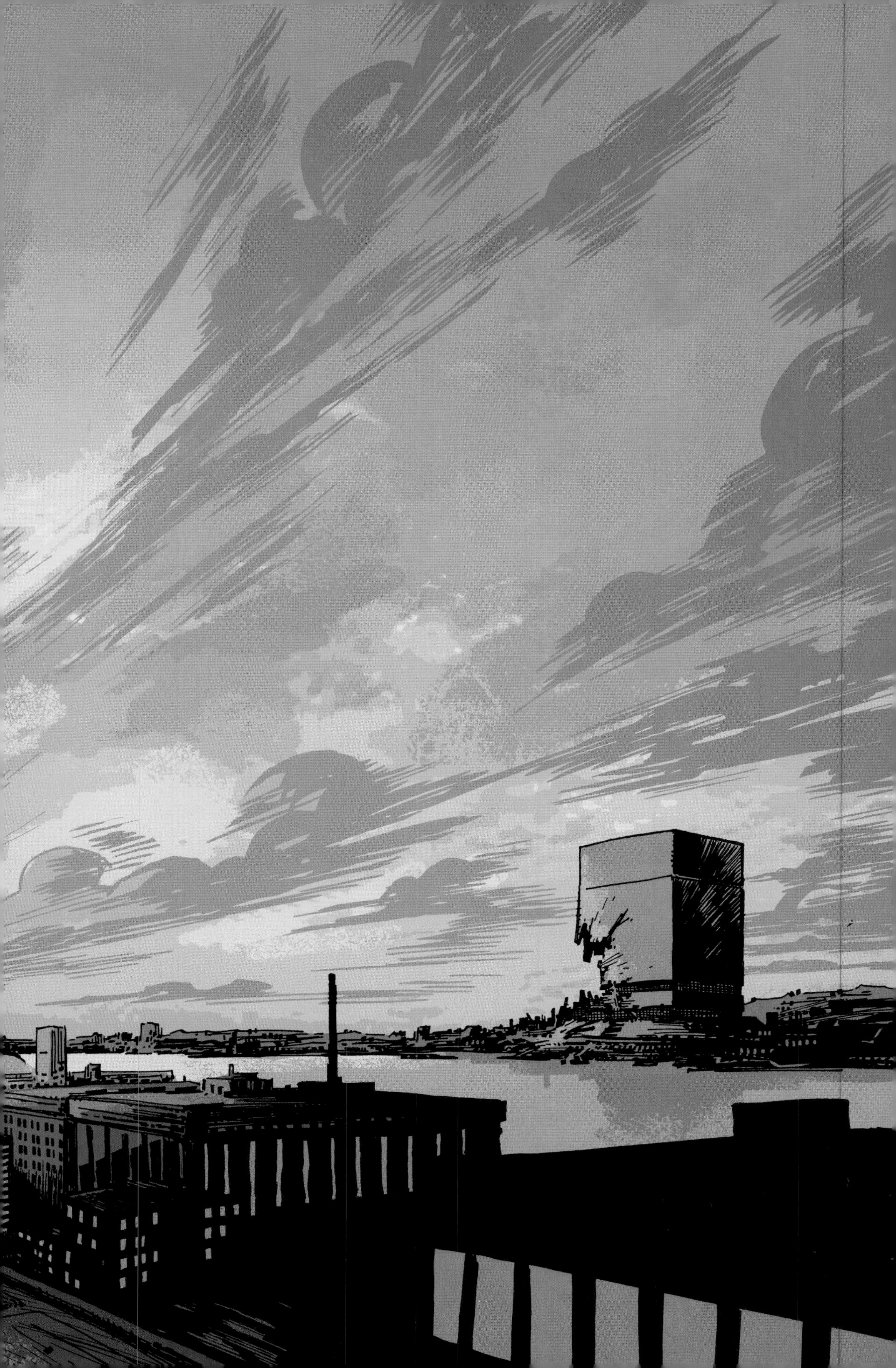

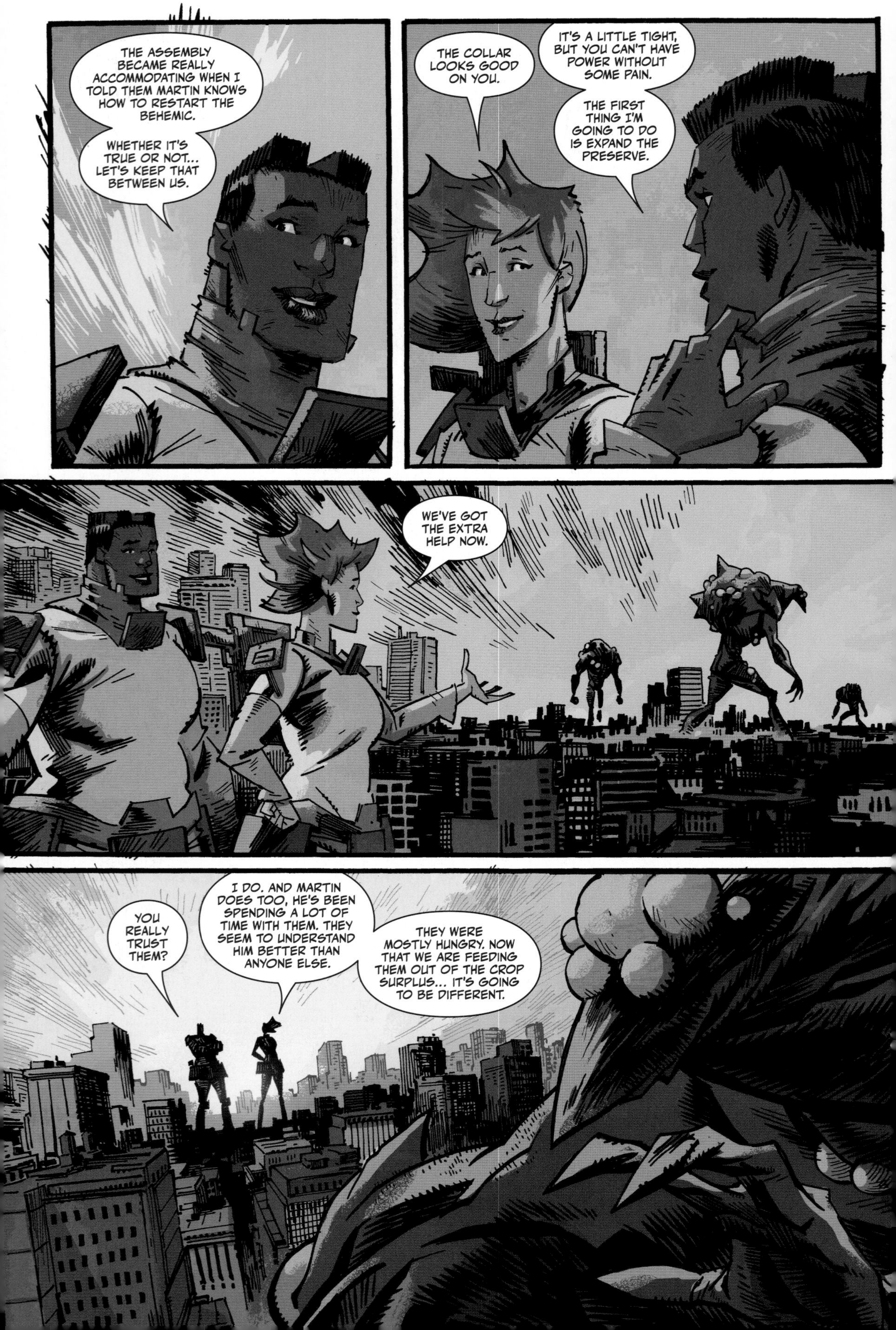
THE ASSEMBLY BECAME REALLY ACCOMMODATING WHEN I TOLD THEM MARTIN KNOWS HOW TO RESTART THE BEHEMIC.
WHETHER IT'S TRUE OR NOT... LET'S KEEP THAT BETWEEN US.
THE COLLAR LOOKS GOOD ON YOU.
IT'S A LITTLE TIGHT, BUT YOU CAN'T HAVE POWER WITHOUT SOME PAIN.
THE FIRST THING I'M GOING TO DO IS EXPAND THE PRESERVE.
WE'VE GOT THE EXTRA HELP NOW.
YOU REALLY TRUST THEM?
I DO. AND MARTIN DOES TOO, HE'S BEEN SPENDING A LOT OF TIME WITH THEM. THEY SEEM TO UNDERSTAND HIM BETTER THAN ANYONE ELSE.
THEY WERE MOSTLY HUNGRY. NOW THAT WE ARE FEEDING THEM OUT OF THE CROP SURPLUS... IT'S GOING TO BE DIFFERENT.

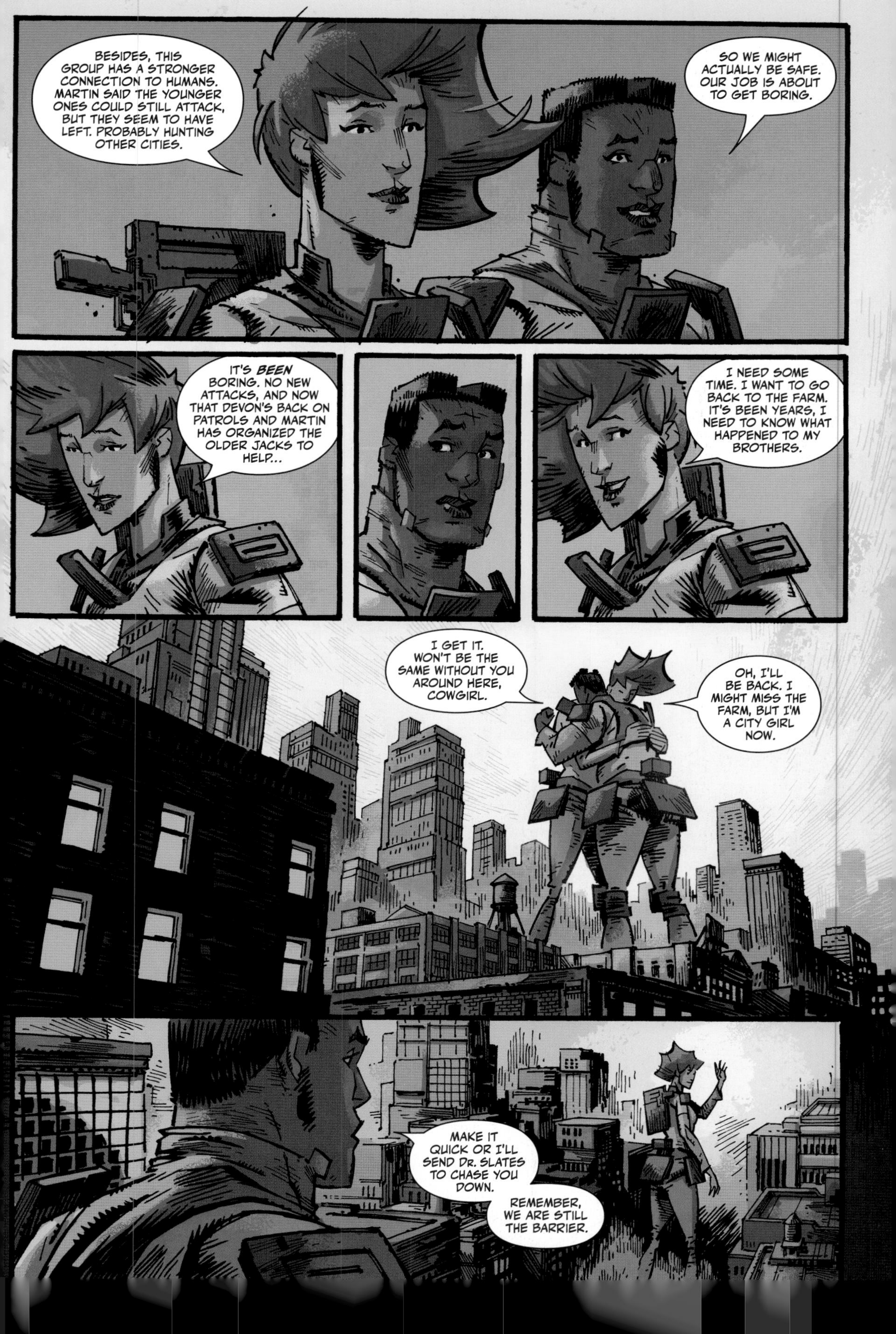
BESIDES, THIS GROUP HAS A STRONGER CONNECTION TO HUMANS. MARTIN SAID THE YOUNGER ONES COULD STILL ATTACK, BUT THEY SEEM TO HAVE LEFT. PROBABLY HUNTING OTHER CITIES.
SO WE MIGHT ACTUALLY BE SAFE. OUR JOB IS ABOUT TO GET BORING.
IT'S *BEEN* BORING. NO NEW ATTACKS, AND NOW THAT DEVON'S BACK ON PATROLS AND MARTIN HAS ORGANIZED THE OLDER JACKS TO HELP...
I NEED SOME TIME. I WANT TO GO BACK TO THE FARM. IT'S BEEN YEARS, I NEED TO KNOW WHAT HAPPENED TO MY BROTHERS.
I GET IT. WON'T BE THE SAME WITHOUT YOU AROUND HERE, COWGIRL.
OH, I'LL BE BACK. I MIGHT MISS THE FARM, BUT I'M A CITY GIRL NOW.
MAKE IT QUICK OR I'LL SEND Dr. SLATES TO CHASE YOU DOWN.
REMEMBER, WE ARE STILL THE BARRIER.

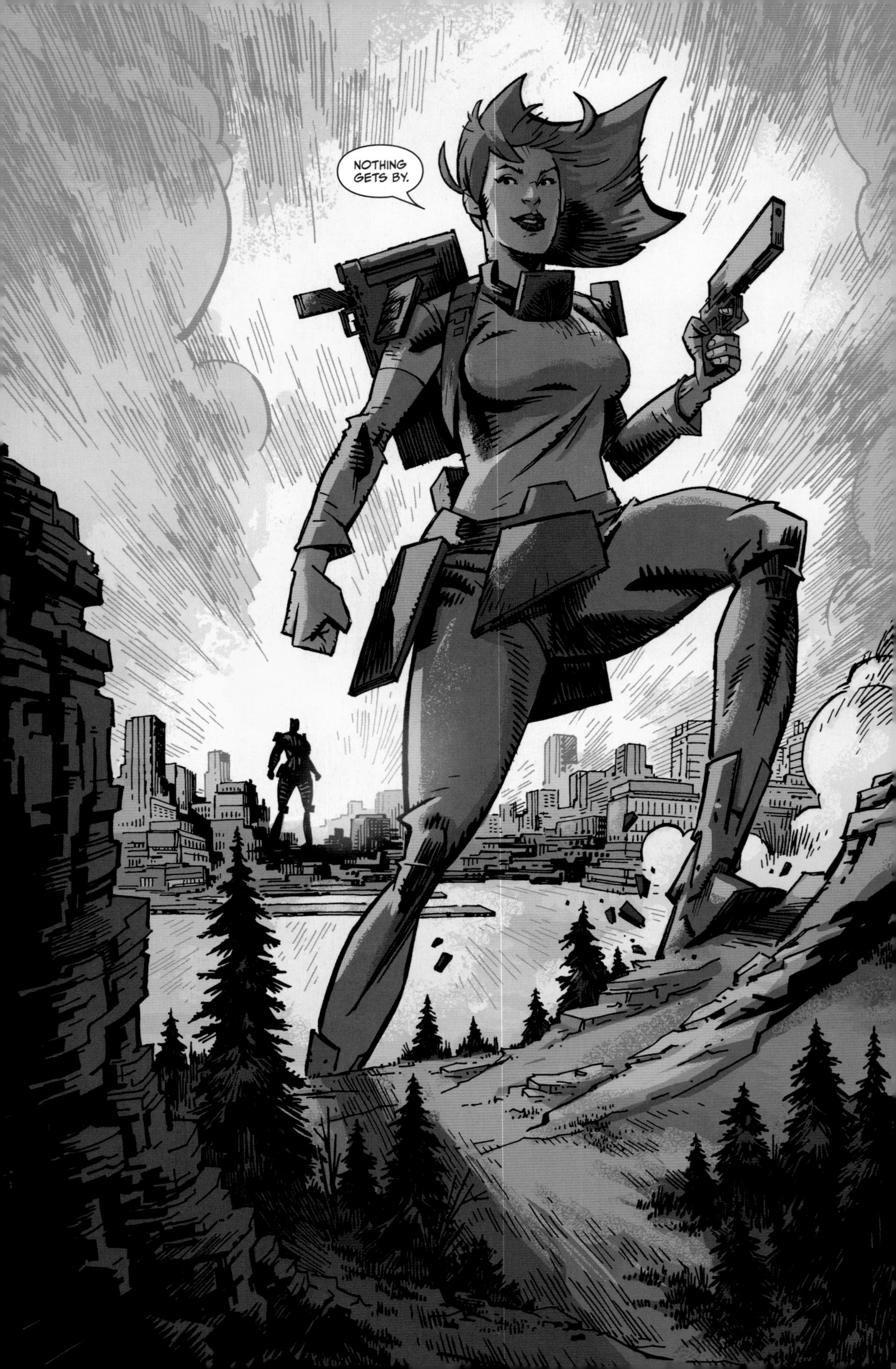
NOTHING GETS BY.

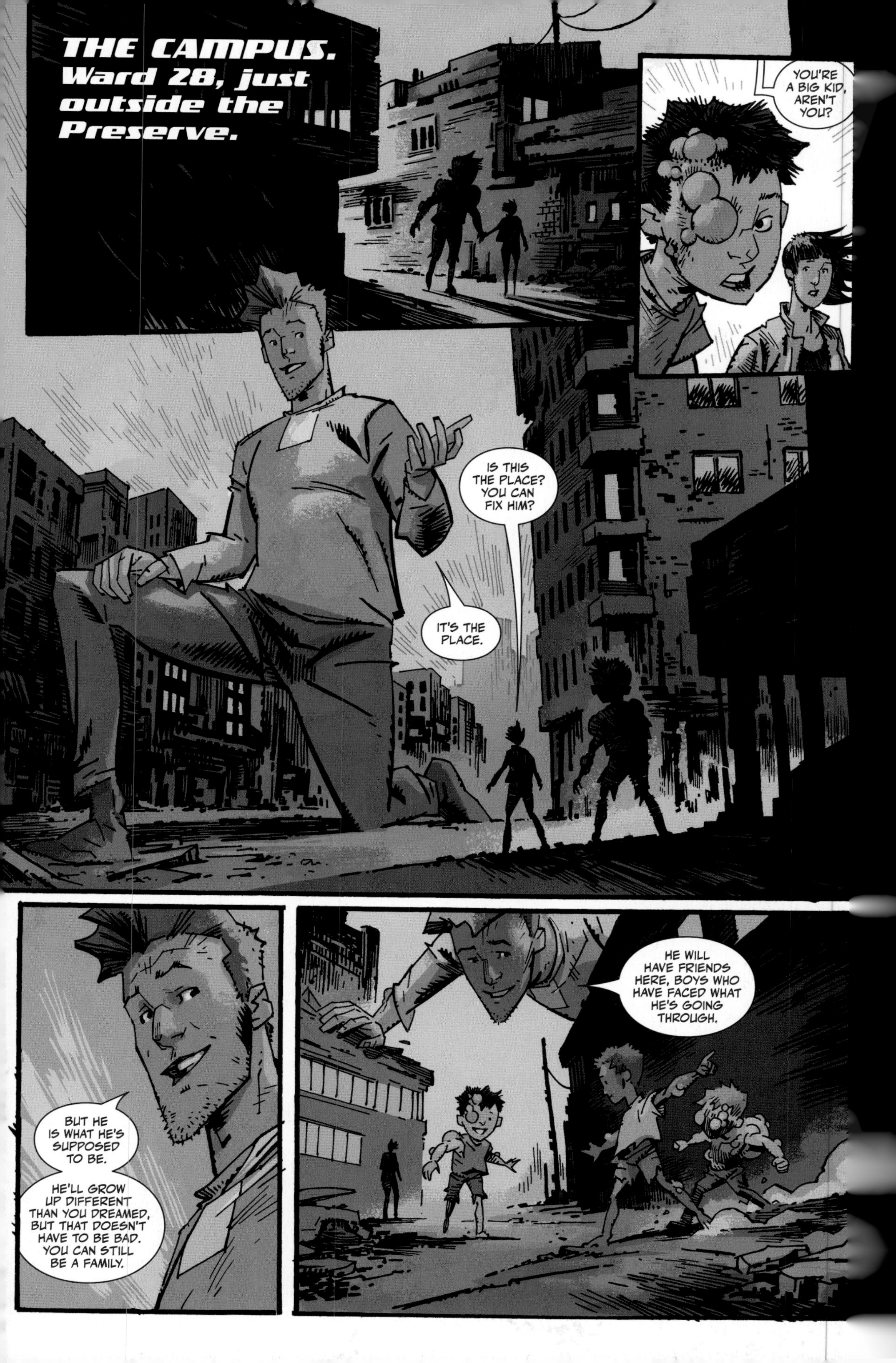

THE CAMPUS. Ward 28, just outside the Preserve.
YOU'RE A BIG KID, AREN'T YOU?
IS THIS THE PLACE? YOU CAN FIX HIM?
IT'S THE PLACE.
BUT HE IS WHAT HE'S SUPPOSED TO BE.
HE'LL GROW UP DIFFERENT THAN YOU DREAMED, BUT THAT DOESN'T HAVE TO BE BAD. YOU CAN STILL BE A FAMILY.
HE WILL HAVE FRIENDS HERE, BOYS WHO HAVE FACED WHAT HE'S GOING THROUGH.

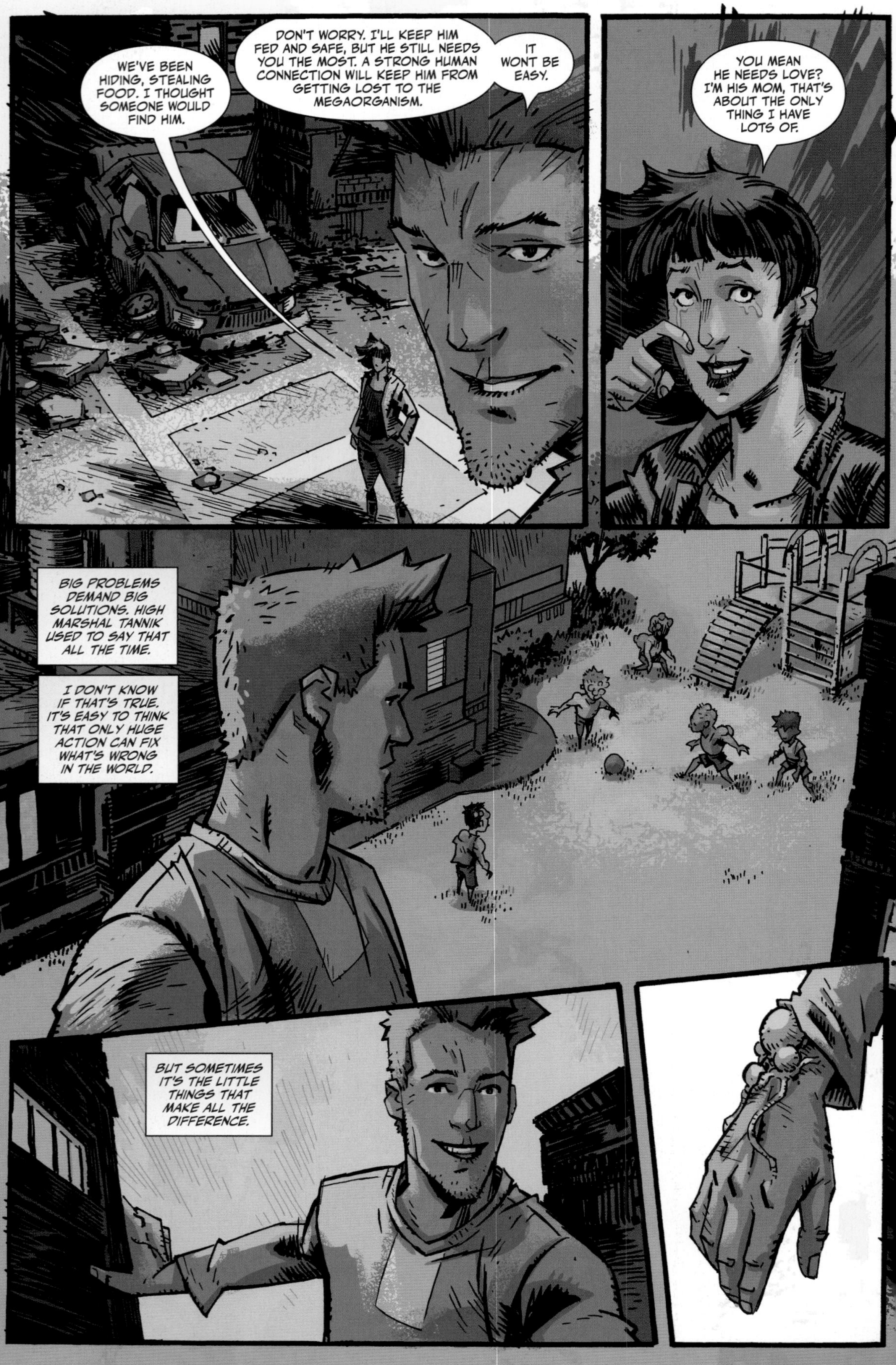
WE'VE BEEN HIDING, STEALING FOOD. I THOUGHT SOMEONE WOULD FIND HIM.
DON'T WORRY. I'LL KEEP HIM FED AND SAFE, BUT HE STILL NEEDS YOU THE MOST. A STRONG HUMAN CONNECTION WILL KEEP HIM FROM GETTING LOST TO THE MEGAORGANISM.
IT WONT BE EASY.
YOU MEAN HE NEEDS LOVE? I'M HIS MOM, THAT'S ABOUT THE ONLY THING I HAVE LOTS OF.
BIG PROBLEMS DEMAND BIG SOLUTIONS. HIGH MARSHAL TANNIK USED TO SAY THAT ALL THE TIME.
I DON'T KNOW IF THAT'S TRUE. IT'S EASY TO THINK THAT ONLY HUGE ACTION CAN FIX WHAT'S WRONG IN THE WORLD.
BUT SOMETIMES IT'S THE LITTLE THINGS THAT MAKE ALL THE DIFFERENCE.

JASON HOWARD

Jason Howard is an American comic book artist and writer. He's a creative force in comics, but he's probably most known for co-creating and illustrating the groundbreaking and critically acclaimed TREES graphic novel series. He also wrote for and was a creative executive on the SUPER DINOSAUR animated series, based on the graphic novels he co-created and illustrated. His other comics work includes co-creating and illustrating the series THE ASTOUNDING WOLF-MAN and CEMETERY BEACH. His newest project BIG GIRLS sees Jason take full creative control, both writing and illustrating it.

FONOGRAFIKS

The banner name for the comics work of designer Steven Finch, 'Fonografiks' has provided lettering and graphic design to a number of Image Comics titles, including SAGA, NOWHERE MEN, INJECTION, TREES, and CEMETERY BEACH. He lives and works in the north east of England.

BIGGIRLSCOMIC@GMAIL.COM

ISSUE ONE

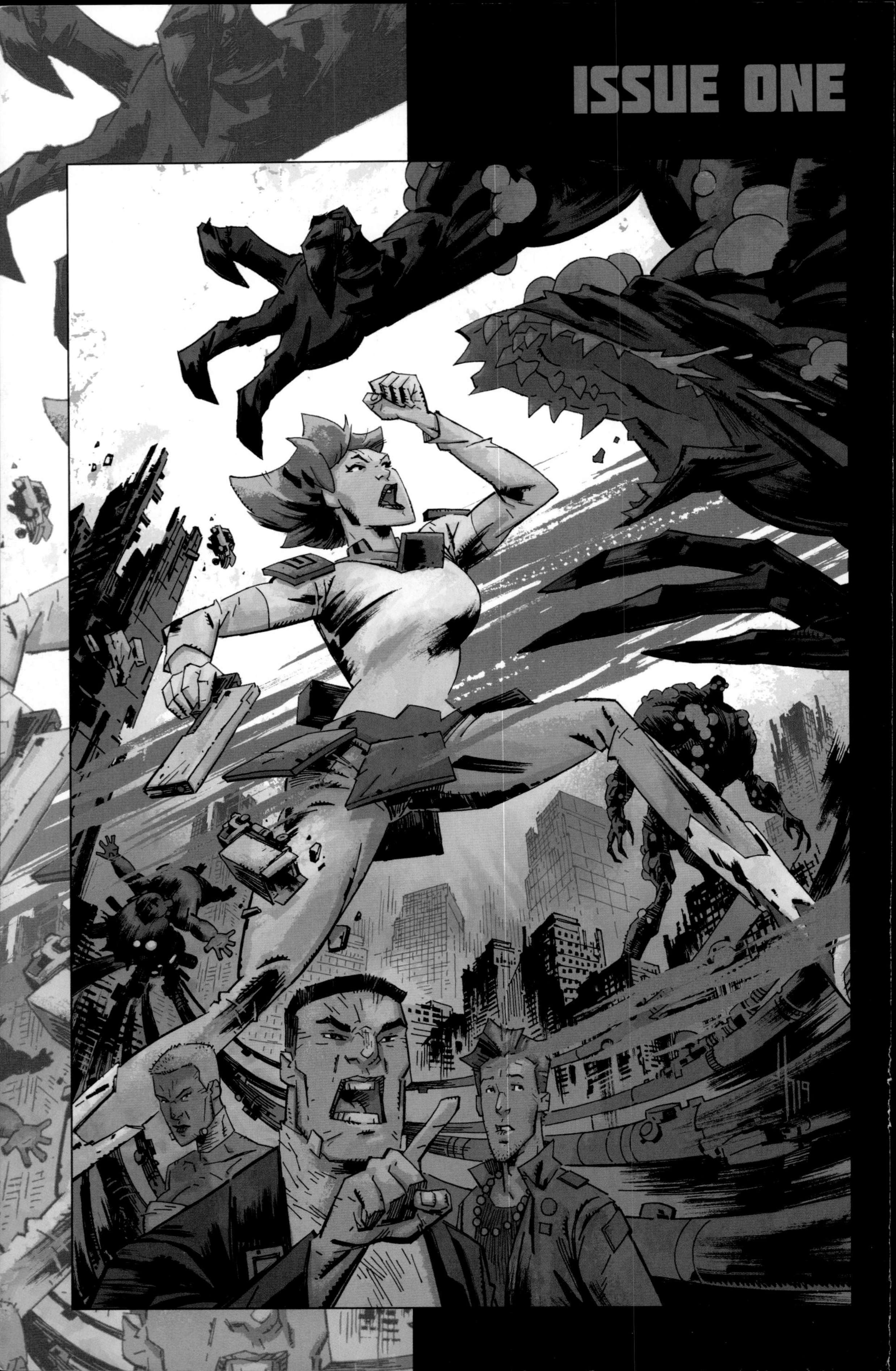

ISSUE TWO

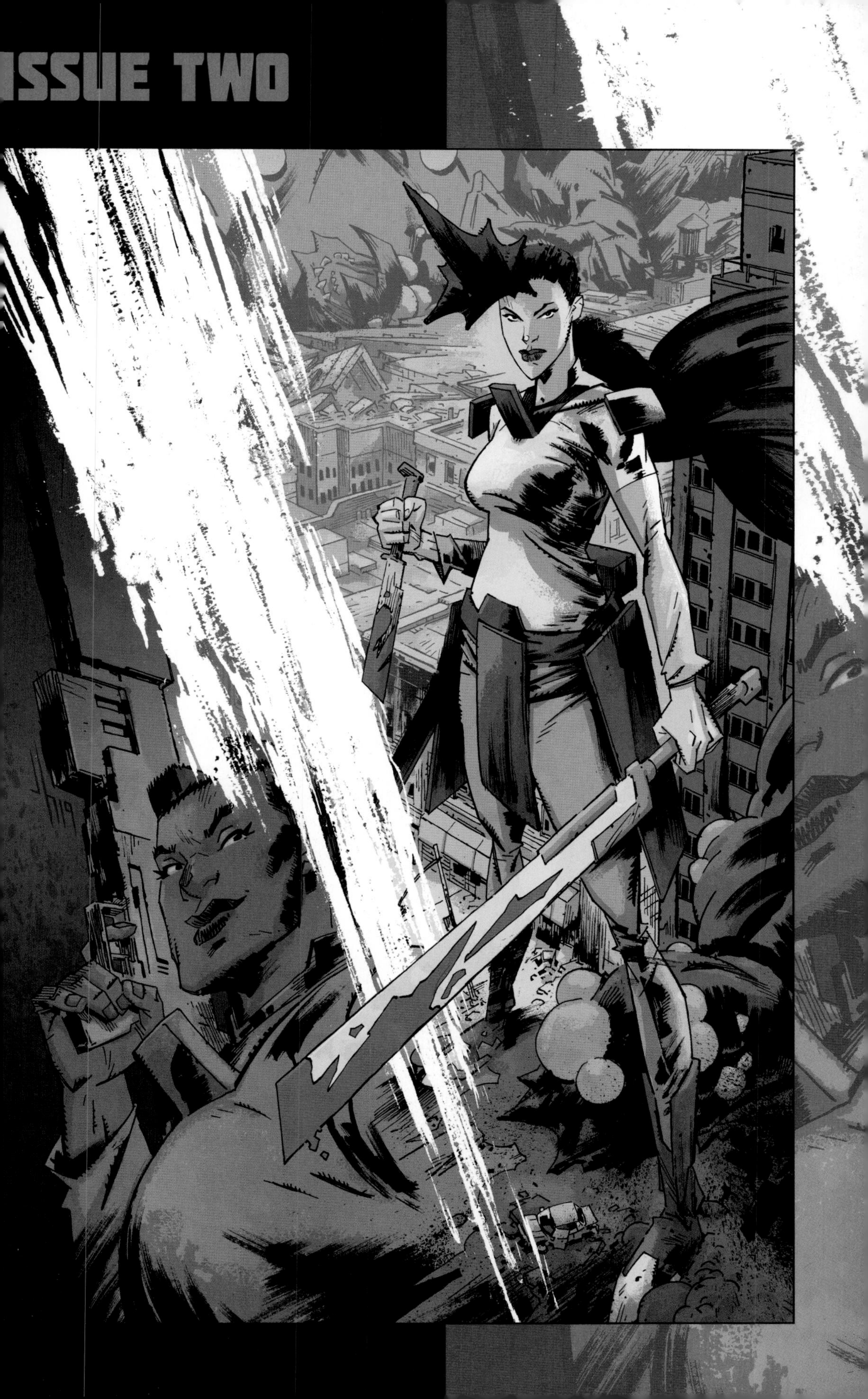

ISSUE THREE

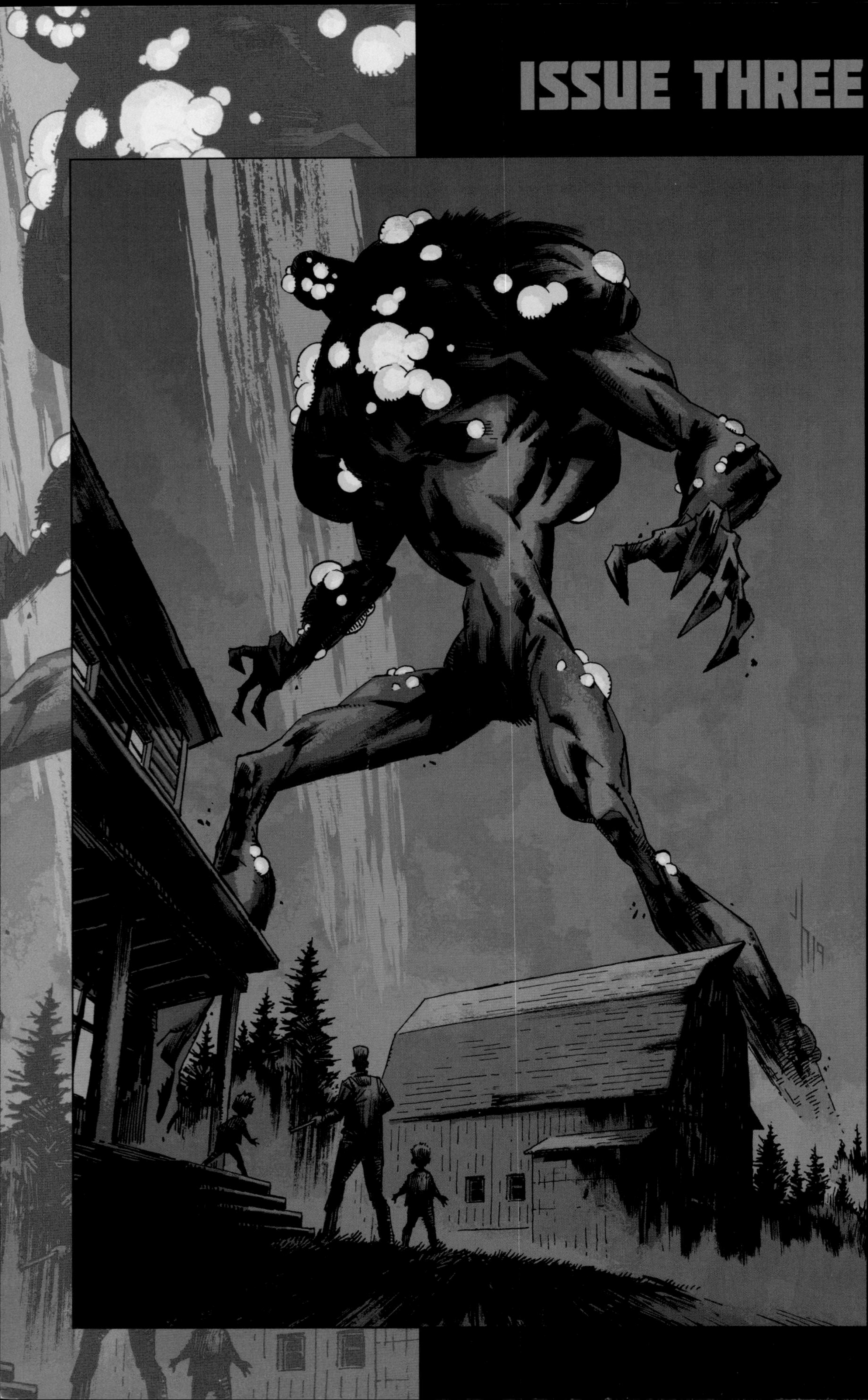

ISSUE FOUR

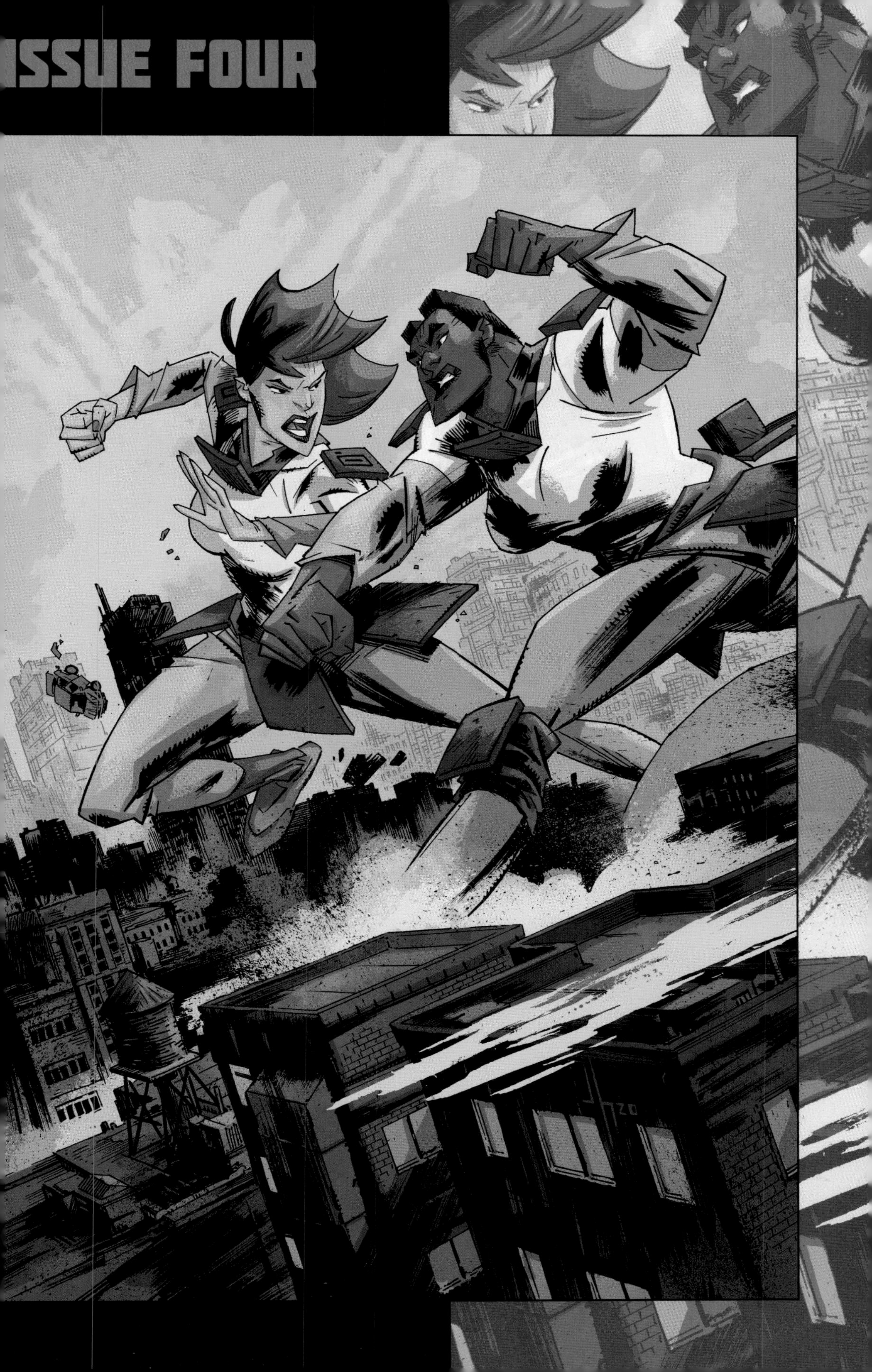

ISSUE FIVE

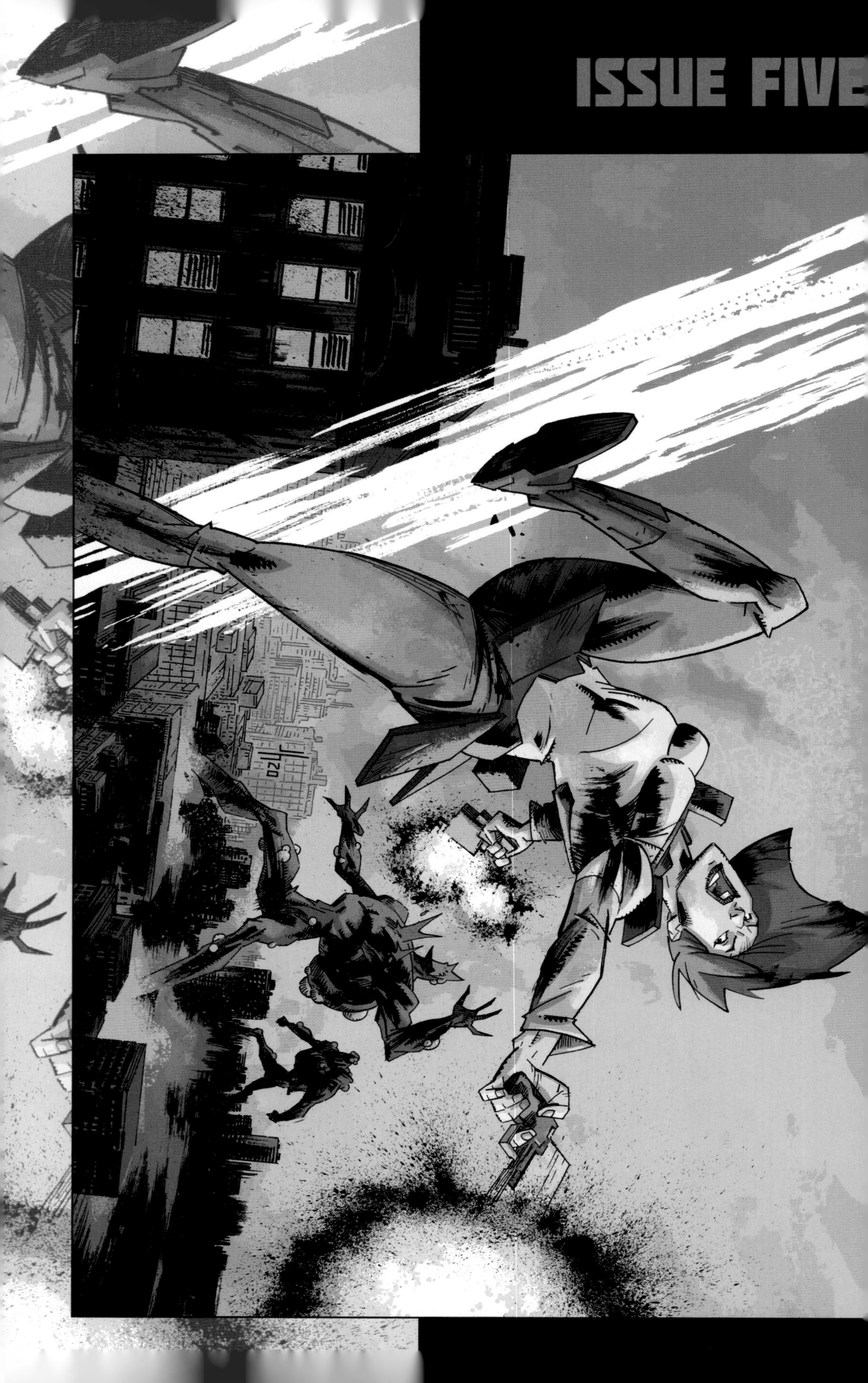

ISSUE SIX

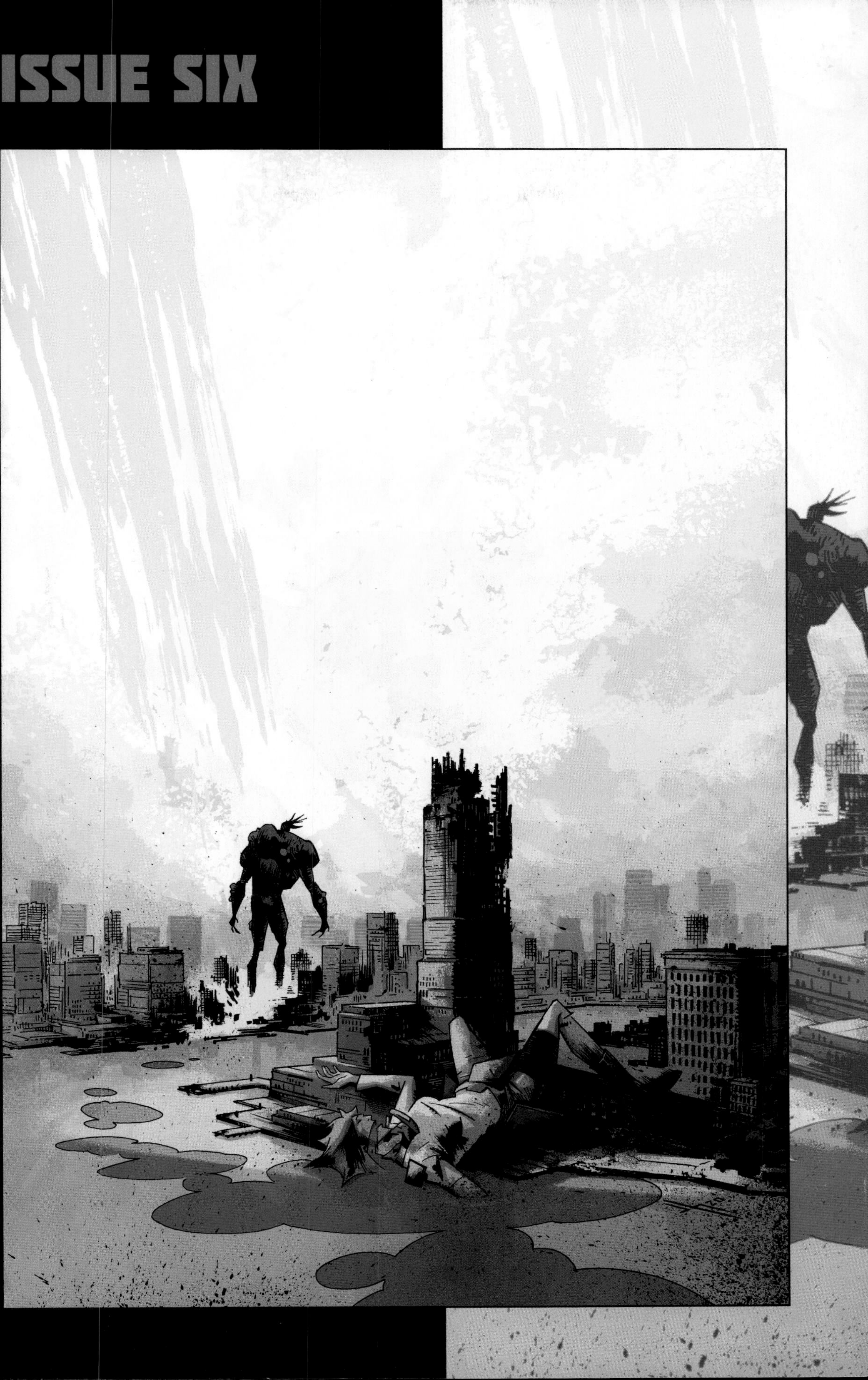

ISSUE SIX

SKOTTIE YOUNG VARIAN

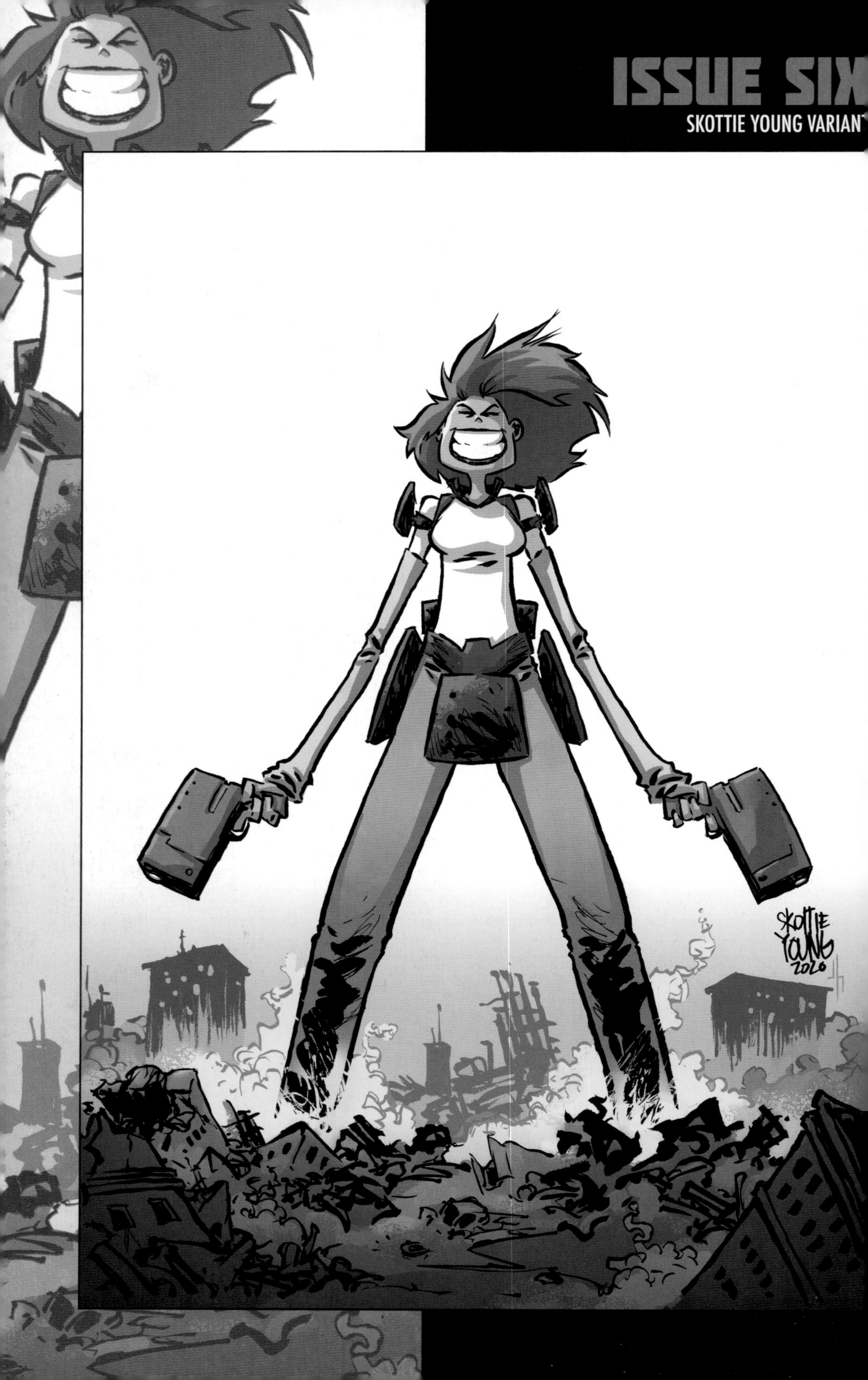
SKOTTIE YOUNG 2020

OTHER GREAT IMAGE COMICS FEATURING JASON HOWARD ART!

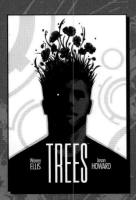
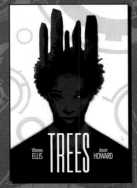

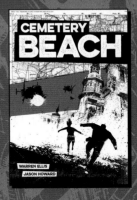

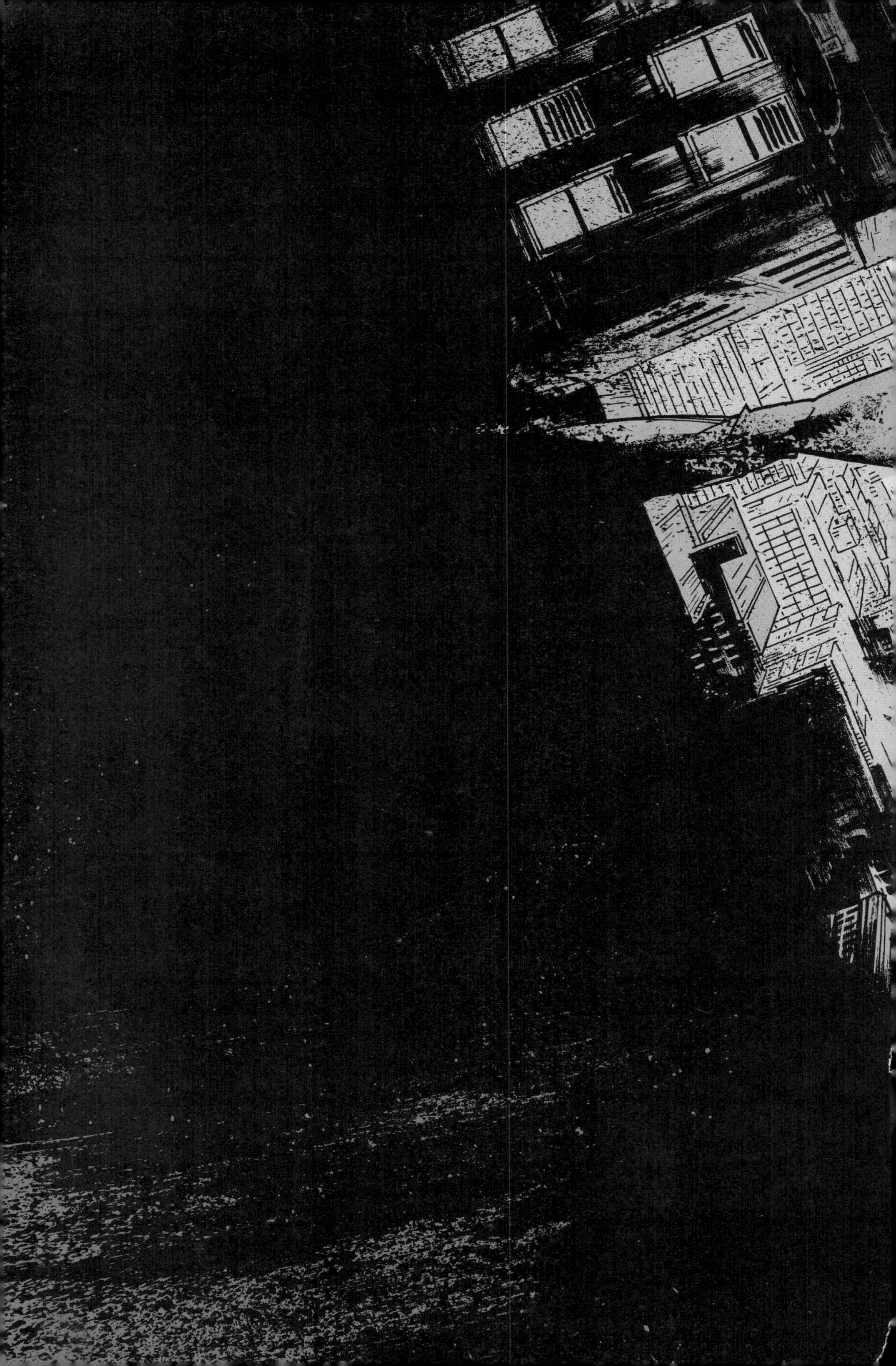